THREE IS THE LUCKIEST NUMBER

Catherine Cloud

ISBN-13: 9798617649026

Visit thesameoldstreets.tumblr.com for more stories and extras!

For Julie

1

The day before the Draft, they agree that this will be the last time.

It's a decision that's made for them, by life, by common sense, and by however many miles will be between them once the next few days are over.

They could spend the rest of the summer together, in a neatly-kept backyard in Connecticut, or in a basement with black marks on the wall in Ontario, but they'll be training in different places for what comes next, for what will likely be the next twenty years of their lives.

God, Blake hopes it'll be twenty years.

Twenty years of hockey. It seems impossible. He's eighteen. He hasn't even made it through twenty whole years. Elliot's a few months younger than him, a gigantic pimple blooming on his forehead, hair hiding it badly. He'll play twenty years of hockey, too. Hell, he'll play twenty-five if they let him.

Elliot Cowell is a prodigy. He'll be an All Star, a leader in the room, and maybe, one day, a captain.

Sometimes Blake can't believe that Elliot is the same guy who's been kissing him whenever he's sure that no one is looking, who's been stealing his shirts, who's been slipping into his bed, quiet laughter in the air, lips always eager, and his hands even more so. They never talk about it, never say a word, it's just dark corners wherever they can find them, shared rooms on the road, sleepovers that end with them on the same mattress, with hands under shirts, with them shushing each other, and there's no room for conversations in between.

They don't talk about it until the day before the Draft, when they're in a dark stairwell in a hotel in Ottawa. First it's Elliot's lips on his, then it's, "This is the last time we're doing this."

Blake says, "I know," because he did know. He knew all along. He heard the way Elliot was talking about the NHL, about what he thought his life would be like, and Blake never had a place in the future he was

1

imagining. Elliot wants to play until he drops dead on the ice, he wants five Cups and three gold medals, wants everything the hockey gods will grant him. There's no room for Blake between all that. There's no room for error. No room for rumors, for scandals, for PR disasters. So, yes, Blake knows. It doesn't take him by surprise.

Elliot is going to go second or third, there's no consensus, really, all they know is that he won't be first, because Yuri Petrov will go first, to the Texas Wildcats. So for Elliot it'll be New York, if he's second, or Hartford, if he's third.

"Where do you want to go?" Blake asked him this morning.

"It's not my choice to make," said Elliot and tugged his fingers through his hair, like that would tame it somehow. It's starting to curl a little at the tips. Blake overheard Elliot's mom say that he should have gotten a haircut and Elliot looked at her like she'd gone insane, because how could she possibly think of something as mundane as haircuts at a time like this. She muttered at him in Spanish and Blake had no idea what she was saying, but going by the look on Elliot's face, she was telling him off.

"But if you could?" Blake asked.

"I can't," was Elliot's reply and that was it for their conversation.

Blake would choose if he could. For him it would be the Cardinals, always the Cardinals. Somewhere in his grandma's basement is a box full of old Cardinals gear that Blake would never let her throw away, even when he'd long outgrown it. But the Cardinals are picking third, a pick that wasn't even theirs until last season's trade deadline. The Cardinals don't need a goalie. And Blake isn't going third. Maybe he'll go in the third round. That's probably his most realistic outlook, even though Elliot is dead-sure that he'll go in the second. He doesn't mind speculating about where Blake might end up, but as soon as it's about him, he starts shutdown procedures. He's scared, but he won't say it. Elliot remains cheerful, smiling at everyone, but there's other stuff going on underneath that he won't let anyone else see.

If Blake was getting the kind of attention from the media that Elliot is getting, he probably wouldn't want to talk about anything anymore either. It's all stats, the tiniest of flaws being compared, speed and puck movement, every little weakness laid bare for the world to see as they try to figure out which team should pick him.

The two of them in a dark stairwell in a hotel in Ottawa the night before the Draft? Another weakness, but not one that anybody knows about.

Nobody will know about it.

Because this is the last time.

Elliot kisses him the same way he always does, like they snuck away again, like there's no significance to any of this. His touches are featherlight against Blake's sides, skimming along the hem of Blake's shirt, reluctant, like he knows he shouldn't take this too far, not when they're hiding in a stairwell, dark as it may be. In the beginning, Elliot always kissed him like he wasn't sure if he was allowed to, slow and reluctant, but Blake quickly figured out that Elliot just wasn't ready to take things further.

Blake tried to be patient with him, waited for Elliot to make up his mind, could tell that Elliot was constantly torn, never sure what he wanted. Elliot was scared of someone finding out, but he always came back to Blake. It's his choice, though. It was his choice from the start.

Now Blake is much too aware that this is the last time he gets to kiss Elliot and for weeks he's been wishing they had more time, but the days kept slipping away and now this is it and Blake can't decide where to put his hands, a knot in his stomach because he wants to remember everything as much as he wants to forget it all the second they go their separate ways.

Elliot pulls away with a sigh, ducking his head.

"Hey," Blake says, his hand still on Elliot's back, "don't…" He doesn't quite manage the *don't go yet*, but he doesn't have to anyway.

Elliot tilts his head, bumps into Blake's chin. Blake kisses his temple. It occurs to him now that he's never done that before, or at least he doesn't remember ever doing it. There are so many things he wishes they could have done together, so many things they did that he'll miss.

"I should go," Elliot says.

He kisses Blake again. And Blake starts to count. That's one.

"Already?" Blake asks.

"I'm sorry," Elliot mutters and then his lips are back on Blake's, careful, gentle, hands in Blake's hair.

This time, when they pull apart, neither of them says a word.

That's two.

Another kiss, one that lingers, and that's three.

Elliot always had this thing about kissing Blake three times for good luck before games. There was never a fourth, so Blake knows that this is it. Blake takes Elliot's hand before he can walk away. "I…" He takes a deep breath. There's nothing he can say now that'll make a difference. He wouldn't know how to say any of it anyway. "Good luck tomorrow," is what he settles on. It's easy and it's safe.

"Thank you," Elliot whispers, like his voice might crack if he said it any louder.

He steps away and the motion sensor catches him and the lights flicker back to life like they did when Elliot first pulled him out into the stairwell.

Blake doesn't want to look at him, forces himself to look down anyway. Elliot's always smiling, only now he isn't, and it's not Blake's fault, not really, but he hates that he had a part in this.

"Don't forget about me when you're a big star," Blake says.

It tickles the smallest of laughs out of Elliot. "Never," he says. He means it, Blake can tell.

Then Elliot tugs his hand out of Blake's, and they're done.

Elliot tells himself that he's relieved when the New York Ravens select him with their first round pick. No other feelings. He isn't happy, he isn't sad, just relieved. He goes second and his mother hugs him and his dad has tears in his eyes and Elliot walks up onto that stage and plasters a smile on his face and shakes hands with important people whose names he knew five minutes ago and can't remember now that he's standing right in front of them.

He's handed a black and red jersey and a baseball cap and he smiles for the cameras and tries not to think about why he's so lost.

This was supposed to give him direction. He finally knows where he's going to spend the next few years of his life. And maybe a few more years after that. He wonders if Blake can see him right now, if he's taken one look at Elliot's face and seen right through him. He barely remembers it after, sees a replay on TV and silently congratulates himself for looking 100% delighted and 0% terrified, when it was, in fact, the other way around.

Once he's off the stage, someone hands him a phone and his fingers only shake the tiniest bit when he takes it.

"Elliot, I just wanted to say welcome to the Ravens," says someone extremely French-Canadian on the other end of the line.

Jacob Desjardins. Captain.

Elliot is glad that he managed to remember his name. He thanks him, tries to retain all the information he's given during that two-minute phone call and forgets everything as soon as he's said goodbye.

He's whisked away to take pictures with the Wildcats' first rounder, Yuri Petrov, who looks about as lost and confused as Elliot feels, and David Santana, who was selected third by the Connecticut Cardinals and who looks so delighted to be here that Elliot finds himself smiling when Santana pats his back in passing.

That could have been him.

Elliot could have just as well gone to Hartford. He tried not to think about it before, didn't want to pick a favorite, because he didn't want to end up being disappointed, but he can't help but wonder now how

Blake would feel if Elliot had gone to the Cardinals. He gave Blake a Zach Goldman shirt for his birthday once and he wore it so much that it literally fell apart. The Cardinals aren't a bad team. They got their pick in a trade and Elliot might have had a better chance to at least make the playoffs with them, but the Ravens have potential, too, especially if they make the right moves in free agency. They have already signed a new coach for next season and they have drafted some good players during the last couple of years, so Elliot is tentatively excited.

Blake finds him later and hugs him and Elliot doesn't want to let go, wants to pull him with him, but last night in that stairwell was the last time. Elliot's stomach turns, thinking about hiding a secret that big and they don't even know where Blake is going yet. He might end up on the other side of the country.

No, they made that decision and he's not going to take it back. It wouldn't be fair for either of them.

Blake goes in the second round.

He goes in the second round and he almost laughs, because Elliot was right, and because it's the New Jersey Knights who pick him, and they play in Newark, across the river from the New York Ravens.

It's almost a blessing that Blake already knows that he'll be spending some quality time with the Knights' AHL team in upstate New York, because that way he won't be thinking about how bad of an idea it would be to visit Elliot in New York on a daily basis. Because Elliot is definitely going to New York. The Ravens need a guy like him on the roster, don't have time to send him down.

It's not like Blake is desperately in love with Elliot. He didn't let himself fall desperately in love with a boy who would have refused to love him back. Whatever they were until they kissed goodbye in that stairwell had an expiration date so bold and glaring that having any feelings whatsoever would have been nothing but torture.

So, no, Blake is not desperately in love, but it's easier to be somewhere that's not just *across the river*. Rivers are too easy to cross, with all those bridges and ferries and tunnels.

After he's drafted, Blake gets a call from Jason Renwick, one of the Knights' alternate captains. He's thirty-five, just signed a one-year extension, and he gives Blake his phone number, his address, and invites him over for dinner, "Whenever you're next in town, kid. We're glad to have you on the team."

Honestly? Blake is glad that he ended up in New Jersey. People don't usually have too many good things to say about the place – Blake has never been, except for the airport – but looking at the team they have actually gives him hope. They made the playoffs last season, none of their players are outright assholes and their management seems to be at least somewhat competent. Jersey has a good room that welcomes new guys with open arms. Blake's phone is blowing up with messages all day – the Knights' new captain, Brian Kelly, and their starting goalie, Jake Matthews, other teammates, coaches and trainers.

There's one from Elliot in there, too, a very formal *congratulations*, and not a word about the river, or the bridges and ferries and tunnels. Of course not, because they broke things off the other night. Being so close to one another won't change a thing; they could be on the same team again and it wouldn't change a thing.

He wonders for how long he'll think about Elliot, about how small he seemed when he leaned against Blake in that stairwell after Blake told him that he knew, that he'd known all along that this was it for them. There were wrinkles in the shirt Blake was wearing from where Elliot's fingers were clenched in the fabric, like he didn't want to let go. He did let go, though, and so all Blake gets is *congratulations*.

His grandma hugs him tightly when they know that he's going to New Jersey and she pats his cheek and Blake lets her, because she's the only one around to be proud of him, except for his brother, Evan, who insists on giving him "the highest of fives". They'll probably be here again, two years from now, to see where Evan will end up.

Blake tries not to wish his Mom and Dad were here. No point in that. He knows that by now.

Blake leaves Ottawa without exchanging another word with Elliot. Which is fine. What would he say anyway? Goodbye? They've said goodbye.

On the way to the airport, on the flight home, he can't shake the thought that he forgot something important.

2

Elliot spends his summer working harder than he's ever worked before. He was the second overall pick and there's a good chance that he'll end up on the Ravens' opening night roster, but he doesn't want to show up acting like he already has a place on the team.

The Ravens had an abysmal previous season, hence the second pick, one of their forwards retired at the end of the season, two moved on to greener pastures. The Ravens signed a bunch of new guys during the off-season, so it's a weird locker room to walk into for training camp, although Elliot is really just excited to be here. He's in his gear before everyone else, eager to get on the ice.

As guys get sent down and the rest of them are fitted into the lineup, Elliot ends up on a line with Magnus Nyström on his left wing and Adam Ishida on his right. Magnus has been on the roster for three years, Adam has been a more recent addition, spent the past season on the farm team. Elliot gets along with them, jokes around with them on the ice, laughing when Adam tries to find nicknames for him.

"El. No, that's weird. Wellie."

"What did people call you in juniors?" Magnus asks.

"Elliot."

"They did not, that's way too boring," Adam says, shaking his head at him, or maybe at the lack of creativity on his junior league team. "There has to be something we can do with Cowell. What about... Hm, Cowie."

Magnus slaps the back of his head. "No."

"Yeah," Elliot says, "that's definitely a no."

"Oh," Magnus says. "What does the cow say?"

Adam's eyes light up. "Moo."

"No."

"Yes."

"No."

"Moo," Magnus says softly. "Beautiful."

Two days later the entire team is calling him Moo and there's no escaping it anymore. Some of the guys will still call him Elliot every now and then, but he likely won't get rid of that nickname any time soon.

He's weirdly okay with it. Things are okay. New York is okay. Adam lets on that he has an unused room, in case Elliot needs one after the preseason. He fits right in. Things are okay.

They're okay until he plays his first preseason game against the New Jersey Knights and Blake Samuels is in goal, on the other side for the first time in their lives. Elliot doesn't score on Blake, disgruntled when he heads off the ice, because he should have been able to sneak one past him in his sleep.

He finds Blake after the game, talking to someone in a hallway outside the visitors' locker room. Once he lays eyes on him, he realizes that he didn't actually mean to find him, just wanted to take a quick peek to see if Blake grew his hair out like he said he would – he did – and, well, maybe to see if he looked happy – he does. The Knights play in dark blue and it does things to Blake's eyes that Elliot doesn't know how to explain, same goes for the suit that Blake is wearing right now, a blue that seems to match his eyes exactly.

Blake freezes when he spots Elliot, excuses himself, and walks over very slowly, like he's not sure if he even wants to.

"Hey," Elliot says and smiles.

Blake's smile is a little slower to appear. Elliot can't blame him. Blake's smiles have always been a bit of a rarity and Elliot has figured out that there are probably three types that make the most frequent appearances – *a friend just scored a goal* is the first, *Elliot just said something stupid and Blake can't help it* is the second, and *just found a really good burrito* is the third. In any case, Elliot has been a terrible friend and probably doesn't deserve a smile. They didn't talk much during the summer, and when they did, their conversations fizzled out after a handful of texts. Elliot never knew what to say, felt awkward when he texted Blake to ask how he was doing.

He never has that problem with his teammates, but he also can't treat Blake like a teammate. That's not what he is. Not what he was either. Or at least not *just* that.

"Hey," Blake replies eventually.

"Great game," Elliot says. The Knights pretty much wiped the floor with them, but it's only the preseason. They have time to get up to speed before the regular season starts. Or so Elliot tells himself.

Blake nods. "Yeah, it was okay." A minuscule shrug and he adds, "They're sending me upstate. Glad I got to play, though. I guess you're playing on opening night?"

8

"I don't know yet," Elliot says, even though he's reasonably sure that the answer is yes. He doesn't know why he doesn't just say that. Maybe because he's sad for Blake, because they're sending him down, even though Blake must have known from the start that the AHL would be his first stop.

"Well, I gotta go," Blake says and holds up his fist, "good luck."

Tentatively, Elliot bumps his fist against Blake's, and thanks him, and watches him walk away, wondering why he feels like he was talking to a complete stranger.

"Ravens again?"

Blake doesn't reply, because Dennis has eyes and can see that he's watching the Ravens again, and Dennis also knows that he's friends with Elliot Cowell – at least hypothetically. It's not like they talk or anything, because Elliot is busy being a rising star and Blake is busy getting used to being in goal for the Knights' AHL team. He gets to start often enough, has won more games than he lost, but it's nothing like the show Elliot is putting on down in the city.

They love him.

Blake, of course, knew that they would love him, because how could they not? After what seems like five minutes in the NHL, Elliot is already so much more grown up than he was last summer. Since Blake loves to torture himself, he also watches Elliot's interviews and not just his games.

He misses him.

That sunny smile, his laughter that sounded a bit like a goose being strangled, the smattering of freckles on the bridge of his nose and his cheeks, the way his eyelids fluttered the tiniest bit whenever Blake touched him, all those little things that Blake barely even noticed when they still saw each other all the time.

"Yikes," Dennis says when he flops down next to him. The score is 4-0 in favor of the Ravens and they're only just approaching the end of the first period. Two of those goals are Elliot's.

"Wanna order pizza tonight?" Dennis asks.

Blake hums something that could be considered a yes to the pizza question, his eyes still on their TV.

He usually keeps himself from wondering if Elliot misses him, too, because the very honest answer to that is that he doesn't know. He indulges himself today when the broadcast cuts to Elliot during a stoppage in play. A strand of brown hair is sticking out at the front of his bucket and he's chewing on his mouthguard, eyes darting across the ice until he seems to find what he was looking for and skates over to Nyström, who's about seven or eight years older than them and also a

Swedish god. Elliot smiles at something that Nyström says to him, glove covering half his face so the cameras won't pick it up.

"So you used to play with him?" Dennis asks after a while.

It takes Blake a moment to tear his eyes off the screen. "Yeah."

"He's unreal, isn't he?"

"Yeah," Blake says again.

Elliot, on TV, is getting ready for a face-off.

Deep down, Blake already knows that he's about to watch Elliot Cowell score his first NHL hat trick. There's two periods of hockey left and there's a lot Elliot can do in two periods of hockey.

It happens in the third.

Next to him, Dennis is losing his mind, on TV, Elliot is swept into the arms of Mikey Walters, a very large D-man, who lifts Elliot right off his feet. Hats rain onto the ice and Elliot's teammates pile a few on his head before the ice crew takes them away.

Order resumes, and Dennis says, "Did you text him?"

"Huh?" Blake's brain catches up a moment later. Right, they're friends, he should probably send Elliot one of those *congratulations* texts that they've become so good at. He got one for his first win, another one for his first shutout, surprised that Elliot was checking the AHL scores, and Blake also sent one to Elliot when he got his first point and two days later his first goal.

Blake hates sending and receiving those texts.

He picks up his phone, says, *Proud of you*, but doesn't hit send, because he's not Elliot's mom. *Awesome goals*, he tries next, but it sounds weird to him, so he deletes that as well. Five more tries and Dennis shoots him a look that's asking if he's writing a novel over there.

Blake grits his teeth and sends, *Congrats on the hatty!*

He hates this one, too.

The Ravens eventually win the game 6-0. It's a fluke, because the Ravens have been terrible since the start of the season, have been terrible for the past two years and are slow to get back to where they'd like to be, but they aren't going to lose every single game of the season either.

Blake does not receive a reply from Elliot until the next morning: *thanks. how's it going?*

Blake tells him that everything's going fine, doesn't mention that he thinks about him all the time, doesn't mention that he misses him and that he sometimes wonders if Elliot misses him, too, doesn't mention that he wishes they had time to really talk more often. Elliot is too far away, not just because Blake isn't across the river in Newark, but because he's living an entirely different life. He gets to be an NHL player already and Blake is still waiting his turn, and that's really just how it is in this business.

They can't all be prodigies who break rookie records.

He gets called up in February.

He mostly sits on the bench, because it's the Knights' backup who's injured, so their starter, Jake Matthews, is still in net for the three games that Blake spends with the Knights.

He joins them for the first one in Florida, then flies back to Newark with the team and Mattie – like there was never even a question where Blake would be staying – takes him home, to his wife, his two kids, and his two Labradors. Blake becomes fast friends with both the kids and the Labradors, lobbing balls around their playroom with tiny plastic sticks.

They have the day off when they return from Florida and Mattie takes it upon himself to show Blake around, because, "You know, in a few years you're probably going to live here."

Mattie is thirty-one. If he plays for a few more years, Blake might be ready for the NHL when he retires. Mattie talks about it like there's really no other way for the Knights to go, like Blake already has a place in this franchise, like, in a few years, he'll take Mattie's place.

When Mattie goes on and on about what a great time Blake is going to have and how well he'll fit into the team, Blake finds himself staring in disbelief.

"What's with the face, kid?" Mattie eventually asks. "Is that why they call you Fish? Because you make that face?"

"No, they call me Fish because Samuels is apparently the same as salmon."

"Sure," Mattie says. "What's with the gaping then?"

Blake gapes a little more and then asks, "Aren't you… I don't know… Wouldn't you rather play forever?"

Mattie laughs like that was the funniest joke he's ever heard. There's some wheezing and snorting. Mattie claps Blake's shoulder. "Yeah, ten years ago I wanted to play forever, but now it's…" Mattie shrugs. "I love hockey, but I'm not getting any younger. I'll go as long as I can, and as long as they'll let me, but… You know, my dad was a hockey player and he had to retire early and he said that hanging up the skates might have hurt less if he'd seen it coming. So, I guess what I'm saying is that I'm seeing it coming."

"Oh," Blake says. He can't even imagine it, retiring.

"No, I get it," Mattie says with a wink. "You haven't even started yet."

In the afternoon, Mattie leaves him to his own devices and, for the first time, Blake considers the river. So easy to cross. And then he'd be in New York City and then what? He knows that Elliot lives in

Manhattan with one of his teammates, but he has no idea where. Manhattan isn't a place you go to on a whim to track down an old friend.

Elliot might not even be in the city.

With Blake getting called up, he lost track of the schedule a bit, so he pulls out his phone to check. Elliot's playing in Toronto tomorrow night, so today might be a travel day for the Ravens.

Elliot's not even in the city. So the river doesn't matter.

It wouldn't even matter if he *was* in the city. Because what was Blake going to do anyway? Give him a call? Ask him if he wants to hang out? Elliot likely doesn't want to see him. They broke up. No, not even that, because they weren't together in the first place. They were something, in the middle of the night, whenever no one was watching, on rare summer days when they happened to be in the same town. That's when they were *something*.

Blake pushes those memories away.

He and Elliot are done.

Blake is in close proximity to New York City and Elliot is in Toronto, which is probably for the best, because Elliot couldn't handle seeing Blake in person right now.

He likes New York. His rookie year is a fairy tale.

When he got his roster spot, Elliot moved in with Adam. They're pretty good at being roommates as long as they don't try to watch a movie together. Hockey games work, because they usually have the same priorities, but their taste in movies couldn't be any more different. Adam likes thrillers and horror movies; Elliot likes comedies and superheroes. They stay out of each other's way, at least movie-wise, and only watch hockey together. It works well enough.

Sometimes Elliot eats food that isn't his and then Adam will give him the evil side-eye, but he usually forgives him quickly when Elliot cooks him pasta. Because Adam will eat pasta for breakfast, lunch and dinner if you let him, and Elliot knows his way around pasta, because he will also eat it for breakfast, lunch and dinner if you let him.

The guys in the room actually seem to like having him around. He got pranked into oblivion early in the season, but it appears as though the guys have finally settled down. Tape balls hitting him in the neck are still a daily occurrence, though, because he sits close to Moby and Moby needs to bother at least one teammate a day and usually that teammate is Elliot.

They're halfway through February and Elliot is tired, sleeps more than he ever has in his life, is skinnier than he's ever been, but there's a buzz under his skin that keeps him going. They're working their way up to a wildcard spot. There's a chance they'll actually make it there.

"Earth to Moo."

Elliot looks up.

Riley is looking back at him expectantly. They've been plane buddies ever since Riley got traded to the Ravens to be their new backup goalie a month ago, with their other backup out long-term. They hit it off instantly, like the same shows, and Riley's from Oshawa, so they grew up pretty close to each other, know the same people.

"What?" Elliot asks. "Sorry, I kinda zoned out there…"

Riley snorts at him. "You wanna come to my parents' house for dinner tonight? You said your parents both have other stuff going on, right?"

"Oh, uh…" Elliot hadn't even thought about it. His mom is working late at the hospital, his dad is out of town for work, so he won't even be able to make it to the game tomorrow. His mom will be there, though, and some of his childhood friends, too.

"It's cool if you have other plans, but I figured I'd ask because you said you weren't seeing your mom until tomorrow."

"Yeah, thanks, that'd be nice."

"Cool," Riley says and goes back to watching whatever he was watching.

Elliot grabs his laptop, too, because his only other choice would be to think about Blake again.

He's not doing that to himself.

In the summer, Blake finally caves.

It's four days after the NHL Awards, where the Carolina Comets' Jamie O'Rielly won the Calder. Blake wouldn't say that Elliot deserved it *more*, but he did deserve it at least just as much and Blake vividly remembers Jamie O'Rielly skating right into him during a game in juniors, so Blake is somewhat biased.

He's sitting in the backyard of his grandma's house, his grandma and Evan out to buy some new clothes for Evan, because the boy can't dress himself, and Blake decided to stay out of it. He didn't want to be the one to explain to his grandma that neither of them has ever developed much of an interest in fashion, but he has at least enough sense to wear shirts without holes when they're at her house. Evan brought this upon himself.

So Blake is left alone with his thoughts, a glass of iced tea, a book he's not going to read, and his phone, replying to teammates' messages, deleting stuff he doesn't need anymore, all mindless things he forgot to do during the season.

He's going through his photos when he stumbles across one of him and Elliot that they took before the Draft, maybe the day before. Elliot, with those big brown eyes and the almost-curly hair, in a shirt that was Blake's once, smiling like he won the Stanley Cup. Something in Blake's

13

stomach twists and after that his brain signs the fuck off and lets his heart do whatever the hell it wants.

So he calls Elliot.

And Elliot, of course, answers after the first ring.

He sounds breathless when he says, "Hey, Blake... uh, hey."

"Hey," Blake replies. And then he says nothing, because... Why did he do this? Hearing Elliot's voice feels a punch in the gut. Or at least he imagines that this is what being punched in the gut feels like. He's never been in a fight.

There's a small pause, a hitch of breath that might be hidden laughter, then Elliot says, "What's up?"

"Well," Blake starts. "My grandma was asking how you're doing and I... wanted to ask... how you're doing." It's not even a lie, Blake's grandma did ask how Elliot was doing and Blake didn't have the heart to tell her that he had no idea, because the only word they seem to be able to say to each other is *congratulations*.

"I'm okay," Elliot says. "How about you?"

"Yeah. Me, too. The team is great and... yeah. All good."

"Good."

"Yeah," Blake says. "Good."

Silence falls, but Blake can't say goodbye yet and Elliot doesn't say anything either. His grandma's cat, Angus, comes over the garden wall and plops down next to him, belly up, waiting for pets.

"Angus is here," Blake says, because Elliot loved Angus more than anyone else in the world.

"Aw, Angus," Elliot coos. "Pet him for me, yeah?"

Blake scratches Angus's head. "Sure."

"Thank you."

"Yeah." Blake takes a deep breath. He should hang up, because he's out of things to say and he still can't figure out why he called in the first place. Definitely not to tell Elliot that he misses him, because that wouldn't be fair.

A few summers ago, Elliot was sitting in this very backyard with him, and he told him a secret that changed everything. Blake can't quite bring himself to wish that Elliot had never told him, had never said, "I think I like boys, sometimes," but it cost him a friend in the long run.

"Blake?" Elliot says eventually.

"Yeah?"

"Why'd you really call?"

Blake sighs. "I was just... thinking about you."

He can hear the breath Elliot draws in at the other end of the line. He shouldn't have said that. It sounded too much like *I miss you*.

Again, there's silence.

Angus meows at Blake when he does a terrible job at petting him and eventually wanders off to murder a mouse or a bird or whatever it is that cats do when their humans fail them.

"I'm sorry, Blake, I gotta..." Elliot trails off. "We can't do this."

"Call each other?" Blake asks.

"No, you just can't..."

He just can't call and say something that sounds too much like *I miss you*. It's been a year. How does this still hurt?

"I'm sorry," Blake says. "I shouldn't have called."

"It's fine," Elliot mutters, even though they left *fine* behind in a stairwell in Ottawa. "I'm glad you're okay, Blake."

Blake doesn't know how to say goodbye.

"Say hi to your grandma from me, okay?" Elliot says.

"I will."

"And good luck next season."

"You, too."

"And..." Elliot pauses again, apparently out of things to say now, too. "Blake?"

"Yeah?"

"I need some time to..." Elliot clears his throat. "We're still friends."

"We are."

"Okay."

"Okay," Blake echoes. "Bye, Elliot."

"Bye."

Blake doesn't hang up right away, waits until the line goes dead, except it doesn't, because Elliot isn't hanging up either and so Blake stares down at his phone and wonders if Elliot is doing the same, until his battery decides that it's had enough two minutes later and his phone dies.

Should have charged it last night.

So he could sit in his grandma's backyard and *not* talk to Elliot on the phone a little while longer.

He's a fucking idiot.

3

Blake doesn't get to play his first NHL game until the end of his second season with the franchise.

The season flew by, game after game, some of which he spent on the bench, some of which he missed because of a groin injury. When he was in net, he won more games than he lost, had a pretty nice streak going for a while, and then it's April all of a sudden. Blake gets called up for the last game of the regular season because the Knights' backup goalie is sick, and since the Knights have already clinched their playoff spot and can't move up or down in the standings, they put Blake in goal.

He's in goal. For his NHL team.

When they first called him up last season, he couldn't wear his usual 31, because that one's taken by the Knights' backup, so Blake wears 33. He only thought of Elliot for a second when he made his choice and doesn't think of him now that he's pulling on the jersey, doesn't think of Elliot wearing number three, or of Elliot kissing him before games, always three times, because three is the luckiest number. It's not about Elliot, it's about the numbers. He thought it might help if he felt like the universe was on his side.

They're playing against the Minnesota Bears, who could definitely use two points, so Blake will be facing their regular roster. He'd lie if he said he wasn't scared shitless, even though all that's being asked of him is that he'll do his very best. In the standings, nothing will happen if they lose and nothing will happen if they win.

Things aren't looking so great when he gets scored on 35 seconds into the game.

Renwick skates over after and gives him a tap with his stick. It's an apology, because the D sort of left him hanging there, and it's an encouragement at the same time. They have over 59 minutes left on the clock, that's plenty of time for the Knights to score. Blake does what he can, keeps the door shut for another ten minutes, then the Bears strike again on a breakaway.

Blake glances at the bench to see if Coach is going to pull him. Nope. It's only two goals after all. He takes a deep breath and fiddles with his water bottle. The goals don't matter. The saves matter. The game matters. He's here right now, in his crease. All he has to do is make the next save.

That's all there is.

The next save.

They make it to the first intermission without any more pucks getting past Blake.

Mattie shoots Blake a look across the locker room, nodding at Blake when he catches his eye. Tonight, this is Blake's place. He belongs here, he belongs in that net. When he was a kid, everyone said he was too small and scrawny to be a goalie and then he somehow ended up being over six feet tall anyway. He grew out of spite.

Maybe he'll win out of spite, too.

Three minutes into the second period, Paulie scores a goal and after that the rest of the guys seem to remember how to score, too. Three more Knights goals in the second, then the Bears get one back early in the third, but they never manage to tie the game. The Knights run away with the game, score one more, and then again into the empty net.

When the guys line up, patting his head and hugging him, Renwick drops a puck into his glove with a smirk, only to be practically pushed aside by Brammer, who hugs him like they just won a playoff series, bouncing up and down as he wraps his arms around Blake.

Back in the room, their equipment guy wraps some tape around his puck and writes 1st NHL WIN on it before he hands it back to Blake.

There's hugs and pictures and interviews and even more hugs and Blake sends a picture of him and his puck to his grandma, who watched the game with her sister back home in Connecticut, hoping that she'll figure out how to open it. He doesn't have time to look at all the texts in his inbox, but he replies to his brother, who's completely losing it, and he reads the text from Elliot — *congrats on the win :)*

It's the first time he's heard from him since they sent each other *Merry Christmas* texts over three months ago.

And that's okay. It's okay that they don't talk, because it's been months since they last actually spoke to each other and Blake is finally at a point where he's across the river from Elliot and he doesn't care.

He's slowly coming to terms with the fact that he won't have what he had with Elliot ever again. He doesn't have much of a love life to speak of, and even that is a euphemism. His teammates try to set him up with girls often enough and Blake tries to be polite and has even gone out on a couple of dates with girls, so the guys would stop bugging him, but he never went out on a second date with any of them. There's no point.

Blake flies to Los Angeles for the Draft.

His brother is projected to get drafted during the first round, so Blake first drives to Connecticut, spends a few days there, and then takes his grandma to LA with him.

There's a good chance that Blake is even more nervous for this Draft than he was for his own two years ago. His palms are sweaty long before they even sit down at the venue and he can't seem to stop jiggling his foot, until Evan puts his hand on Blake's knee and says, uncharacteristically stern, "Stop, you're making it worse."

Evan is quieter than Blake has ever seen him, usually chewing his ear off with hockey stats and rambling about the Cardinals. Today he's barely said a dozen words since they got up this morning.

"Do you think the Cardinals will draft Zach Goldman's kid?" Blake asks, so he doesn't have to sit here and wait for it to start.

Evan shrugs.

Their grandma reaches over Evan to pat Blake's shoulder. She raised the both of them when their parents died, drove them to practices, bought their equipment, cheered them on at every game she could make it to. She still sends Blake a care package every few weeks and she probably does the same for Evan.

During the last couple of years they might have drifted apart, just a little, with them in different junior leagues, staying with different billet families, but it's weird to think that they might end up playing against each other sometime during the next couple of years. Both of them in the NHL, both of them living their dreams.

When it's about to start, Evan lets out a small breath.

Phoenix pick first. Then Philadelphia. Then Ottawa.

The Knights don't get to make their pick until much later – they made it through one round of playoffs before the season was over for them. The chances that they'll pick Evan are comparatively slim, and anyway, Evan will likely get picked up before that.

Or that's what Blake thinks until the Seattle Sailors are making the 27th pick and Evan is still sitting next to him.

Blake can tell that Evan is starting to get anxious, because he keeps picking at his fingernails and Blake is trying extremely hard to keep himself from jiggling his leg again, because that'd make it worse for Evan, but someone should have picked him by now. Blake knows his stats. Evan went to World Juniors, he was second in points on his junior team.

Once the Sailors have left the stage, the Grizzlies make their pick, and then they're on to the Conference Finals losers. First the Seals, then the

Ravens, not because they actually made it to the Conference Finals, but because they got the pick in a trade before the Draft.

"What if I don't get picked at all?" Evan eventually whispers to him when the Seals pick... someone else.

"You'll get picked."

It happens only a few minutes later when the New York Ravens make their selection and their GM finally, finally, says, "Evan Samuels."

Blake doesn't hear anything else, is too busy hugging Evan to pay attention. Their grandma hugs him, too, and then they send him on his way to the stage, where he's handed a jersey and a baseball cap and he's beaming and Blake is so proud of him that he doesn't even realize what else this means until his phone buzzes in his pocket.

It's a text from Elliot — *can I have Evan's number?*

That's right. Because the Ravens are Elliot's team.

Blake sends it to him, as requested. He doesn't get a reply back and isn't exactly surprised, but when they find Evan later, he beams at them and says, "Elliot called me!" He hugs Blake again. "Jacob Desjardins, too. And Mitch Swanson sent me a text!"

"Awesome," Blake says.

"Wow, are you actually smiling? I think you were smiling earlier, too. What's happening?"

"Shut up," Blake says gruffly, but he doesn't stop smiling.

Before the start of his third NHL season, Elliot sort of adopts three newcomers.

They don't move in with him and Adam, but they follow him around like ducklings during training camp. It's not that surprising that one of them is Evan Samuels, because he remembers Elliot from when he was visiting Blake a few summers ago. It's weird at first, to have him around, this kid who looks so much like Blake but couldn't be any more different if he tried. He talks more, smiles more, and is generally more inclined to share information than Blake has ever been. William Isaksson, their new Swedish kid, seems to start following Evan around, and then Andreas Wagner, their new German kid, joins the New Kid Club as well.

Elliot doesn't even notice at first, he tries to help them out, finds them places to stay, calls the bank for Andreas, because he's scared that his English isn't good enough, helps William with his driver's license, gives them pointers on how to navigate the city, which places to avoid, where to go for dinner. It's all stuff that other people did for him when he first came to New York.

He literally went through all of that, minus the language barrier, so it makes sense that he passes on what he knows.

He sits with them during lunch, because he remembers being at a total loss, not knowing where to sit, who to talk to. He'll leave the pranking and chirping to the other guys. He doesn't really mind that those three are basically glued to him and look at him wide-eyed when he talks about last season's playoffs.

They got closer to the Cup than the Ravens have been in the last seven years. They didn't make it past the first round, but the media called it a miracle. Elliot would have rather called it hard fucking work.

Elliot likes the kids. Probably because he's a kid, too, barely older than the three of them. Evan is the youngest, Andreas almost a year older than him, and William has already played a season with the Sailors' farm team out West and got traded to New York during the summer. William talks about Blake MacDonald, the Sailors' Hockey Jesus, all the time and every time Elliot hears his name he thinks about his Blake, except he's not really *his* Blake, not anymore. Evan doesn't usually mention his brother and Elliot can't decide if he's grateful or if it's driving him nuts.

Evan mostly talks about other players he admires and William joins in, hearts in his eyes, and Elliot can see the beginning of a wonderful friendship there. Andreas often sits next to them and looks lost because William's English is so good that he almost talks faster than Evan and uses words that Elliot doesn't know the meaning of, but they usually slow down quickly when they notice that Andreas isn't following.

Their captain finds Elliot before their first preseason game and gives him a pat on the back. "Good job with the kids, Moo," Jacob says.

"I was just trying to help," Elliot says.

"Yeah, that's what I'm saying," Jacob replies and hands him a jersey. "Good job with the kids."

Elliot frowns down at the jersey, because he does have one hanging in his stall, except, when he looks at it, he notices that this one has an A on it. "I…"

"Chris, TJ and I talked about it and we talked to the coaching staff and we agreed that you deserve it," Jacob says, so thankfully Elliot is saved from the embarrassment of being totally speechless. "So we'll have three alternates and you guys are gonna rotate. Sound good?"

"Thank you," Elliot says.

"Put it on, eh?"

Elliot nods and pulls it over his head and the rest of the evening is full of pats on the back and hugs and his three little ducklings are looking at him with stars in their eyes, congratulating him like he signed a 10-million-dollar contract and won the Cup at the same time. They win the game 6-1, and when Elliot falls into bed that night he still has a smile on his face.

He's almost asleep when his phone buzzes on his nightstand. It's been buzzing all evening with people congratulating him on that A on his jersey — apparently the news spread quickly. He didn't even have a chance to tell his parents, they somehow already knew, must have read it on Twitter or maybe his mom was googling his name again. Elliot's mom follows hockey news like it's world politics and her life depends on it.

Elliot isn't sure why he decides to open his eyes and reach out to grab his phone instead of going to sleep and answering that text tomorrow.

When he sees who it's from his heart betrays him before his brain even has a chance to catch up, fluttering in his chest, ruining the most excellent day he's been having. It's a text from Blake — *saw you were wearing the A tonight, congrats!*

Elliot thanks him and the next time his phone buzzes he doesn't pick it up again.

Blake's third year in the NHL begins with a blur of a preseason.

He ends up on the same ice as Elliot during the second game, tries not let it throw him off and wins them the game with only one goal sneaking past him. Elliot seems to be distraught because he didn't get to score on him and Blake almost expects a text after the game, and is only a little disappointed when he doesn't get one.

They don't talk during warmups. They don't talk during the game, not that there's a lot of time for more than a quick hello. Blake considers going to the visitors' locker room, but then realizes that he doesn't have more than a hello in him anyway.

He gets sent back to the AHL together with Dennis and they settle back into their apartment quickly with tons of beer and pizza. Dennis literally won't shut up about how he can buy beer for them now and maybe drinks one too many and then falls asleep on the couch while Blake finishes the *Indiana Jones* movie they were watching.

It's easy to fall back into the routine he's known for the past two seasons and nothing too remarkable happens for a few weeks. His grandma comes by to visit and Dennis is devastated when she leaves, because she was cooking all their food. Blake doesn't mind cooking if it's nothing too fancy, but Dennis has managed to burn a variety of things, including pasta and milk, so Blake won't hold it against him if he stays out of the kitchen.

Elliot scores his second career hat trick and Blake sends him a text to congratulate him.

Blake goes on a 6-game win streak and Elliot sends him a text to congratulate him.

Elliot gets invited to the All Star Game and Blake sends him a text to congratulate him.

Other than that, they don't really hear from each other, not until both the Knights' goalies get injured, one after the other, and suddenly Blake's in Manhattan, on NHL ice, with his NHL team hurling pucks at him, and no one other than Elliot Cowell and *his* NHL team on the other side of the center line.

Blake has never played a regular season game that wasn't on home ice. Hell, Blake has never played a regular season game that mattered as much as this one. Not with the Knights. He goes through his warmup routine and tries to settle down. Because this is just a game like any other. And he'll do what he can. And it doesn't matter at all who's coming at him on the ice, doesn't matter if it's Elliot. All Blake has to do is make saves.

And he does, for a while. He keeps the door shut until the second period, at the end of which they're tied at one. Could be worse.

He tunes out the crowd as best as he can during the third, tries not to listen to what they're chanting at him and his teammates, but things start to get chippy on the ice soon, guys pushing and shoving each other, trying to draw penalties and the whistle goes and goes.

Elliot comes for him on a breakaway late in the third, and shit, he's so fast, there's no way for anyone to catch up, no matter how hard they try, and somehow, through some sort of miracle, Blake gets his stick on it and it deflects up into the netting. The others catch up when the whistle has already gone and there's some more pushing and shoving and yelling behind Blake's net.

Blake doesn't want to get too involved, but Elliot is at the sidelines, holding on to one of Blake's teammates, and Blake can't help himself, he has to poke Elliot in the back of the neck with his stick. Very gently. Just a little tickle. Elliot spins around, eyes narrowed, ready to pounce, but only until he realizes that Blake is the culprit. Blake gets a masterful eye-roll in return.

Elliot is distracted soon enough, giving the refs an earful when they start escorting guys from both teams to the penalty boxes, because the Ravens have apparently never done anything wrong in their lives. They end up playing 4-on-4, but the clock runs down with the game still tied.

The Knights lose it in OT, but Blake is still sent off the ice with his teammates patting his back.

The Ravens give him third star of the game for his 37 saves.

When he's asked why he was bugging Elliot, Blake says, "I was saying hello to an old friend. We used to play together."

saying hello my ass, Elliot texts him a few hours later.

Blake doesn't reply, only smiles about it and pulls the sheets up to his chin and goes to sleep.

He's staying at Mattie's house, so he knows when Mattie is ready to come back. Blake is happy for him when it turns out to be a quick recovery, loses another game and then wins two with the team in the meantime, then he gets pulled aside after practice one day.

"Blake," Coach says and he's making a face that Blake has never seen before, which probably means it's not a good one.

"You're sending me down?" Blake guesses. He doesn't get it. Koivu had to have surgery and is on IR, so even with Mattie back in the lineup, they're going to need a backup. He was playing well.

"You've been great for us," Coach says, "but we need you to play more games, and you're not going to play those here with Mattie back in the lineup."

Okay, maybe he does get it. He needs experience and if they send him down, there's a chance that he'll get to start for the Raiders more than he ever did before. The Raiders are going to the playoffs for sure. Dennis got his first hatty while Blake was in Newark, although that was sadly also the only game they won, being in a bit of a goaltending pickle with both of their regular goalies on the NHL team.

So Blake packs his bags and drives back to the place he shares with Dennis, with a bag full of food from Mattie on the backseat and pictures that Mattie's kids drew for him, of him in goal, and of him and the dogs, and of him with the whole family. Blake was experiencing a few emotions too many when one of Mattie's tiny kids came up to him and said, "I drew you a picture of Shadow, because you always pet him and you'll probably miss him, so you can take this and look at him and not miss him as much."

Dennis doesn't chirp him when he puts that picture on their fridge.

The Knights face the Ravens in the first round of playoffs and if Blake wasn't so preoccupied with their own playoff race, he might find the time to be sad that he's not in Newark to win that series with the Knights. The Knights don't make it past the second round, though, but that only means that Mattie and his entire family are in the stands in Samuels jerseys when Blake gets to lift the Calder Cup.

That night, Blake has an entire bottle of champagne poured over his head and after that he has almost an entire bottle of champagne poured into this mouth, thankfully much slower, but still with little precision. Some insanely smart person has covered their entire locker room in plastic, so no one even blinks when Dennis lies down on the floor and starts making champagne angels, although at this point there's probably some beer mixed in there, too.

They take the party and their Cup to a local club that has likely never seen so many people and someone starts buying shots.

Blake has never been this drunk in his life.

He knows that because he doesn't even protest when the boys drag him onto the dance floor. Someone's shouting something about getting tattoos – Blake got two last summer, is working on a sleeve, but at least his brain is alert enough to consider spontaneous tattoos a terrible idea.

"Blake, this is Elena," someone shouts into his ear and then he's dancing with a girl who smiles at him and laughs when Blake gives her a twirl. He doesn't know how to dance. He doesn't know what to do with a pretty girl.

She wraps her arms around his neck and Blake does his best not to disappoint in the dancing department, then he asks her if she wants a drink, but she shakes her head and they keep dancing. When the song fades into another, he tells her that he'd also buy her mozzarella sticks, or whatever else she wants, because it's not like drinks are the only thing on the menu, and she laughs and says that she's just fine right here.

Blake kisses her, because that's what's expected from him here, right? He kisses her, because maybe it won't be so bad.

He should feel something. Anything. He wants to sleep. The room is spinning and he needs some fresh air. He excuses himself and escapes to the bathroom, slips into a stall and sits down, leans his head against the cold wall, and breathes. The smell makes him nauseous, but he can't go back out there yet.

This isn't him, he can't kiss a girl and pretend that it's okay or that it's what he wants. He left that behind when he was fifteen. Or so he thought. He misses being close to someone, and it's not even so much about sex, a hug would be fine, but maybe one that doesn't end.

He needs to drink some water.

"Yo, Fish, is that you? You okay in there?"

"I'm fine," Blake says.

He's fine.

Everything is fine.

He makes it out of the club, makes it home, curls into bed and gets back up to throw up in his bathroom a little while later, only barely making it to the toilet bowl.

Dennis finds him there in the morning, nudging him with his foot. "Shit, dude, wake up."

Blake blinks at him and glares. Dennis looks like he just crawled out of bed, his hair all over the place. Blake doesn't know how Dennis is standing up straight right now. He wants to be on this bathroom floor forever. "No. I live here now."

"Come on."

Someone behind Dennis snorts. Probably his girlfriend. "I'll get you both some water."

Blake sits up and immediately regrets it. Somewhere, something is buzzing. "What's that noise?"

"Probably your phone."

It's on the floor. Why is his phone on the floor?

24

Blake only stares at it.

Dennis reaches down to ruffle his hair. "It's okay, Fish, we all feel like we're dead, but the show must go on."

"I wanna sleep."

"Yeah, me too. Nap time is later. Breakfast time at Timo's house is now. Come on, Liz is gonna drop us off." Dennis wanders out of the bathroom, muttering, "Fuck, I hope I don't throw up in the car."

Blake takes a deep breath. Yeah, he needs to get off the floor.

"Calder Cup champions, baby," Dennis shouts downstairs. "Braden, Oscar, time to wake the fuck up! And Braden get your fucking shoes off the couch, you savage. Who raised you?"

Blake had no idea that Braden and Oscar were staying over. He grins, but doesn't move yet. Things could be worse. Yes, he's on a bathroom floor and, yes, he's one wrong move away from a slow and painful death, but that's just because they won the Calder Cup.

With a sigh, Blake closes his eyes.

"Don't sleep, Fish!"

Something soft hits him in the face, presumably a clean shirt.

Blake groans.

Elliot can't decide if he should give Blake a call back. To see if he's still alive. He sounded beyond wasted on the phone last night.

Pictures of the Raiders show up on Twitter not too much later, from the team breakfast they were having at their captain's house and Blake is holding a mug that might have once said something like *World's Best Dad*, except someone's put tape over the last word and scribbled *Goalie* on it. He looks tired and rumpled, but he has the smallest of smiles on his face.

Elliot is so proud of him and he told Blake that last night on the phone, but only because he was reasonably sure that Blake wouldn't remember. Blake essentially won the Raiders the final series. He'll play in Newark soon enough.

Elliot's season ended earlier than he would have liked, but he's still happy with how they played, how hard they all fought. He'll be staying in New York, because he can see this team going somewhere. He's signed his contract. Eight years. Eight million a year. It was a lot easier than he thought it would be, making all those choices, asking for what he wanted. His agent did most of the work, of course, but Elliot wasn't completely out of his depth.

Nothing is going to change, really. Maybe, in a year or two, he can find himself his own apartment, but for now he'll be Adam's roommate. Adam almost looked relieved when Elliot asked if he could stay in his room for another year. "For sure," Adam said, "We kinda need each other to keep each other alive, you know?"

He has a point there, because one of the two of them always remembers that they should maybe buy some food, and it works really well for them. They're both still alive.

Elliot spends some time in Toronto with his parents after the end of the season, then he goes to Sweden with Adam for Magnus's wedding. They stay for two weeks and then head back to the city together. Adam has a trainer in New York that he really likes, so Elliot sticks around to train with him and a few of the other guys this summer.

He likes the city. He lets Adam drag him along to baseball games, they try new restaurants, they hang out at the park and elbow each other when they see a dog.

They find their new favorite takeout place that summer, down the street from their apartment. They have the best dumplings in the world and Elliot goes way too often, especially when Adam is out with his girlfriend and Elliot isn't in the mood to cook.

It's where he meets Natalie. She's a college student, pre-law, works in the café across the street a few times a week, and is also weak for dumplings apparently. They start talking while they wait for their orders and then end up eating together at one of the tiny tables by the window instead of taking their food home.

Natalie has never been to a hockey game, but has heard about the Ravens. Her college friend's dad works for the Comets down in North Carolina. She likes basketball, but isn't tall enough to play professionally and has a black cat called Vader that lives with her parents and she shows him pictures and he offers to buy her dessert because he doesn't want to stop talking to her yet.

"I know a place," she says and they walk five minutes to a bakery that Elliot has never seen before, even though he's lived here for three years. They get cupcakes and coffee and they talk until the place closes, after they've also tried the brownies and the red velvet cake.

Elliot is gonna have to watch it for the rest of the week, but it was worth it.

He walks her to the Subway after and she thanks him and he says, "Can I give you my number?"

He's new at this, except for the few dates that his teammates set him up on, one disaster after the other, and maybe he should have asked for her number instead, but she only laughs and hands him her phone. Elliot is almost surprised when she doesn't say no, is pretty sure that he made a complete ass of himself. He talked about hockey way too much, even though she told him that she didn't know much about it and then he got distracted by two dogs on the way to the Subway while she was talking. When he puts his number in her phone, he gets the numbers mixed up twice, his face going red when he finally hands back the phone after what seemed like an eternity.

Natalie has dimples when she smiles at him. "I'll call you," she says.

"Looking forward to it," Elliot replies.

As he turns to walk back home, he realizes that he actually meant it, that it wasn't just something he said to be polite, like he usually does. He genuinely wants to spend more time with her, get to know her, hear more about that murderous cat of hers.

Even now that the streets are dipped in a bright orange glow, the summer heat still clinging to the city streets, the air heavy and thick, Elliot feels light.

4

Blake gets an invitation to Brammer's house on Long Island for an end of summer party before they have to report for training camp, so Blake leaves his grandma's house in Connecticut a few days earlier than planned, kisses her goodbye and pretends that he doesn't notice all the food she's sneaking into his bags as he gets ready to go. Evan has already taken off, only spent two weeks at home around the time when Blake had his day with the Cup.

The drive down to Long Island isn't terrible, so Blake gets to Brammer's house about an hour earlier than planned, but Brammer waves him off when he apologizes and pulls him into the house, which is already full of people.

Most of them are Knights, some are their girlfriends, some of them Blake has never seen before. When Brammer introduces one of the strangers as Noah Andersson, Blake realizes that he probably does know most of them and doesn't recognize them without their gear on.

Noah Andersson plays defense for the Brooklyn Mariners. He got drafted the same year as Blake. And Elliot. They weren't really friends or anything, but as far as Blake knows, no one's ever uttered a single bad word about Noah. Blake doesn't particularly like the way he plays, but he doesn't particularly like the way anyone on an opposing team plays when they're putting pucks into his net.

"Almost didn't recognize you without the pads," Noah says. He's tall and blond and when he smiles, his eyes crinkle.

"Same," Blake says.

Noah winks at him. "I'm the guy who kept taking your net off."

"Yeah, as if I could forget," Blake says.

"Here, let me get you a drink and we'll call a truce until tomorrow morning," Noah says and nudges him further into the house. Brammer has disappeared to fuck-knows-where. "What've you been up to?"

28

Blake shrugs. "Hockey, training, you know…"

"Yeah, hockey, training, winning the Calder Cup… That kinda stuff, huh?"

For some reason, Blake's face goes hot under Noah's scrutiny when he doesn't reply right away. There's something sheepish about Noah's smile. "Yeah, stuff like that," Blake eventually says.

"Did you have a good day with the Cup?"

Blake nods. "I took it back home. Put some ice cream in it."

"Where's home?"

"Norwalk."

Noah's eyebrows twitch. "Connecticut?"

"Yeah," Blake says. Noah would know it, of course, because he spent a little over two seasons playing for the Mariners' farm team in Bridgeport. They played against each other quite a bit and Noah somehow took his net off every time they played against each other, until the Mariners' entire D-corps completely fell apart last season and Noah got called up and never got sent back down again.

Blake follows Noah through the kitchen and a set of doors and then they're next to the pool, where they instantly get soaked by one of Noah's teammates – if Blake remembers correctly – who is chasing one of Blake's teammates around the pool with a water gun. Blake and Noah get caught in the crossfire.

"Oh, great," Blake says gruffly.

Noah laughs and grabs a drink from a table that's probably supposed to be safe from the fighting in the pool area. The drinks are very blue. "Try these. Brammer's girlfriend made them and they're amazing."

A light breeze ruffles Noah's hair. He has a scar that cuts through his eyebrow and it makes him look a little like a pirate. Who's also a Disney prince. And a model. All at the same time.

"What did you do this summer?" Blake asks, mostly to distract himself.

"Went to the Caribbean with some of the boys, said hi to my mom. She lives in LA, because Dad used to play there way back in the day and after they got divorced, she didn't want to stay in Vancouver, so she went back."

Ten minutes later they're deep into a conversation about how Noah wouldn't call himself Swedish, having grown up in Canada, with a few trips to Sweden sprinkled in here and there. His dad is working in Vancouver, for the local broadcast crew, but it seems that Noah isn't too keen on talking about his famous hockey player dad and quickly changes the topic back to his mom. She is probably a model or a movie star, and that's why Noah looks like he should be playing a character on *Baywatch*.

They watch the water gun battle come to end with all parties jumping into the pool, splashing everyone who hasn't managed to duck behind something. Blake is only fast enough to shield his drink, but ends up getting splashed from head to toe. Noah, next to him, has somehow mostly stayed dry.

"Great," Blake says again. He's wearing swimming trunks, but his shirt is pretty much soaked through.

"Sorry, Fish," Henny shouts from the pool. Going by the shit-eating grin on his face, he's not sorry at all.

"Fish," Noah echoes.

Blake waves him off, because he doesn't want to explain the salmon thing again. He wipes a few wet strands of hair out of his face.

Noah gives him an approving look, eyes dipping to the sea monster tattoo on Blake's arm. "You know, that's a good look on a guy whose nickname is Fish."

"Thanks," Blake says dryly.

"Maybe we should hop in, too."

"Huh…" Not the worst idea. Blake, pale even after spending a decent number of days in the summer sun, looks like a ghost next to some of the other guys, but he's used to it. He's never been self-conscious about the way he looks. His height was an issue for a while, but he literally grew out of that.

When Noah tugs off his shirt and leaves it by the side of the pool without a care in the world, Blake can't help but feel… something. Blake quickly looks away, spreads out his own shirt on a chair so it'll dry in the sun while he's in the pool, and jumps into the water alongside Noah.

Blake ends up on a floating unicorn, feet dangling into the water, then someone puts heart-shaped sunglasses on him that likely belong to someone's girlfriend, next is a drink in his hand and then Brammer is snapping a picture, cackling as he keeps fiddling with his phone, probably putting that picture on Instagram for the entire world to see. Blake quite likes the unicorn and stays where he is, but gives back the sunglasses when a blonde girl at the side of the pool asks if she could please have them back. She blows a kiss his way when he hands them over.

Noah eventually tips over his unicorn and takes off, legs kicking, but Blake catches him quickly and pulls him under, laughing when Noah tries to retaliate but goes under again because he's not tall enough to stand.

"You always look so serious on the ice, I didn't realize you even…," Noah grins, "know how to smile."

Blake huffs.

"Honestly, your murder eyes are scary."

"I don't have murder eyes," Blake protests.

"Yeah, you do," Henny throws in, now chilling in the hot tub at the side of the pool. "I'd be so scared if we weren't on the same team."

Noah nods. "Now imagine how I felt."

"Next time you come at me with the puck, I'll smile," Blake says, even though he has no idea when they'll even be on the same ice again.

Noah laughs and clambers out of the pool, bathing suit hanging low. Blake doesn't look. Except that he does, but only for a second. He hasn't allowed himself to find anyone attractive in a while. Too big of a risk to hook up with random guys, too big of a risk for anyone to know when they don't have as much to lose as he does.

So usually he doesn't look, considers nothing, and walks away when he starts thinking about doing something stupid.

Not that he's thinking about anything of the sort right now.

It's just… Noah Andersson is hot and maybe Blake is allowed to notice that.

"Summer went by fast, didn't it?" Noah says as he plops down on a chair, dripping all over the place.

Blake hums in agreement. His summer was shorter than he was used to from his first two seasons, but he's excited to get back to playing, too.

"I mean, I would have obviously preferred it even shorter, but…" Noah shrugs. "There's always next season."

Blake nods. "You guys have been good."

"High praise from the Calder Cup champion."

"You make it sound like I'm the only one."

"Aren't you?" Noah asks and Blake gives him a shove. "No, but seriously, they wouldn't have made it without you. You were a beast. I hope they don't put you in goal against us next season, I'm already quaking in my boots."

Blake huffs at him, although he is cautiously excited for next season. He re-signed with the Knights, got a pretty good pay raise out of it, and was told that he'd have a chance of backing up Mattie in Newark next season if he performed well during training camp. He's ready for it, confident that he can compete on the level they need him on.

Mattie is expecting him at his house tomorrow. Blake called him to ask if he was coming to Brammer's party and Mattie laughed at him for a full minute before he went dead-silent and eventually said, "No." When he looks around, Blake does realize that most of the guys at the party have played less than ten seasons, don't have kids at home, and can easily spend an entire day at a pool party because they don't have any other obligations.

Noah gets them another round of drinks. They're sweet and you can barely taste the alcohol in them, but Blake starts to feel them eventually, his cheeks turning hot despite their spot in the shade. Two girls, friends of Brammer's girlfriend, join them when Brammer shows up with enough pizza to feed three entire hockey teams, and start asking them about their teams. Noah does most of the talking, which Blake is grateful for, and listens to him as he tells a story about when they filled their goalie's trunk up with pucks last season.

Blake lets out a pained groan at the thought and Noah laughs and claps him on the back, his hand lingering for a moment, fingers warm against his skin. He still feels it after Noah has pulled his hand away.

Blake shakes it off by taking another sip of his drink, which doesn't help at all, only makes his face even hotter. He must look like a tomato sitting here and probably has a bit of a sunburn on his face and shoulders as well.

One of the girls keeps shooting him looks even as Noah talks and Blake has had to deal with this long enough to know that there's some interest there. He doesn't want to be rude, but also keeps himself from smiling back at her, because he doesn't want to give her the wrong idea. He keeps his eyes on his drink, and on Noah as he talks, and eventually excuses himself to find the bathroom.

When he returns, it's just Noah, handing him another drink as he sits down.

"Weren't feeling it, huh?" Noah asks.

"I… what?"

"Aw, come on, don't tell me you didn't notice. She was basically undressing you with her eyes. Not that there's a lot left to undress, but you know what I mean."

Again, Blake's face goes red and he wishes he could stop it somehow. It's more about Noah's eyes on him, slowly traveling down his naked torso and less about the girl who couldn't take her eyes off him. And of course Noah doesn't know it, but Blake does and it's mortifying.

He wants someone's hands on him so badly.

He takes another sip and resigns himself to getting stupidly drunk, because he doesn't usually drink much during the season and he deserves one last party and, maybe just this once, he can allow himself to cope with being in the closet the unhealthy way.

"You seeing anyone?" Noah asks.

"No, it's not that…" Blake shrugs, at a loss. "I'm not really in a good place to be in a relationship right now."

Noah laughs. "Pretty sure that she would have gone for something less permanent, too."

Blake shrugs again. Takes another sip of his drink. And then nearly drops it when he sees a familiar face on the other side of the pool.

Elliot wasn't going to let Adam drag him to a party out on Long Island a few days before the start of training camp, but Adam's girlfriend is out of town – he took her to the airport this afternoon – and he didn't want to go alone, so he was nagging at Elliot until he caved. "You don't have to drink," Adam said as they left their apartment. "You can just eat the food and have a good time and hop in the pool and... I don't know."

It wasn't until they were almost there that Adam mentioned that they were on their way to Johnny Brammer's house.

"Johnny Brammer who plays for the Knights? That Johnny Brammer?"

"I've known him for ages," Adam says. "He's been throwing that party for like... the past three years, I think? I was gonna take you last year, remember? And then you pretended that you had a mysterious illness."

Elliot laughs, because he does remember that. He isn't much of a party person, likes hanging out with the guys, but not at clubs. Bars are mostly okay, although he always felt bad when he got into places before he was twenty-one, because he knew he wasn't supposed to be there. "Seriously, though, we're going into enemy territory. You should have warned me." He's wearing a Ravens baseball hat that he's probably going to leave in the car.

"Oh, don't worry about it, Bram usually invites guys from other teams. I think Riley said he was going. Bunch of Mariners are gonna be there, too."

"That's just asking for trouble."

"Nah, the boys can behave, it's not even the preseason yet."

Elliot decides to trust Adam on that; he's been to that party before after all.

They're greeted by a heavily inebriated Johnny Brammer who shouts at a fellow Jersey Knight to hand them drinks. Elliot does know most of the guys at the party, sees Riley talking to a blonde girl in the kitchen. He waves at them when he sees them, but all it takes is a shared look with Adam for them to decide that they're not saying hello right now.

The doors at the back of the kitchen are open, leading them out onto a terrace where people are lounging on beach chairs, eating pizza, drinking, laughing, and there's people in the pool, throwing a ball back and forth. A guy Elliot doesn't recognize is floating around on a slowly deflating unicorn.

Adam has already finished his drink, so Elliot hands over his own, because he didn't really want it in the first place and takes a bottle of water from a nearby table. When he looks around, Adam has disappeared and Elliot is stranded by the pool. He's never had much trouble getting to know new people, but he hasn't shaken off the feeling of being in enemy territory, so for a moment he stands there by himself, not sure where to go next.

Elliot's eyes wander across the crowd gathered around the pool and eventually settle on Blake, who is sitting on a beach chair next to the Mariners' Noah Andersson, who's laughing at something Blake just said. Elliot didn't even know those two knew each other, but he has to admit that he knows very little about Blake in general these days.

They text sometimes, never much, and even less this summer, after Blake won the Calder Cup. Elliot assumes that he's embarrassed and wants to tell him that it's fine, that he gets it, that he has nothing to be embarrassed about. Maybe today's not the best day for that, though.

Blake, of course, immediately catches him staring, and before Elliot can disappear, Andersson catches him looking as well and waves and now Elliot has to head over there to say hello. Anything else would be rude.

"Hi," Elliot says.

Blake looks at him for a long moment before he nods at him and says, "Hey."

"Hey, what's up," Noah says and nods at an empty chair. "Have a seat. I'm Noah. Andersson."

"I know," Elliot says. "Sorry." He doesn't even know why he's apologizing, probably because he's been mostly looking at Blake and only spared Noah the briefest of glances.

"You guys know each other, yeah?" Noah asks. "OHL?"

Blake nods.

"Cool," Noah says and pulls a pizza carton off a table next to them. "Want some?"

"Thanks," Elliot says. He takes a slice and lets Noah carry the conversation, mostly about off-season training and Elliot chimes in here and there, talking about his and Adam's trainer, who's been torturing them all summer.

Blake is quiet, but that's hardly surprising. He's never been much of a talker, especially when there was someone else around who didn't mind doing the talking and that clearly hasn't changed. He looks different, though. Broader somehow, tattoos covering his arms, and his hair longer, falling down to his shoulders, disheveled, and it's a good look on him. Elliot has seen pictures of him, has even seen him in person throughout the season, and yet Elliot is surprised that Blake isn't the exact same person he was three years ago. Sitting next to him like this, like they're old friends who happened to come across each other at the same party, seems wrong somehow.

"How do you know Brammer?" Blake eventually asks.

"Oh, I don't, really," Elliot says. "Adam's girlfriend's out of town and I'm... a mediocre replacement, I guess."

"I'm sure you're..." Noah trails off with a grin. "Sorry, I gotta go say hi to someone. I'll see you guys around."

Elliot only nods, his eyes settling on Blake, who looks like he wants to bolt. He fights down the urge to ask Blake if he's okay and instead says, "How was your summer?"

"Good," Blake says. "How about you?"

"Also good," Elliot replies. "I went to Sweden for Magnus's wedding and it was... Have you ever been?"

"No. Liked it, huh?"

Elliot nods.

"Did you swing by Iceland while you were in the general area?"

"I wouldn't say that Iceland is in the general area," Elliot says with a laugh.

Blake's lips twitch, like that was his plan all along, making Elliot laugh. The thought pulls at something in him, so he tries desperately not to think at all.

"So Iceland's still on the list?" Blake asks.

"Yep, still on the list."

Elliot doesn't really remember that conversation, only remembers being on the road, sharing a room with Blake, curled up in Blake's bed instead of his own, mumbling nonsense between kisses and one of those things was, "I want to go to Iceland."

Blake promised he'd go with him. They obviously never went. Blake shifts in his seat, restless.

Elliot would bet that they're going to exchange about two or three more pleasantries and then Blake will find a reason to escape from him.

"Excited for the season?" Blake asks.

"Yeah, it'll be good to get back on the ice."

"Tell Evan I said hi if you see him."

Again, Elliot can't help but laugh, because of course Blake is telling him to say hi to his brother. "Sure."

With the straightest, most offended face, Blake says, "Can't be assed to call me. Like, ever. Little shit."

Elliot grins.

"Anyway, I'm gonna go, uh..." Blake nods at the house. "Find a bathroom."

He walks away, pulling a shirt that's presumably his off a different chair on his way into the house.

Elliot is still smiling for some reason, maybe because Blake looks more grown up but hasn't changed so much after all, maybe because they had an actual conversation that wasn't horribly awkward.

He grabs another slice of pizza and leans back. He's almost glad that Adam convinced him to tag along.

Elliot finds Blake a while later when the sun has almost set and Brammer's girlfriend has started lighting candles and torches around the pool. The crowd has thinned a little and some of the partygoers have wandered down to the beach. Elliot sincerely hopes that no one's going to go swimming.

After Adam introduces him to some friends, Elliot wanders back outside, watches the waves, then notices Blake sitting on a low stone wall, down the hill behind the pool, his shoes behind him, feet in the sand. He looks up when Elliot approaches and tucks a strand of dark hair behind his ear, eyeing Elliot like he's contemplating if he should walk away and drown himself in the ocean.

"Hey," Elliot says. "Can I sit?"

"Sure."

Elliot clambers onto the stone wall and realizes he's way too close to Blake, but now it's probably too late to scoot away, so he stays where he is, with a mere inch between them. It's gotten so dark that he can barely see Blake's face, the only light coming from the house behind them, a little further up the hill.

Again, Elliot keeps himself from asking Blake if he's okay. Instead, he says, "Congrats on the contract." He sent exactly that to Blake when he signed that contract, but he can't think of anything else to say.

"Thanks," Blake says. "You, uh… Yours is pretty good, too."

Elliot laughs. "Yeah, pretty good."

"Ravens are treating you well?"

"They're a good group of guys," Elliot says and now he sounds like he's talking to the media. "I like playing with them. I never felt like I didn't belong, you know?"

Blake hums.

"How's your grandma doing?" Elliot asks.

"She's okay. Worse than a nutritionist, though. Her sister showed her how to use Google, so she put together a meal plan for the summer and she got really serious about it."

A snort escapes Elliot and Blake elbows him in the side.

"Not funny," Blake grumbles. "I just wanted some cookies."

Elliot pats Blake's back, because that's what he does when he's around friends and Blake freezes, goes rigid and Elliot pulls his hand away quickly, resolving to leave it in his lap.

"Guess I'll have to make my own cookies," Blake mutters.

Elliot assumes that Blake's relationship with his grandma isn't at all like the one Elliot has with his own, because Blake's grandma practically raised him, with his parents not being around anymore. Blake never talked about it much and Elliot didn't ask, because it would have felt much too personal, like he was prying, but it must have been hard for him.

This time, Elliot doesn't manage to keep the words from slipping out. "Are you okay?"

"Why wouldn't I be?" Blake asks, no emotion whatsoever in his voice.

"It's... When you called me that night, you sounded like... I don't know. I just wanted to ask."

A moment of silence, then Blake says, "When I called you?"

"After you won the Cup."

"After I won the..." Blake takes a deep breath. "I called you. I'm sorry. I was really drunk and I... I don't even remember calling you."

"Oh. Yeah." Elliot shrugs, tries to laugh it off. "Don't worry about it."

"I'm sorry," Blake says again.

"Really, it wasn't... It's okay."

"Okay."

"Just, if you ever need someone to talk or anything..." Elliot trails off. They've barely talked at all recently, so maybe this offer rings hollow, but he doesn't want Blake to think that he doesn't care either. "We're still friends."

"Yeah," Blake says. "Thank you."

Elliot nods, not even sure if Blake can see it in the dark.

"Do I want to know what I said to you on the phone?" Blake asks, voice low.

"It was... You know, I barely understood half of it, you were really, really drunk, but it kinda sounded like you... needed a friend. I don't know." Again, Elliot shrugs, wondering how much he should tell him. Blake was probably having a rough night, and when you're drunk everything seems like the worst thing in the world at a certain stage.

Blake doesn't say anything, but then he's closer all of a sudden, his arm pressed against Elliot's, solid and warm, and it could be an accident, just him shifting, but then he doesn't pull away.

"I..." Blake doesn't finish, never does, but his pinkie knocks against Elliot's wrist.

Elliot knows this move, but he can't do this right now, so he pulls his hand away and says, "Blake."

"Sorry."

"No, don't be sorry, it's okay. It's okay. But... I'm seeing someone, so I can't... It wouldn't be fair."

"Oh," Blake says. The warmth disappears and that inch between them is back within a second. "You're seeing someone?"

"Yeah, Natalie, she's… my girlfriend."

"Oh," Blake says again.

It's been three years, so Elliot probably doesn't have to worry about hurting Blake by telling him this. It's not like they were together. They were… something else. Something undefined, something unfinished. Still, he wishes he could see Blake's face right now, to be sure. "We can talk about this stuff, right?" Elliot eventually asks.

"Yeah, of course we can," Blake says. His voice doesn't waver.

"You're not seeing anyone?"

Blake huffs. "No." And he makes it sound like it should be obvious, and maybe it is. Elliot doesn't know what it's like for Blake, if he's even told anyone, or if he's hiding it. He thinks about the night Blake called him, telling him that he needed to talk to someone who knew, someone who could even remotely understand how lonely he is.

"I know it's hard," Elliot says.

"Oh, do you know that it's hard, huh?" There's something vicious in the way Blake says it and it's not something Elliot is used to at all. Blake has always been gentle with him, always so patient.

Elliot bristles, involuntarily, at the implication of it. "What are you trying to say?" he hisses, fighting to keep his voice low, because even though no one's close enough to hear what they're saying, they're not alone out here. "That I have it easier somehow, because I like women, too?"

"Well, things seem to be working out fine for you," Blake says.

"Fuck that," Elliot says and stands up, because he doesn't want to sit next to him anymore all of a sudden. "Do you think if I had it that fucking easy, I would be–" He stops himself before he says something he's going to regret. Like, if he had it that fucking easy, would he be with anyone other than Blake? If they could have been together, wouldn't he– Elliot takes a deep breath. No need to go down that road. Blake never really had feelings for him anyway, it was just convenient for both of them, and it was good while it lasted, but maybe Elliot caught himself wishing that it didn't have to end every now and then in the course of the last three years.

That doesn't matter now. He's with Natalie. She makes him laugh and he misses her when he can't see her and he'd actually rather crawl into bed with her instead of having this fight with Blake about who has it harder, like it's some sort of competition. He shouldn't have brought it up, Blake is drunk and Elliot is on the way there, because he decided to have a few beers with Adam after all. This conversation was never going to end well.

"I'm gonna go," Elliot says. "Have a good season."

Blake doesn't reply and picks up his drink.

"What, you're not even gonna say anything?"

It's very Blake.

Elliot hates it. "Fine, be a fucking ass," he says. "Drink some water," he adds, because he can't help himself.

He's pretty sure that Blake scoffs at him as he walks away, but Elliot doesn't turn around again.

Blake has been staring out into the darkness for so long that he can actually see the waves now, his eyes used to the dark. Out there, two people are chasing each other around the beach, both of them laughing, and a little further to his right, two people are whispering to each other, too far away for Blake to understand a word.

He wants to go home, wherever the fuck that is supposed to be. He doesn't really have a place, because he doesn't have a guaranteed roster spot with the Knights, but if he doesn't fuck up during training camp, Dennis will have to find a different roommate. Blake is going to move in with Mattie for the time being and live in that little apartment he has in the basement. He hates that he doesn't really have a place to go, not that he could drive anywhere with how many drinks he's had. Brammer has told him from the start that there'll be more than enough couches to sleep on, so maybe Blake should find himself one of those.

He's mad at Elliot, though, and he doesn't want to come across him on accident, so he stays where he is and listens to the faint sound of the crashing waves.

Elliot had to go and ask him if he was seeing anyone. After he told Blake that he had a girlfriend now. It stung a little, even though Blake wasn't exactly surprised, because Elliot is... pretty. He has those eyelashes and that hair and he's very nice to look at, all in all, and he's always smiling, always nice to everyone, except when he's being an insensitive douchebag. Anyway, Blake wasn't surprised. Elliot is remarkably easy to love. He's so quiet, not that he doesn't talk, he really talks more than most other people do, but in that strange way of his that always pulled Blake in.

Blake empties his drink and decides that it was the last one.

Next to him, someone clears their throat.

"I thought you might have wandered off and drowned," Noah says.

"Nah. I was thinking about it five minutes ago, but..."

Noah raises his eyebrows at him, like he can tell that it wasn't *just* a joke. "Here," he says and hands Blake a bottle of water. "Can I sit?"

"Sure," Blake says, hoping this will be more pleasant than the conversation he had with Elliot.

"I wanted to, uh..." Noah clears his throat, takes a sip from his water bottle, and then stares out at the dark waves for a moment. "There's no

39

good way of saying this, really, and I honestly wasn't sure if I should say anything at all, but… yeah. Anyway." Noah shakes his head and then turns to Blake. "I know about you and Elliot."

If Blake had to make a list of all the things he'd least like to hear another person say to him, that right there would probably be on top of the list.

Blake is frozen on the spot, doesn't know what to do with that information, wants to know how that's even possible, but he knows that he can't ask any questions right now. He has to deny it, so he says, "I don't know what you're talking about."

"I think you do know," Noah says, voice low. "I saw you guys together. After the Combine? I guess you thought there was no one else around, but–"

"What are you trying to do here, exactly?" Blake asks and it comes out sharper than intended, but if Noah is trying to pull some shit here, Blake needs to– Well, what does he need to do? There's nothing he *can* do. If Noah wants to go and tell everyone, it's not like Blake can stop him. All he can do is hope that no one will believe him, it's not like he has evidence.

"No, no, I'm not… That came out wrong," Noah says and laughs nervously. "I didn't tell anyone. I'd never… I swear."

"Nobody else saw?" Blake asks.

"It was just me. And I didn't stick around too long, no worries."

Blake tries to breathe evenly, because this is his worst nightmare right here, someone else knowing, someone he barely knows, with the power to fuck up his entire life. And Elliot's, too, if he wanted to.

"Blake," Noah says, and something soft has crept into his voice that wasn't there before. "I'm saying this all wrong. I'm sorry. I didn't mean to freak you out, I wanted to tell you, because I talked to you earlier and you seem like a good guy, I like you, and I… Back then, I was just so glad that I wasn't the only one."

"That you weren't– Oh."

"Yeah."

"You're…?"

"Yeah," Noah says and winks. "Don't tell anyone."

"No, of course not."

"Good." Noah gives him a nudge. "I honestly didn't want to freak you out and I don't know if you and Elliot are still a thing–"

"We're not."

"Okay, all the better for me, because I was going to say, if you're not, and you need, uh, a friend, you know, a *friend*, I'm available. Very much available."

"Are you serious?"

"Yeah, why wouldn't I be?" Noah says. "Listen, it doesn't have to be... I'm not asking for your hand in marriage here. No strings, if you're not one for strings. Probably easier that way. But you'll be with the Knights and I'll be with the Mariners, so I'm assuming we'll see each other around."

Blake can't do much more than gape at Noah right now.

"Think about it." Noah pats his back. "I'm free tomorrow evening and this," he pushes a piece of paper into Blake's hand, "is my number."

"Okay," Blake says, numb.

"Okay," Noah echoes, somehow amused. "Good talk. See you later."

5

Blake arrives at Mattie's house just after noon, looking a little worse for wear. He slept well enough on a couch at Brammer's house, but a quick glance in the rearview mirror of his car tells him that he still looks like he just rose from the grave. He stopped for a cheeseburger on the way, because he passed on the breakfast that Brammer was cooking up, whistling as he handed out cups of coffee to those who'd spent the night at the house.

He didn't come across Noah or Elliot before he left, which he considered a blessing, but that didn't stop his thoughts from jumping back and forth between them on the entire ride to Mattie's.

When he rings the doorbell, he's greeted by screaming children and excited dogs, Mattie's wife trying to get the kids to leave Blake alone long enough that he can make it into the house. "If you don't let Blake get to his room, he might not want to stay," Mattie says and the girls immediately back off and offer to carry things for him.

Mattie hands him a set of keys and Blake knows the drill, has been here before, so he takes his stuff downstairs, Mattie's kids at his heels, carrying the lightest things he had in the car, carefully setting them down on his bed, both of them beaming when he thanks them for the *Welcome, Fish!* banner they put in his room. They painted the Knights logo on it, the sword glittering, surrounded by extremely colorful fish.

"They worked on it for a week," Mattie mumbles to him. "They used up all their glitter."

He says *glitter* like it's a deadly weapon.

Blake grins.

"Yeah, you're grinning now, but you won't be when it somehow ends up on your gear. That shit gets everywhere."

Blake unpacks, takes a quick shower and considers a nap, but decides to hang out with Mattie and catch up before he turns into a hermit. Katie makes them coffee, because she probably took one look at Blake's face and saw how close to death he is. Mattie offers to make him something to eat, but Blake waves him off.

He found the scrap of paper with Noah's number on it in the pocket of his jeans when he took them off earlier and now it's downstairs in his room and he doesn't know what to do with it, almost wants to throw it away and never think of it ever again, but part of him wants this, just one time, just to take the edge off, because it's been just him for so long and he's almost forgotten what it's like to have someone else touch him, to be kissed and actually want it.

"Blake?"

"What? Sorry."

"You have any plans for tonight?" Mattie asks. "We were gonna take the girls out for dinner at their favorite place, but you're welcome to come with us."

"I was actually thinking about hanging out with a friend later."

"You have friends?" one of Mattie's kids asks.

"Uh, yeah?"

Mattie's shaking with laughter, trying to hide his face behind his hand. "It's okay, kiddo, Blake will be having dinner with us a lot."

Blake spends the next fifteen minutes discussing his favorite food with the girls and they hug him when he admits that he doesn't like kale. Afterwards, Katie sends them upstairs to clean their rooms and Mattie tells Blake to go downstairs and take a nap.

"You kids and your parties," Mattie mumbles good-naturedly as he sends Blake on his way.

Blake flops onto his bed, but doesn't close his eyes right away. He grabs his phone and saves Noah's number, then he scrolls around on Twitter for a few minutes before he goes back to his messages and sends one to Noah – *I'm not driving back to LI today.*

understandable, Noah replies about a minute later, and adds, *dinner in the city? i live in brooklyn, meet u halfway?*

Blake almost wants to ask him if that's it, wants to ask and then what? It didn't sound like Noah just wanted to have dinner when they talked last night, but maybe Blake is getting ahead of himself. He agrees to meeting Noah in the city at a place Noah suggests, because it's not like Blake has spent too much time in the area.

He gets there thirty minutes early, because he must have misread the train schedule or he miscalculated something along the way, so he walks around for a bit and eventually returns to the restaurant, still five minutes early, but Noah is now waiting for him outside the door. Blake doesn't know how to greet him, dismisses a handshake, then dismisses a hug almost as quickly, and then ends up *waving*, which is even worse than anything else he could have done.

Noah grins, throws an arm around him and steers him into the restaurant. They have a booth in the back, which gives them some privacy and Noah's legs brush against Blake's under the table as they sit down. Blake doesn't move for a moment, keeps his eyes on Noah, who's looking back at him, the features of his pirate Disney prince face soft in the low light.

"Order whatever you want, my treat," Noah says. "I have recommendations if you need any."

Blake raises his eyebrows at him. "Why are you paying?"

"Because this was my idea."

Blake hums, because he can't really argue with that and picks up his menu. "They have chicken parmesan."

"A classic," Noah says, nodding approvingly. "Best I've ever had, honestly."

They both end up ordering it, talking about the upcoming season while they wait, like they're old friends and are catching up before training camp starts for both of them. Blake was afraid that things would be awkward, that their conversation would be stilted, that he'd run out of things to say, because he *always* runs out of things to say, but Noah comes to his rescue every time, always has another question to ask, and so they make it through dinner without any drawn-out silences.

Noah tries to talk him into getting dessert, but Blake declines, and so Noah waves their waiter over for the check.

"So," Noah says when they head out into the street, "that wasn't as awkward as I thought it was gonna be."

Blake lets out a huff that's maybe also a laugh, relieved that he wasn't the only one who had second thoughts.

"Listen, I don't usually do stuff like this," Noah says, "but you seem like a nice guy and, like, I'm about to ask you if you want to come home with me and if the answer to that is no, it'd still be cool if we could hang out again."

Blake stares at him, wondering how he can just say stuff like that without tripping over the words.

"Too forward?"

"No, no, I mean, we were talking about this yesterday," Blake says. Or at least Noah was talking about it. Blake was quietly freaking out as he listened.

"It's okay if you don't want to. My ego will only be a little bit bruised and life will go on and… we're all good."

"Okay," Blake says.

"Okay as in okay you want to come with me or–"

"Yeah."

"Shit, all right, I didn't think you were actually gonna agree to this," Noah says. "Let's get a cab, I'll pay. I'll make you breakfast in the morning, too."

Noah holds up his fist and it takes Blake a very long moment to understand that he's supposed to bump it. Not exactly a fist bump kind of situation, but Noah grins and hails them a cab.

Blake doesn't know what the hell he's doing.

They don't touch in the cab, they don't touch until Noah has led him into his apartment, until the door is closed and Noah turns to him with a smile. "Can I get you anything? Glass of wine? Coffee? A snack?"

"I'm good," Blake says.

"Okay, then, I guess we're getting straight down to business?" Noah says and shrugs off his jacket, takes Blake's in passing and throws them on a chair by the door. He's back in Blake's space a moment later, eyes on Blake, expectant. "You still okay with this?"

"Still good," Blake says and hopes it comes out confident and not terrified. It's been a while since he last did this and he's scared that he'll fuck it up somehow and then Noah Andersson, that handsome pirate Disney prince, will laugh at him. Except Noah is probably not the kind of guy who'd laugh at someone else because of that. He's this good-looking guy who probably has people all over the league groveling at his feet just because of his last name and he's loud and outgoing, but also surprisingly polite and generous.

When Blake leans a little closer, Noah suddenly snorts. "I'm sorry," he says, still with a smile on his face.

Blake takes a step back. "What?"

"You..." Noah says and reaches out to reel him back in. "You have glitter on your face."

"Oh... Mattie's kids..."

"It's a nice look on you," Noah says. "Like a broody unicorn. Love it."

"Shush," Blake says and leans in to kiss Noah.

"Wait a second," Noah mutters before Blake can actually do it. "So, for the record... I'm not... let's say I'm not the most experienced guy."

"Okay." Blake won't lie, it's not what he was expecting. He knows it's not exactly easy to get into another guy's pants when you're a professional hockey player, but Noah struck him as someone who has all the experience in the world.

"Just... don't be mad if I don't know what the fuck I'm doing," Noah says.

"Are you..." Blake tilts his head, not quite sure how to say *a virgin* without saying *a virgin*. "Have you *ever* done this?"

"I slept with my girlfriend when I was sixteen and then pretty quickly realized that sleeping with girls wasn't actually my thing."

"I see," Blake says. "Hey, if you don't want to–"

"No, see, the whole point of this is that I want to," Noah says and grabs a fistful of Blake's shirt. "So, you know, give me some directions along the way and we're all good."

Blake hesitates, only for a second, because they should spend a few more minutes talking about this to make sure that they're really on the same page. Before he can say a word, Noah smiles at him and Blake kisses him and he's clumsy about it, but then Noah makes a soft noise against his mouth and Blake forgets about the twinge in the pit of his stomach and it's replaced by that swooping, falling feeling, Noah's hands on his back, lips insistent, eager.

Noah pulls him down the hall with him, into his bedroom, pushes him onto his bed, and then hovers over him, his hair messy, like Blake had his fingers in there. He doesn't remember, maybe he did.

"Okay," Noah says, "what now?"

"Whatever you want."

"That's not helpful, Blake."

"Uh, clothes off?"

"Okay," Noah says and pulls off his shirt with enthusiasm. "Clothes off."

Blake snorts. Maybe this wasn't as terrible of an idea as he initially thought.

"Hey, you..."

"Hey," Elliot says and it doesn't come out as delighted as Natalie's greeting. He's cooking, because he didn't know what else to do, and it looks like Natalie brought takeout, because Elliot didn't tell her that he was cooking. Everything's going wrong today.

Blake was a dick to him last night. They never fought, not about anything important, it was just bickering and quickly resolved misunderstandings, but this is bigger, this one hurt. Still hurts.

"Oh," Natalie says when she drops her takeout bags on the counter, "I didn't know–"

"Sorry, I should have called, I dug up this cookbook earlier and I wanted to try a recipe and now here we are…"

Elliot's kitchen is a mess. Every surface is covered in pots and pans, some in use, some a little dirty because Elliot tried to use them and then realized they were too small. There's food wrappers, spices, empty plastic bags, food that dropped out of pans that he hasn't managed to clean up.

"Can I help?" Natalie asks.

"This is probably not edible," Elliot mutters.

Natalie wraps her arms around him from behind and gives him a squeeze. "We'll try it and if it's really terrible, we'll figure out what you can do better next time."

He waves at his mess of a kitchen. "Are you suggesting that I should do all this again at some point in the future?"

"That's usually how you learn how to do things," Natalie says, amusement creeping into her voice. "You do it several times."

"I know… It just wasn't…"

"What?"

Elliot sighs. "This is stupid."

Natalie's arms disappear and she leans against the counter next to him. "So, I'm guessing there's something else going on here and you definitely don't have to tell me, but if I can help… even if it's by cleaning up some of those pans, let me know, yeah?"

"I'm cooking because I'm stressed, I thought this was going to help, but now I'm even more stressed, because… look at this mess."

Natalie's fingers curl around his wrist. "It could be so much worse. Not that this isn't a pretty impressive mess, but…" She reaches up to run her fingers through his hair.

Elliot sighs and leans into it. "I met an old friend last night and we fought. He… he said something that was… I don't know… I probably shouldn't be mad."

Except he is, and it's burning low in his stomach, even when he's not thinking about it. Doesn't help that he's tired and maybe a little hungover.

"It's okay to be angry. He clearly hurt you."

"Yeah, but…" Elliot shrugs. He shouldn't be as affected by this, they've barely been talking anyway. He thought that Blake wouldn't be so ignorant, that he'd understand that this was as hard for Elliot as it was for him. It's not the *same*, but–

"Hey," Natalie says and pulls him into a hug.

Elliot's food burns and Natalie quickly lets go to pull it off the heat, but there's likely nothing salvageable about it now. Not that it was a culinary masterpiece in the first place, but now half of it is black and crusty. Elliot turns off the stove and pushes the window open. He'll have to accept that the last twenty-four hours were an absolute disaster and move on with his life.

"I'm so glad you brought food," Elliot says and peers into the bags Natalie put on the counter. It's from their favorite place and it looks like she got them a generous amount of dumplings. "You're the best."

"We can have them with…"

"Extremely charred vegetables and chicken? Yeah, sounds delicious."

Natalie cackles and grabs them plates. "You'll get there. Next time you'll know which pans to use and maybe you can banish your girlfriend to the living room, so she doesn't distract you."

Elliot gives her a nudge. "I'll try."

He doesn't let her help clean up the kitchen later, because it's his mess and if his mom taught him one thing it was that he had to clean up his own messes. He wasn't always good at it, still isn't good at it sometimes, but he needs to do one thing right today. He asks Natalie to pick a movie and digs up some ice cream for them instead. Elliot is pretty sure that it's Adam's; he'll buy him a new one tomorrow. Maybe he'll get him two. Adam had to deal with his shitty mood this morning, so he deserves them.

Natalie curls against him on the couch and Elliot starts to slowly get his shit back together. The kitchen is clean, he can close his eyes now, and he'll figure things out with Blake somehow. Not right now, not at any point in the near future, because the season is about to start and he doesn't need this kind of distraction and he doesn't know how to stop being angry yet, but somehow…

He eventually falls asleep, head on Natalie's shoulder, so he at least gets a good ending to a shitty day.

The season doesn't start well for Blake. He's doing fine in the preseason, but once the Knights give him the nod and he gets to start in net in the second half of back-to-back games, he somehow can't get it together. The D kind of leaves him hanging, too, the guys tired from the night before.

When Blake lets in the third goal within ten minutes, Coach Franklin pulls him.

It's a mercy.

Mattie gives him a tap with his stick as Blake heads to the bench. He can't decide if he wants to smash something or cry, so he sits down in the spot that Mattie just vacated and pulls his baseball cap down low so no one can see his face. He gets a pat on the back from one of the assistant coaches and that makes his mood even worse.

During the first intermission, Coach Franklin is poking his finger in every direction, yelling at them to get off their asses and start playing. They're down 5-0 and they still have forty minutes left to play, but it would be a mighty comeback and they all know it. The least they can do is break the shutout. Blake tries to disappear because half of that score is basically his fault, terrible defense or not.

The game ends with a score of 7-2, the team quiet on their way into the locker room. Blake tries to look at absolutely no one, but still has to talk to the media. The first question he gets thrown his way is how he felt when he got pulled.

"Not too great," Blake says. What the hell kind of question even is that?

"Do you feel like you got pulled too early?"

Blake looks up at the face of the reporter who's implying that Blake is in a position where he has any choice whatsoever in when he gets pulled by his coach. "I feel like Coach Franklin did what he felt would give us a chance to win this game."

It goes on and on like that and once the crowd of reporters finally disperses, Blake wants to curl up on the floor and never move again. He'll stay here until the next game. Which he'll be spending on the bench. And then they'll send him down again. Because he wasn't ready for the NHL after all.

"Hey."

Blake looks up and finds their captain hovering over him. Brian Kelly is a huge dude, only 28, doesn't look old, but still somehow like he already has 50 years of NHL experience on his back.

"Hey," Blake says, and even that sounds defeated.

"Not your fault, kid."

"I—"

"We left you hanging," Kells goes on. "We'll do better next time, all right?"

"All right," Blake says.

Doesn't mean that Blake didn't fuck up out there, but he appreciates it nonetheless. Being a goalie, people tend to either give you too much credit or unload all the blame on you. Kells ruffles his hair and then wanders away, patting backs on his way to the shower.

Blake stays in the shower way too long, is still in there when all the other guys are done. He belatedly remembers that Mattie gave him a ride to the arena and is waiting for him out there, probably tired because he had to play two nights in a row, both of which is Blake's fault.

Mattie is indeed sitting in his stall, fully dressed, most of the guys already heading out.

"Sorry," Blake mutters and gets dressed as quickly as he can, keeping his head down.

Mattie doesn't talk on the way to the car, doesn't talk as they get in, doesn't talk as they leave the parking garage. Blake should apologize, but doesn't know how, and while he chews on that, Mattie seems to remember how to talk.

"I'm not really sure what to say to you and I'm thinking about what would have made me feel better when I was your age and got pulled during my first start of the season and I... I got nothing."

Blake sighs. "I'm sorry."

"No, listen, we all got bad nights and you didn't stand a chance with the first one and you were kinda alone out there for the other two, so I can promise you that no one's blaming you. Hell, no one would be blaming you if all three of them were your fault."

Blake has a hard time believing that, but he nods anyway.

"There's always the next game and the next and you're still growing, you're at the very beginning of this and not every game's going to be a win, but you know that already."

"Yeah, but…"

"No, I get it. I've been there. We've all been there. You just keep going, okay?"

"Okay," Blake says. It sounds small. He feels small.

"What do you need? You need to go back in next game or do you need a break?"

"I don't think that's really my choice."

"No, it's not really your choice, but we have Tanner on our side and if we tell him that you'll fucking drop dead if they don't put you in net the day after tomorrow, he'll talk to Coach."

Blake doubts that Tanner has that much say in the final lineup, only being the goalie coach, but Mattie has been around longer than him.

"So, what do you need?" Mattie asks.

"Go back in."

"I thought you'd say that. You're a tough kid."

Tough is just about the last word he'd use to describe himself right now, but if he gets benched for a few more games, he'll get more and more scared of the next time they'll put him in net, to a point where he'll believe that losing is the only option. He's been there before. He wishes he was over it.

There's no way of telling if it's really Tanner who talks to Coach Franklin, or if Coach Franklin sees that Blake is working his ass off at practice the next day, but Blake is between the pipes again for their next game, on the road, in Hartford.

They win 4-1 and when the guys line up to pat his head after the game, Brammer hugs him so hard that he nearly lifts him off his feet.

For Elliot, the new season begins with an ankle sprain.

He gets injured in their last preseason game against the Foxes. It's nobody's fault, just an accident. It's not as bad as it could be, but he would have preferred to be on the ice for their first regular season game instead of watching it from the press box.

It's unfortunate that it happened at the beginning of the season, because they have a bunch of new guys on the roster that Elliot wants to get to know better and it's hard when he's not practicing with them. He tries to spend as much time with the team as possible, travels with them, hangs out at the rink, gets there early, has lunch with the team.

Through it all, Andreas Wagner still follows him like a duckling, much like last season. He cracked the regular season roster this time and Elliot suspects that he's a little scared of Jacob and that's why he comes to Elliot with all his questions.

He misses their first game of the season, a road game against the Knights. Elliot gets on the bus with the rest of the guys, even though they're literally going one city over and will all sleep in their own beds tonight. Blake is on the bench, stone-faced, glaring at the puck as he follows it around the ice with his eyes. He saves one of the trainers from taking a puck in the head during the second, still stone-faced. He throws the puck to a little girl behind the bench and she straight-up kisses the glass, which finally tickles a smile out of him.

Elliot tries not to look his way too much, even though Blake probably doesn't even know where he's sitting. The fight they had a few weeks ago still doesn't sit well with him and the only thing Elliot currently wants to tell Blake is to go fuck himself, so maybe it's not the best time for a conversation. It still hurts, and Elliot can't tell what hurts worse – what Blake said to him, or that it was Blake who said it.

He goes down to the locker room after the game to make sure the rookies are okay, because after an evenly-paced first period, the Knights snatched the game from them in the second, outshot them, outscored them and eventually won the game, 5-2.

"Come back soon," Adam says when they're on their way home.

"As soon as I can," Elliot promises.

When it's time for Elliot to return and he starts skating again, first on his own, then with the team, he often stays after the official end of practice, usually with at least a few other guys, amongst them Adam and Andreas, often with Riley still in goal, swearing at them loudly every time they score on him.

The night Elliot returns to the lineup, he leaves the ice without a single point, and he's not exactly disappointed, but he was hoping for at least an assist and even wouldn't have cared if it was secondary. Natalie is waiting for him at home, hugs him and tucks him into bed, holding on to him like she knows that it's exactly what he needs.

It's not like she's ever seen him during the season. He'd hate for her to realize that this isn't what she wants after all, now that everything's changing after the summer. Elliot will be gone for roadies, sometimes for nearly two weeks at a time. It's a tough schedule, even when they're at home. It takes him ages to fall asleep that night and he grumbles at his alarm in the morning.

The next game goes better. A goal, only an empty-netter, but it's better than nothing.

After that, they're on the road for two games and it's another two games without a point. Elliot is starting to get frustrated, but not quite as frustrated as Riley, who hasn't won a single game this season and, being their backup, also doesn't get too many starts, and also not quite as frustrated as Andreas, who hasn't scored a single goal, despite being in the lineup since the beginning of the season.

"They're going to scratch me soon," Andreas mutters. He was on the third line at the beginning of the season, now he's on the fourth, slowly slipping down the ranks.

Elliot is still centering the second, but he's not producing so who knows how long that'll last. He was hoping that at some point he'll get bumped up to the first line, but that's pretty much a distant dream right now.

When he gets home, ridiculously late at night, Natalie is at his and Adam's place, waiting for him and he hugs her for about fifteen minutes without saying a word and she lets him, gently rubbing his back. Adam sneaks away, doesn't stick around to chirp him and doesn't say anything about it when they're going to practice the next day.

Before practice, while they're skating around, waiting for the rest of the guys, Andreas catches up with him, face red, and says, "You want to stick around after practice?"

"Yeah," Elliot says.

Slowly, so slowly, he starts racking up points.

December begins with a hat trick on the road, and it's like he can't stop scoring after that. Their line is on fire, Adam and Magnus on his wing, giving him the most beautiful passes as early Christmas presents. Another hat trick three games later, and he's now on a seven-game point streak and when he gets out on the ice, it's like he's flying. After the second hatty – this one at home, hats raining down onto the ice – the amount of messages he receives is completely insane.

Nothing from Blake, not that it matters, but a year ago he would have at least sent him one of those *congratulations* texts.

He sees Blake in late December, a few days before Christmas. The Ravens are playing against the Knights in Newark and it's the first game of a back-to-back for the Knights, and of course they decide to put Blake in goal against the Ravens, because the Ravens are, objectively, doing a lot worse than the Grizzlies, who will be in town the next day. Despite Elliot's point streak, the Ravens aren't winning enough games. Elliot is one goal away from overtaking Morozov, even though he missed several games at the beginning of the season and Morozov hasn't missed a single game.

The game against the Knights is dirty, but they always are, same with the Mariners. They're too close, the fans riled up as much as the players. Less than five minutes in, Moby drops the gloves with the Knights' Ian Hennings for something that happened in a previous game, but the fighting doesn't stop there. Power plays and penalty kills are chasing each other and they go into the third tied at three.

Elliot scores on Blake halfway through the third and Blake looks fucking pissed, slams his stick against the goal and glares out at the ice, past Elliot, like he's not even there.

The Knights tie the game again, not a minute later, no power play this time.

Things somehow get even uglier, one of Elliot's teammates – he's not even sure which one – takes Blake's net off and trips Blake in the process. Blake seems to be okay, but someone touched the goalie, and when someone touches the goalie, any goalie, you can expect gloves to go flying. It's Moby again, now exchanging blows with the Knights' captain, the most terrifyingly large D-man in the Eastern Conference. Another Knight tries to jump in, Elliot tries to pulls him back, then someone tries to pull *him* back. Elliot shoves his elbow back blindly and is shoved back in return. Elliot turns around and finds that it was Blake.

"Fuck off," Elliot shouts in his general direction, but Blake won't and practically cross-checks him out of his crease.

Before Elliot can retaliate, he has two Knights on him, then Blake pulls one of them off of Elliot saying something that sounds like, "It's okay, we're all good, all good..."

Then one of the officials gets between them, but not before Johnny Brammer can lay one on Elliot.

The officials start dealing out penalties, minor and major alike, and the Knights end up on the power play. They convert within twelve seconds and the Ravens don't manage to tie up the game again.

Elliot is on the ice when the final horn goes, Blake's teammates taking off, surrounding Blake, about five of them trying to hug him at the same time and Blake hugs all of them thoroughly one by one. As Elliot gets off the ice, memories gnaw on him, memories of being in that line, Blake crushing him against his chest after games.

He doesn't dwell on the thoughts of Blake, mostly because thinking of him also makes him think of last summer, of what Blake said, and just like that he's done with his trip down memory lane.

6

When Elliot gets selected for the All Star Game, he's not sure if he deserves it.

Adam, when they drive home that day, lays it all out for him, all the stats that likely contributed to that decision, and Elliot knows the stats, knows he's overtaken Morozov in scoring, knows he's leading the team in points, but maybe Swanson would have been more deserving. Sure, his save percentage has suffered, but that's just because the rest of the team was playing like shit in front of him for the first three months of the season.

They've recovered a little, keep slipping in and out of a wildcard spot, but Elliot shouldn't even be thinking about making the playoffs right now, except he thinks about making the playoffs every single second of every single day.

He can tell that Natalie isn't too happy with him constantly on edge, but when he apologizes she'll always say something along the lines of it's fine and she understands and she'll support him, like he supported her when she had to finish a paper before Christmas and didn't talk to him for three days straight. But there's an edge to her voice when she says it, like it still bothers her and she won't say it for some reason and it has something simmering low in Elliot.

The All Star Game is somehow more fun and also more exhausting than Elliot remembered from the last time he went, but he gets to play with people he's been looking up to for years, so you won't find him complaining for a single second. It's a lot of talking to the media, some of which is about as boring as it is at home, some of which is a great deal more fun. They let him play with puppies, they let a little girl interview him and he somehow makes it home with four sticks signed by other players. One of them is Josh Roy's. When they swapped sticks, Elliot asked Josh if he could sign a shirt for him, because– He doesn't really know why. It's not like he's going to give it to Blake for his birthday, because they're not talking, and this long stretch of silence makes it pretty clear where they're at.

But he takes it home and puts it in the back of his closet, together with some other things that'll likely stay in there and never come out.

He wishes he could say that the season goes better for the Ravens after the All Star break, but they still only barely manage to hold on to their wildcard spot.

Then Jacob gets injured and the mood in the locker room goes from bad to worse.

Elliot isn't on the ice when it happens, can barely even see it, just sees one of the Wolves jam his stick between Jacob's legs and maybe it's an accident, maybe he didn't mean to trip him, but Jacob falls and goes hard into the boards.

And then he doesn't get up.

Elliot is on his feet, along with the rest of the bench, all leaning forward, the guys on the ice hovering close by as one of their trainers is bent over Jacob. He waves for a stretcher.

The arena has never been this silent since Elliot started playing here.

It's only the beginning of the second so he has to keep it together, no matter how much his hands wants to shake. Adam, white in the face, eyes wide, lets out a shuddering breath as they carefully get Jacob on the stretcher. That's their captain out there and they don't even know if he's conscious, because there's so many people in the way and Elliot wants to jump over the boards and check on Jacob himself.

It looks like Jacob waves, only the tiniest bit, when they wheel him off the ice and the crowd cheers and Elliot taps his stick against the boards like everyone else, numb, knowing that they'll have to finish this period, and they won't have news yet during the intermission, and then they'll have to make it through the third, and after that someone might be able to tell them what's going on.

"Elliot, I want you out there with Adam and Kenny."

Kenny's usually on Jacob's wing. Elliot, still rattled when he climbs over the boards, lines up for the face-off. The Wolves don't give them too much trouble for the rest of the game and the Ravens walk out of it with a 4-2 win, but they don't celebrate after they return to the locker room.

Nobody goes back out for the three stars of the game, they all gather in the locker room, and the look on Coach Warren's face doesn't bode well.

"We don't know enough yet…" he starts and is interrupted by questions and *buts* and guys talking over each other until Warren yells at them to shut the fuck up. "As I just said," he continues on, the *before you so rudely interrupted me* going unsaid, "we don't know enough to say how bad it really is, but we're looking at weeks."

They're all smart enough not to ask how many weeks and Coach Warren tells them to hit the showers.

Elliot ends up talking to the media, doesn't know what to say when they ask him how he felt when he saw Jacob getting injured. He tries to pull out something generic, how it was hard to see that, how it's always hard when a teammate gets injured, that they hope he'll be able to come back to them soon. He doesn't know what his face is doing as he says it, if they can all see that he's shell-shocked.

They let him go sooner than they might on any other given day and Elliot is pathetically grateful.

The next day, the Ravens announce that Captain Jacob Desjardins will undergo surgery and will be out for four to six months.

Blake isn't a hundred percent sure what's going on when Evan texts him a fuckton of exclamation points. Blake is at practice when he gets it, so he isn't exactly quick to reply.

The exclamation points are followed by, *aw shit do u hav the day of.*

Then, *ur asleep aren't u.*

And, *THEY CALLED ME UP!! STOP SLEEPING!!!!*

And then a few more exclamation points.

I was at practice you dipshit, Blake replies.

Before he can say anything else, Evan is already calling him, which means he must be really excited. "Dude, I just got here," he says. "You're not playing tonight, right? Because I am. Can you come?"

"Sure, I'll–"

"I'll get you a ticket," Evan practically shuts. "Elliot said we could do that. So you can pick it up… somewhere."

Someone mumbles something in the background.

"Oh, do you need more than one? You wanna bring someone? Girlfriend? Teammate?" Evan falls silent for a moment. "It's probably too late for you to go pick up grandma, right?"

Blake glances at the clock. They had an 11:30 practice and he stayed on the ice as long as he could and then had a few meetings, so it's the afternoon and it's definitely too late for him to drive up to Norwalk and pick up their grandma. "Sorry, man."

"No, it's okay. But you're coming?"

"I am…" Some of the guys are still hanging around, but they're all supposed to hate the Ravens with every fiber of their being, so he's not asking anyone to come. He sure as hell won't ask Mattie, because they're home for a week and he'll want to spend as much time with his family as he can.

Maybe Bram would come with him if Blake asked, but then Bram would probably also get into a fist fight with a Ravens fan and Blake doesn't need that tonight.

"One ticket is good," Blake says.

"Sweet," Evan says. "Come see me after, yeah?"

"No."

"Blaaake."

"Do you want me to die?"

"You're gonna be there as my brother, not as, like, the enemy."

"He's still gonna be the enemy," someone shouts.

"I heard that," Blake says.

"Please."

Shit, has Evan ever said please to him in his entire life? "Fine," Blake says.

"Yay," Evan says and hangs up before Blake has a chance to say goodbye.

"Who was that?" Paulie asks.

"My brother," Blake grumbles. "He's playing his first NHL game tonight and I apparently just agreed to go."

"He close?"

"Ravens," Blake says and Paulie laughs at him as Blake packs up his shit.

Mattie laughs at him too when Blake tells him an hour later. Blake is sensing a pattern here.

He makes sure not to wear anything with the Knights logo on it as he heads out for the game. He digs up an old baseball cap that has his junior team's logo on it, because that's probably safe enough and pulls on a gray hoodie that can't be mistaken for any team gear.

Blake gets there early enough so he can watch warmups, but only from afar. He keeps his head down and tries not to look directly at anyone. Someone made a sign for Evan, which Blake tries to snap a picture of for their grandma and Evan throws a puck over the glass for whoever made it. Elliot gives his head a pat in passing.

Now on the first line, Elliot is still a joy to watch. With Desjardins on IR and Morozov probably having the worst season of his career, all the lines got shuffled. Elliot scores a goal and sets up two others, his smile bright when his teammates rush in for a hug.

During the first intermission, Blake goes and buys a burger, because he's a bit hungry and also prone to stress-eating. Who would have thought that watching his brother play would make him so nervous? Evan isn't getting a ton of ice time, but Blake's still waiting, at the edge of his seat, hoping he'll at least get an assist.

While he waits for his burger, he looks down at his phone, his teammates chirping him because, *haha, rip Blake, he isn't dead, he's just at a Ravens game.* A little girl, waiting with her mom next to him, is staring up at him and when he catches her looking, he smiles at her. She smiles back at him and waves. Blake waves back, because who the fuck doesn't wave to a little kid?

The mom notices, frowns at Blake, and he can actually pinpoint the second she recognizes him. Blake tries to keep smiling, then his order is ready and he quickly goes to grab it, waves at the little girl before he leaves, because she's still watching him, and then escapes back to his seat.

Evan does get an assist in the third period and Elliot's on the bench waving to one of his teammates to grab the puck, which is swiftly delivered to the Ravens' equipment manager. Blake cheers for Evan, but for nobody else. He didn't show too much enthusiasm for the Ravens' other goals, but when it's Evan, he'll make an exception.

After the game, he goes down to the locker rooms as promised and they let him pass when he gives them his name, some of the arena staff going a little bug-eyed when they see him. He waits outside the locker room and Evan comes out a moment later, sweaty, only half out of his gear, and jumps right into Blake's arms.

"You came," Evan shouts.

"I said I would."

Evan squeezes him.

The locker room door opens and Elliot peers outside while Blake is still hugging Evan. It takes embarrassingly long for Blake to convince himself to at least wave at him. He pushed off apologizing to Elliot until it was too late and now Elliot probably thinks he's the biggest douchebag to ever walk the planet. Elliot, with some reluctance, waves back at him, then disappears again.

"Some of the guys are taking me out for drinks," Evan says and lets go of Blake. "You wanna come?"

Blake doesn't comment on Evan being underage, because that's none of his business, and shakes his head. "I have a game tomorrow. Also not really in the mood to supervise your underage drinking." Okay, so he did say something. Like he wasn't the king of underage drinking, like, two years ago.

Evan grins and punches him in the arm. "Thanks for coming, though."

Blake nods, gives him another hug and escapes before he can think too much about whether or not he should ask someone if they can find him Elliot.

Blake is almost convinced that he'll get to the other end of the season without playing a single game against the Mariners. He's mostly okay with that, although he'd like to get a few more starts in general, which is unlikely now that it's almost playoff time.

When they wrap up their season series against the Mariners, the Knights have already clinched their playoff spot, but they have a chance to get home ice tonight, so the way this game ends is still important. Noah grins at him during warmups, but it's fleeting, in passing, not enough to be a distraction. Blake is on the bench until Mattie, after over twenty minutes of being a brick wall, absolutely fucking falters in the second, letting in four goals in a matter of minutes.

"Blake," Coach only says and Mattie comes off the ice, glaring daggers.

Someone needs to score right the fuck now, which Coach is probably shouting about on the bench right as Blake gets settled in the crease. He hates coming into games like this, after sitting on the bench for ages, but when he saves the first shot, which, admittedly, just goes right into his glove and doesn't require any acrobatics, Blake is more grounded.

The game goes on like nothing happened and the Mariners pepper him with shots and Blake is mad. He's mad, because they have their playoff spot, but they still need to win this game, and his guys need to get off their asses and the next time he gets his stick on the puck, he hurls it down the ice, and somehow, miraculously, Kells is right there in the back, taking he hell off with that puck. The Mariners' goalie never stood a chance.

The Knights manage to get another one, and in its execution the goal isn't pretty, but Blake doesn't care if it's pretty as long as it gets them closer to tying up the game. They don't.

Not in the second.

The third starts with two guys in the box with matching minors. The Knights score on the 4-on-4 and their entire bench is jumping up and down.

The Knights score another one, get it taken away because it's offside, and with four minutes left in the game, Blake is ready to murder someone. He wants to win this. He can't go out there and score a goal himself, so one of the guys needs to do him that favor now.

"Fancy seeing you here," Noah says as he glides past him before a face-off.

Blake gives him the evil eye and the smile drops right off Noah's face. A strange wave of satisfaction washes over him, but he doesn't examine it any further, because he needs to focus on the face-off.

Blake doesn't know how they win the game. Well, objectively he does know. He doesn't let in any other goals and his team scores four, and it's that kind of ridiculous comeback that happens maybe once a season. Brammer barrels into him no two seconds after the final horn and Blake lets it wash over him, the taps, the hugs, while the Mariners' crowd quickly disperses.

As they head down the tunnel, Blake hears that the Mariners gave him second star, and someone pats his back, and Mattie is actually smiling at him in the locker room, despite the murder eyes earlier. "Well done, kid," Mattie says.

"Hey, Fish!"

Blake turns around just in time to find himself face to face with Paulie, who hands him the knight helmet they've been passing around the locker room all season. Blake puts it on because someone will put it on him if he doesn't, says *thank you* and *good game, boys,* but takes it off again quickly, a little embarrassed by all the eyes on him.

Before Blake can get out of his gear, before he can get put on media duty, Mattie comes shuffling back over, already mostly out of his pads, and drops a puck in his hand.

"Wait…"

Blake has had his first win, he has the puck at home on a shelf. He frowns down at the writing on the tape and realizes it says nothing about saves or wins. 1ST NHL POINT, it says.

Because he got a point. When he passed the puck to Kells and Kells scored. He didn't even notice at the time.

"You didn't realize, did you," Mattie says, deadpan.

"No."

Mattie snorts and walks away, leaving Blake to get eaten alive by the local media. Except they're not so bad today and one of them congratulates him on his performance and PR takes pictures of him and his first point puck.

He takes his time changing – most of the guys are probably going to hit the city to celebrate, because now their last game of the season is pretty much a formality, but Blake has other plans. A game in Brooklyn isn't as much of a road game as, say, a game in California, so they don't have a curfew and if they want to make their own way back to Newark, no one will bat an eye.

Blake does check his phone, because maybe he will go back on the bus with the team. It's up to Noah.

There's a text from his brother – *shit u have ass many points in the nhl as i hav* – and there's so much to unpack there, starting with the 'ass' and ending with the two different 'haves', his grandma sent him one as well – *So proud of you, Blake! Love, Nana!!* – and he smiles about that one a little bit. He keeps scrolling until he finds the text from Noah he's been looking for.

come 2 mine? pity bj?

Blake tells him that he's on his way, takes a cab, and finds that Noah is already at home, already out of his suit, waiting for Blake. They don't do this a lot, only when they both happen to have at least half a day off at the same time, when Blake is in Brooklyn, not when Noah is in Newark, because Blake lives with Mattie, and it's not like he can bring a guy home and hide him in the basement.

It works well enough, meaning that Blake has someone's hands on him often enough that he doesn't have time to think about how fucking lonely he is when he's sitting in Mattie's basement on his own. This is pretty much as good as it gets for him. Noah gets him, gets the situation they're in, and he never asks for more than Blake is willing to give. They're not boyfriends, they don't owe each other anything, although if asked, Blake would probably say that they're friends.

Noah texts him all the time, pictures and jokes and whatnot that Blake more often than not rolls his eyes at, but he'd also miss those texts if Noah wasn't sending them, so he won't complain.

Before Noah pulls Blake into his bedroom, he asks him if he wants anything to eat, hangs up Blake's suit jacket and then starts chirping Blake's teammates. There's no way around that, and Noah doesn't really mean anything by it, just runs his mouth until Blake shuts him up. Blake enjoys shutting him up; maybe he's a little smug about it.

Noah peels him out of his clothes, pushes him into bed, but Noah isn't the kind of guy who takes his time and it's not like they lovingly gaze into each other's eyes or anything, they're not... that. Noah does usually tell him to stay, doesn't kick him out in the middle of the night, but they don't cuddle or anything. Sometimes Blake will wake up with Noah's leg hooked over his, sometimes they'll bump into each other during the night, but it's not like Noah wraps himself around Blake like... certain other people that Blake has shared a bed with.

In the morning, Noah will make him breakfast, he's good at that, and then Noah will send Blake on his way.

It's good enough.

The playoffs aren't going well for the Ravens. They only barely managed to get into their wildcard spot, ended up playing against the Grizzlies, and they absolutely destroyed them in their first game.

Shutout for the Grizzlies, the final score 3-0.

The second one didn't go much better, again, they played in Boston, again, they lost, this time 5-2.

The third one was a little closer, but they still didn't manage a win, walked down the tunnel after a 4-3 loss, quiet, knowing that they had to win the next one or it'd be over. After three losses, the faces in the locker room are stony. They're missing Jacob, one of their D-men is injured and the guys the Ravens traded for before the deadline don't really fit into the lineup. It's a fucking disaster. Elliot goes and talks to Andreas, who looks like he's given up on life, not sure afterwards if it helped or if he made everything worse.

They need to win four times, and it's not impossible, but it's not exactly realistic either. Natalie looked up the stats for him when he told her exactly that over breakfast yesterday, to see if any team had ever pulled this off before, and the answer was yes, it's happened before, but Elliot didn't ask how often, only kissed the top of her head and left to contemplate whether drowning himself in the shower would be preferable to playing another game against the Grizzles.

They're on home ice for Game 4, but it's worth little when the crowd goes dead silent after the Grizzlies' first goal early in the first. Elliot manages to tie it up, but only halfway through the third.

They go into overtime.

They lose the game and Elliot wants to lie down on the ice and never get up again, but he doesn't get to.

He hugs Swanson, even though they usually only bump helmets. He tries to ignore the Grizzlies who are celebrating at the other end of the ice. They all want to get the fuck off the ice and lick their wounds, but Jacob isn't here and someone's going to have to start the handshake line. Andreas is standing next to him, still looking totally defeated, and Elliot can't look at him anymore, so he goes, on autopilot, and skates to the middle of the ice.

The Grizzlies' captain, Nikolai Ivanov, doesn't keep him waiting, detaches himself from his teammates, who are a little slower to follow, and comes to shake Elliot's hand.

"Good game," Elliot says. He remembers that part from last year.

Ivanov nods, serious, pulls him in a little, pats his back. "Well done," he says and Elliot isn't sure if they did anything well, but this is not the time to correct Ivanov on that. "Was hard without Desjardins."

Elliot nods, keeps going when Ivanov lets him go, and somehow makes it through that handshake line. He waits until everyone's done and they all follow him to the middle of the ice and they raise their sticks for whoever stuck around until the very end.

On the way off the ice, Elliot hands his stick to a kid who's wearing his jersey, because maybe today doesn't have to be total disappointment for *everyone*.

Jacob is waiting for them in the locker room and he pats Elliot's back as he passes, says, "Well done," and once again Elliot isn't sure which playoff series Jacob has been watching, but they didn't do a single fucking thing well.

Elliot's face must be telling Jacob exactly what he was thinking, because Jacob smiles a little.

"*You*," Jacob says. "You did well."

Elliot isn't too convinced, but shuffles away to his stall in silence.

It's late when he leaves the arena that night. Thankfully he's not too far away from home. He takes a cab, because he can't bring himself to go on the Subway. He shares it with Adam, drops him off at his girlfriend's apartment, and then heads home. He told Natalie to come over, because he wants to sleep in his own bed tonight.

"I'm so sorry you lost," Natalie says when he gets home. She must have looked up the score. She isn't really turning into much of a hockey fan, but Elliot won't hold it against her. He's not interested in law either.

But she stayed up for him, which is nice of her, although he almost wishes she hadn't so he could just curl up next to her in bed without saying a word. He talked to the media after the game and now he's done talking for the night.

"It's fine," Elliot mutters and tries, and almost succeeds, to put a smile on his face. "It happens. There's always next year."

"Do you need anything?"

Elliot is too tired to figure out if he needs anything, so he shakes his head, because it's easier. "No, just… bed."

"Okay," she says and leads the way.

He kisses her and they stumble a little and she laughs. He tells her that he loves her and she blushes, like he said it for the first time. It's still a new thing for him say, it's not like he's ever said it to anyone else before, but it never seemed hard to him.

Natalie tucks him into bed, kisses his forehead and runs her fingers through his hair until he starts to drift off. "Oh, and Elliot?" she says.

"Huh?"

"I love you, too."

He smiles into his pillow.

The loss still stings, because losses like that always sting. He'll carry it around with him for a while, will be reminded almost daily until June, when someone will finally lift the Cup and they'll slide into the oblivion of summer for a while.

7

Blake can tell that his phone keeps buzzing in his jeans. He had it out when he left the rink, but then stumbled across a horde of fans in the parking lot and quickly stuffed it into his pocket so he wouldn't accidentally drop it while he was signing stuff.

They're playing their first preseason game tomorrow and he sort of wants to get home and make dinner, but he's been signing stuff all throughout training camp, so what's one more day, really? When fans ask him for photos, he suffers through those as well, well aware that people always say that he looks like he's waiting for the ground to swallow him up in every picture that's taken of him. He'd rather sign jerseys for half an hour than take even just one selfie. He eventually manages to detach himself and walks back to his apartment.

He moved out of Mattie's basement during the summer and found a pretty nice place about a 10-minute walk away from the rink, bought the largest bed and the largest couch he could find and then found out that the couch is more comfortable to sleep on than the bed. No, he's exaggerating, but when he falls asleep on the couch, he actually stays on the couch.

As he walks away, he finally manages to check his phone. Noah has been texting him.

did you forget about me?

shit wait i'm like 30 mins early

i'm getting food u want anything?

Blake replies that no, he hasn't forgotten about him and that he's on his way home, and he also says yes to the food, hoping that Noah will pick something that wouldn't make every NHL team's nutritionist cry.

He makes it to his place before Noah does, but Noah is close behind, since he was already in the area and got food at the Thai place down the street. They eat in front of the TV, Noah chirps him because he still doesn't have any video games, and then plucks Blake's takeout box from his fingers and gets his hands in Blake's pants so fast that Blake's mind doesn't even have time to catch up.

They eventually end up in Blake's bed, maybe two hours later, Blake eating the rest of his now cold takeout, Noah upside down on the bed in nothing but his briefs, eyes half-lidded, lips red.

"Is your mom a model?" Blake asks, because, honestly, she has to be.

Noah laughs. "She was. Not anymore, though. She does tons of charity stuff now."

"Yeah?"

"Human Rights Campaign," Noah only says.

Blake looks back at him, wondering if it's too personal if he asks Noah if his parents know. He had Noah's dick in his mouth about twenty minutes ago, so maybe personal isn't the right word, but–

"They know," Noah asks. "I'm assuming that's the question you were chewing on?"

"Yeah."

"I told my mom pretty early on. When I was fifteen maybe? She helped me tell my dad. He was, uh... He has some issues with it."

Blake doesn't like the present tense there. "Oh."

"We don't talk about it."

"Sorry."

"It was a bit awkward when they were still together, but now it's..." Noah shrugs half-heartedly. "Don't look like that. This isn't, like, tragic or anything. He cheated on her. A couple of times. She forgave him the first few, but..."

"That sucks."

"Well..." Noah stretches. "You know, it's okay to ask me stuff. I literally spent an entire week in your bed when you got this place, we're at a point where we can swap life stories, I think."

Blake laughs, finishes his veggies.

"You ever tell anyone?" Noah asks.

"Not really."

"Seriously? No one?"

Blake shakes his head.

When his parents died, he didn't have anything to tell them yet. He was eleven. He doesn't remember when he started to realize that he wasn't as into girls as he was apparently supposed to be. He kissed a girl when he was thirteen and it was... underwhelming. He thought maybe he was just bad at it.

It dawned on him eventually.

He didn't say a fucking word. Not to anyone.

He never told his brother, never told his grandma. He has no idea how Evan would react; they didn't spend enough time together during the last couple of years for Blake to have him all figured out. His grandma would be okay with it, she has friends who are lesbians and makes them pride flag cookies for their birthdays, and Blake has *nearly* told her so many times that he's lost count but he can never bring himself to say it. Sometimes he works up to it for days and when the time comes, he never manages to say the words, even though he knows that it would be fine.

"It's hard," Blake says.

"I know."

Blake puts down his takeout container. "Well, I guess you know now."

Noah's grin is blinding. He nudges Blake's ankle with his foot and says, "Guess I do. I'm, like, your gay buddy, Noah."

Blake shakes his head at him.

"Well," Noah says, "I guess Elliot knows, too."

Right, Elliot knows, too.

"I mean," Noah goes on when Blake doesn't say anything, "I do suppose he noticed that you had your tongue down his throat and your hands on his ass? Or at least he did that one time I saw you guys together."

Blake groans and throws a pillow in Noah's direction. He misses and it slides off the bed.

"How did that even happen?" Noah says. "I mean, I almost didn't figure out that I was gay, and, like, I never would have figured out that you are gay, so how did you…"

Well, Elliot told him, for starters. And then Blake told him, too. And then nothing happened for a while. And then one night, on the road, Elliot kissed him, in their room, after a game and Blake kissed him back and it was *everything*. For a month, maybe even two, it was just that, just kisses, and then suddenly it was more, and after that Blake didn't know how to stop. Not that he had to, because Elliot clearly didn't want to stop either.

Not until the Draft.

"It just happened," Blake says.

"Got it, you don't wanna talk about it."

"There's not really a lot to talk about." Blake shrugs. "We weren't together or anything. We were a thing… and then we weren't."

"He's literally…" Noah waves in the vague direction of Manhattan.

"I know."

"But?"

"But… that didn't happen."

"Well, his loss, I guess," Noah says.

Blake doubts that it was that much of a loss for Elliot. He didn't have any problems walking away from this.

Noah makes a face. "He really broke your fucking heart, huh?"

"No, it wasn't like that."

"Yeah, I can hear you saying that, but your face is like... in pain."

"I'm not in pain," Blake says gruffly.

He's not.

"Sure." Noah rolls onto his side, watching Blake. "Are you still in love with him? It's okay if you are, I won't be, like, offended or anything."

"I wasn't in love with him," Blake mutters.

"*Okay.*"

Blake huffs at him.

"It's okay to have feelings, you know?" Noah says. "Like, even if they're... mushy, or whatever."

"Mushy?"

"You know what I mean."

"I really don't."

"I'm sorry," Noah says.

Blake shrugs it off.

"No, not about the chirping," Noah says. "I'm sorry that he hurt you. You're a good guy and good guys don't deserve that."

Blake glares at the ceiling. "Can we talk about something else?"

"Sure," Noah says. "You think Desjardins is gonna retire?"

Blake can deal with that extreme shift in topic, even though they're technically talking about Elliot's team. "I don't know, he's kinda young to hang up the skates, but..." Blake shrugs. Desjardins is turning 35 later this year and he obviously doesn't know him, but they've all heard the rumors. That his recovery isn't going as well as the Ravens were hoping, that he probably won't ever get back to where he used to be. "They haven't really said anything about him in a while, so..."

"Yeah, can't help but wonder what's going on behind closed doors there," Noah says. "Sucks. I really liked him as, you know, a person."

"Evan was scared of him, but, like... just because he grew up watching him and then he was suddenly on the same team as him and apparently he hung around the locker room a lot even when he was on IR."

Noah laughs. "Wow, okay. I mean, I guess Desjardins is kinda intimidating with the beard and the scowl and everything, but, like, your brother grew up with you, so he should at least be used to the scowling."

Blake hurls another pillow at him. Misses again.

"You'll run out of pillows if you keep that up."

"Ugh," Blake says and flops down.

Noah considers him for a moment, then he gives him a poke. "Nap?" he asks.

"Yeah, sounds good."

"Cool if I stay for a bit?"

"Yeah, sure."

Noah still doesn't cuddle, but it's nice not to be alone.

"Dumplings?" Elliot asks when he picks up Natalie at the Subway.

She told him not to, said he really didn't have to about five times, and he does it anyway, because he knows it'll make her smile and the next season – his fifth, if you can believe it – is just around the corner. He's not going to have too much time for stuff like this.

"Yay, dumplings," Natalie says.

He wraps his arm around her and she tells him about what she's working on for law school, the reading she has to do, and he tries really hard to follow, but some of it goes way over his head. He tries to ask questions, so it doesn't seem like he completely clocked out and Natalie answers with enthusiasm. It's the least he can do. She does the same for him when he's overcome with the need to spew hockey stats for half an hour.

Elliot kisses the top of her head as they walk and she smiles as she talks and it's all good. He made the right choice when he asked her to move in with him.

It's not that Adam kicked him out, he just very quietly mentioned that he's been thinking about asking Lou to move in with him, which was basically Elliot's cue to vacate the premises. Permanently. Adam helped him move, into an apartment two blocks away, a place that Elliot can afford easily with his contract. Natalie insists on chipping in. He tried to argue with her about it, but it didn't end well and he eventually came to the conclusion that it means a lot to her. He was trying to be nice and it took him a few days to stop being sulky about it, as much as he hates to admit it.

Their favorite Chinese place is packed when they get in line, Elliot's eyes on the menu, loudly wondering if getting twenty dumplings is a bit overkill, Natalie poking him in the side, laughing into his shirt.

He almost doesn't notice how she suddenly goes still, almost doesn't hear the unfamiliar voice that says, "Hey, Nat."

"Hey," Natalie says, voice strained.

Elliot tears his eyes off the menu board to look at the guy she's talking to. Tall, blond, scruffy. Looks like he belongs on a beach.

"Hey," Elliot says.

Natalie clears her throat. "Elliot, this is Cody. Cody, this is Elliot."

"Nice to meet you," Elliot says.

"Yeah," Cody only says, eyes back on Natalie. "How have you been, Nat? Haven't seen you in a while."

"Good, how about you?"

"All right."

The line moves up and Natalie nods at him, then at the line. "Sorry, we need to…"

"Sure," Cody says, gives Elliot an appraising look and wanders away.

"Cody, huh?" Elliot says. "How do you know him?"

"He's my ex," Natalie grits out.

"Ah."

That's it for that conversation, at least for now, because they order, and Natalie keeps Elliot from getting twenty dumplings, but he gets twelve, because that way he can maybe have two for breakfast tomorrow morning. They get veggies and fried noodles and too many spring rolls and then wander home, in a silence that seems strange to Elliot until he remembers Cody.

"So, is Cody a douchebag or…?"

"He cheated on me," Natalie says.

"So that's a yes."

Natalie hums.

Elliot is supremely uncomfortable about the teammates who have a girlfriend in New York and then screw around on the road, or, even worse, who have a girlfriend in New York and then screw around in New York on top of that. He's not about that at all.

He's never talked to Natalie about her exes, they just sort of established that they both had them but that there was nothing really worth mentioning.

Natalie asked him once, if he used to take girls home a lot, and he told her the truth, that sometimes he did when the occasion arose, but that it was never serious, and nothing that happened regularly.

Of course that wasn't the *whole* truth.

Sometimes he wonders if he should tell her, that he's bi, that he's been with men. Or, one man, he should say. He couldn't mention any names, but sometimes it sits on the tip of his tongue, until he dismisses it, because it doesn't matter, does it? Or maybe it does, because it's part of him, and he's… well, he's not hiding it, isn't actively lying about it, but he won't mention it either.

He knows it should tell him something, should maybe tell him that he doesn't trust Natalie enough, but he never gets to the end of that train of thought.

"I'm sorry," Elliot says. "That he did that."

"I'm pretty much over it," Natalie says and squeezes his hand. "Kinda sucks, though. I dated another guy for a while after I broke up with Cody and I had such a hard time trusting him, you know?"

"I'm sorry," Elliot says again, because what else is he supposed to say?

Natalie leans against him a little, the bag with their takeout bouncing off her legs. "Love you. And, Elliot, don't… don't think I don't trust you, okay? I do. I'm not… permanently scarred by one asshole who decided to cheat on me."

"Okay," Elliot says quietly and holds on to her hand until they're home.

As Natalie unlocks the door, taking her shoes off by the door, which is something Elliot needs to make a habit of but constantly forgets, Natalie says, "Hey, I have this friend from law school who wants to maybe go out on a double date with us, what do you think?"

"Uhh, sure?"

"If it works with your schedule?"

"Yeah," Elliot says, wandering back to the door to take his shoes off before he goes back into the kitchen.

"Okay, I'll let her know and she can talk to her girlfriend and… Elliot."

"Huh?"

"What's with the face?"

"What face?"

Natalie frowns at him. "*Your* face."

"Nothing? It's just my face."

"Yeah, and you… Elliot, you don't mind that she has a girlfriend, right?"

"No, what, of course not," Elliot says and he basically trips over the words, they come out way too fast and Natalie can definitely tell that something is up. Elliot could tell her now, there's never been a better moment for this, but Natalie has the angry face on, so maybe it's safer for him if he talks his way out of this. "It's just…"

"It's just that you hate gay people?"

"I don't hate gay people," Elliot says. Sounds way too defensive.

"But?"

"Nothing."

"Uh-huh."

Natalie shakes his head at him. "Elliot, seriously, like, grow up."

"I don't care," Elliot says. Too whiny. "I swear, I don't–"

"So you won't be weird around them? If we go somewhere with them, you're not gonna act like they have the cooties?"

"Natalie, we're not five."

"Then why are you acting like it?" Natalie snaps.

"Hey." Great defense, really. *Hey*.

"No, honestly, gay people exist, they're out there, get with the times. It's nothing that should make you uncomfortable," Natalie says. "You know, there's a good chance that someone on your team likes men."

Yes, that person would be Elliot. Somehow he still can't say it, even though Natalie would be on his side. Clearly. How hard can it be? He's told Blake. Telling Blake, in all honesty, was probably the hardest thing he'd ever done. He almost cried when Blake hugged him after and said, "Okay." He hugged Elliot for like five minutes and Elliot wasn't going to tell him to let go. Then Blake said, "I like guys, too. But not just sometimes." And then Elliot hugged him back, and said, "Okay," too and Elliot was so relieved that Blake understood, that he still wanted to be his friend, gay or not, that he accepted him, no matter what.

Elliot didn't tell him that he only noticed because he suddenly found himself daydreaming about kissing Blake. Maybe he'd noticed before, had noticed guys who looked hot, but he'd never noticed anyone as much as he noticed Blake. He didn't want Blake to think that Elliot only wanted to kiss him because Blake happened to be gay and it was convenient for him.

He fell for Blake when he had that unflattering, really short haircut and pimples all over his face and when he glared at everyone, even Elliot, all the fucking time.

But he can't tell Natalie any of that. It's like he's carrying around half of a secret. He could share his half, obviously, but even just the thought scares the crap out of him. So he stays quiet and starts unpacking their dinner, somehow unable to look up, and he lets Natalie think whatever she's thinking, because right now it somehow seems better than the alternative.

Natalie doesn't say much to him for the rest of the evening and he probably deserves it.

8

When the Ravens announce Jacob Desjardins's retirement before the start of training camp, they call in Elliot for a meeting and tell him that they want to make him captain. This is somehow surprising only to Elliot and nobody else.

Jacob calls him to congratulate him and the first thing he says is, "You'll be great at this."

Elliot is freaking the fuck out, but obviously he can't tell Jacob that. "How do you know?" he asks instead, because that sounds a lot better than, *I'm actually really scared that I'll fuck this up and that the team will suffer because of it and that we'll be even worse than last season and everything will fall apart.*

"Moo," Jacob says. "You've been their captain ever since I got injured."

But that's not right, because Jacob was still their captain, was still around, was with them in the locker room. "But—"

"You didn't have the C on your jersey, but that doesn't mean you weren't it. I saw that and everyone else saw it, too. Keep doing what you were doing and you'll be fine. I trust you to take care of my guys, yeah?"

"Okay," Elliot says.

"I was scared shitless when they gave me the C."

"Yeah?"

"Yeah. And I'm sure you'll fuck up here and there, but everyone fucks up here and there. Try to remember that. You get to fuck up, too, like everyone else."

"Thank you, Jacob."

"Sure, kid."

He catches himself smiling when he hangs up the phone.

He can tell that the guys are sad about Jacob, but he's also getting more hugs than ever when he shows up for training camp. It's strange to pull on the jersey with the C on it, PR taking pictures for the announcement, meeting the media after, getting all those questions about how he feels, what it means to him.

The guys take him out that day to celebrate and he lets them buy him way too many drinks. This is probably one of the things he fucked up as a captain. He let them play him. It made them happy, though, so he clearly only fucked himself over.

Natalie is already asleep when he sneaks into their apartment and promptly knocks over something that makes a shitton of noise when it falls. He's pretty sure that it's the frame they got for the black-and-white print that Natalie picked. They haven't managed to hang it up yet, because Elliot doesn't know how to hang up pictures. He's absolutely useless. He turns on the lights and bends down to pick up the frame, makes a little more noise and then has to sit down on the floor to get off his shoes, because apparently untying your laces is really hard after a few drinks and he... wants to lie down.

Which is a terrible idea.

He knows that.

He falls over when he takes his second shoe off, but he's already sitting on the floor, so he doesn't fall far.

His phone chimes somewhere.

Elliot should probably check that. Maybe someone's wondering if he's dying. Maybe he *is* dying. He's on the floor and he can't get up.

Fingers clumsy, he starts digging for his phone. It's in his pocket, which isn't that hard to access, but it still takes him an eternity to dig it out. Elliot squints down at it and finds a text from Blake.

For a second there, he's pretty sure that he's hallucinating, but then he reads it and realizes that it couldn't be from anyone else. *Congrats!* it says.

Elliot struggles to sit up and stares down at it, phone in his lap, at that one word and suddenly, for some reason that his inebriated brain can't understand, he wants to call him. He just wants to hear his voice, wants to hear Blake say congrats in person, wants to pretend, only for a moment, that they still have a chance at being friends.

He leans his head against the wall and sighs, phone still in hand, not drunk enough to fucking do it, and to hell with how his sober self will feel about this tomorrow.

He's about to do... something, when the picture frame behind him falls over again.

The lights come on in their bedroom a few seconds later, and Natalie comes padding into the hallway, feet bare, wearing one of her Columbia University shirts, looking at first confused, then amused. "Elliot, babe, what are you doing?"

Elliot frowns. What is he doing? He points at the shoe he's still wearing. "I'm taking off my shoe."

"Okay," Natalie says and comes over, pulls off his shoe and then gently helps him up and maneuvers him into their bedroom, gets him out of his clothes, and pulls him into bed with her.

The next morning, Elliot stumbles over Blake's text again.

He doesn't reply.

Blake gets to start in net at their home opener.

Part of him knew this was coming, knew he'd be getting more starts now, but it still takes him by surprise. He did well last season, had a good save percentage, and he knows that Mattie's contract runs out at the end of this season, and he's sort of torn about it, because he loves Mattie and he never ever wants him to leave, but being the starting goalie for an NHL team has been his dream for as long as he can remember.

And… he's getting there.

The boys don't let him down, they win, and win, and win, holding the top spot in their division until Christmas, then a few lost games put them into the second spot, but they're still okay, as long as they don't lose ten in a row.

Everything's going well.

His grandma adopts a ginormous orange kitten and the next time Blake is on the same ice as Elliot, he almost wants to skate to the center line and wave him over to tell him, but then he remembers that Elliot didn't reply to his text at the beginning of the season, which either means that Elliot changed his number and didn't tell Blake, or Elliot saw his text and decided not to reply. Either way, Elliot has made it pretty clear that he doesn't want to talk to him.

Okay, so, the hockey part of his life is going well.

Now that Blake has his own place, Noah can actually come over every once in a while, and they still work pretty well together. They don't fight. They have sex and then go their separate ways. Sometimes they order food. Sometimes they'll even manage to get halfway through a movie.

Noah still chirps him whenever he sets foot into Blake's apartment, but Blake can deal.

"You know," Noah says, wearing a Santa hat he found fuck-knows-where, prancing into Blake's kitchen, "if I was your boyfriend, I'd judge you for all the dishes in your sink. But I'm not your boyfriend."

"So you're not judging me?"

"No, I mean, I am, I'm just not saying it out loud."

"I think you just did," Blake says.

Noah shakes his head. "Nah."

Blake only now realizes that the Santa hat is the *only* thing Noah is wearing. He wordlessly hands Noah the glass of water he came to the kitchen for and then heads back to his bedroom, Noah at his heels, laughing when Blake pulls the Santa hat off his head.

So the Noah part of his life is going well, too.

He drives to Norwalk for Christmas, picks up Evan on the way and he spends two nights in his childhood bedroom before they get back to work. He spends New Year's Eve on the road with the team, then it's back to New York for one game, and then it's Blake's least favorite time of the year.

The Knights and their fans love the annual dads' trip, love the stories that come to the surface, the footage of their dads celebrating on the road. Like last year, Blake's dad won't join them on the dads' trip. Of course not, because Blake's dad is dead. Maybe it's a little easier this year, because he knows that this is coming, not like last year, when it felt like running into a brick wall when he was asked if his dad would be joining them for the trip.

The Knights tell him that he can invite an uncle, any mentor, really, they're kind about it, but Blake says no, he won't have anyone on the trip. Last year, Michelson's dad wasn't on the trip either, so Blake wasn't on his own, but this year, with Michelson getting traded in the summer, Blake is the only one who doesn't have his dad on the plane.

After last year, the guys know that Blake's dad is dead, don't ask any questions when he gets on the plane on his own and tucks himself away in a seat in the back.

He doesn't have to speak to the media once during the entire trip, because their media relations guy knows what's going on and he's merciful. Even after Blake's shutout in DC, Blake gets to hit the showers and doesn't have to say a word to anyone.

Sometimes he gets caught up in how unfair it is that his parents never got to watch him play in an NHL game, that they never got to see how far he made it. It's so obvious now, with all the dads talking to the Knights' camera crew, saying how proud they are, sharing stories about taking the boys to hockey practice, about buying them their first skates, their first stick. He wishes the Knights had a moms' trip, because then he could have at least invited his grandma. She was the one who drove him to practices, who bought his gear, who sat with him until midnight, making him hot cocoa, when he was sad about a loss.

He makes it through the trip, like he did last year, talks to the guys' dads when they start a conversation, and breathes out a sigh of relief when they're back in Newark and he can finally go home.

"Hey, kid," Mattie says, hand on Blake's shoulder as they head to their cars. "You wanna come over for dinner?"

"No, I'm good. Thanks, though."

"You sure? Wouldn't be a problem. The girls would love it."

"I…" Blake shakes his hands. He knows that Noah is already on his way over, texted him as soon as their plane touched down. "Sorry, I sort of have plans."

"Oh," Mattie says, lips twitching. "You have a girlfriend?"

Blake doesn't know what the fuck is wrong with him, maybe he's tired, or maybe he just had the worst few days of the season, maybe not on the ice, but definitely in his head, but he hesitates. And not in an *oh, no, it's nothing serious* kind of way. More in an *I'm trying to hide something from you* kind of way. So he can't just give Mattie an extremely delayed and extremely untrue yes.

Maybe Mattie will think that Blake lied about having plans, but Blake's face is probably several shades of red right now and he's being cagey and there's no way Mattie doesn't at least figure out that there's *something* going on here.

Mattie's lips stop twitching and he grows serious. He wraps an arm around Blake and gives him a hug. "Dinner tomorrow?"

"Okay," Blake says.

"Okay," Mattie echoes.

Dinner the next day is comfortable and the girls pull Blake into their playroom downstairs and put him in their tiny goal and start shooting balls at him with their tiny sticks. Mattie doesn't talk about the day before, but he insists on walking Blake out to his car later, so Blake already knows what's coming.

"You know," Mattie says, "I know when something's none of my business, so I'm not going to ask. I'll say, though… that it seemed like there was something you might want to talk about. And… I have ears."

"Mattie…"

"That's literally all I wanted to tell you. I'm not gonna ask any questions. All I'm saying is… well, you know what I'm saying."

"Thank you," Blake says.

Mattie sends him on his way with a mumbled, "Drive safe," and then wanders back to the door, giving him a wave before he heads back inside.

Blake drives back to his apartment, parks in his spot, sits in his car for a good ten minutes, staring into space, his thoughts all over the place, until a car door slams shut somewhere and he snaps out of it.

Elliot sort of bullies his team into making it to the second round of playoffs. He doesn't know how else to describe it. The Ravens haven't made it past the first round in actual years, often didn't make the playoffs at all, and during a team meeting before the playoffs start, he tells his guys that it's not going to happen this year.

They're going to make it past the first round.

No one expects it. Again, they only barely managed to hold on to their wildcard spot. The media is talking about them like they've already lost, think they can't make it past Montreal in a hundred years.

It's not like Elliot doesn't have doubts, he just doesn't allow himself to acknowledge them, because he has to walk into that playoff series like he believes that they can make it to the other end of it with four wins.

They lose the first game, because of course they do.

The guys are a lot quieter than they should be after one loss. Because that's it. One loss.

"Stop acting like we lost the entire fucking series," Elliot says.

He's so mad, he's pretty sure he scores all the goals that follow out of spite. Two in the next game, another two in the third one, and after they win those two, the rest of the team catches on. They win the fourth, too.

They drop the fifth, but this time the locker room isn't as quiet as it was after the other loss. They're taking it back to New York. They're going to *win* in New York.

Elliot scores the game winner, and just like that, they're going to Round 2.

They don't make it past the Grizzlies, but this time nobody dares to even insinuate that they're not good enough. They made it past Montreal, knocked out a serious contender, and when they do their exit interviews this year, Elliot doesn't waste any time on talking about how they weren't good enough.

He talks about how hard his guys fought. He talks about how proud he is of them. How he can't wait to do this all over again, hopefully minus losing the second round.

Elliot takes his entire team out for dinner before they all leave town for the summer. He doesn't like the thought that some of them won't be back in the fall, despite their performance in the playoffs. It's a good group.

"Thanks, Moo," Andreas says when he hugs him goodbye. "You know, for... everything."

"Thanks, Andi," Elliot echoes.

He watches Andreas and Evan walk away, nearly shoving each other into traffic as they leave.

"They grow up so fast," Adam says and throws an arm around Elliot. "Okay, listen, now that all the children are headed home, I need your help."

"Yeah? What's wrong?"

"Nothing's wrong, really," Adam says. "I need your not-so-professional opinion. Are we too young to get married?"

"I, uh..." Elliot hadn't really thought about it. "I don't know?"

Adam is a year older than him, and even if he wasn't, Elliot knows plenty of players his age who are engaged, even some who are married already. Most of those guys have been with their girlfriends since they were teenagers, though. Like Magnus. He met his wife when he was fifteen, but they didn't get married until they were together for over ten years.

"You're not helping," Adam says. "Have you never thought about it?"

"Getting married?"

"Yeah."

"I... No?"

"I mean, you and Natalie have been dating for nearly two years, don't you... I don't know. Maybe I'm weird, but I started thinking about marrying Lou, like, two months after I first met her."

Elliot only blinks at him.

"No, don't look at me like that, oh no, Adam is being ridiculous again," Adam says and slaps Elliot's arm. Which kinda hurts because Elliot's entire body is covered in bruises. "I just really love my girlfriend, Moo."

"I also love my girlfriend," Elliot says and it comes out almost petulant.

"Good for you." Adam slaps Elliot's back this time and it doesn't hurt as much. "Can you help me with the ring?"

"I'm not sure if you're asking the right person for help."

Adam makes a face. "I don't want help picking the ring, I want moral support."

"Oh."

"See, you're exactly the right person for that."

Elliot can't really argue with that. He *is* pretty good at the moral support thing.

It almost seems too easy how early the Knights clinch their playoff spot, how little they have to fight for home ice. Mattie is going to get the start during the first round, despite Blake sitting on the bench less often. There were some mumblings around the trade deadline, about Mattie getting traded, about the Knights having Blake as their starting goalie for good, but Mattie gets to stay. He might re-sign at the end of the season and Blake will likely be the Knights regular starter next season with Mattie as their backup. Or at least those are Mattie's musings.

Blake isn't surprised when they give Mattie the nod for the first round of playoffs.

They end up playing the Mariners and Blake and Noah still chirp back and forth, never really go silent, even though their texts become less frequent. They mostly talk about the weather, and food, and Noah's insane neighbor. Not hockey, never hockey.

The first game is going remarkably well for the Knights – after the first period they're up 4-1. Blake isn't one to be suspicious when things go too well, because that's just life. Sometimes everything goes well. On other days everything goes to shit. Sometimes it's both.

On the day of their fifth playoff game, it's definitely both.

They have a chance to win this series, in front of their fans in Newark. All they need is one more win.

Then, during the second, Mattie takes a knee to the head, one of the Mariners barreling into him, tripping in front of the net. It takes a while for Mattie to get up, the guys quiet as he walks down the tunnel, leaning heavily against one of their trainers.

Blake tries not to think about what they're looking at here. A concussion? Hopefully nothing worse. Whatever it is, Blake can't think about it right now, he needs to make sure that they walk out of this with a win, one save after the other.

The clock runs down and they win, only barely, after an empty netter with a score of 5-3. Three guys jump into Blake's arms as soon as the final horn sounds, shouting into his ear.

The next morning, it's just Tanner and Blake on the ice, no Mattie in sight. One of the kids gets called up from the Raiders. Mattie has a concussion, will likely be out for a few weeks. No one says it out loud, but they all know it's a bad one. "It's all you now," Tanner says to Blake. He's not trying to scare Blake; he's telling him the truth.

They make it past the Comets in Round 2, take it to seven games, three of which end in overtime.

Then it's Round 3, Conference Finals, against the Grizzlies.

They lose the first, win the second, win the third, lose the fourth, lose the fifth, and somehow manage a win in the sixth, in double OT, after which Blake is so tired that he wants to sleep for a fucking week. They lose Game 7 in Boston, fall to the Grizzlies, just like the Bobcats and the Ravens did.

Blake knows that his grandma is in the crowd with Evan, and they both meet him after the game and Evan gives him a hug and says, "Sorry, man. Been there. Sucks."

Blake only nods and lets his grandma hug him, too.

In the room, the guys are all quiet and subdued, although they keep patting Blake's back as he moves around and when Kells talks to him later he says, lowly, "I hope you know that we wouldn't have made it this far without you."

He wasn't really thinking about it.

It's nice to hear.

9

Blake is two months into his sixth season of playing professional hockey when things go to shit fast and unexpectedly.

It's a day off for the Knights because they just got back from a roadie in California and Nevada and he's on his way home from the grocery store when his phone starts to ring. He almost ignores it, but then finds that it's Aunt Beth – his grandma's sister, so she isn't really his aunt – and Aunt Beth never calls him, so he answers. "Aunt Beth? What's up?"

"Blake, honey," Aunt Beth says and she sounds all choked up, which is when Blake knows that it's bad, so, so bad, and he stops dead in the middle of the fucking sidewalk, someone walking into him, grumbling at him in passing.

"What happened?" Blake asks.

He must sound like he's scared shitless. He is. This is his worst nightmare. Blake is already running through all the things that could have happened. His grandma tripped over one of the cats and hit her head, she fell down the stairs, had a car accident on the way to Aunt Beth's house.

Aunt Beth takes a breath on the other end of the line.

"How bad is it?" Blake presses.

"I got worried when she didn't answer the door this morning, we were going to have breakfast together, and you know how she keeps a key under that pot out front and... I found her. Blake, sweetheart, I'm so sorry."

"She's..."

"She didn't wake up this morning."

Blake is going to– He doesn't know what the fuck he's going to do. Throw up? Cry? He needs to go home. Not to his apartment, but to Norwalk. He needs to get Evan, then he needs to go home. Aunt Beth

80

can't take care of this alone and there's no one else left, except for Aunt Beth's kids who are nowhere even close to home.

So he needs to go home, except he's supposed to play a fucking hockey game tomorrow, so how the hell can he go home now?

Do they let players go home when their grandparents die?

"Will you..." Aunt Beth's voice cracks. "Will you give your brother a call?"

"Yeah, yeah, I'll... I'll talk to..." Fuck, he doesn't even know who to talk to about this. "I'll see if we can come home, okay?"

"Thank you, Blake. Give me a call when you know, will you?"

Blake promises he will, hangs up the phone, and stands on the sidewalk for a moment longer, frozen to the spot.

He doesn't remember the night his parents died. Not well.

He woke up in the morning, and he was at his grandma's house with Evan, because his parents had been on a trip to Boston, and she told them that their dad was at the hospital. Told them that their mom didn't make it. He doesn't remember what exactly she said.

Blake remembers endless days at the hospital, weeks, he would have sworn, but a few years ago his grandma told him, no, it was only five days after the accident that his dad died.

He remembers the funeral, realizing that they weren't coming back. But his grandma was there, Blake's hand in hers, promising him that she'd always be there for them, and now she's gone, too, and—

He needs to go home.

He calls Kells, because he doesn't know if he should talk to Coach or if he should call their GM or whoever the fuck is in charge here. So he calls Kells, because Kells knows this kind of stuff.

Kells answers after a few rings. "Fish? What's up?"

Blake doesn't say anything for a moment, because he doesn't remember how. He should have called Evan first. Not that Aunt Beth will; she doesn't have to do this twice.

"Everything okay?" Kells asks. He doesn't sound concerned a lot. That probably means something.

"I..." Blake squeezes his eyes shut. He can do this. "I need to go home."

"Okay," Kells says, "did something happen?"

"My grandma, she... she died last night."

"I'm so sorry, bud. I... Why don't you give Coach a call? Tell him what happened, he'll understand. You can go home, take care of everything. It's okay. Don't worry about the team, okay? Just do what you need to do."

"Okay. I'm sorry, I didn't know who to call and... I'm sorry."

"Hey, don't worry about it. Call if you need anything."

"Thanks, Kells."

Blake calls Coach Franklin next, talks himself into moving. When Coach Franklin answers his phone, sounding gruff, Blake somehow manages to choke out what happened. After that, Coach Franklin doesn't sound so gruff anymore. His team knows that his parents are dead, they've all met his grandma, know that she basically raised him and his brother.

Coach Franklin tells him to go, tells him to take all the time he needs. Blake thanks him, tells him that, yes, he's okay to drive, apologizing for whatever inconvenience this is going to cause for the team. He almost cracks when Coach says that there's no need to apologize, that they're a family here and that they'll always look out for him.

By the time he's hung up the phone, he's back home. He texts Mattie to tell him he won't be able to come over for lunch after all. He sends another text to Noah to tell him that he can't come to his place tonight. He says it's a family emergency and doesn't wait for replies.

He doesn't know how the hell he's keeping it together right now.

He sits down and calls Evan.

He doesn't answer. He's probably on the ice for practice. Blake sends him a text and asks him to call him back as soon as he can. He tells him that he doesn't have good news.

It takes about twenty minutes for his phone to ring, Evan's voice small when he asks Blake what happened. Blake just says it. There's nothing that could soften the blow, no gentle way of putting it. Fuck all those euphemisms; there's nothing poetic about the death of someone you love.

The way Evan's voice cracks when he asks if they can go home almost does him in, but Blake makes it through that, too, and says, yes, they can go home. "Is Elliot there?" Blake asks.

There's some shuffling, then there's Elliot's voice, worried when he says, "Blake?"

"Yeah."

"Your grandma?" Elliot asks.

"Yeah," Blake says again, quieter. He clears his throat. "Listen, can you… I don't know, can you talk to your coaches, see if Evan can come home with me?"

"Of course, whatever you need."

"I…" Blake squeezes his eyes shut. He's at a total loss. He's an adult, but no one ever taught him how to deal with this. "I'll drive your way and you guys can give me a call when you've figured things out on your end?"

"Sure."

"You guys at the rink?"

"Yeah, we just got off the ice."

"Okay…" Blake lets out a deep breath. "Okay, so… I'll be there in… Give me an hour? Are you still gonna be there in an hour?"

"Yeah, we have lunch and meetings and… I'll stick around with Evan," Elliot says. "We'll go talk to Coach Warren in a minute."

"Thank you," Blake says. "Elliot…"

"Yeah?"

Blake doesn't know what to say. They haven't talked in such a long time and Elliot is still dropping everything to help them out. "Thank you," Blake says again. That's all he has in him right now.

"Of course. We'll give you a call when we've figured things out."

Ten minutes later, Blake has packed a bag and he's in his car, headed for the Ravens' practice rink.

When Evan started talking to Blake on the phone, Elliot pulled him out of the locker room, sensing that something was going on. He heard part of the conversation, then Evan handed him the phone and suddenly he was talking to Blake

They hash out the details, then Blake hangs up, already headed their way.

Evan is still on the bench in the hallway that Elliot pushed him onto, silent, staring at Elliot like he wants to ask him for help and doesn't know how. Elliot can't say that he's ever been in a situation like this, but he can handle it.

"Do you need a minute?" Elliot asks.

Evan nods.

Elliot watches him take a deep breath, like he's trying to keep himself from bursting into tears, and Elliot wants to tell him that it's okay if he needs to cry, that no one's going to judge him. Instead, he sits down next to him and waits for Evan to get it together enough that they can go find Coach Warren.

He's still holding Evan's phone.

They'd just gotten off the ice when Evan checked his phone and gave Blake a call. Both of them are mostly out of their pads. They need a shower, but that's not the most pressing issue right now.

"Do you want me to do the talking?" Elliot asks.

Evan only nods.

Elliot nods back at him, then interrupts a meeting to get Coach Warren. If there's ever been a time for interruptions, it is right now. Coach Warren doesn't look too happy with him at first, but is quick to get up when Elliot tells him that it's an emergency. He explains the situation as quickly as he can — he's pretty sure that Coach knows that both of Evan's parents died when he was nine, but makes sure to mention it and Evan's breath hitches the tiniest bit when he does.

Coach tells them to consider it taken care of and asks, "You need anyone to drive you to the airport? Need us to book you a flight?"

"His brother's on his way, he'll pick him up," Elliot says.

Coach nods. "Find Samuels something to eat, yeah?"

Elliot tugs Evan away and calls Blake with Evan's phone, tells him that Evan is good to go and that he'll stay with him at the rink until Blake gets here.

"Don't speed," Elliot says before he hangs up.

"I'm not. Promise."

"Okay." There's something else Elliot should say, but he can't think of the words right now. He almost wants to stay on the phone with Blake while he drives up here, which is ridiculous, so eventually he says, "We'll see you in a bit."

"Yeah. Thank you."

Elliot wishes Blake would stop thanking him, like he's making some huge sacrifice here.

He ushers Evan into the showers first, because they both need one, then he marches Evan to the buffet, makes sure he gets a decent amount of food and nudges him over to a table. He wanders back over to get some water and some food for himself, which is when Adam sidles up to him, eyes narrowed.

"Everything okay?" Adam asks, thankfully keeping his voice low.

"Evan's grandma died."

"Shit, isn't he like… an orphan?"

"Yeah."

"Oh, crap."

"Don't…" Elliot looks around, at Evan, at the corner of the table that Elliot nudged him over to, poking at his food. "Tell the guys not to bug him, okay? But, like, do it quietly."

"Sure, no worries."

Elliot goes and sits with Evan, who doesn't say a word. He puts Evan's phone on the table, in case Blake calls them again, but the phone stays quiet and so does Evan. Elliot talks him into eating at least some of his food.

"I'm okay," Evan eventually says.

Probably because Elliot has been staring at him. Elliot nods, even though Evan definitely doesn't *seem* okay. It starts with the lack of constant word-vomit that's pretty much Evan's trademark, and then there's that pinch to his mouth, replacing the usual easy smile that definitely doesn't run in the family.

Elliot was legitimately scared of Blake's grandma the first time he went to visit Blake in the summer. He soon figured out that she was very concerned, not only for Blake and Evan, but literally everyone else, made sure Elliot had everything he needed, asked about his family, kept putting food in front of him, but food he was actually supposed to eat, not just milk and cookies or whatever Elliot's grandma makes for him when he swings by.

Blake actually laughed at him when Elliot pointed that out, and then said, "Yeah, no cookies here. Although if you ask really nicely she might make us some."

They did ask really nicely and she did make them cookies and they ate all of them before anyone could stop them.

Elliot jumped on any invitation to the Samuels' house, at first because he felt so comfortable there, almost like he was home, then because he also wanted to spend every possible second with his lips attached to Blake's. He always slept in Blake's room, Blake on a mattress on the floor, Elliot in Blake's bed, except when Blake was in his bed with him. One time they watched a movie downstairs, Evan at a friend's house, Blake's grandma out playing cards with her friends that Blake called the Casserole Brigade, because they apparently were always out giving their neighbors casseroles at every possible occasion. When she got home, Elliot was fast asleep, Blake's head on his chest, but jerked awake when the front door closed. Blake, of course, didn't fucking wake up and Elliot didn't manage to get him off his chest either, so Blake was still plastered against him when Elliot's grandma poked her head into the living room.

Elliot was still scrambling for an explanation when she nodded, like she was pleased that they didn't trash the house, and wished them a good night. Elliot let Blake keep on sleeping. He never told him about that.

Blake's grandma turned into one of his favorite people eventually, with her big black cat and all the kale in the fridge and her lesbian friends.

"You don't have to sit there, you know?" Evan says.

"Do you want me to go?"

Evan chews on his bottom lip. "I'm just saying you don't have to."

"Okay," Elliot says. "Well, if you don't want me to leave, I'll sit here."

Evan nods, fiddles with his phone, and Elliot thinks he made the right choice.

It's strange, pulling into the parking lot of the Ravens' practice facility. It's even stranger to get out of the car and awkwardly hover in front of the door, because he can't just walk inside.

The parking lot is dotted with your typical hockey player cars — Blake's Jeep fits right in. But he's literally standing here in a Knights shirt. He pulls out his phone and gives Evan another call, tells him that he's outside and waits.

Evan shows up a few minutes later, escorted by Elliot, who's looking at Blake like he's a ghost.

"Hey," Blake says.

Evan doesn't say hello, he just walks right into him and hugs him. And Blake is still keeping it together. He mouths a *thank you* at Elliot over Evan's shoulder.

Elliot nods.

"Okay, let's go..." Blake says and nudges Evan over to the car.

Evan nods at Elliot, who lingers in the door for a moment, then slips back into the rink as Evan and Blake get into the car.

"You okay?" Blake asks.

Evan doesn't look at him, only shakes his head and starts crying and somehow Blake is still keeping it together. He needs to get them home first. It's almost like it hasn't really sunken in yet.

Blake reaches out, squeezes Evan's arm, and turns the key in the ignition. They're not that far from home and the stop they make at Evan's place to get some clothes for him only takes them ten minutes. By the time Blake pulls into the driveway of the house they grew up in, Evan has stopped crying, his eyes still rimmed red. The place looks like it always does; Blake isn't sure why he thinks that it should be different.

They go in, the cats running to greet them, and Blake keeps it together.

He keeps it together all day. They meet up with Aunt Beth, they help her organize the funeral, they're running from one office to the next all day and when they get back to the house in the evening Blake is absolutely exhausted, ready to drop into bed, and it's only seven. He didn't even do much, because Aunt Beth clearly knew what had to be taken care of. Blake was just driving her where she told him to go while she was making phone calls, Evan in the backseat, quietly wiping away tears.

Blake doesn't know why he hasn't cried yet. He isn't a crier in the first place, but he knows that it's coming and he wants to get it over with already. It's been building up all day.

They drop off Aunt Beth at her house and they pick up dinner on the way home at a diner they used to go to when they were kids and they sit down at the kitchen table and Evan doesn't eat and Blake doesn't have it in him to make him, because he can barely convince himself to take a bite right now.

"I..." Evan says. He picks up his pickle and puts it down again. "I feel like I should have come home more often. I was barely here during the summer and... I just thought... I don't know... Shit."

Blake was here for a few weeks during the summer, but it makes no difference at all. They probably could have spent every single day of their lives here and it wouldn't feel like it was enough.

"And…" Evan draws in a shuddering breath. "It's just us now."

"I know," Blake says. He was thinking about that while he was on his way to pick up Evan. It's just them now. Aunt Beth will still be around, they grew up with her popping in several times a week, but it's not the same.

"I don't even remember the last conversation I had with her, like, she called me on my day off and I was so distracted because I was about to go out with this girl and I—"

"Evan, don't do that." Blake puts his pickle on Evan's plate because he always does, even though it looks like Evan isn't going to eat anything.

Evan stares at him, then stares down at his burger. "She'd tell us off for having fucking burgers right now."

"She'd also tell you off for saying fuck," Blake says. "And she'd tell you off for not actually eating your food and just poking at it."

"I hate this."

Blake takes a deep breath. "Me too."

He eats his food, watches Evan until he's eaten his as well, including the pickle Blake gave him, then he shoves Evan out of the kitchen, cleans up their mess, and feeds Angus and the orange cat, Squid. His grandma always had the radio on in the kitchen, so now it seems too quiet. He can hear the murmur of the TV down the hall and finds Evan curled up on the couch, hugging a pillow.

Blake sits down by his feet, phone in hand. He pretty much ignored everything all day, has a few missed calls, a bunch of notifications from the team's group chat, texts from Mattie and Noah. While he's staring down at his phone, trying to figure out if he has it in him to reply to any of them tonight, his phone starts ringing.

It's Elliot.

Blake wonders briefly if Elliot is calling the wrong Samuels brother.

He almost doesn't answer but changes his mind when it's nearly too late. Fuck knows why. "Hey," he says.

"Hey," Elliot replies. "I'm sorry. Is this… I was about to ask if this is a bad time and, like, of course it's a bad time… I…"

"It's okay," Blake mutters. He glances at Evan, whose eyes are fixed on the TV. "Let me… Give me a second to go upstairs."

Blake gives Evan's foot a gentle pat, then he sneaks out of the room. He doesn't want to have this conversation with Evan listening in.

Elliot thinks about calling Blake all day.

After Evan leaves, Elliot is distracted in the meeting he has in the afternoon, is distracted when he drives home, is distracted when he lies down for a nap and can't even convince his eyes to stay closed. He should have said something to Blake. Anything. Even if it was just the standard *my condolences*. He wanted to hug him so badly. He doesn't know why he didn't do it.

The fight they had aside, he behaved like a soulless asshole.

So he keeps fiddling with his phone all day. He gets distracted when he makes dinner, burns his chicken, and then eats the charred chicken because it's his own damn fault. Natalie isn't home yet to judge him for it, so he suffers in silence. He's actually become pretty good at cooking, except when he tries new recipes. There's still a fifty-fifty chance of him hurtling towards a major disaster when he tries something new, but there are some dishes he's made so many times that he's perfected them.

He keeps thinking about Blake.

Eventually, he can't deal with himself anymore, grabs his phone and calls him. He likely has more important stuff to do and won't answer anyway, so Elliot will leave a message and tell him that he's sorry for his loss, because then he at least said something. Blake probably doesn't even want to talk to Elliot, which is confirmed a moment later when Blake doesn't answer his phone.

Except then he does.

"Hey," Blake says.

"Hey," Elliot says. For a moment, he can't remember what he called to say. "I'm sorry. Is this... I was about to ask if this is a bad time and, like, of course it's a bad time... I..."

He's an idiot. He shouldn't have called.

"It's okay," Blake says, voice low. "Let me... Give me a second to go upstairs." Elliot can almost see him stomping up that narrow staircase. He hears a door creak, then Blake says, "Okay."

"I'm so sorry, Blake," Elliot says.

Blake takes a deep breath on the other end of the line.

And then Elliot's mouth just runs away with all the thoughts he's had all day for some reason. "I wanted to hug you so much when I saw you earlier and... I should have. Blake... I..." Elliot pinches the bridge of his nose, because he can't cry right now, this is not about him. "And I'm so sorry I called, I just wanted to check on you... and on Evan... and... I'll hang up now, but I'm sorry and I hope you're okay."

Which is ridiculous, because of course Blake isn't fucking *okay*.

All he gets from the other end of the line is a shuddering breath and a very quiet, "Don't hang up."

"Okay... Okay, I won't."

"It's..." Blake trails off. "She had a stroke, she wasn't... She just went to sleep last night and... Yeah. That's good, I guess? It didn't hurt, I don't think. And the funeral is the day after tomorrow and..." His voice cracks. "Fuck, I'm sorry."

"It's okay." Elliot still wants to hug him. He does entertain the absolutely insane idea of driving to Norwalk to give Blake a hug. He knows Blake is crying on the other end of the line, can hear him sniffle. Fuck, he'd drive to Norwalk to bring him a tissue right now. "Blake?" Elliot says.

"Can you... talk to me? About... whatever?"

"Sure. You wanna hear about... I don't know." All he does is play hockey. Blake probably doesn't want to hear about his personal life and Elliot doesn't have much else going on. "I can tell you about my teammates."

"Yeah."

"Okay," Elliot says.

And so he tells Blake about Andreas's ridiculous pregame ritual that involves a lot of muttering in German, and about Moby, who keeps taping dicks on people's jerseys, even though he's way too fucking old for that kind of shit, and Swan, who lost a bet and had to get a tattoo of an actual swan, and their rookie, baby-faced Keith Taylor who keeps getting pranked by Dima and gets so red every single time that the guys have started calling him Crab.

Natalie gets home, peers into the bedroom, where Elliot is sitting at the foot of their bed. He points at his phone, gets up and closes the door. It's not something he'd usually do, he doesn't hide his phone calls from her, but this is different.

He talks about the Ravens' latest road trip, about a restaurant he found in Nashville that he liked. He can't remember the name, knows he has a napkin somewhere, but he gives Blake directions on how to get there from the arena.

He tells Blake about Adam and picking a ring for his girlfriend. He tells Blake how much he misses Magnus, who's a Comet now.

He keeps talking. He doesn't know for how long, slipping from one story into another, trying not to think about how Blake is probably all by himself in his old room, crying quietly while Elliot prattles on and on about nothing in particular. Somehow, he doesn't run out of things to say.

Eventually, Blake says, "Thank you."

"Of course."

"I'm not supposed to like any of the guys on your team, but I guess I'm, uh... weirdly fond of some of them now."

"They're jerks."

"Yeah, my guys are jerks, too," Blake says. "I love them a lot."

Elliot laughs.

"Thanks for calling," Blake says softly.

"If there's anything I can do..."

"Thank you." Blake clears his throat. "I should go check on Evan."

"How is he?"

"He'll be okay. You'll keep an eye out for him when we're back, yeah?"

"I will," Elliot promises.

They're both quiet for a moment. They both have other things to say, but now is not the time. If Elliot makes one wrong move, something will break.

"Blake?" Elliot finally says.

"Yeah?"

"When you're back, can we... hang out?"

"Yeah," Blake says. "I'll..."

"Whenever you have time." Elliot drags his fingers through his hair. "Take care of yourself."

Again, Blake says, "Yeah." Then he says goodnight.

Elliot stays where he's been sitting for the past hour or so, staring at the floor, trying to piece himself back together into a presentable person.

He resurfaces eventually, because Natalie got home about forty-five minutes ago and the longest Elliot usually spends on the phone is ten minutes. He makes an exception when he's on a long roadie and calls her, but even then they're usually done talking after half an hour.

She's on the couch, watching that TV show with the vampires she likes, munching on a bowl of popcorn. "Hey," she says and it sounds like a question.

"Sorry," Elliot mumbles. "Old friend. Got some bad news today."

"Oh," Natalie says. She's looking at him like she's expecting him to say something else, but he doesn't really know what else to say, so he asks if he can have some popcorn and then nudges the remote back to her so she can go on watching her vampire show.

Blake sits in his old room for a few more minutes. There's not too much left in his closet and on the shelves, just some old gear, some clothes he left, stuff from when he was a little kid that his grandma apparently didn't want to throw away.

He rubs his eyes. They're dry now, after he cried for half an hour while Elliot was talking about stuff that Blake barely even registered. Elliot has always been a talker, even during difficult situations, never tried to wiggle his way out of a conversation, because he could deal. There's something soothing about the way Elliot talks, now even more than six years ago. He has that captain thing down.

He talks himself into moving, because he really should check on Evan. Looking at it now, Evan's intermittent crying is probably a much healthier way to deal with this than Blake trying to keep it together until he just couldn't do it anymore and then letting it go while he was on the phone with his fucking ex.

Evan is still exactly where Blake left him, watching TV. There's a tear clinging to his eyelashes, like he stopped crying into the pillow he's hugging to his chest no two minutes ago. He sits up when Blake joins him on the couch, eyes lingering on Blake's face.

"Who was that?" Evan asks. "Girlfriend?"

The thing with the truth is that in some moments it seems easier to say than in others. Considering the situation they're in, this should not be one of the easy ones, but Blake will take it. "Ex-boyfriend," he says. It's the worst time to say it, but it's never felt easier.

What Blake isn't expecting is Evan's, "Why'd you break up?"

"What?"

"You and the boyfriend? Why'd you break up?"

"Really, I tell you that I'm gay and that's what you want to know?"

"You didn't technically say you were *gay*," Evan says. "What was I supposed to say?"

"I… don't know."

"Did you think I'd pass out because I couldn't deal or some shit? I'm not a total douchebag, Blake."

"No, but…"

"Believe it or not, but you're not the first gay person I've met," Evan says. "Chill."

"Okay," Blake says, taken aback.

"So?"

"What?"

Evan pokes at Blake's knee. "Why'd you break up?"

"It just wasn't… working. At the time."

Evan seems to accept that as an answer and then says, "You have a boyfriend now?"

"Not really."

"Not really is not a no."

"It's a thing."

"A *thing*." Evan shakes his head at him, like he's deeply offended by the term. "Can I meet him?"

"It's not… no."

"So you're saying you have, like, a dirty mistress."

Blake rolls his eyes at him, even though Noah would probably find this whole conversation hilarious and would in no way object to being called a dirty mistress.

"I'm curious, since we're talking about your love life for the first time *ever*. I thought you just hated talking to me about it, you know? I always told you about my girlfriends."

"You told me *too much* about your girlfriends."

Evan cackles. "When things get serious with... your guy... can I meet him?"

"It won't get serious," Blake grumbles. "But I guess if there ever is someone serious, you can meet him."

"I can live with that."

Evan fiddles with his phone and Blake nearly has a heart attack when Squid jumps into his lap, purring as he makes himself comfortable. Evan changes the channel, then gets up to get himself some water and picks up Angus on the way. He almost disappears against Evan's black shirt.

Evan hugs Angus to his chest and nods at the orange fur ball on Blake's lap. "What's gonna happen to them? Aunt Beth doesn't really like cats and I don't want to put them in a shelter, I mean, they don't deserve that, do you think one of the neighbors–"

"I'll take them," Blake says without even thinking about it. They got their first cat when Blake was three, a tabby called Cheese, and since then they've always had at least one or two cats, so he knows how to take care of them. He made sure he could have pets in his apartment in Newark, because he was playing with the thought of maybe getting a dog one day.

He'll take Angus and Squid instead. Works just as well.

"Yeah?" Evan says. "You sure?"

Blake scratches Squid's head and his purrs get impossibly loud. "Yeah."

"Thank you," Evan says. He hesitates, looks around. "Blake?"

"Hm?"

"You know what Aunt Beth said, about the house, that it belongs to us and that we need to figure out what to do with it and... I don't know, we need to decide what to do with *everything* and..."

"Yeah," Blake says. He's not looking forward to the part where they figure out who gets what. He doesn't want any of it, not the money or the house or their grandma's car.

"I don't want to sell the house," Evan says, almost timid.

Blake hadn't even thought about selling the house, although he supposes that's a thing that happens after somebody dies. He frowns at Evan. "You want it?"

"It's just... *our* house," Evan mumbles. "I can have it?"

"All yours," Blake says.

"You can keep your room," Evan says, and that's probably the nicest thing he's ever said to Blake.

10

Blake rejoins the Knights on the road, in Raleigh.

He tells Coach that he's ready to play.

Coach puts him on the bench.

Blake gets it, was pretty much expecting it, so he lets the guys welcome him back, tries to talk to them, lets Mattie give him a hug, and lets Kells give him a hug, which is weird, because he's pretty sure Kells only hugs people after goals and Mattie hugs the rookies when they need it.

Blake wasn't the only one who was relieved that Mattie recovered from his concussion and re-signed with the Knights for another two seasons. He's backing up for Blake now, which still seems weird, but Mattie was already talking about this years ago, always believing that Blake would one day be the Knights' starter.

When they get back to New York, they immediately get back to it, this time with Blake in net, and they walk out of it with a win. In OT. It's an optional practice the next morning and Blake is on the ice for it, because he did miss two games and it's not that he feels guilty, but… maybe he does feel guilty. He knows it's ridiculous, knows that no one's blaming him, but he still sticks around for longer than strictly necessary with their rookie, Williamson, and their most recent call-up, Lehtinen.

Talking to the media after the game last night was daunting, and even though no one outright asked him why he was gone for a few days, he still got questions like, "Is it hard to get back on the ice after being away from the team?" Blake answered that one with a very simple, "No," since they'd just won a game.

When Blake gets home after practice, he has a missed call from Noah. He hasn't exactly been in touch, only sent Noah a quick text to tell him why he had to leave town and that he'd be in touch when he's back.

He's back now.

He still hasn't called Noah.

94

Blake calls him back, on the couch, where Squid joins him no five seconds later, meowing at him before plopping down next to him, purring before Blake has even started petting him.

"Hey," Noah says when he picks up.

"I'm sorry," Blake greets him.

"Uhhh… what did you do?"

"I… I don't know, I said I was gonna call and then I didn't."

"Don't worry about it, honestly, you had… stuff… lots of stuff happening. Just wanted to ask if you want me to come over. I got out of practice like an hour ago and I don't have plans. Figured I'd ask."

"I…" Blake closes his eyes. "I don't think I'd be very good company."

"Okay."

"Sorry."

"It's cool, Fish. But, for the record, I wasn't, like, talking about me coming over for sex. Just… you know, I'd bring food and braid your hair and shit."

"Oh," Blake says. "We don't really do that, though."

The whole point of their arrangement, despite the friendship that has come out of it, is that they have someone they can get off with without risking anyone else finding out about either of them. They don't cuddle. They don't– They're not boyfriends.

"What the fuck, dude. We hang out. You know, before or after the sex. Sometimes before *and* after the sex. We're friends. Sex friends, yeah, but… What kinda food do you want me to bring?"

"Are you sure you want to come over?"

"Do I want to drive all the way there even though I'm not getting any dick in return… Well, Blake, I think I just offered, so tell me what the fuck you want to eat and stop being an idiot."

Blake's brain is capable of making that choice right now. "I…"

"Chinese."

"Yeah."

"I'll text when I'm close."

"Thank you," Blake says.

They hang up and Blake stays on the couch, petting Squid. He seems to like Blake's apartment and has found himself a spot he likes, but Angus mostly hides in the guest room and doesn't interact with Blake. The way he brought them here probably wasn't ideal, just put them in their carriers, put a cat tree and their litter box in the trunk, grabbed a bunch of food and here they are. He found someone to feed them while he was in Raleigh at the very last minute; a girl that Paulie recommended. He lives down the street with his girlfriend and they have a demonic tabby who'll attack anyone who even so much as looks her way. Paulie loves her dearly.

Blake takes a nap and when he wakes up, Squid is still next to him, also taking a nap.

Noah rings his doorbell not too much later, carrying four bags full of Chinese food that they'll never be able to eat, which is what Blake tells him when Noah drops them all on the living room table.

"I figured you could use some leftovers, I don't know… when my sister died, I didn't really feel like cooking for… a while."

"Your sister died?"

"I was twenty, it was before… We didn't really know each other yet, so you wouldn't know." Noah shrugs. "Anyway."

"I'm sorry," Blake says.

Noah squeezes his wrist, then he says, "Uh… Fish?"

"Yeah?"

"There's a cat, like, right there."

"Oh, yeah, that's Squid. He was my grandma's, and Angus, too, and they sort of needed a place to go, so I took them with me." Blake frowns at him. "You're not allergic, are you?"

"Nope, just a dog person." Noah sits down on the couch, eyeing Squid warily. "No worries, we'll stay out of each other's way." He points at Squid. "No scratchies. No attackies."

Blake snorts. "Weirdo."

"Shut up. Eat these amazing mini spring rolls I brought you. Mostly dough, minimal veggies, just the way you like them."

"Thank you."

"Sure."

"For coming over, too."

Noah winks at him and grabs one of the cartons, probably something with fried beef. Squid seems to be more interested in whatever Noah is eating and starts climbing into his lap.

"Uh…"

"Squid, come on," Blake says and tries to lure him away, but he seems to be having an excellent time in Noah's lap. "Guess he likes you?"

"Orange beast, if your claws get anywhere close to the goods, I'll take issue."

"He'll be good," Blake says.

Noah huffs and starts eating his food, Squid in his lap, eyes closed. "I guess he's okay," Noah eventually says.

"Hey… Hey, Moo! Where do cows live?"

"If you say Moo York, I'm gonna fucking strangle you," Elliot mutters. He's trying to get off his practice jersey and it got caught on his pads somewhere and now he's wiggling around like an idiot.

"Here," Adam says and frees him. "But fuck you for hating on my joke."

Elliot huffs at him and starts pulling off his pads, putting them back with a little too much force.

"You okay, dude?" Adam asks.

"Yeah."

"You wanna go grab a bite?"

"I'm fine," Elliot says.

"No offense, Moo, but, like… You're not subtle. And you're the happiest, sunshiniest person I know and right now you look miserable and also kinda mad and it's unsettling, so… let's go grab a bite. Actually, come to my house, so we can talk. I have food."

Elliot doesn't say yes, because Adam is going to drag him with him anyway. He tried to keep it off the ice, but he clearly didn't manage to keep it out of the room, and he'll be the first one to tell his guys that it's okay to have a bad day, but he doesn't *want* to have a bad day and he's angry at himself for– What? Allowing himself to have emotions?

Yeah, sounds about right.

He showers, angrily, and he gets dressed, angrily, and then they head out together and Elliot follows Adam to his place. Adam makes them steaks and veggies and they talk about their game against the Bobcats tomorrow and for a while Elliot isn't even in that terrible of a mood. At least until Adam says, "So, what's wrong?"

"It's not… It's personal shit."

"Well, tell me about the personal shit. Unless it's… Is it, like, weird sex stuff?"

"Dude," Elliot says. He's pretty sure that he's blushing; his face is on fire. "No. It's nothing like that."

"So?"

"I had a fight with Natalie last night after I got home."

Honestly, who picks a fight with their boyfriend when he just got home from a fucking matinee game in Boston? That they lost? And it wasn't even close, the score was 7-1. They lost 7-1 and Natalie decided that it was a good time for a fight. Breaking news: it wasn't.

"What'd you do?" Adam asks through a mouthful of steak.

"I didn't do anything," Elliot snaps, indignant.

"Okay, but… What was the issue?"

"I don't know, she was talking about this friend of hers who got engaged the other day and I was fucking exhausted, so maybe I wasn't really… receptive to any of that? And I guess I wasn't excited enough? So she got mad because I wasn't really listening and… I wasn't, I'll give her that, but then she sort of…"

Adam tilts his head, clearly willing to let Elliot figure out the end of that sentence.

"I don't know, it happened really fast, first she was saying I never listen and it's like I don't even care and then suddenly it was about us and our future and... yeah. So she's mad at me."

"I mean, I get exhausted after games, too, it's not really the best time to talk about serious stuff," Adam says with a shrug.

"Exactly."

"But you also said that you weren't listening."

"Because I was tired."

"Did you tell her that?" Adam asks, eyebrows raised, like he knows that Elliot didn't.

"No. I sort of figured that'd make her mad, too."

Adam chews on his bottom lip. "It shouldn't. But I guess..."

"What?"

"No, I don't want to, like—"

"Just say it."

"Don't be mad at me now," Adam says, "but you kinda always tell people you're okay and that everything's just peachy and... I guess what I'm saying is maybe you should say when you're not okay, and when you're tired and shit, because then people know where they're at."

"I don't do that."

"Uh-huh."

"I don't."

"Earlier you tried to tell me that you were fine. You're not fine, Moo."

Elliot takes a deep breath and silently continues to eat his steak, because maybe Adam has a point. He probably could have avoided that fight yesterday if he'd apologized and told Natalie that he was tired and pissed off because they lost that game in Boston, but the thought that he could do that didn't actually cross his mind.

He's not really spending a lot of time at home either and that's probably hard for her, and he's been terrible about calling her on the road, because he's been keeping an eye on Evan and their youngest rookie, who needs a little more moral support every now and then. He's a little shy, but he seems to be okay talking to Elliot, so Elliot has been going out with the team on most nights on the road, so the kid would have someone to hang with before Elliot eventually pushed him towards other teammates.

And then there's that other thing that's been bugging him for a while.

"Adam," Elliot says. "Can I ask you something?"

"Sure?"

"Do you tell Lou everything?"

"Everything?"

"I mean, like, everything about yourself?"

"We've been together for years and we're getting married, I'm pretty sure she knows me better than anyone else."

"No, I mean… Let's say here's something about you that's not relevant to your relationship, but something that's… sort of important. Would you tell her even though it doesn't really matter?"

"Dude, I think you're gonna have to tell me what this is actually about, because I'm not following."

Elliot takes a deep breath. Maybe this could be a practice run for when he tells Natalie? Because he has to tell her. Eventually. He doesn't even know why it's so important to him. Maybe, to him, it's something you should tell the person you love.

"Moo."

"Yeah?"

"You're my best friend. You can tell me shit. All the important stuff and the stuff that doesn't really matter."

Elliot nods.

"Moo."

"Yeah?"

"Did you kill someone or what?"

"No, fuck."

"I was kidding," Adam says, frowning. "I think."

Elliot stares down at his food, like it's going to tell him what the hell to say next. The food, of course, isn't helpful in the slightest.

"It's not… So, a couple of years ago, before I even got drafted, there was this guy and I… We were sort of… I don't know. It doesn't really matter now, because I'm with Natalie, right?"

"There was a guy," Adam echoes.

Elliot can't look at him.

"Were you in love with that guy?"

"I… Maybe."

"You're saying maybe, but it kinda sounds like yes," Adam says. "Anyway, regardless of… gender or whatever, it's just another ex, right?"

"Right," Elliot says and it comes out sounding like a question. "We talked about our exes, but I sort of didn't mention that one of them was… not a girl."

"So you feel like you're lying to her?"

"I guess."

"Then tell her?"

"I don't know how, though?" Elliot stabs a bit of broccoli with his fork. "It's not like I can randomly bring it up? Oh, by the way... I'm... not... straight."

Adam clears his throat. "You know that I'm cool with this, right? Because you're sort of trying to murder your food with your eyes there and that steak is already dead, so it's not... Moo. Come on. You know I'm not homophobic or something."

"I'm not gay."

"Yeah, but you just said you're not..."

"Straight," Elliot mumbles. "Yeah."

"Listen, if it really bugs you, tell her, but..." Adam shrugs. "I don't know. I guess if knowing that changes anything, that's her problem, not yours."

Elliot spears a piece of carrot. He needs to breathe. *Breathe.* Everything's okay. "Yeah, I guess."

It takes Blake actual weeks to finally call Elliot. At first he's trying to get back into his routine and suddenly they're hurtling towards Christmas, then the Knights go on the road and it's not until Blake is on his own in a hotel room in Winnipeg that he finally gets around to it.

He didn't really want to go out with the guys, it's fucking freezing and he's tired, then he started looking for a movie to watch, started scrolling through Twitter and stumbled across an interview with the Ravens' coach this morning.

Blake isn't sure why the hell he decides to watch it.

It's about the Ravens' games against Dallas and Arizona and he's talking about how the Ravens practically destroyed both teams on the road, then one of the reporters asks about Elliot.

"Yes, of course, Elliot has been great for us, obviously, even if you just look at his numbers, the way he's producing. He's on a six-game point streak right now, and he's had two points or more in all of them. But, you know, he's just great to have in the room as well. Ask any of the guys and they'll tell you that Elliot is a fantastic teammate."

Blake hits pause there, because all that talk of Elliot and what a great person he is reminds Blake that he's being a terrible person, because he still hasn't called him.

He could do it right now.

His phone is right there.

Elliot doesn't have a game tonight. It's not that late yet.

When he finally calls him, Blake is actually hoping that Elliot won't answer, but he does, after the second ring, with a soft, "Hey, Blake."

"Hey," Blake says. "How's it going?"

"Just... having a quiet night in. Give me a sec, I'll..." There's the murmur of a TV show or a movie in the background, some quiet mumbling, then it's quiet and Elliot says, "How are you?"

"I'm okay."

"Yeah?"

"Yeah," Blake says. "It wasn't... It was a rough couple of days, but... being back with the team helped, I guess." He lies back, stares at the ceiling. It's going to hurt for a while. His parents died over ten years ago and he still misses them. And now he has another person to miss. "I have cats now."

"Your grandma's cats?"

"Yeah," Blake says. "You should come by and say hi to Angus. He's not really adjusting well and he always liked you."

"He's sad, too," Elliot says.

Blake pinches the bridge of his nose. He's not going to cry again. "I'm a bad cat dad," he says. He doesn't like the way his voice sounds, but it's not like this can get any more embarrassing than their last phone call.

"I'm sure you're doing your best," Elliot says. "Just don't feed them any chocolate. Or is that dogs? I don't know."

Blake snorts.

"See, I'd be a way worse cat dad. But I'd love to say hi. To Angus. And the... other... How many other cats did your grandma have? I just know Angus."

"She got another one not too long ago. His name is Squid. He's... orange."

"Can't wait to meet him." Elliot clears his throat. "You wanna have dinner at some point? I don't mind coming to Newark."

It takes them a few minutes to go through their schedules and find a date at the beginning of January when they're both in town and both have the evening off. It's not that Blake didn't know how hard this can be. He's constantly doing this with Noah, comparing schedules, setting up secret meetings. Although with Elliot it's not much of a secret, they're literally just two old friends meeting up for dinner. Well. Exes, too. But that doesn't matter. That was years ago.

"Thanks for calling, Blake."

"Yeah, sure, I'll see you..."

"January 12th."

"I'll find us a place for dinner."

"Send me the address," Elliot says. "And we'll– What?"

Someone says something in the background on Elliot's end.

"Can you give me a few more minutes?" Elliot says, clearly not to Blake.

101

"Hey, if you need to go..." Blake says.

"No, it's fine," Elliot says immediately. After a pause, he adds, "Where are you right now? Winnipeg?"

"Yep," Blake says. "It's cold. I chose being warm over going out for dinner with the guys."

Elliot laughs.

Blake laughs, too, because he'd forgotten how much Elliot's laugh used to make him laugh. It's not even... He's not being mean about it. It's endearing, the way Elliot laughs.

Elliot chirps him for being cold, even though Elliot, who's actually from Canada, is a big baby when he gets too cold. Or at least he used to be. That was years ago, too. Blake almost forgot how much time has passed since they last had a proper conversation. For a few minutes, they talk about the games they both have coming up and Elliot is actually excited about playing against the Mariners. Blake isn't surprised; the Ravens will probably have tons of their fans invading the Mariners' arena. Blake isn't too worried about the game against Winnipeg, but they're going to Montreal next and they've been strong this season.

They wish each other good luck before they hang up.

They'll save the animosities for when they're on the same ice again in March.

Elliot swings by his place before he heads to Newark to meet Blake. He'd be early if he went straight there and he ended up spilling half a of a smoothie over his shirt after practice, so he'll find himself a different shirt.

He says hi to Natalie, who's on the couch, reading something law-related that makes Elliot's brain hurt when he looks at it, kisses the top of her head and then points at his shirt to indicate that he needs to change. He throws the stained shirt in his laundry basket and wanders into his closet and on any other given day he'd grab another shirt and be done with it, but today he sort of lingers in front of his pile of shirts, not sure which one to go for.

Blake told him that the place he picked for dinner is pretty lowkey, so it's not like he needs to worry about that. He just doesn't want to show up in a Ravens shirt or something. He eventually pulls a blue-and-white striped shirt out of the pile and grabs a pair of jeans, because no matter how lowkey that restaurant is, Elliot isn't going to wear sweatpants.

"You look nice," Natalie says when Elliot wanders back into the living room.

Elliot hums and plugs in his phone.

"Wanna go watch a movie later?" Natalie asks.

"Oh, I'm meeting a friend for dinner."

"What?"

It's not a *sorry, I didn't catch that* kind of what. More of a *what the fuck did you just say* kind of what. "I told you, I'm having dinner with a guy I used to play with."

"No, you didn't."

"Yeah, I did."

"Elliot, you didn't."

Elliot did tell her, but she was sort of on her way out the door and she was a little frazzled, so maybe she forgot. "I'm sorry, okay?" Elliot says, because maybe it's his fault for not telling her at a different time.

Natalie gives him a look that tells him that the apology is not accepted.

"Why is this such a big deal all of a sudden? You go out with your friends. And I can't?"

"I go out with my friends while you're on the road."

"Okay?" Elliot doesn't get it. Does it matter when exactly they meet their friends?

"Are you just acting dumb now?" Natalie says. "I bend over backwards to make sure I'm around when you're in town so we can see each other and you… make plans with your friends without even talking to me about it."

"Why…" Elliot still doesn't get it. "Since when do we need each other's permission to see our friends?"

"Oh my God, Elliot." Natalie throws her book on the table and it lands with a thud. "This is not about either of us asking permission for anything. You're never home to begin with and now you're running off again?"

"When the hell am I supposed to hang out with my friends, then?"

Natalie purses her lips, which means he has a point and she doesn't like it.

"So what you're saying is that you'd rather hang out with your friends than spend time with me?" Natalie says.

"No, that's really not what I'm saying." Elliot picks up his phone, which has been charging for all of two minutes and grabs his wallet. "Don't wait up."

"What, you're just leaving?"

"Yeah, I guess I am," Elliot says and then *leaves*. He forgets his gloves and regrets it on the way to the Subway. He sends Blake a text, even though he's likely still at the arena, tells him that he'll probably be early and if Blake's done early, too, can they maybe meet up somewhere?

Blake was playing a matinee game against the Sailors today and the Knights only barely walked out of it with a win. Elliot got a notification when the game ended. He's had the Knights on notifications ever since Blake made the NHL team. Out of curiosity.

Blake replies no five minutes later and tells him to give him a call when he's at the station and that he'll meet him at the restaurant he made a reservation at.

It takes Elliot a little over an hour to get there and he's not exactly looking forward to the hike back, but he sort of forgets about it when he makes it to the place Blake suggested for dinner – a tiny Italian restaurant that Elliot might have not even noticed if he hadn't had the address. Blake is waiting for him outside, bundled into a coat, wearing a scarf in Knights colors that his grandma might have knitted for him. Before… Yeah, Elliot is definitely not going to ask. It looks like Blake is still wearing his game day suit, so Elliot is majorly underdressed compared to him.

Elliot doesn't actually mean to hug him when Blake says, "Hi," but he does it anyway.

Blake sort of goes with it, doesn't move for a moment, frozen to the spot, then hugs him back. Blake's smile is small when he pulls away. "You made it," Blake says, like he didn't believe Elliot actually would.

"Yeah. Took a while, but…"

"Sorry, I didn't want to pick anything too close to the station right after the game."

"No, I get it, don't worry," Elliot says.

"I talked to them and they said that they could move up our reservation, so if you wanna go eat right now…"

"Yeah, sounds good." Elliot is actually starving.

"I'm kinda overdressed now," Blake mutters as they head inside. "I was gonna go home and change in between, but…" He shrugs. "I already took off the tie, so maybe it won't be too bad."

Elliot can see the tie, it's purple and it's sticking out of Blake's coat pocket. "You look good," Elliot says, which… Blake does look good, but he still has a bit of an *I shouldn't have said that* moment afterwards.

Blake thankfully isn't weird about it, just leads the way and greets a waitress who takes them to a table in the back.

Blake picked his favorite pizza place for dinner, far away from the arena, where he'll be left the fuck alone, because the owners know him and won't ask for pictures, and where most fans are unlikely to end up after the game.

Elliot's smile is nervous when he sits down across from Blake. He's actually dressed for this place, unlike Blake, who came here right after the game. He could have told Elliot to wait twenty minutes so he could go home and change, but Elliot asked if they could meet up earlier and for some reason saying no didn't even seem like a valid option to him. Blake sort of wants to ask what happened there, why Elliot ended up being nearly an hour early, but they're not in a place where he gets to ask these kinds of questions.

"Listen," Elliot says, before he's even looked at his menu, "there's stuff we need to talk about."

Blake nods. He was expecting that.

"Later, though," Elliot says, glancing over his shoulder. No one's listening, but Blake gets that this isn't a conversation they should have in public. "If that's okay?"

"Okay with me," Blake says.

They both order pizza and they talk about hockey, because hockey is safe and there's a lot to talk about, especially with the Olympics coming up.

Hockey gets them through dinner and Blake asks Elliot for some dirt on Evan and obviously Elliot won't give him any because he's too nice for that. So Blake asks him about the kid the Ravens call Crab instead and Elliot laughs and tells him that the Crab is doing fine and isn't being pranked so much anyone.

"You told them to lay off, didn't you?" Blake says.

"I might have mentioned that we want the new kids to feel welcome and that excessive pranking could be counterproductive."

"Of course you did."

"They taped my gloves together the next day."

Elliot looks so genuinely disappointed when he says it that Blake can't help but laugh.

They don't stick around for too long after they're done eating. Elliot grabs the bill before Blake even has a chance to reach out. He played today; he's a bit slow. Elliot leaves the most ridiculous tip, because of course he does, and they head out together.

Elliot's breath clouds in the air when he huffs as he buttons up his coat.

"Offended by the weather?" Blake asks.

"It's freezing."

Blake shakes his head at him. "You're a terrible Canadian," he says. "My car's right down the street. You want my gloves?"

"No, it's fine."

Blake tries not to roll his eyes, because Elliot used to say *it's fine* a lot, even when things were really not fine, but maybe in this case Elliot can make the one-minute walk without gloves.

When they get to Blake's place, they're greeted by Squid and Elliot starts cooing at him before he's even taken off his coat. He lets Blake take it, takes off his shoes and then picks up Squid, who purrs happily.

"Your place is nice," Elliot says.

"You want anything?"

"Water is good." Elliot wanders into the living room, looking around. "Where's Angus?"

"Probably hiding. He'll come out eventually." Or at least Blake hopes so. He gets two bottles of water, then excuses himself to get out of the suit. When he's in a pair of sweatpants and a shirt, he returns to Elliot and sits down next to him. He's made himself comfortable on the couch, with Squid still in his lap, looking up, offended, when Elliot stops petting him.

"Sorry," Elliot whispers to Squid and start scratching his head again.

Blake watches them for a moment, trying to see the kid he was friends with. Elliot is bigger than he used to be. Not really taller, but... he's clearly been working out. He doesn't have as much of a baby-face anymore. And he's figured out how haircuts work. The smile is the same, though.

"Blake," Elliot says and the smile vanishes.

"Yeah?"

"Can we talk about this?"

"This."

"You know what I mean," Elliot says, soft. "Can we talk about how we... ended up here?"

Blake knows how they ended up here. He knows that it was his fault. Because he remembers the last proper conversation he had with Elliot and it ended with Elliot walking out of his life for a couple of years. He wants to tell Elliot all that, too, but what comes out of his mouth in the end is, "I'm sorry. I said some stupid shit."

Elliot sighs. "It's f—"

"No, don't do that," Blake says. "Don't say it's fine because you feel bad for me, because my grandma died or whatever. It's not fine. What I said wasn't okay."

Elliot chews on his bottom lip, eyes fixed on Blake. "Okay, you're right, it wasn't. I didn't need to hear that shit from you," Elliot says, voice level.

"I know. I don't even know... I was drunk and I guess I missed you. Not really an excuse, but..." Blake shrugs. Sometimes he's an ass, sometimes he doesn't think enough before he talks. None of that, of course, makes this any better. "And then I didn't say sorry and... yeah. I'm sorry."

Elliot leans his head against the back of the couch. "Do you think we can be friends again?"

Blake's heart flutters dangerously. "We can try."

There's something so soft about Elliot that Blake can't really describe. It's funny, because Elliot, at first glance, mostly looks like a little shit who's here to wreak havoc, but as soon as he smiles it's all sunshine and rainbows. "I was mad at you," Elliot says and even that sounds soft.

"I know."

"I'll stop now. We'll start over," Elliot says, determined, like that was the plan all along. "Clean slate?"

"Yeah?" Blake asks. It seems too easy. Then again, Elliot wouldn't be here if he wasn't willing to forgive him for what he said.

"Yeah." Elliot looks at him for a long moment, like he's chewing on something and doesn't know how to say it, but he eventually dips his head down to coo at Squid again, which Squid replies to with a loud meow.

It's weird to have him sitting in his apartment after only really seeing him on the ice for the last few years.

"Elliot," Blake says.

Elliot looks up.

Blake has no idea what he was going to say. Maybe thank you, for being willing to talk and to fix this, for being better at this than Blake will ever be. He probably wouldn't have reached out.

Elliot nods, even though Blake didn't say a word.

"Hey," Elliot says, "look who's joining us."

Angus has made it as far as the living room door, watching them from afar, but at least he came out of the guest room.

Elliot sticks around for another half hour, eventually handing Squid to Blake so he can coax Angus onto the couch with them. He hugs him to his chest, like he used to, and smiles down at him, cooing a little more.

"I should head home," Elliot says eventually. "My girlfriend was kinda mad at me when I left, so I have to go and... grovel."

"Is that why you showed up early?" Blake asks before he can stop himself.

"Yeah," Elliot says. "I'm not the best boyfriend sometimes." He frowns at Blake when he follows him to the front door. "Where are you going?"

Blake, one shoe already on, the other one in his hand, looks up. "Oh. I'm driving you to the station."

"No, Blake, it's fi—"

"It's cold," Blake says, and Elliot doesn't argue.

11

Being in the NHL for nearly six years, Elliot knows that the rollercoaster doesn't only go up.

After the Olympics, after playing for Canada with the best in the league, after winning that gold medal, Elliot gets back to New York and life goes on. In the first game back, Elliot gets high-sticked in the face and comes home with a huge cut on his cheek. A few days later, Evan Samuels gets traded to the Wildcats.

They're on the road when it happens and Evan gets pulled off the ice during morning skate one day before the deadline. They're sending him straight to Dallas. The Ravens got a pick and a prospect in return, so no one new is joining the team right now. They'll call someone up from the farm team, but they'll still miss Evan in the room. He was one of those universally liked guys and Andreas looks like a lost puppy when they get on the plane after their game in Calgary. He sat next to Evan on every single flight.

Since Elliot doesn't really have a plane buddy, he sits down next to Andreas.

"I know this happens a lot," Andreas says, voice low enough that none of the other guys will hear him. "But it's…"

Elliot nods. He has a pretty airtight no trade clause, at least for the first five years of his contract, but he's been watching guys come and go for the past six years. It never really gets easier and it stings all the more when it's guys like Evan.

The last game of their roadie is a game against the Knights in Newark and it's a fast-paced and filthy one. They still have some games left before the playoffs start, but right now they're set to play against each other in the first round, with the Knights in second and the Ravens in third place. The Knights might catch up with the Eagles, who are in first place right now, the Ravens might overtake the Knights, might drop into a wildcard spot. It's all up in the air right now. Nothing's decided yet.

Blake gets knocked over early in the second, loses a skate blade and has to get that fixed on the bench, but he's still good to go after.

When he gets injured, Elliot isn't out there.

Their third line is on the ice and they're skating into the offensive zone and Crab gets tripped up by one of their own guys and he crashes right into Blake, who goes down with Crab. And Crab is quick to scramble off, but Blake is still down on the ice and the Knights are ready to kill Elliot's entire team for touching Blake. Crab gets shoved out of the way by Brian Kelly. He bends down to talk to Blake, who seems to be saying something back.

Behind the net, there's still some pushing and shoving, but the arena has gone quiet, all eyes on Blake.

"Is he okay?" Adam mutters. He sounds worried, even though Blake isn't one of their own guys. No one ever wants to see anyone get seriously injured out there.

"I don't know," Elliot says, standing up to see better, but the Knights crowded around Blake are blocking the view.

Kelly eventually helps Blake up and gets him across the ice with Johnny Brammer, who's saying something to Blake as they skate to the bench. Blake goes straight down the tunnel and doesn't return.

Crab watches him go, face blotchy.

The Ravens win the game, but their celebration is subdued, and Crab in particular looks like he's about to burst into tears, so Elliot pulls him aside before they get on the bus.

"It wasn't your fault," Elliot says. It really wasn't. There's nothing Crab could have done, unless he'd spontaneously learned how to fly. "He got up and he skated off the ice, which means it could be way worse," Elliot goes on when Crab doesn't say anything. What he's telling Crab right now is what he's been telling himself, too.

Blake made it off the ice on his own. That's a good sign.

Elliot has been checking the Knights' Twitter ever since the game ended, but all they posted was that Blake Samuels wouldn't be returning to the game after getting injured in the second period. On the bus ride home, they put up another update, which is just that the Knights' coach will be giving an update on Blake the next day after he's been evaluated.

Crab is sitting next to Elliot on the bus, the guilt is eating him alive. Elliot doesn't know what to tell him. That hockey is a sport where injuries happen? Crab knows that. It's different when you're the one who caused the injury, even though it was nothing but a freak accident.

"Let's see what they say tomorrow," Elliot says. Again, that one was also for himself. As much as he wants to call Blake right now, he probably wouldn't even answer his phone and it's not like... Well, they've been texting a lot since they hung out in January and they managed to grab a coffee a few weeks later, right before Elliot left for Sochi, so maybe they're tentatively back to being friends, but it might be weird if Elliot called him today. Tomorrow is better.

Crab nods. "I hope he's okay," he whispers.

"I'll give him a call tomorrow."

"You know him?"

"We used to play together," Elliot says.

Crab's eyes go impossibly wide. "Can you tell him I'm really, really sorry?"

"I will," Elliot says. "Promise."

After that, Crab is little less upset. Elliot's still vaguely nauseous, thinking about Blake going down.

He checks Twitter again.

Nothing.

"You still alive?"

"Stop," Blake groans and picks up his TV remote to throw it at Noah, then quickly decides against it.

Noah's fingers curl around his wrist, then the remote is removed from his hand. Blake's on his couch and he's pretty sure that there's a cat on his feet, but he has his eyes closed so fuck knows.

He has a concussion because Keith Taylor decided to fucking come for his life yesterday, or at least that's what it felt like when he barreled right into Blake. He hasn't watched the replay because he's not allowed to watch anything right now. Noah has watched the replay and has assured him that Taylor *probably* didn't mean to plop his ass right on top of Blake's head.

Blake is lucky, because he didn't pass out on the ice, his symptoms aren't severe, but he has a murderous headache and he just wants to lie here with his eyes closed and with Noah's fingers curled around his wrist, thumb brushing slowly back and forth against his skin.

He's pathetically glad that Noah came over. He was going to come over anyway, because Noah has the day off, just came back from a West Coast roadie last night, and they were going to hang out, and maybe that's what they're doing, except they're doing it quietly, because Blake isn't a fan of loud noises right now.

"You want anything to eat?" Noah asks, voice low. There's a good chance that he's had one of these before and knows what he's doing.

"I wanna take a nap," Blake mumbles.

"Okay, I'll..." Noah trails off, because something's buzzing. "Your phone, Fish."

"Who is it?"

"Uhhh... Elliot."

Blake sighs. Of fucking course it's Elliot. Blake can't really not answer. "Can you pick up?" Blake doesn't want to open his eyes right now and he also doesn't want to move or even talk, but he'll spare ten seconds to tell Elliot that he's still kicking.

"Me?" Noah asks.

"Or hand me the phone, I don't—"

"No, I got it," Noah says. He shifts away. "This is Blake Samuels's personal phone answerer, how can I help you?"

"Noah," Blake grumbles.

"Shut up, Fish." Noah gives his arm a squeeze. "Elliot asks if you have a minute."

"Yeah, just…" Blake squints at him and regrets it, closes his eyes again and Noah pushes the phone into his hand.

He gets up and mumbles something about Blake's fridge. There's nothing in there and Noah will figure that out in a few seconds, too. He'll probably order them takeout, not that Blake is actually hungry.

"Hey," Blake says. "Are you calling with a formal apology from your out-of-control rookie?"

"Are you okay?" Elliot asks, ignoring him.

"Concussion."

"Yeah, we saw as much, but… How bad is it?"

"Not so bad that I won't be able to murder your entire team during the playoffs," Blake says. "On my own." He regrets that sentence. It was long. Doesn't even know if it made sense. Took it out of him. He really wants to take that nap.

"So it's not…"

"They're hopeful that it won't last too long, but it's still a concussion, so…"

There a moment of silence and Blake isn't sure if it's awkward or not, but then Elliot says, "Crab wanted me to tell you that he's really sorry and that he obviously didn't mean to hurt you."

"Tell the kid that I'll kick his ass," Blake mumbles.

"I…"

"No, don't tell him that." Blake huffs. "I've never been in a fight, Elliot."

Elliot laughs. Blake would be glad to hear it if it didn't make his head hurt even more today. "I think you could take Crab."

"Of course I could, he's tiny. But still. Tell him I *won't* kick his ass, how's that?"

"He'll be so happy to hear that."

"I'm sure," Blake says. Shit, he's so tired. He rolls onto his side and it doesn't hurt so much, but his head still hurts like it did before.

"I'll let you rest, but… Blake?"

"Hm?"

"I'm glad that you're... well, that you're gonna be okay."

"Mm, hopefully."

"We're in town for a couple of days, in case... I don't know, if you need anything..."

"It's okay, I have..."

"Your personal phone answerer?" Elliot asks.

"Yeah. That."

Blake opens his eyes long enough to hang up his phone after Elliot has said goodbye, then he closes them again with a groan. A moment later the couch dips, and fingers gently brush his hair back.

"'m gonna nap," Blake says.

"I'm gonna go out and buy some food," Noah says, fingers lingering in his hair. "Can I borrow a key?"

"Mmm."

"Okay, I'll see you in a bit."

Noah gets up, footsteps barely audible, then something soft lands on Blake. Blanket maybe. He doesn't need a blanket, but he doesn't tell Noah that. He's too tired to say anything.

He's asleep before Noah's even out the front door.

When he wakes up, Angus is on his feet and Squid is next to his head, staring at him like he's about to eat him, which reminds him... He's about to start sitting up when a hand on his arm stops him.

"Where are you going?"

Noah.

"Cats need food."

"I can do that. I think."

"Thank you."

"Drink some water. You want food?"

"No, I don't know, maybe," Blake mumbles and sits up enough that he can drink the water Noah just handed him.

"I bought soup, because I don't know how to make soup," Noah says.

"I don't have the flu."

Noah gives him a look that shuts him up quickly and then wanders off to feed the cats, who both dart away as soon as they hear the sound of food hitting their bowls in the kitchen.

Blake needs to buy Noah a present and write him a thank you note because he doesn't mind spending his day off doing essentially nothing at Blake's place, feeding his cats and buying him food, even though that definitely isn't part of their deal. He returns to Blake, sits down with some space still between them, smiling down at Blake.

"He sounded really worried," Noah remarks.

"What?"

"Elliot," Noah says. "He sounded worried."

"I think his rookie was scared that he killed me and that I'd come back to haunt him or something."

Noah hums. "Poor kid. When I was still in Bridgeport, I clipped a guy's neck with my skate and it wasn't, like, deep or anything, but knowing that if it had been in a different spot or if it had been just a little deeper, he could have…"

"Yeah," Blake says. He doesn't blame the kid. Two seasons ago, he tripped up a guy with his stick, it was Remi Flaubert from the Seals, and he went into the boards head-first and he walked out of that game with a concussion, too. Blake apologized, and Flaubert turned out to be fine, is still playing.

They play hockey, they get injured.

Noah's fingers are back in his hair and Blake can't decide if it makes his headache better or worse.

Eventually, because he doesn't know how to bring himself to ask Noah to hold his hand again, he plucks Noah's fingers out of his hair and holds them and falls asleep, Noah's hand still in his.

Elliot tells Crab that Blake won't come for him the next time they see each other. All Elliot gets in response is nervous laughter, a frown and a, "He'll be okay, though?" And Elliot tells him that Blake will be fine, because that's what it looks like right now.

He won't lie, he's still worried about him, because concussions are brain injuries and even if the symptoms go away, the long-term effects can be… Elliot won't even think about that. Blake will be okay.

Elliot goes home and his apartment is quiet – Natalie's still out – and he curls up on the couch, because it's high time for a nap, except his eyes keep fluttering open. Elliot is not someone who has trouble sleeping. Ever. Maybe when he has a cold. But for him it's usually a lie down, close eyes, fall asleep kind of affair.

He thinks about the game last night.

Thinks about Blake.

About the way he sounded on the phone, exhausted, but mostly all right. And he has someone there with him, the guy who answered the phone. Whoever that might have been. Probably one of his teammates, except the Knights likely had practice this morning, just like the Ravens, so it must have been someone else.

Elliot almost wants to reach for his phone to look up the Knights' practice schedule.

Which is ridiculous.

Maybe Blake has a boyfriend. Doesn't have to be another player. It could be some guy. Some guy Blake met somewhere far away from the rink. Maybe at the movies, Blake always liked going to movies. Or maybe when he was playing golf. Does Blake even like golf? He likes baseball. Or at least he used to. Maybe he met a guy at that Chinese restaurant that he was telling Elliot about.

"We'll go sometime, but not on a game day. It's too close to the arena," he said to Elliot when they met up in January. Elliot, in return, told him that he'd take him to a place that as the best dumplings in the world.

He squints at his phone. He's been lying on the couch for twenty minutes and he still isn't asleep.

Elliot groans, rolls over, and presses his face into a pillow.

It shouldn't matter to him whether or not Blake is seeing someone, but it seems weird that Blake never mentioned it. They've been talking constantly for the past two months and it should have come up in a conversation. If it was serious. Maybe it's not serious. Elliot has mentioned Natalie plenty of times and Blake said he'd love to meet her, which seemed strange to Elliot, although he didn't say so. Blake can meet Natalie if he wants to.

His nap is shorter than usual that afternoon.

The rest of the regular season passes in the blink of an eye, like it always does in the end. They don't end up facing each other in the first round, with the Knights staying in the second seed and the Ravens slipping into a wildcard spot.

The Ravens exit the playoffs after seven hard-fought games. The Knights play thirteen before they lose in the second round. Blake was back on the ice for the Knights, looking rock solid, but good goaltending isn't everything. There's so much that plays into a playoff success, circumstances beyond anyone's control. Injuries. Luck.

Blake takes him to that Chinese restaurant after the playoffs are over for them. Elliot is still in town, because Natalie's here. They're going to her parents' beach house for two weeks in the summer, but for now they're in the city and Elliot has been trawling through children's hospitals, handing out Ravens gear, because he needs to do something with the time he has on his hands. Other than going to the gym with Adam. He does a few things that Ravens PR asks him to do, a few signings, a few appearances at events for charities the Ravens support and Elliot is happy to do it, but he's glad to have a few off days in between, too.

Getting food with Blake turns into a sightseeing tour, because Blake tells him that he's never gone to Manhattan to look at... pretty much anything. So Elliot takes him to the top of the Empire State Building and they stand next to each other and look out at the city, neither of them saying a word as the sun sets in the distance.

Elliot has been up here with his parents and they loved it. Maybe that's why his eyes keep darting over to Blake, trying to figure out if he likes it or if he's torturing him with tourist crap. He paid for Blake's ticket, in case he ended up hating it. The expression on Blake's face is, as usual, a mystery, but at least it's not the murder eyes, so Elliot will consider it a success.

Elliot loves coming up here. It reminds him just how small he is, just how many people are out there, and how lucky he is that he ended up here, of all places.

"What do you think?" Elliot whispers.

"I think..." Blake is still staring out at the city. He doesn't finish the sentence.

Maybe Blake feels small, too.

"You wanna go?" Elliot asks, just in case.

Blake shakes his head. "Not yet."

"Okay," Elliot says, and watches the smallest of smiles work its way onto Blake's face.

Once they're back in the street, they wander to Penn Station, which is where Blake will catch a train back to Newark, but they walk slowly, neither of them in a rush, the night air pleasant.

It's then that Elliot can't keep his traitorous brain from saying, "Are you seeing anyone?"

"Uh..."

"It's just... when I called—"

"Yeah," Blake says. "That was... yeah."

"Oh. Good for you," Elliot says and doesn't pause to examine whether or not he actually means that. He might not like himself very much if he let himself reach the end of that train of thought.

"It's not... a relationship or anything," Blake mumbles. "Not like... I don't know."

"But you have someone."

"I guess. He's..." Blake snorts. "Yeah."

"You wanna tell me about him?"

Blake's face quickly returns to the default, his smile gone. "I can't. He's... I can't, really."

Fellow player, then.

Elliot nods, because he gets it. He shouldn't have asked in the first place.

Blake's summer begins the way it's begun for the past couple of years, with a playoff loss.

He sticks around for a while, because he doesn't have anywhere to go back to, other than the house in Norwalk that's technically Evan's now. He meets Elliot in the city a few times, but it doesn't quite chase away the emptiness in the pit of his stomach.

115

Catherine Cloud

It's about to get worse, because the day after the Mariners have cleaned out their lockers after a third round loss, Noah calls him and asks him if they can talk. Blake says yes, offers to come over, but Noah insists that, no, he'll come to Blake's. Probably so Blake won't have to drive home after Noah breaks things off with him.

Because that's definitely where this is headed. No one asks to talk to you in person for any other reason.

Blake's suspicion is pretty much confirmed when Noah shows up with a bag from Blake's favorite bakery.

"Noah," Blake says when Noah gives him a hug before he shuffles into Blake's apartment.

"Yeah?"

"You don't have to pretend that I don't already know what this is about."

"What gave it away?" Noah asks.

"Mostly that you asked if we could talk."

Noah sighs. "I'm sorry."

"It's okay. This doesn't work for you anymore. I get it, honestly. Don't even... Don't worry about it." Blake gives him a nudge. "We had a good time."

Noah grins at him. "We sure did." He puts down the bag with the baked goods on Blake's coffee table and sits down next to Angus. "Sup, dude."

Angus eyes him with suspicion.

"I should explain," Noah says.

"You don't have to."

"I'll feel better if I do, though? I know this isn't really about me feeling better, but can I?"

Blake nods, sits down next to him.

"I know we said that we'd keep feelings out of this and that you and I were gonna be strictly professional or whatever, but maybe I had a few feelings along the way and... Anyway. I was sad, but that's beside the point. So I met this guy. He's... a piece of work, but I really like him. And, like, we were never exclusive, but I can't do this with you and like him at the same time. It wouldn't seem fair to anyone."

"You never said–"

"Blake, let me stop you right there," Noah says, hand on Blake's knee. "If I'd told you about whatever feelings I was having, what do you think you would have done? Asked me to be your boyfriend? I think the fuck not. Because you're still hung up on Elliot Cowell, and that's okay, I knew that from the start, so we're all good here."

"I'm not hung up on Elliot."

116

"Really? When you think of him, don't you get all warm and fuzzy inside?"

"I…" Blake thinks about Elliot, about seeing him the other week, about Elliot dragging him to the Empire State Building like they're tourists, not even letting Blake pay for the ticket, and what he's feeling is not warm and fuzzy. Maybe warm. Definitely not fuzzy.

"Yeah," Noah says. "So you see why I never said anything. I'm not him."

Blake remains silent. He's not in love with Elliot. It's been six years. He wasn't in love with him six years ago either. He was eighteen, for fuck's sake. He didn't know what love even is. He still doesn't.

"We'll still be friends, yeah?" Blake eventually asks.

"Dude, you're never getting rid of me," Noah says.

Noah definitely means that.

He still texts him afterwards, the exact same amount of silly shit that Blake is used to receiving from him.

Blake eventually goes back to Norwalk to help Evan sort through what's left at the house and donate some of the things they won't need anymore. They meet with way too many lawyers to sort out who owns what, at the end of which he isn't in the mood to deal with his contract negotiations, even though his agent will do most of the work.

If he doesn't re-sign with the Knights, he'll be a free agent in July, except he'd rather stay in Newark for the rest of his career, although a part of him, the smallest, tiniest part, wonders if the Cardinals might be interested. If he could play in Connecticut, the way he always wanted to.

He doesn't even tell his agent about it.

He inks a contract with the Knights in the end. Five years, five and a half million AAV. They work in a no-trade clause and he gets to hand in a list of teams that he wouldn't mind getting traded to. He puts the Cardinals on the list.

He goes on vacation with Evan. Warm and sunny, lots of days at the beach, cocktails, not a lot of talking. Just for a week, otherwise they'd kill each other.

He returns to Newark with Angus and Squid and his apartment is the same it was before. He agrees to put in a few appearances at the Little Knights camp while he's in town. He makes an Instagram account for Angus and Squid when he doesn't know what to do with himself. He watches Elliot win the Lady Byng trophy on TV, two cats judging him as he shoves chips into his mouth and drinks too much beer.

Since he has nothing better to do, he keeps an eye on the Draft and on the free agency madness that follows. It's more entertaining when you're not involved.

Charlie Trainor, previously a D-man for the LA Lions, ends up signing with the Knights. It's a big one. Trainor was one of the Lions' top D-men and for some reason wasn't willing to stay. Blake is pretty sure that the Lions didn't offer Trainor much less than what the Knights offered him.

Kells is already typing in the group chat when Blake grabs his phone.

Trainor comes to town about a week later, and Blake is the only one around, or at least the only one who's been on the team for longer than a year or two, so he offers to pick him up at the airport. Five minutes later he also offers up his guest room, with a warning that he has two very loving cats, one of which likes to sit on people he's just met. Trainor is a huge guy, smiley, but a little shy.

"Dude, thank you so much for picking me up," Charlie says when he finds Blake at the airport. "I'm fucking useless with this kinda stuff."

"No worries," Blake says. "Let's head to mine, yeah? Or do you wanna grab a bite on the way?"

They decide to go to Blake's first and that Blake can show Charlie the culinary hotspots afterwards. As soon as they're in through the door, Charlie asks about the cats, and then follows Blake around his apartment as he gives him the tour, both cats cradled against his chest. Blake snaps a picture of it, for the group chat, and maybe for Instagram, if Charlie doesn't mind.

They pretty much spend the next two weeks in each other's pockets, except for when Charlie goes apartment hunting, recounting the pros and cons of the ones he saw. One day he leaves only to look at an apartment one floor above Blake's. He likes it. Later he asks Blake how he'd feel about being neighbors. "I'll come by to borrow ingredients twice a week, but I'll also share the cookies when I'm done."

"You bake cookies?"

"I'll bake you cookies right now," Charlie says and then does exactly that.

He ends up picking the apartment upstairs.

They meet up with a bunch of the guys – a total of three of them are in town and they all congregate at their favorite pub, not too far from the arena, and they buy Charlie welcome drinks and also welcome onion rings and fries, so Blake doesn't have to carry him home. They go to a baseball game, then Charlie abandons him to go to a few museums – Blake is most certainly not a museum kind of person. They try a bunch of restaurants, one of which looks like it'll give them food poisoning. They survive, but decide that it might be in their best interest if they never go back.

Charlie eventually leaves to spend some time with his relatives in Toronto, where he's also staying for camp. Probably the same camp that

Elliot goes to every year. Blake has found himself a trainer in Newark, so he's staying for the rest of the summer.

He drives Charlie back to the airport and gets a hug for his troubles.

Elliot goes from the NHL Awards to being a groomsman in Adam's wedding, to Natalie's parents' summer house on the Cape in the span of about a week, then has to make it through drinks, a barbecue, meeting the neighbors, and several conversations about boats before he can finally go to bed.

He's pretty sure that Natalie says something to him before he falls asleep, but he doesn't reply. He's exhausted and is honestly looking forward to a few quiet days on the beach, but Natalie's family apparently doesn't really do quiet. They play tennis. They have afternoon tea, they play board games, they talk about boats even more than the night before, and they organize parties and big dinners.

Elliot has obviously met Natalie's parents before, but this is the first time he's seeing them outside of the city, with no one having to run off to meetings or other appointments or work and Elliot... doesn't fit in.

He doesn't know shit about the stock market. Natalie's dad works on Wall Street. Her mom is a successful lawyer. Elliot is painfully aware that he never even went to college. He's out of place here. Especially when they talk about boats. Many of Elliot's teammates love fishing, but he is definitely not one of them.

"I'm sorry," Natalie says, looking amused after her mom held Elliot hostage with a conversation about porcelain for half an hour. "They get excited about weird stuff."

Elliot has never met anyone who was excited about porcelain.

He'd be more certain that he's absolutely capable of making it through a week of this if Natalie's parents weren't also constantly mentioning childhood friends and cousins of Natalie's who were just so happening to be getting married and having babies this summer. It's all, did you hear about this friend who tied the knot, and did you hear about that cousin who just gave birth. The baby's called Banjo.

Who the hell names their kid Banjo? Banjo and his brothers, Piano and Trumpet?

This is so not part of Elliot's world.

The worst part is that every time the words *marriage* and *babies* are mentioned, someone, usually Natalie's mom, throws a meaningful glance in Elliot's general direction.

"Is your mom trying to tell me something with all the baby talk?" Elliot says as they crawl into bed together halfway through the week.

Natalie doesn't reply. Doesn't even laugh.

Elliot was cracking a joke here, he wasn't trying to insult Natalie's mom, which is what he tells Natalie, too.

Natalie still isn't saying a word.

"What?" Elliot asks.

"Elliot, no one's trying to pressure you," Natalie replies.

"Okay?"

Natalie gives him a *look*, and he should probably know what it means, but Elliot is too tired to figure it out.

The next day, Natalie is acting weird around him, pulls her hand away when Elliot tries to take it, keeps her answers short and leaves Elliot on his own as he struggles through a few more conversations about things he knows absolutely nothing about, including wine, investment portfolios, and caviar.

"Did I do something wrong?" Elliot asks in the evening.

Natalie hasn't said a word to him since she asked him to pass the bread during dinner.

"No," Natalie says, but it was clearly meant to be a yes.

"Are you sure?"

"Are *you* sure you want to have this conversation right now?" Natalie asks.

"Uh… what's the conversation?"

"Every time anyone brings up getting married, you act like it's somehow a big mystery to you why anyone would think that we might get married one day," Natalie says.

"Well…" Elliot shrugs. "It's mostly that they're acting like we'll get married… I don't know… tomorrow."

Natalie gives him that stare she always does when she's trying not to roll her eyes. "Humor me for a second," she says. "Have you ever thought about getting married? Not that I'm saying that I want you to promise me that you'll propose soon or anything like that. I'm asking about your general stance."

"On getting married?"

"Yes."

"Oh," Elliot says.

"I mean, is that something you can see in our future?"

Elliot should say yes. He knows that there's only one right answer to that question. Because if he doesn't say yes, it means that…

"You look freaked out," Natalie says, eyes turning towards the ceiling, definitely annoyed with him now. "Please stop looking freaked out. We're adults, we've been together for three years and it's something you talk about when you're in a relationship. Getting married, having kids… It's not in our immediate future, but, you know, it might be relevant one day."

"Right," Elliot says. He needs to say more than that. His face is burning hot. He's about to fucking panic. About getting married.

"Elliot."

"Yeah?"

"Correct me if I'm wrong, but I sort of assumed that this was the direction we were headed in?"

Elliot can't really blame her for assuming that, because that's usually the direction that you're headed in when you love each other and you're in a serious relationship.

Natalie gets back out of bed, which means that shit's about to hit the fan. She's better at arguing when she's standing up. It must be some sort of lawyer thing. In any case, Elliot's in trouble. "Listen," Natalie says, "I'm going to be straight with you here. I want to get married. And I want to have kids. And I want those things with you. I love you, Elliot. But if we're looking at two different futures here, I don't know if…"

Elliot looks at her, that girl he met while he was buying a ridiculous amount of dumplings. He knows what this is. He can recognize an ultimatum when he sees it. If he doesn't tell her that he wants to get married eventually, this is it for them. Natalie has obviously been waiting for him to propose and never said a word about it until now, and maybe Elliot should have known, but he didn't even think about it. He thought he had more time.

He should have an answer to all this. He should know if he wants to spend the rest of his life with her, but he doesn't. He should tell her that he loves her, too, that he needs a little more time, but will he know in a month? In a year?

Does he even want kids? Most of the guys have families, a kid, or four. Dima's wife is often at their games with their son, who waves at Dima through the glass and it's cute, but Elliot can't really see Natalie behind the glass with *their* kid. It's not even that he thinks he'd make a bad father, he'd probably be a decent one, at the very least, but the idea is still foreign to him.

"Nat, I…" Elliot bites down on his bottom lip. He can't even tell her that he loves her right now, because he'd say it to deflect, to somehow make things right.

Natalie nods. "I see."

"I'm sorry, I just… This is a lot right now."

"Just tell me if you want to get married," Natalie says. "Yes? No?"

Elliot doesn't know.

"Yes, but not to me?"

Oh. This is bad. Because… what if she's right?

"Okay," Natalie says when Elliot says absolutely nothing, because this is only just sinking in for him now, too. She has tears in her eyes and it's his fault. She nods. "Okay."

"Nat."

"You should go."

"No, come on, let's talk about this," Elliot says, even though there's no fixing this. He can't make himself love her enough to give her what she wants, and he also can't promise her something that he doesn't really want. He can't propose to her to end an argument.

"Elliot, I don't think we have anything to talk about."

Maybe they don't.

"You want me to leave?" Elliot asks. Hell, *he* wants to leave. He's wanted to leave ever since they got here.

Natalie nods.

Three years together and now he's packing his bags, pulling his clothes back on. His car is downstairs, so he can drive… somewhere. It's almost ten, so he won't make it that far before he gets tired. It's like he's on autopilot, throwing his stuff back into his suitcase, Natalie sitting in the window seat, wearing a silk robe, watching him, tears running down her cheeks.

This was the worst time to have this conversation.

"I'll explain things to my parents," Natalie says. She takes him to the door, like she wants to make sure that he's actually leaving, the house quiet. That's the last thing she says to him.

The last thing he says is, "I'm sorry." Not that it does much good, not that it fixes anything.

He goes back to New York for a few days. He doesn't hear from her. He flies to Toronto like he was supposed to, stays with his parents, and takes two weeks to tell them that he and Natalie broke up when they won't stop asking about her. She was supposed to join him while he was training, but she's obviously not coming.

When he gets back to New York, Natalie's stuff is gone from Elliot's apartment, and her key is on the kitchen counter without a note.

12

The first time Blake sees Elliot's apartment is a week before training camp starts for both of them. Elliot just got back into town and asked him if he wanted to hang out. Blake has been in town all along, mostly hanging out at Mattie's house.

He invited him over for dinner the other day. Told him he'd retire at the end of the season. Mattie's wife said he'd probably change his mind another twenty times, but Blake knows that Mattie's made his choice. He hasn't forgotten about what Mattie told him all those years ago, about seeing it coming. Blake is going to miss Mattie like hell, but he understands why Mattie told him.

So Blake will see it coming.

The invitation to Elliot's is a good distraction, because otherwise Blake would spend another day wondering how he'll deal with being on a team that doesn't have Jake Matthews on it.

Elliot's apartment is uptown and Blake takes the train, because he isn't insane enough to drive, takes a book and reads on the train. He's never been a huge reader, only picked up a book here and there and mostly stuck to audio books, but Charlie asked for the closest bookstore when he first came into town and they went and Blake has gone back there twice over the summer, looking around, picking up a bunch of fantasy novels.

Some kids recognize him at Penn Station and he stops to take pictures with them, other people looking at him like they're trying to figure out who the hell he is, eventually wandering off when they realize that he's not a Hollywood star.

Elliot meets him at the Subway, about ten minutes after Blake texts him that he made it and Elliot drags him to a takeout joint that sells Chinese food. Elliot walks in there with the confidence of someone who comes here more often than would make the Ravens' nutritionist happy. He orders thirty dumplings.

"Seriously?" Blake asks.

"Don't worry, I know what I'm doing."

"Have you invited ten other people?" Blake says drily, then remembers that Elliot has a girlfriend. "Oh, wait, is your girlfriend gonna be there?"

"Oh, uh, no. She's kinda... not my girlfriend anymore," Elliot says quickly and then turns away to order even more food, like the thirty dumplings, which are apparently just for the two of them, aren't more than enough.

"Sorry," Blake says as they head back out into the street. "That was a bit... I didn't know you'd broken up."

"Yeah, I didn't want to... I don't know. I guess I could have mentioned it, but then time passed and... yeah."

"Sorry, that sucks. I'm not gonna ask what happened, but if you wanna talk about it..." Blake trails off, because Elliot probably doesn't want to talk about it, because if he did, he would have mentioned it way earlier.

Elliot shrugs. "She wanted to get married and I... didn't."

"No?" Blake tries not to sound surprised. They never talked about it, obviously, it wasn't something that was on their minds when they were eighteen, but why wouldn't Elliot want to get married?

"I don't know," Elliot says. "Maybe at some point, but maybe... not to her. Shit, that sounds terrible. I'm a terrible person."

"You're not," Blake says. He means that. Elliot is one of the kindest people he's ever met in his life.

"I don't even know how this happened, I mean, I was in love with her, but then it also wasn't enough somehow? I didn't trust her with my secrets and I couldn't see us together, I wasn't sure about her."

Blake doesn't ask about the secrets. He already knows what Elliot is talking about. It's them, what they were back then, the one thing Elliot never wanted anyone to know about him. So he says, "Yeah, you can't just get married, because... I don't know, because it's what you're supposed to do."

"Exactly, but maybe I'd have been sure about her in two years, but I don't know and I don't know if I want kids either and it turned into this huge mess, and I guess it was good that we broke up, because now she can go find someone who loves her so much that he thinks about marrying her two months after he meets her and I can... I don't know. Figure out what it's like to love someone enough to want to marry them, I guess."

Then Elliot falls silent and takes a sharp left into a building. Blake has some trouble keeping up. Elliot's building has a doorman, and his apartment is on a totally different level than Blake's, really bright and polished, but Elliot's crap is lying around everywhere, shoes in a pile by the door, a jacket slung over a chair here, a tower of cookbooks on the counter there, and socks all over the place.

"Nice," Blake says, despite the socks.

"Yeah, it's, uh… I was gonna clean up, but then Adam invited me over and I didn't have time. Sorry." Elliot shrugs and leads him to the couch. "How's your, I don't know, your… significant other doing?"

Blake was really hoping that Elliot wouldn't ask. "Not so significant anymore."

"Shit, sorry."

"It's okay."

Noah got traded before the Draft, first to the Seals, who almost instantly flipped him back to the East, to the Foxes, so Noah's in Philadelphia now. He seems to like it well enough and told Blake that he might stay if he likes it and they still want him after the end of the season.

Elliot hands him a box of dumplings and suddenly Blake understands why Elliot got thirty.

While they eat, Elliot tells him that he's been trying to cook more and bought a few new cookbooks over the summer, and that he destroyed three pans in the process, because he gets distracted when he cooks, because he doesn't have the patience to stand next to the stove and watch, so he starts looking at his phone and suddenly stuff is burning.

"How are you still alive?" Blake asks. He's truly baffled that Elliot hasn't burned this place down.

Elliot laughs. "Sheer dumb luck, I guess. My food is actually pretty good, though. When it's not burnt."

"Crispy," Blake says.

"Oh, I forgot, you actually like crispy stuff. Although sometimes there's really too much crisp."

"No such thing."

"I'll cook for you sometime," Elliot says. "I'll make it extra crispy. So crispy it's unrecognizable."

Blake huffs at him.

"I can cook, though."

"Didn't say I didn't believe you," Blake says. "I'm sure you're very talented. Especially when it comes to making things crispy."

Elliot shakes his head at him. "I bought you dinner and this is how you treat me?"

"Sorry, I totally appreciate the dumplings."

"You'd better."

"Hey, tell you what," Blake says, "whoever ends the regular season with the most points, like our teams' points in the standings, buys the loser fifty dumplings."

"Fifty?" Elliot laughs, eyes crinkling. He reaches out to shake Blake's hand. "I'm in."

The Ravens' home opener this season is a game against the Knights, because of course it is. They saw a lot of each other during the preseason already, but Elliot has to admit that it's a good matchup for a home opener.

These games have potential to get nasty, although it's early in the season, the third game for both teams, so they're starting with a clean slate.

The Knights have already won two games on home ice, the Ravens have won two on the road, but tonight one of them is going home with their first loss of the season. The Ravens are off to a good start, score five minutes into the period and it goes back and forth from then on out, until they're tied 3-3 at the beginning of the third.

Elliot said hello to Blake during warmups when Blake was stretching close to the center line, but Elliot hasn't otherwise interacted with him. He hasn't scored on him yet, only has an assist on Adam's goal and another one on Crab's that they got during a power play. Towards the end of the third, when both of their teams are getting antsy, things start to get a little rougher.

Elliot ends up sliding into Blake's net – thankfully not into Blake – about forty seconds before the end of regulation and Adam gives Blake a nudge, so Elliot can get back out of the net, which Trainor takes issue with, pulling Adam away by his jersey. Blake, unimpressed by the pushing and shoving, gives Elliot a poke with his stick. Elliot can barely feel it, that's how gentle of a poke it is.

"Get the fuck out of my net, *Moo*," Blake says.

Elliot fights the insane impulse to stick his tongue out at him and crawls out of the net without provoking another fight.

Their game goes into overtime and Elliot so very nearly scores the game winner. He has no idea how Blake gets his stick on it. Elliot thinks he has him, shoots and can practically see it going in, except it doesn't. He stops after, stares at Blake, who's staring back at him, unimpressed. Elliot shakes his head and skates off.

The Ravens win in the shootout. After six rounds.

It's Andreas who finally scores.

Elliot texts Blake after the game, says he'll buy him a drink.

When Blake meets him outside the arena, he looks a lot happier than Elliot thought he would.

"Why are you so happy?" Elliot asks, even though it's rude as shit.

Blake actually laughs. "I'm sorry, I know I just lost a game and I should be crying on the floor, but we watched a replay of when you nearly scored on us in OT and your face…"

Elliot rolls his eyes. "How the fuck did you do that?"

"I don't even know, but it was the highlight of my night. I should be buying *you* a drink."

Elliot elbows him in the side.

He takes him to a bar not too far from the arena that'll have a table for them because he's a Raven. They won't have to wait.

"You have curfew?" Elliot asks.

"Nah, we're practicing in Newark tomorrow and we're flying out after that. I told them that I'd find my own way home, they're usually cool with that unless we have a game the next day. I mean, this was practically a home game."

Some people shoot them looks when they slide into their booth, but no one comes over to talk to them. Maybe no one cares about hockey anyway; maybe no one even recognizes them.

Blake doesn't really look like he does in the promotional photos the Knights keep using. In those pictures, Blake's face is clean shaven, his hair pulled into a bun, but the Blake across from Elliot is scruffy, beanie on his head, hair loosely hanging down to this shoulders, the tips still damp.

He looks good with the longer hair. More like himself.

"By the way," Blake says, "tell Crab he's back on the shit-list."

Elliot grins. "Please be nice to the child, Blake."

"He actually does look like he's twelve. He's probably like you, he's gonna look like he's twelve until he's forty."

"I don't look like I'm twelve."

"You do. And right now you also sound like you're twelve."

Elliot kicks him under the table.

"Dude, if I walk out of here with an injury, my team's gonna murder you."

"I know that was a joke," Elliot says, "but I'm pretty sure they actually would kill someone for you."

Blake's lips twitch. "They're good guys. Even the insane ones."

"Looks like Trainor's fitting in well," Elliot says.

"Yeah, although the guys keep calling him Choo Choo and I think he's gonna snap one of these days. I'll be surprised if we all make it back from that roadie in one piece."

They finish their drinks and Elliot walks Blake back to Penn Station, like he always does. He'll take the Subway from there.

"Hey, when's the next time we see each other?" Blake asks.

"December, I think?" Elliot says, even though he knows it's December 2nd. He doesn't want it to look like he has all of their games memorized. He just happened to stumble across the date the other day.

"We should hang out before that."

"Yeah," Elliot says.

"You can cook for me. Something crispy, yeah?"

Elliot gives him a shove in reply.

"I swear to God, if we weren't friends, I'd think you're trying to injure me."

"Sorry," Elliot says and goes in for a hug. "I'll see you soon, okay?"

"Yeah, we'll compare schedules," Blake says and hugs him back, ruffling Elliot's hair before he goes.

They manage to hang out a couple of times, but their schedules usually clash and most of the time there's no point in going to each other's places when they can't hang out for that long anyway. They try to meet in the middle, which is somewhere around Penn Station. It's not actually the *middle*, but it's better than the alternative.

Blake spends most of his time off at Charlie's, or Charlie will come downstairs, hug both of Blake's cats and then complain because Blake's grilled cheese is not as good as his. It's true. Charlie's grilled cheese is a revelation and Blake's grilled cheese is… just regular grilled cheese.

Charlie now sits next to him on the plane, always gripping the armrest, knuckles going white as the plane takes off. Blake offered his hand on their second flight together and Charlie took it, head ducked, probably hoping that no one would see. Blake is pretty sure that only Mattie noticed and Mattie generally couldn't give less of a shit about chirping anyone. He keeps telling Blake that he's getting too old for all sorts of stuff, chirping included.

They go to Toronto, then Winnipeg, then Minneapolis and Charlie's parents come to the game and Charlie's mom gives Blake a hat she knitted, in Knights colors, and thanks him for showing Charlie around in the summer. Which is funny, because Charlie's a year older than him and doesn't need a babysitter.

"She thinks I'm absolutely useless as an adult," Charlie says to Blake on the plane. "And she's right. But does she have to say it?"

"You're doing okay on your own."

"I had to call my dad the other day because I didn't know what a roux was. And don't ask me what happened when I got a Costco membership."

Blake can't help but snort.

"See?" Charlie says. "I *am* useless."

"You make really good cookies, though."

"True. My only redeeming quality."

Brammer's head appears between the seats in front of them. "Choo Choo, you make cookies?"

"Yeah," Charlie says, "but only for people who don't call me Choo Choo."

Brammer sticks out his bottom lip and disappears again.

"My mom hates cooking, she only bakes, so the first thing I learned how to make were cookies," Charlie says, voice lower now. "And then there's obviously the hat thing... Don't feel like you have to wear it or anything, by the way."

"I like it," Blake says.

Charlie's smile is soft and sheepish. "Okay." He wiggles in his seat. "Where do your parents live? Do they ever come to games?"

Brammer resurfaces, glaring. "Hey, Choo Choo—"

"Bram, sit down," Blake says.

Brammer pulls a face, but does sit down.

"My parents died when I was eleven," Blake says lowly.

"Oh no, I'm so sorry..." Charlie chews on his bottom lip. "I shouldn't have asked, I'm really sorry."

"It's okay, you didn't know."

Charlie wiggles again. He's so nervous on planes, poor guy, and this conversation isn't making this flight any less awkward for him.

"It was a really long time ago," Blake says, "and I... I mean, I miss them, and it sucks that they can't come and see me play, but... I'm all right. It's not like you can't mention your parents around me or talk about families or whatever."

During the season, it always hurts the most during the dads' trip, but after a few years of this, Blake knows that it's coming and their PR team has made sure that Blake could pretty much disappear.

Charlie shoots him a glance, then he whispers, "My dad isn't actually... He's my stepdad. The other guy left when I was four."

"Sorry, man," Blake says.

"Like, I'm not trying to go for pity points or whatever," Charlie mumbles, "just... if you wanna talk about stuff. I don't know. I'm probably not the first person you'd go to, but..."

Blake has never really talked to anyone about his parents, other than his grandma and Evan. When they were home, him and Evan, usually Evan, would say, "I miss Mom and Dad," and Blake would say, "Me, too." And then sometimes Evan would pull out stories, mumble them to Blake, and then say, "Sometimes I don't know if the way I remember them is actually the way they were." And Blake never really knew what to say in return. When they were little, their grandma would talk about their parents a lot, when they got older, it was a lot more of, "Your parents would be so proud," and, "I wish they could see you right now." And Blake never knew what to say in return to that either. That he wished they could see him, too? Of course he wanted them around. Of course he wanted them there to see him do all the things he was proud of, wanted them there for the Draft, still wants them at games. But wanting all that won't bring them back.

"Thank you, Charlie," Blake only says.

Charlie nods.

He falls asleep a few minutes later and Blake hopes he'll snooze right through them landing in New York, because Charlie once told him that that's his least favorite part.

Blake grabs his iPod, puts on Fleetwood Mac and eventually falls asleep as well.

Blake calls Noah after the Foxes' game against the Lions, after Noah dropped the gloves with Pierce Martin.

"Are you calling to ask if my face is still unblemished and beautiful?" Noah says when he picks up. "To answer your question, yes, it absolutely is, but I look... *rugged*. How's that?"

"So you're okay?"

"Oh, Fishy, were you worried?"

"The only reason I'm letting you get away with calling me Fishy is because you got your bell rung by fucking Pierce Martin."

Noah laughs, delighted.

"Why the hell did you think that was a good idea?"

"He called one of my guys a... derogative word for what you and I might refer to as a person who's gay and knowing what you know, I guess I don't have to explain to you why I found that offensive."

"Yeah, I get that," Blake says.

"The Lions are fucking insane, man," Noah grumbles. "Half the roster is assholes. Anyway, my hand hurts. Fuckin' Lions. But, hey, thanks for calling to check on me, that's so sweet."

Blake huffs.

"Don't be embarrassed, I already know that you're all soft on the inside," Noah chirps. "It's okay, I won't tell anyone."

"Thanks," Blake says gruffly.

"How are things in Jersey?"

"Pretty good, we're on a seven-game win streak."

"I know that, Fishy, I mean, like... How are things in Jersey, you know what I'm saying?"

"I... don't."

"Have you managed to replace me, is what I'm asking," Noah says.

Blake rolls his eyes, mostly for his own benefit, because Noah can't even see him. He probably knows, though. He's spent too much time with Blake not to know. "It's not like I've even tried to replace you."

"Yo, Fish, wrong answer."

"I didn't realize there was a right answer."

"The right answer," Noah says, "is that I'm irreplaceable and that you miss me."

"I do miss you," Blake says. "You know, not... in that way, but..."

"Aww," Noah says. "I know what you mean. I know. We'll hang out when I'm in town in two weeks, okay? Drinks after the game? Or dinner the day before?"

"Both," Blake says.

"You really do miss me."

"Shut up."

"Never," Noah says. "Hey, have you talked to Elliot recently?"

"No," Blake says, defensive, even though he sent Elliot a text this morning. "Yes."

"Oh-hoooo."

"We're friends."

"You're—"

There's a knock on Blake's door. It's probably Charlie, because anyone else would ring the doorbell. "Noah, give me one second, there's someone at the door."

"Ohhh, suuure, there's someone at the door."

"There literally is someone at the door," Blake says as he yanks the door open.

Charlie waves at him with one hand, holds up a plate of cookies with the other. Blake waves him into his apartment, pointing at his phone.

"Who's at the door, then?" Noah asks.

"It's Charlie," Blake says and kicks the door shut. "I gotta go."

"I swear to fucking God, if you're making up—"

"What, do you wanna talk to him?" Blake says.

"Can I?"

"No," Blake says. "I'll see you in two weeks."

"Can't wait. Bye, babe."

"Don't—" Blake shakes his head. No point in telling Noah to stop calling him babe. "Bye."

Charlie isn't quite frowning at him, probably more confused than anything else. "I can go, you know? I just wanted to drop these off."

"No, don't..." Blake nods at the living room. "Noah was just being a dick, it's cool."

"Noah?"

"He plays for the Foxes. He, uh… got into a bit of a scrap with Pierce Martin, I wanted to make sure his head was still on straight."

"He fought Piercer?" Charlie asks, eyebrows raised. "Fuck."

"Yeah, apparently he was saying some shit…" Blake trails off, not sure if he should mention what kind of shit exactly, because with stuff like that guys can surprise you, and not in a good way. You'll think that a guy you've been playing with for years is great, because he's been nice to little kids, throwing pucks, helping out with charity stuff, inviting people over for barbecues, and then he'll turn out to be a homophobic asshole.

That particular guy retired two years ago, but still. Blake has learned his lesson. Just because someone's nice doesn't mean they're a good person.

"Ah," Charlie says. He grabs Squid when he comes to investigate. "He's always been…" He shrugs. "Let's say we weren't friends."

Blake hums.

"He was…" More shrugging. "LA wasn't… It's not a good room… Anyway…"

"Hey, if you wanna talk about it…"

Charlie pulls a face. "There were a bunch of really shitty people in that room. Like, people who could really get you down. You could tell that those guys didn't like each other much. And they're still good players and the Lions, I mean, if you look at the on-ice performance, the Lions are a great team. But in the locker room? None of that."

"That sucks."

"You know how it is in our room? The guys chirp each other, but it's… it's fun. It's not actually hurting anyone. And the shit Piercer was spewing sometimes… It was bad. I don't know if you know Leon Danvers?"

Blake nods, he's met Leon. He was the Lions' backup goalie and got traded to the Comets in the summer.

"His sister's gay. And she came to a game. With her girlfriend. And Piercer was all… weird about it."

"Weird as in…"

"Weird as in I nearly punched him in the face," Charlie says.

Blake grins.

Charlie grins back at him, then gets serious again. "That's why I wanted to leave. The guys here aren't like that. They wouldn't… I don't know. Like, I don't have a gay sister, but I have a gay uncle and he couldn't give less a shit about hockey, but what I'm saying is, I wouldn't be scared of introducing him to you guys, you know what I mean?"

"Yeah, I get it," Blake says. He doesn't know why he's so eager to change the topic. Maybe because it's hitting a little too close to home.

He still hasn't told anyone on the team, even though the guys probably know. They have to know. He doesn't have a girlfriend, never had one, not a single one of them ever saw him flirt with a woman. They used to chirp him, especially when he still used to disappear after games to meet Noah, jokingly and *loudly* whispering about Blake's secret girlfriend, but no one's said anything in a while.

Sometimes he wants to ask Mattie. If he knows. If he's figured it out. Sometimes he wants to find out if Mattie will look at him differently if Blake actually tells him. To his face.

Blake gives Charlie's leg a flick. "Glad you came to the Knights."

"Me too," Charlie says. He chews on his bottom lip and looks around Blake's apartment, at Angus, who's sitting on top of the cat tree, glaring in their general direction. "You wanna hang out tonight?"

Blake was pretty sure that that was what they were already doing. He laughs. "Sure."

It's a supremely bad idea to get wasted after a game, even when you have the following day off. Because they don't get a lot of days off. And Elliot doesn't want to spend the entire day in his bed, convinced that he'll throw up all over his entire life if he moves even just an inch. He's been there. He should know better.

He still lets the guys drag him to a club after the game.

It was a good one, an 8-2 victory over the Mariners. They fucking hate the Mariners. The guys are overjoyed, the media is less nasty than usual and Elliot doesn't even dread talking to them after the game. The boys want to go out after, Elliot promises to buy all the goal scorers a beer, but then they decide that a bar is too boring, and then suddenly Andreas and Crab are talking about this club they like, and Crab's not even twenty-one yet, so what business does he have, having favorite clubs?

Elliot tries to talk his way out of going with them, but it looks like half the team is going, pretty much everyone who doesn't have kids at home, even one guy who does have kids at home, so Elliot's feeble protests are ignored and he's going with them after all.

He doesn't mind clubs so much, except it's loud and he hates dancing, so he stays at a table with Adam, who also doesn't like dancing, and Moby, who tells them that he has to get drunk before he goes dancing.

He orders three rounds of shots to start with and Elliot hasn't even moved on to the second one when he starts to regret that he agreed to any of this, especially because the Elliot who's had three shots doesn't protest when Moby drags him on the dance floor with him.

Elliot does not dance.

He can't.

He sways back and forth awkwardly in a gaggle of his teammates and… a bunch of other people. He recognizes a wife and two girlfriends, but doesn't know any of the other people. It's not until someone's hands land on his ass with keen interest that he makes an escape, finding Adam exactly where he and Moby left him, somehow not drunk enough to give in to Moby.

"Had enough already?" Adam asks when Elliot scoots back into the booth.

"Someone touched my ass. And I'm pretty sure it wasn't an accident."

Adam cackles and pats his shoulder. "I'll buy you a drink."

Elliot does not need another drink right now, but he doesn't tell Adam that, so he can't exactly blame Adam for getting him one anyway.

While Adam is gone, Elliot fiddles with his phone and pulls up his latest text conversation, which was just him telling Blake that he can't wait to wipe the floor with the Mariners. He could tell Blake something like hey, we actually did that, but ends up sending, *help they dragged me to a club :(*

Blake replies within the next minute, says, *not coming to ny to rescue you,* which is honestly just mean.

Elliot tells him exactly that. *they made me dance,* he adds, so Blake will see how terrible of a time he's having right now.

Then Adam returns, hands him a drink and Elliot forgets about his phone for a bit.

Elliot isn't very good at getting drunk. He doesn't drink a lot, and if he does, it's a beer, on some occasions two, but that's usually it. He gets clingy when he's drunk, always wants to lean not against something but someone, because people are generally more comfortable than things.

He's also a lightweight.

"You okay, buddy?" Adam asks, with the shit-eating grin of a best friend who knows that Elliot is currently having at least a dozen regrets.

"Fine," Elliot says. "Where's Lou?"

"Asleep on the couch," Adam replies. "Can't wait to be asleep on the couch with her, to be honest. But she thinks it's important that I do stuff with the team. Like I didn't want to stab every single one of these fuckers after our last roadie."

Elliot snorts. He gets it. The guys can be… a lot. Moby was calling everyone *mon cher* by the end of it and Chris and Dima kept stealing each other clothes. Elliot nearly lost his shit when Dima tried to hide Chris's jockstrap in his bag.

Adam tilts his head, which means he's about to ask something personal. "How are… Have you been seeing anyone since you broke up with Natalie?"

"She broke up with me."

"Either way…"

"Nah," Elliot says.

"You want to?"

"I don't know." Elliot thinks about going out on dates and getting to know another person and being awkward around them before you settle into the whole relationship thing and… nah. Then again, his apartment is really quiet. And he thinks a lot about his apartment being less quiet. He doesn't know how to make it less quiet, because it's not like he's going to put another person in it from one day to the next.

"You miss her?" Adam asks.

"No. Yes. No. I… I miss having someone around."

"We can find you someone… to have around." Adam wiggles his eyebrows. "The entire world is at your feet, Moo. You're a hot guy in your twenties. You're a millionaire. This shouldn't be hard."

"I… I don't know. I fucked things up with Natalie. It was my fault."

"Because you didn't want to get married yet?" Adam asks.

Elliot told him the whole story. He sort of had to explain what happened. The thing is, it wasn't so much about getting married now. It was more about… "Because I didn't want to get married to *her*." Elliot scrunches up his nose. "Do you think there's like… you know, in romcoms and shit… there's always, like, that one person that's exactly right for you. But that's bullshit, right?"

"Yeah, probably bullshit. They're trying to scare us."

"But don't you think Lou is the one?" Elliot asks. "How did you know you wanted to marry her?"

See, he would not even be asking this if he was sober. Sober Elliot would be too polite to ask questions that personal.

"Moo, I know that you know that relationships are hard fucking work. And with Lou… I guess she wanted to do the work."

"And I guess I didn't want to do the work with Natalie?"

"It's not always just about doing the work, though," Adam says. He shrugs and gulps down the rest of his drink. "Sometimes it's about other stuff. You can't make yourself love someone more just because you want to make it work."

"Is this a weird conversation to have?" Elliot asks.

"No, dude, it's not. You guys were together for a while and then you suddenly weren't."

"I tried to call her after and she didn't pick up."

"Can't make her want to do the work either," Adam says. "Here…" He takes Elliot's empty glass. "I'll get us another one."

Before Elliot can protest, Adam's gone. He returns remarkably quickly, handing Elliot another drink. "There were cute girls at the bar."

"Good for them."

"Okay, not in the mood for that. I get it. But right now you're moping and that's sad. Moo. You–"

They're interrupted by Moby, who's come to drag Elliot back on the dance floor and Elliot goes, because if he sits next to Adam, he'll mope and it's too early to go home. He has to be a good captain. Adam follows them, with great reluctance, hovering at the edge of the dance floor, slowly shifting his weight from one leg to the other.

Unsurprisingly, Adam is the first one to beg off, followed by Moby and his girlfriend, then the rest of the guys head home one by one, some on their own, some with a girl in tow. Elliot heads out of the club with them and hails a cab. He miraculously manages to stay awake until they're at his apartment building and he somehow makes it into the elevator and somehow makes it through the door, tugs his shoes off and then faceplants into bed.

He's not as wasted as he feared he would be.

Maybe he should set an alarm. He'll get up before noon, so he won't waste his entire day off.

When he fiddles with his phone to set an alarm for a reasonable time, he finds a text from Blake. Two, actually. The first one says, *I think dancing is one of your duties as their captain*, the second one says, *try to have fun for like a second I dare you*.

It makes Elliot smile.

It also makes Elliot call him. For some reason. He can't explain it to himself.

"You're so lucky that I'm in Seattle," Blake says.

"Sailors tomorrow?" Elliot asks. It doesn't come out steady.

"Yeah. Did you just get home?"

"Mmm, I made it. Finally."

Blake coughs. Hiding a laugh. What an ass. "You're an old man."

"So what?"

"No, I mean, I get it, I'd choose a pub over a club at all times," Blake says. "Did you have fun for a second, though?"

"No." Elliot sighs. "Someone touched my butt, Blake."

"Well, I'm sure that person had a great time."

"You're not funny."

"That was the worst chirp ever," Blake says. "Go to bed, Elliot. But drink a glass of water first."

"No."

"Seriously. You'll thank me tomorrow morning."

"S'already tomorrow."

"Maybe where you are."

Elliot groans. "Blake…"

"Yeah?"

"I…" Elliot squints and tries to remember what he was going to say. "Did I wake you up?"

"No… Seattle, remember?"

"Yeah. Right. I'm gonna cook for you when you're back in town."

Blake laughs and it's soft and it makes a knot unfurl somewhere in Elliot's stomach. "Okay."

"I'm sorry. I didn't wanna call you but I wanted to."

"Makes perfect sense," Blake says and there's some amusement in there. "You're all good, Elliot. Don't forget to drink water."

"Water sucks," Elliot mumbles.

"You're about to fall asleep right where you are."

"Bed."

"Yeah, I hope that's where you are."

"Mmmm."

"Good night, Elliot."

"Hm."

Elliot barely notices when the line goes dead, doesn't look up when his phone gives one last chime.

In the morning, after half an hour of groaning, he reads the text that Blake sent him last night – *do you regret that you didn't drink any water.*

fuck off, Elliot replies.

But, yes, he does regret it.

13

The first time their schedules line up again, they meet for dinner in the city. Elliot has a matinee game that day and after games he's usually not in the mood to play masterchef, but he wants to hang out with Blake. So he tells Blake there's a restaurant he wants to try and then spends an hour finding a restaurant that he actually does want to try.

Blake goes on a roadie the day after; Elliot plays one more home game and then leaves for two games in Canada.

When he comes back, Blake is still on the road in the West, but they set up a dinner date – well, not a date, but an informal meeting – for when Elliot has time to cook for Blake. Blake has a day off on a day that coincides with a day when Elliot only has practice in the morning and no obligations in the evening.

Elliot makes lasagna the first time Blake comes over for dinner, because he's made it so many times that he can cook it in his sleep. Not a lot that can go wrong there. He can prep it in advance before Blake even gets to his place. Blake said he'd bring dessert and he promised that he wouldn't try to make it himself.

Elliot does remember Blake cooking him eggs and bacon for breakfast when Elliot came to visit him during a summer many years ago, but maybe eggs and bacon aren't exactly hard, so he doesn't have much of a grasp on Blake's cooking skills. Elliot can't imagine that Blake's grandma would have let him move into his own place without teaching him the basics, though.

Blake arrives carrying a box that probably has pie in it, snowflakes melting in his hair, after walking through an early December flurry. His hair is not in a bun today, just loosely falling down to his shoulders, ink-black, soft.

"Hey," he says.

Elliot stares, only for a moment, before he, too, says, "Hey. Come on in."

Blake hands him the box, takes off his boots, hangs up his coat, and then he's standing in Elliot's hallway in jeans and a blue sweater that matches his eyes exactly and Elliot is probably having some kind of aneurysm, because he saw Blake not too long ago and he didn't want to stare at him for an hour like he does right now.

He doesn't know what changed.

"Thanks for... this," Elliot says and lifts up the lid of the box. It's cherry pie.

"Still like cherry?" Blake asks.

Elliot nods, can't believe that Blake even remembered.

Blake is clearly pleased with himself. "What's for dinner?"

"Crispy lasagna," Elliot says and wanders into the kitchen, Blake at his heels.

Elliot pushes the lasagna into the oven with Blake looking on like he still isn't sure if he trusts Elliot's abilities, which is fair, because Elliot's first attempts at cooking pretty much anything ended in at least minor disasters. He had to buy some new pans and pots when he ended up burning food and there was no scrubbing those black marks away.

"Where do you wanna eat?" Elliot asks. He has a small table in the kitchen that seats three and another table around the corner where dining and living room share the same space. The dining room table is too formal, too big, would put them too far away from each other, but then he thinks about knocking his ankles against Blake's under his small kitchen table and suddenly he wants that space between them.

Not his choice, though, because he just asked Blake.

"Uh, wherever is easiest for you," Blake says. "I'm not... you know. No need to pretend you're fancy or anything."

"Hey, I can be fancy."

Blake grins and nods at the kitchen table. "That one's fine."

"Okay," Elliot says and the demon that possessed him when he saw Blake with snowflakes melting in his hair on his doorstep wholeheartedly agrees.

It takes a while for the lasagna to heat up and for the cheese to melt, so Elliot throws together a salad in the meantime, Blake being extremely helpful by eating all the grape tomatoes before Elliot can even put them in the salad bowl.

"Stop it," Elliot says and swats at Blake's hand when he goes for another one.

"They're good."

Elliot sighs at him, grabs a handful and washes them, puts them in a bowl and hands them to Blake, who's leaning against the counter, eyes gleaming like he's a small child who got handed a bowl of freshly baked cookies.

"Do you want wine?" Elliot asks.

Blake wrinkles his nose.

"I guess that's a no."

"If your lasagna is only good with wine, I'll have a glass, but…"

"My lasagna is good no matter what you have with it, thank you very much."

Blake smirks and shakes his hair out of his face.

"How's Evan doing?" Elliot asks as he turns his attention back to his salad.

"He's okay," Blake says. "He's… He spent some time in Norwalk in the summer, even after I left and… I think he misses Grandma a lot. Like, not that I don't miss her, but he was even younger when Mom and Dad died, so he has even fewer memories of them and now she's gone, too, and…" Blake shrugs. "It's not that I'm worried about him, because he's all grown up and I'm still around, you know, if he needs anything, but…" Another shrug. "Sorry, that was a lot of family drama."

"No, I mean… I asked," Elliot says. He realizes that it's been about a year since Blake's grandma died. He doesn't mention it.

Blake looks at him for a long moment. "It's weird…" Trails off again.

"What?"

"No, it's… it's depressing."

"Tell me anyway."

"Well…" Blake considers his bowl and eats a tomato. "I usually went home for Christmas, but then last year, I obviously couldn't and Evan came over and it was… so fucking sad. We had the worst Christmas of all time. And this year I'm going to Mattie's, because I'm his charity case, and maybe it won't be sad, but it's weird, because I'm only just starting to realize that every Christmas is gonna be like this from now on. It'll just be me. I'm basically on my own now."

"I'm sure you're more than a charity case," Elliot says.

Blake chews on his bottom lip. "I mean… yeah. I guess."

"But, yeah, it's… I'm sorry, Blake. That she's not around anymore."

Blake ducks his head. "Told you it was depressing."

The thing is, though, Blake never talked about jackshit. Never even mentioned his parents to Elliot, other than that they'd died. Blake always liked to pretend that he'd never had a feeling in his entire life, and now he's in Elliot's kitchen, actually talking about this. Elliot wants to hold him as tightly as he possibly can right now, but that's the worst idea he's ever had and he has a salad he needs to work on.

"How are your folks doing?" Blake asks.

"Oh, they're okay," Elliot says. He doesn't keep himself from talking about his parents anymore. He used to. Especially when they came to their games.

"Yeah? Are they coming down for the holidays?"

"They're coming a week before Christmas. For those two home games we have before the break. And they'll stay here for Christmas, and they'll come up to Boston for that one away game we have and they'll fly back from there. And I'll come back here for the New Year's game."

"Matinee?" Blake asks.

"Yeah, thank fuck. Are you playing?"

"Nope. First time since I started playing in the NHL that I get to sleep in my own bed on New Year's Eve."

"Seriously? Where were you last year?"

"Edmonton."

"Ew," Elliot says, with feeling.

Blake laughs.

The demon that possessed Elliot never wants him to leave.

The second time Elliot cooks for Blake, it's Blake who has the matinee game in Brooklyn and Elliot who has the day off because he came back from a roadie the night before.

Blake isn't sure if he actually wants to go to Elliot's after a game, is convinced that he'll be terrible company, especially if he ends up losing the game, but then Elliot sounds so excited when he tells Blake that he found another day when their schedules might match up that Blake doesn't have the heart to say no. He has a day off the next day, the first one in a while. He'll sleep in.

At first Elliot only asks if Blake wants to hang out, then he calls him a few days before and says, "I'll cook for you again, but you'll have to come to mine."

"You're just saying that you'll cook for me because you don't wanna hike all the way over to my place, aren't you?"

"I like cooking," Elliot said, defensive.

Anyway, they could have met up somewhere in Manhattan. Would have been easy to get to from the Mariners' arena. It's also easy to get to Elliot's, so Blake isn't really complaining.

He leaves the arena in high spirits, after a shutout, technically on the road, even though it's just Brooklyn. They're having a great season so far, are at the top of their division. They've had to deal with some injuries in November – Blake missed four games, Kells missed six, Charlie missed three – but they quickly got back on track.

Blake takes a cab to Elliot's. He isn't insane enough to go on the Subway after a game, not when their fans are making their way back to Jersey. A bunch of them recognize him when he heads out of the arena, even though Blake did his best not to look like he'd just played a game. He left his suit with Mattie, put on jeans and the most nondescript hat he owns, but they somehow figure him out, so Blake takes a picture with them, signs their jerseys and then quickly flags down a cab before anyone else has a chance to get a good look at him.

When he gave his suit to Mattie, he grinned and said, "You got a hot date, kid?"

"If I had a hot date, I'd keep on the three-piece suit," Blake deadpanned.

Brammer, next to them, was howling with laughter.

Mattie chucked a ball of tape at him that hit him square in the eye, so Brammer shut up pretty quickly after that.

"I'm hanging out with a friend," Blake said, more quietly, so only Mattie could hear.

Mattie hummed, like he didn't quite believe him. "Old friend on the Mariners?" he asked.

"Uh… no." It did dawn on Blake eventually why Mattie had asked. Blake used to disappear very regularly after their games against the Mariners to hang out with an *old friend*. "Different friend."

"I'm surprised you have more than one," Mattie said drily and wandered off with Blake's suit, but not without inviting him over for dinner the next day.

The ride to Elliot's place takes longer than expected and when Blake gets to his apartment, Elliot is already in the middle of making dinner. When he opens the door for Blake, he's wearing an apron. Striped. Like his shirt. But different stripes.

"Hey, you're, uh… stripy," Blake says, which is probably not the best greeting. He didn't even bring pie this time because he came straight from the game.

Elliot grins and waves him into the apartment. "Nice game today. Don't tell anyone I said that, though."

"Thanks," Blake says as he hangs up his coat. "Hey, do you want me to go get something for dessert, or…"

"No worries, I've got it covered. I found something at the bakery that I wanted to try."

"Oh. Cool."

"Come on, sit down."

Blake doesn't sit down, because it'd be weird, watching Elliot cook from the kitchen table. So he leans against the counter next to the oven and watches from there. It's an unfamiliar sight, seeing Elliot flit about the kitchen like he actually knows what he's doing. It looks like they're having steak tonight and if it's even half as good as the lasagna Elliot made last time, Blake has a real treat to look forward to.

"I made fries, too," Elliot says, like he does this every fucking day. "I'll leave them in a little longer, so they get crispy."

142

"Thanks," Blake says. He starts digging through Elliot's kitchen cupboards for plates and glasses, so he's not completely useless.

Elliot's done with dinner not too much later and the steak is amazing, but Elliot won't tell him what exactly he put on it, just keeps grinning and telling him that it's a secret. Elliot bought cupcakes for dessert, two with white chocolate and raspberries and two with dark chocolate and mint. Elliot seems to like the dark chocolate one so much that Blake lets him have the second one.

They end up on the couch, with a game on TV. Elliot's couch is huge and he has one of those footrests that you can push around, so they can both put up their feet. Blake definitely needs this today, although he'll probably nod off halfway during the game, so he tells Elliot to wake him up if he does. It's the Cardinals against the Grizzlies. Likely to be a bloodbath. Neither of them would have picked a movie over this.

The score is 1-0 in favor of the Cardinals when they turn it on.

Elliot frowns at the TV for a second, head tilted.

"What?" Blake says. "Don't tell me you're rooting for the Grizzlies."

"Please..." Elliot says, shaking his head. "I just remembered something. I'll be right back."

Elliot vanishes and returns a few minutes later, carrying a balled up... something. He drops it in Blake's lap.

"What's this?" Blake asks and holds it up. It turns out to be an All Star Game shirt from a few years ago.

"Turn it around."

Blake does, finds that it's a Josh Roy shirt. It's signed. "No way."

"He gave me a super weird look when I asked him to sign it for me."

"I bet he did," Blake says. He's met Josh Roy before, took a picture with him, tried to be cool. Josh is only a year older than them, was made captain when he was only twenty. He's been so valuable to the Cardinals ever since they got him. The thing with this shirt is that Elliot got it for him when he was still mad at him. They weren't even talking at the time when that All Star Game happened. Blake almost wants to give him a hug, but they're pretty much lying next to each other on Elliot's couch and Blake doesn't want this to turn into some kind of awkward full-body thing, so he says, "Thank you," and leaves it at that.

Elliot smiles.

They watch the game and Elliot mumbles about how much he hates playing against Santana. Blake also hates playing against Santana, because he scores too much for a defenseman, at least in Blake's humble opinion. He doesn't care so much when it's Charlie who scores a ridiculous number of goals, but Charlie isn't putting the pucks in *Blake's* goal. Only at practice.

Blake falls asleep before the game is over. He doesn't mean to but there's a commercial break and he wants to close his eyes for a second, which should be a sign for him to get up and go home, but tells himself that he can stay awake until, what, 9:45?

He can't.

When he wakes up, the light in the corner is still on, but the TV is off. Elliot is next to him, curled up on his side, fast asleep. Blake doesn't exactly stare at him, but he spends at least a few seconds considering Elliot's eyelashes before he scoots forward to grab his phone from the table.

It's 1:20 in the morning. Are there even still trains running? Probably. Maybe not as frequently as during the day. He could take a cab home. He doesn't want to think about how much that would cost, despite him being… a millionaire. Basically. It's still a waste of money.

Blake gives Elliot a nudge. "Hey…"

Elliot blinks at him and frowns. "Time's it?"

"Past one," Blake says.

"Ugh…" Elliot pats the couch. "No worries, just stay here."

"Yeah?"

"Hmm."

Blake lies back down, grabs himself a blanket and scoots away a little, wondering if he should get a blanket for Elliot, too, because he clearly isn't in the mood to get up and sleep in his actual bed. He's gone right back to sleep. Blake snatches a second blanket off the back off the couch and drapes it over Elliot as best as he can.

In the morning, Elliot wakes him up with a gentle shake, holding up a cup of coffee in front of Blake's nose.

"Sorry," Elliot says, "I need to head out for practice in a bit."

"Oh…" Blake sits up quickly and takes the cup of coffee. "I'm sorry, I didn't mean to–"

"It's fine," Elliot says, waving him off, like it's nothing, like they do this all the time. But Elliot says it's fine a lot and that usually means that it's not.

Elliot makes omelets for breakfast, even though Blake tells him twice that he doesn't have to, that he can buy something on the way to the Subway, that he'll get out of Elliot's hair.

That would only make things awkward, though. Elliot doesn't want Blake to think that he wants him out of his apartment or that him sleeping here was a problem. Because it wasn't. People sleep at Elliot's place all the time, mostly teammates, but that's basically what Blake is anyway, except he's on a different team.

"You want some coffee for the way back?" Elliot asks when Blake is getting ready to leave.

Blake shakes his head.

Elliot should be ready to go already, but Adam will forgive him if he's five minutes late. Adam is five minutes late all the time, so he might not even notice. He leaves the dishes in the sink and grabs his jacket. Might as well head downstairs with Blake.

"Hey, uh... thanks again for dinner and... for the shirt," Blake says before they part ways. "And I guess we won't see each other before Christmas so... Merry Christmas."

"Thanks, you too," Elliot says. He gives Blake's arm a nudge before he walks away, towards the Subway. When he looks the other way, he finds Adam's car, pulled over a few spots away.

Elliot sincerely hopes that Adam was too busy looking at pictures of puppies on his phone to look at the entrance of Elliot's building, but Elliot's hopes are squashed when he gets into the car and Adam says, "Is there something wrong with my eyes or was that Blake Samuels?"

"It was," Elliot says, which is all the information he's willing to offer.

"How did you never mention that he lives in the same building as you do? That's fucking weird. It's a bit of a commute to Newark."

"He doesn't live here." Elliot can't start a rumor that Blake Samuels lives on the Upper West Side. Shit like that travels fast, especially when it's to make fun of an opposing player.

Adam looks at him, shaking his head. "Moo. What's with the extra short sentences? Explain?"

"We're friends," Elliot says with a shrug.

"You and Blake Samuels."

"Yeah."

"And you had a sleepover?" Adam asks.

Elliot very sincerely hopes that Adam won't come to a conclusion that's not even the right one, because Elliot has mentioned to him that he used to see a guy in juniors and Adam is pretty smart and has an extremely active imagination. They haven't talked about it ever since, but Elliot hasn't forgotten that Adam knows.

"You sleep at my place all the fucking time," Elliot says. Anyway, It's not like he's the only hockey player in the world who has friends on other teams. Which is also what he tells Adam.

"Okay, but..." Adam narrows his eyes at him. "Wait, is he the friend you made the lasagna for?"

Elliot's cheeks are hot. He hates everything about this. "So what?"

"Where's *my* lasagna?"

Elliot snorts. Thank fuck. It's just about *food*. "Are you jealous?"

"Yes? Because Blake Samuels apparently gets all the good food. Make me food, Moo."

"You're such an idiot. Start driving."

Adam huffs at him, but does start driving, muttering about ribs and burgers and steak. Elliot does not mention that he did, indeed, make steak last night. Adam would never forgive him.

"Honestly…" Adam says ten minutes later, when he's done giving Elliot ideas for their next dinner together, "I can't see you being friends with a guy like Blake Samuels."

"What is that supposed to mean?"

"Well, you're all sunshine and he's all… gloom and murder eyes."

"He's a really nice guy," Elliot says.

"He's hiding it well."

"Dude, you've never even talked to him."

"Yeah, because he's scary." Adam cackles. "Is he… secretly like a puppy?"

Blake really couldn't be any less like a puppy, he's more like an old dog who's done with everyone's shit, but still cuddly if you ask nicely. There's something about Blake that makes Elliot want to be close to him. He knows it's because he's sort of lonely and because Blake is familiar and Elliot won't turn it into a huge thing. It can't be.

He just managed to figure things out with Blake and he's so glad to have him in his life again and he won't ruin that because he needs a hug.

"Sorry," Adam says before Elliot has a chance to reply, "I don't wanna be mean or anything, I swear. I'm sure he's a great guy."

Elliot only nods and makes a mental note to cook dinner for Adam at some point soon so he doesn't have to be jealous of Elliot's other friends.

"Hey," Adam goes on, "if I get a puppy, will you help me convince Lou that Skywalker is a great name for dog?"

One of these days, Lou is going to murder Adam and Elliot won't even be surprised.

Blake is waiting for his train at Penn Station when Charlie calls him. He's asking if Blake wants to hang out later and sounds slightly disappointed when Blake tells him that he can't.

So, once he's on the train, Blake calls Mattie, because Mattie probably won't mind if Blake brings Charlie over for dinner, especially if Blake mentions that he's not sure if Charlie can actually feed himself. At the age of twenty-six. Because, really, the only things that Blake knows Charlie can make are chocolate chip cookies with so many chocolate chips that you have to send a search party to find the cookie part, grilled cheese that is better than anyone else's grilled cheese, and pretty much anything you can safely stick into a microwave. Mattie will likely take pity.

Mattie answers his phone after a few rings with a way too cheerful, "Hey, kid. How was your hot date?"

"Mattie," Blake says at the same time that Mattie's wife, in the background, says, "*Jake.*"

"Katie thinks I'm a nosy old man," Mattie says, still cheerful. "But I think if I have to babysit your suit, the least you can tell me is whether or not your date went well. I'm just concerned for your wellbeing."

"It wasn't a date," Blake says.

"Okay. Good talk, kid."

"Wait, I actually called for a reason."

"Oh, did you? Thought you wanted to check up on your suit."

"Can I bring someone to dinner?" Blake says, immediately regretting that he said *someone* instead of mentioning that it's Charlie he wants to bring.

"Who do you wanna bring? Your girlfriend?" Mattie asks.

Blake rolls his eyes. "No."

"Boyfriend?"

"*Jake,*" says Katie, voice muffled.

Blake really needs to think of something to say, and eventually goes with another, "No," because it was obviously a joke, Mattie didn't mean anything by it, but it caught Blake off guard. He tries to laugh it off, and says, "I wanted to bring Charlie."

"Oh, Choo Choo. Yeah, you can bring him. Doesn't look like he knows how to even make a Kraft dinner, poor kid."

"Thanks, Mattie."

"Sure thing. I'll see you later. Same time as usual."

Blake thanks him again and hangs up, texts Charlie and then rests his head against the window with a sigh, still hung up on the boyfriend comment.

He considers calling Noah, then decides to wait until he's home, because he can't say shit on the train where people might be listening. At home, he flops into his bed, where he's immediately joined by Squid, who meows at him accusingly. Right. Food. Blake gets back up again, takes care of that and then flops back down, this time on the couch, because it's the closet comfortable surface.

He's eternally grateful that Noah answers pretty much immediately.

"Couldn't wait to see me in person tomorrow, huh?" Noah says.

"Can I talk to you about something?"

Noah sighs. "I hate that you're even asking me this question. What's up, babe?"

"Are you alone?"

147

"Yeah. What's wrong?"

Squid hops onto the couch, making himself comfortable on Blake's stomach. "Do you think..." Blake stares at the ceiling for a moment, trying to find the right words, even though he knows that with Noah he doesn't really have to talk his way around the issue. "Do you think my entire team knows that I'm gay?"

"I don't know, have you *told* your entire team that you're gay?"

"No, but... I've never had a girlfriend. Doesn't that make it pretty obvious?"

"Okay, but... Think about it this way... Most of those guys haven't even known you for your entire career. Some of them have maybe only been around a year, two years... There's barely anyone who's known you from the start. And the guys who did know you from the start are probably, like, the core guys, like your captain and Matthews, and, honestly, I don't think they'd feel like it's any of their business."

"I think Mattie knows," Blake says lowly. He's still convinced that the boyfriend thing was a joke, but, in all honesty, how could he have not figured it out by now?

"Listen, if anything, he suspects. Is he being a dick or something?"

"No, he's not."

"Then what's the issue?"

"I don't know," Blake says. Everything's off-kilter and this secret is getting too big for him. There's nothing he can do about it, though. "How's your, uh..." Noah said there was someone, but Blake never asked, figured Noah would tell him if there was anything to tell, but Blake is somewhat desperate to change the subject, because he thought he knew how to talk about this, but, as it turns out, he doesn't.

"Ohhh, wait a second, are you deflecting?" Noah says. "I'm working on my... whatever it is. We'll get there. I'm an optimist. Now back to you."

"No."

"Yuh-huh. You called me, Fishy. Tell me what's wrong."

"I..."

"Out with it."

"I stayed at Elliot's last night."

"Oh, *shit*."

"Nothing happened."

"Nothing happened, my ass," Noah says, gleeful. "You slept there? How'd you end up there in the first place?"

"We had dinner and I fell asleep, it's not a big deal, but..." Blake covers his face with his hand, because he's pretty sure that his cheeks are flaming red and it's not like Noah can see him, but Blake is so embarrassed that he doesn't even want Squid to see. "Fuck."

"Oh, Fish."

"He's still Elliot, you know?" Blake says, like that explains anything at all.

"I wish I could help you with this, but I don't think you have too many options here."

"I have options?"

"Well, either you get over him, or you... don't. But if you choose not to get over him, you're either going to suffer or you need to talk to him."

"Yeah, no."

"Is he seeing someone?" Noah asks.

"That's not even... It doesn't matter. He doesn't want to be with... a guy. We broke shit off before the Draft. He didn't want to take the risk. Which is... It's what he wanted and I said it was okay."

"But that was years ago."

"So?"

"So people change their minds," Noah says.

Blake blows out a long breath.

"Listen," Noah says, "I need to head out in like two minutes, but here's my incredible advice on this... Figure out what you want and either take yourself out of this or jump right in."

"I don't think that's helpful."

"Never said I was helpful. Love you, Fishy. I'll see you soon, okay?"

"Okay," Blake says.

Doesn't really matter what he wants. He's fucked either way.

14

Blake gets invited to three New Year's Eve parties.

Three.

He doesn't want to go to a single one.

One of them isn't even a party. Mattie invited him over, but Blake already spent Christmas at his place, so he can't impose on Mattie and his family any more than that. The other two are parties, though. The rookies are having a party at their house, which Blake, even though he's not even one of the oldest guys on the team, is way too old for, the other one is a party that Brammer's girlfriend's friend is throwing. It's in the city. Blake isn't going to that one either.

He'll hang out with Squid, and maybe Angus if he's having a good day, and go to bed at ten.

In all honesty, he's never been a fan of all the New Year's stuff, people asking for your resolutions, like they don't forget all about what they promised themselves about three days into the new year. It has no significance, January 1st is just another day, and everyone will be the exact same person that they were on December 31st. "It's just a fucking reason to have a good time, Fish. It's not that deep," Brammer said when Blake told him exactly that.

To be fair, Blake wasn't being grumpy for no reason, it was because Brammer wouldn't stop bugging him.

They play in Hartford the day before New Year's and return home late, so Blake sleeps in, two cats in his bed with him, walking all over him, and then screaming when he won't get up and feed them. They won't get to sleep in his bed the next time he tries to sleep in.

He makes himself breakfast, scrolls through Instagram for a bit and posts a picture of Squid, because the people love him. The whole Instagram account for the cats thing was a joke in the beginning. He needed a distraction from being miserable, but then Blake actually kept posting photos and now his cats have followers.

Angus doesn't make too many appearances, because he usually only glares when Blake takes a picture of him, but Squid is a natural and tries to look extra pretty when Blake points his camera at him. He's still fiddling with filters when someone knocks on the door.

It's Charlie, smiling when Blake opens the door.

"Hey," Charlie says.

"Hey, you wanna come in?"

"I actually wanted to ask what you're doing tonight," Charlie says, but comes in anyway.

"Hanging out here, I guess."

"You're not going to the party Brammer was talking about?"

"No, why?"

Charlie shrugs. "I was just wondering."

"Oh," Blake says. He's a little suspicious, because Charlie isn't much of a party-goer either. When they go out after a game, it's usually Charlie and Blake who lead the way to the next best pub. They don't do dancing. He'd suspect that Brammer put Charlie up to this, but then Charlie isn't the kind of guy who'd do Brammer's dirty work.

"It's just…"

"Yeah?" Blake prompts.

"I… Okay, this is embarrassing, but…"

"Yeah?" Blake says again.

"I haven't really… I kinda want to go to the party. Because it's been so long since I…" Charlie's face is redder than Blake has ever seen it, which is quite the feat. "I'm bad at talking to girls. And, like, I'm not asking you to be my wingman or anything, but the other guys are always so… They're not subtle. And they're mean. And they're gonna be assholes about this if I show up alone, but if you're there… it might not be so bad."

"So what you're saying is that you want me to come so Brammer won't embarrass you in front of a girl with his juvenile bullshit?" Blake says.

"I guess?"

"I…" Blake really doesn't want to go. Especially if he's going to have to watch Charlie pick up a girl.

"I'll pay for the cab fare."

Blake presses his lips together. Still doesn't want to go.

"I bet they'll have really good food. And free drinks."

Not really enough to sway Blake. He has food and drinks in his fridge. It's right there in the kitchen and he doesn't have to go to some Upper East Side party to get it.

"Please?" Charlie says.

"Fine," Blake says, because he can't stand the look on Charlie's face. He has actual puppy eyes.

Charlie honest to God hugs him. "You're the best."

"Come on, it's gonna be fun."

"I don't know…"

"Moo, it's time."

"For what?" Elliot asks as he fiddles with his elbow pads.

"To get back in the saddle," Andreas says with a wise-beyond-his-years kind of voice.

Elliot rolls his eyes. They shouldn't have taught Andreas idioms.

"No, he's right," Adam says. "Moo, it's time to get laid. Come on. You're not seventy years old. Honestly, seventy-year-olds probably have more sex than you. It's been months. I mean, what else are you gonna do? Be alone forever?"

"Yeah," Elliot grumbles. He's not in the mood for a party. They just played a hockey game and he wants to take a nap. "I'm tired."

"Go home, take a nap, then come to the party."

"Whose party even is this?"

"Oh, it's…" Andreas looks at the ceiling, clearly thinking hard. "It's my girlfriend's friend. They were in the same soro… soriety?"

"Sorority," Elliot says.

"Yeah, that. What even is that? It sounds like some sort of sect when she talks about it."

"I think that's exactly what it is," Adam says.

"She told Carly that she could invite me and that I could bring as many of my teammates as I want."

"Are you sure she didn't say *single* teammates?" Elliot asks.

Adam snorts. "Probably what she meant. But you are a single teammate, Moo. The ladies will love you."

"I'm going to the party, but only if you promise that you won't give a shit whether or not I go home alone," Elliot says.

"I can live with that. But you have to talk to girls."

"Okay, maybe I will, but don't be weird about it, okay?" Elliot says. His worst nightmare is his teammates setting him up on dates and introducing girls to him at bars, because he's currently not at all sure what he's looking for. It's awkward to have someone pushed at him and it's even more awkward to talk to someone he didn't choose to talk to, someone who probably also didn't choose to talk to him, but was lured over by one of his teammates.

"We're never weird," Andreas says, solemn.

"Don't give anyone my phone number."

"Of course not."

"Don't like… pull one of those weird moves–"

"We're never weird," Andreas interrupts.

"Let me find people to talk to."

"But can we give you suggestions?" Adam asks, hope in his eyes.

"Maybe."

Andreas grins. "Yay, Moo is coming. Hey, I'm gonna double-check with Crab to see if he's still planning on dropping by."

Elliot lets out the deepest sigh.

"Come on, old man," Adam says and gives Elliot's ear a flick. "Four point game. Captain of a hockey team. You're a catch. You gotta put yourself out there."

"Hey, I agreed to come to the party, didn't I?"

"Yeah. But when you did it, you looked like you wanted to stab us. We're trying to help. You keep telling me that you're lo–"

"I'm not lonely."

"Well, then sexually frustrated. Same difference."

"I will pay you to stop talking," Elliot says.

"Really, how much?"

Elliot almost throws his jock at him. Almost, because he's a good captain and Adam is his best friend, and maybe he deserves it, but he also doesn't want to subject the locker room to Adam screeching like a little kid.

"Hey," Adam says and leans over, keeping his voice low, "do you want me to come over before the party and help you pick something to w–"

Elliot has a sock off his foot so fast that Adam doesn't have time to duck out of the way before Elliot slaps it right into his face.

"MOO!"

"You deserved that one," Elliot says.

"Hey, Elliot?"

"Yeah?"

Tara, one of their social media people, holds up a phone. "Could you say 'Happy New Year' to our fans real quick?"

"Yeah, for sure," Elliot says. "Anything in particular you want me to say?"

"No, you just go for it," Tara says.

It's Elliot's least favorite thing to hear. He isn't bad at talking to the media, not at all, but he likes doing stuff like this a lot better when they give him clear instructions. Tara usually does a few takes, so Elliot tries a few different things, says he hopes everyone is safe out there tonight, says he hopes they'll see them all at the arena next year, thanks them for supporting them, even does one with Adam, who gives him bunny ears.

"Are you using that one?" Adam asks.

Tara smiles at him, like you might look at a small child who asked you if the Easter Bunny is real. "No, but I'm sure it'll go into the outtakes compilation that we're planning on doing."

"Outtakes," Adam mutters and trots away to take a shower.

Elliot puts on a striped shirt for the party, because when he doesn't know what to wear and a suit it too fancy, a striped shirt is usually a good idea. He puts on jeans, dismissing the thought that he could be on his couch in sweatpants. His hair is… curly. Messy. As always. He had the sides cut a little shorter and he likes it well enough. His mom is still appalled every time she sees him.

Adam comes by to pick him up, in a cab, because he's not driving, but he clearly doesn't trust Elliot to actually show up at the party if he doesn't have an escort. Elliot wouldn't trust himself either. Lou smiles at him when he slides into the cab and tells him he looks nice. She looks nice, too. Sparkly.

The party is in a penthouse on the Upper East Side, the place already teeming with people, mostly girls. One of them detaches herself when they arrive – she's tall, blonde, her teeth so white they seem to sparkle with her silver dress. "Hey, Andy's teammates. Glad you could come. I'm Chrissie."

"Oh, hey!" Andy's girlfriend comes over as well, clearly a few drinks ahead of them.

"Hey, Carly," Lou says and hugs her, their dresses sparkling together.

"Come on in, Elliot, Adam, you look dashing, come meet my friends," she says and ushers them further into the apartment. She very quickly introduces them to about fifteen girls, whose names Elliot has no chance of remembering, then she hands them over to Chrissie, who offers them drinks, then food, and then darts off to greet more guests.

The party is thankfully big enough that no one will notice if Elliot tucks himself into a corner with a plate full of food. It's all excellent, probably from a catering company. He doesn't want to know how much it cost, because even with the money he makes now, he doesn't understand how some people spend theirs so freely, when he's more concerned with saving it all up for whatever comes after his playing career is over. He bought the apartment, but that was his only expensive purchase, apart from the stuff he bought for his mom and dad.

Whoever lives in this apartment – probably Carly's friend, although maybe her parents own the place – likely has a few more millions to spend than Elliot does. It's all marble and golden picture frames, soft carpets, and dishes that most certainly didn't come from IKEA, like Elliot's.

They eat, Elliot gets himself another drink and talks to two Broadway actors, one of which practically undresses Elliot with his eyes. Elliot shoots him a smile, then excuses himself, because he can't walk out of here with a guy. The idea is... Shit, he loves the idea of taking that guy home, even though he's not really Elliot's type, and it bugs him that he can't.

"What crawled up your ass?" Adam asks when Elliot returns to him.

"Nothing," Elliot says. Which might be part of the problem.

"Okay, so..." Adam nods across the room. "What about her? Red dress. Veeeery high heels. She's single. Ready to mingle."

"How do you *know*?"

"Lou gave me a scouting report."

Lou apparently also fled the scene after delivering said report, which was pretty smart of her, considering that Adam agreed that he'd leave Elliot the fuck alone with this.

"She's hot," Adam says.

"Are you allowed to say that? You're married."

"If Lou is allowed to sit in front of our TV and tell me how beautiful and luscious Blake Samuels's hair is, I'm allowed to say that that girl is hot." Adam's eyes go wide. "Oh, I forgot that you know him. Please don't tell him that my wife thinks he's hot? I'm pretty sure she'd leave me because he has way better hair than I do."

"I won't say a word if you leave me the fuck alone," Elliot says.

"Fine," Adam says and leans back.

Elliot eventually loses Adam when he leaves the safety of the couch he was sitting on to get some more food. He finds chicken sliders and is still working on his third one when a girl sidles up to him.

"Hi," she says. That's it.

Elliot doesn't immediately know what to do with that. "Hi," he says. "Sorry, am I in your way?"

"No, don't worry," she says. She's sparkly, too, but not as much as some of the other girls. Her hair is really long. *Really* long. He almost wants to tell her that he's impressed, but then she asks, "Are you here on your own?"

"Uh, with friends."

"Friends," she echoes, like he told her a secret. Maybe he did. "Are you one of the hockey players? Carly said that her boyfriend brought some friends."

"Oh. Yeah."

"Awesome. Thought you looked like a hockey player," she says. Then grins. "My sister's actually a goalie. She plays in Michigan."

"Oh, that's great."

"They tried to get me into it, too, but I was always more of a runner. You know, solid ground and all that."

Elliot laughs, can't help it.

They talk for a while. She's nice. At some point, he realizes that he never even asked for her name. Probably too late now. They keep talking. Adam catches his eye at some point and gives him a thumbs up. Elliot doesn't dignify it with a response. He enjoys talking to this girl, but only about as much as he'd enjoy talking to literally anyone else.

Eventually he says, "Sorry, I think I saw someone I know. Just wanna say hi real quick."

"Oh, of course," she says.

Elliot escapes before she can look too disappointed.

He does say hello to Crab, who has a blonde girl sitting in his lap. Her cheeks are red and her words are slurred when she tells Elliot to sit down and teach her friends about hockey.

Elliot tries to give them some interesting facts, then someone's hand ends up on his thigh and he excuses himself to get another drink before someone ends up in his lap, too. He eventually sneaks into the kitchen, where they're hiding even more food. He's not the only one in here. A girl is crying quietly in a corner, another girl, presumably a friend of hers, is whispering to her. Over by the counter, the guys he met earlier are mixing drinks.

"Hey," one of them says, "I didn't catch your name earlier."

"I'm Elliot," he says.

They introduce themselves as Marcus and Jayden. They mix him a drink and share their plate of appetizers with him.

Jayden, the one who was undressing Elliot with his eyes earlier, says, "So, how do you know Chrissie?"

"Oh, my teammate's girlfriend knows her. Carly. She invited us all."

"Teammate? What do you play?"

"Hockey."

"Like, not to be too forward, but do hockey players all have… glutes like you do?"

"Jay, shut the fuck up."

"Uh," Elliot only says. "I guess?"

"You're straight, right?" Jayden says, already looking devastated.

Elliot could say no. Except he can't say no. What he does say is, "Sorry."

"Aw, too bad." Jayden winks at him. "If you change your mind—"

"Idiot," Marcus says and turns to Elliot. "Ignore him. You have a girlfriend?"

"No, but my teammates think they need to change that."

"They trying to set you up?"

Elliot shrugs. "I think I got them to stop."

"It's okay, you can hide with us," Jayden says. "You're pretty."

"I swear to God, Jay."

"Are you uncomfortable? I promise I'll stop if you're uncomfortable."

"No, you're fine," Elliot says. Honestly, he doesn't mind so much. Jayden is clearly just having fun and he's keeping his hands to himself, which is more than he can say for the girls he was talking to. It's nice to be flirted with.

"Marcus, did you hear that?" Jayden whispers. "I'm *fine*."

"That's not what he meant."

"I know." Jayden nods at Elliot's glass. "Drink up, darling. I'll make you another one."

"Stop flirting with him."

"You're not my mom, Marcus."

"Yeah, thank fuck for that."

Elliot laughs. He likes these guys.

It's where Adam eventually finds him, on to his third drink with his new Broadway friends. "Dude, there you are. Come on, some of the guys just got here."

"Gotta say hi to my guys," Elliot says.

"Oh, *your* guys?"

"I'm the captain."

"Nooo, you didn't tell us you were the *captain*."

"Hey, if you ever want to come to a game, tell Carly to let me know and I'll get you tickets, okay?" Elliot says as Adam tugs him away.

"Thank you, Captain," Jayden says and blows him a kiss.

Adam laughs. "Who were they?" he asks when they're out of earshot.

"New friends," Elliot says.

The party they're invited to is... a party.

They get there pretty late and it's exactly as bad as Blake was expecting, but at least they have good food. Like those tiny burgers. He loves the tiny burgers. He eats about ten of them and is only mildly disgruntled when Charlie hands him a beer.

"How do you talk to girls?" Charlie asks.

"I…" Blake is distracted, because he's pretty sure that he saw Brammer talking to Adam Ishida. Who plays for the Ravens. On Elliot's line. "I don't know," Blake eventually says, because that's the truth. "You just talk to them."

He tries to find Brammer again. Yeah, that's definitely Adam Ishida. Elliot mentions him a lot. Obviously, that doesn't mean that Elliot is here. Elliot cries when he has to go to nightclubs, so he probably wouldn't jump on the opportunity of going to a New Year's party.

A guy nods at them as he passes them. It's Keith Taylor. The kid the Ravens call Crab.

"Oh, hey," Blake says.

The kid freezes. "H…i."

Blake grins at him.

"I'm so sorry about when I, you know… I'm really sorry about that. I honestly didn't mean to."

"No hard feelings, kid," Blake says, because he scared the crap out of him, he had his fun, and he knows that the kid really didn't mean to give him a concussion.

Keith Taylor smiles uncertainly and then practically runs away from them.

"What was that all about?" Charlie asks.

Blake only shakes his head.

Maybe half of the Ravens are here. No Mariners. They're out of town. As he and Charlie walk around, they also come across a few more of their own teammates, but it looks like most of them ended up going to the rookie party. Or they're home with their families.

Blake would also prefer being home with his family of two cats.

"Okay," Blake says, "find someone to talk to."

"What?"

"That's why we're here, right?"

"I mean, yeah, but…"

"Excuse me," a girl says, smiling at them as she passes, "could I… You guys are right in front of the tiny burgers. Which might be your plan, you know, hiding the tiny burgers, so you can have them all."

"That's exactly what we're doing," Blake says. "But I think we'll share. Right, Charlie?"

"Right," Charlie says.

Blake steps aside so she can get some burgers, then he gives Charlie a pointed look.

Charlie gives him a pointed look back, looking absolutely helpless.

Blake waves. *Just say something.*

"You should try the ones with chicken," Charlie tells her. "They're good."

"Oh, I will, thanks for the tip," she says.

"I'm Charlie," says Charlie.

"Nice to meet you, Charlie, I'm Emma."

"Hi," says Charlie.

"Hi," says Emma.

That's Blake's cue to leave. He grabs another small burger and sneaks away. Charlie doesn't even seem to notice that Blake is begging off. He's not going home immediately, because he didn't come all the way here from fucking Newark to spend half an hour at a party.

The good thing is that there are so many people at this party that it's easy enough to hide, the partygoers spread out across several rooms, no one really paying any mind to Blake as he wanders about. He slips past a bunch of Ravens players who apparently just arrived, hangs out in a corner, scrolling through Twitter on his phone for a bit, and then ducks into the kitchen when a girl across the room keeps smiling at him.

In the kitchen, he finds a teary-eyed girl and her friend and two guys who are bickering.

"–can't believe you wouldn't stop flirting with him. Fuck's sake, Jay."

They look up when Blake wanders into the kitchen and fall silent.

"Sorry, didn't mean to interrupt," Blake says.

"No worries, tall one," says the guy named Jay.

The other guy shoots Jay a murderous look.

"You want a drink?" Jay asks.

Blake holds up his beer. "I'm good." He does grab a plate and some appetizers, though.

"You a hockey player?" the nameless guy asks.

"Yeah," Blake says.

"There are so many of you," Jay says.

Blake snorts.

"And all so handsome," he continues. "We were talking to one of your fellow... hockeys. He was pretty. But so are you."

"I swear he's not harassing you." The long-suffering guy holds out his hands. "I'm Marcus. The one without a brain-to-mouth filter is Jayden."

"Blake," Blake says and shakes his hand. "What do you guys do?"

"Jay's in Wicked, I'm in Jersey Boys."

"Oh, so you're... actors?"

They nod. Jay winks at him and Blake is weirdly pleased.

"I have to admit, I've never been to a Broadway show," Blake says.

"Well, I've never been to a hockey game, so I guess we're on the same page," Jay says. "Although our new best friend did offer us tickets. What do you do in the hockey? Score a lot of goals?"

"I'm a goalie, actually."

"Ohhh," Jay says. That's probably the first time that *I'm a goalie* elicited such delight. "Is that why you're so tall?"

"You need to stop drinking," Marcus says.

"Shhh," Jay says and gently puts his hand on Marcus's face. "So do you play with Captain Elliot?"

"You guys know Elliot?"

"Yeah, we just met him," Marcus says.

"He's actually on a different team," Blake says. He can't run off and try to find Elliot, right? That would be ridiculous. "But I know him." He really wants to talk to him. He'll say hello real quick. Then he'll make sure that Charlie is doing okay. Then he'll go home. "Maybe I should find him and say hi."

"Yeah," Jay says, "and tell him we love him."

Blake laughs. "Sure, I'll do that."

"Hey, it's your best friend."

"Wha–" Elliot looks up. He was distracted, scrolling through Instagram. "Oh." It's Blake. He's across the room, looking over at one of his teammates, Charlie Trainor, who seems to be deep in a conversation with a girl over by the food.

"And he brought his luscious hair," Adam grumbles.

"Ohhh, it's Blake Samuels," Lou says, across the table.

Adam looks like he's about to crawl under the couch.

"You wanna say hi?" Elliot asks, because Adam was a dick to him earlier and he deserves it.

Lou tilts her head, eyes on Adam. "Will you still love me if I ask him for a selfie?"

Adam rolls his eyes dramatically and says, "There are maybe two things that would make me stop loving you and that's not one of them, so I guess it's fine."

"Love you," Lou says and makes grabby-hands for Elliot, who offers her his arm and leads her over to Blake.

Blake sees them coming and smiles when he spots Elliot.

"Hey, Blake," Elliot says. "This is Lou, she really wanted to meet you."

"Hi," Blake says and shakes Lou's hand. "Nice to meet you…" His eyes flicker to Elliot for the briefest of seconds, then back to Lou.

"She's Adam's wife."

"Yeah, he's having a breakdown right over there," Lou says and points at where Adam is sitting, glaring at them.

That tickles a laugh out of Blake.

"Could we take a picture?" Lou asks.

"Yeah, sure," Blake says.

Lou hands her phone to Elliot, beaming when he snaps the picture. "Thank you so much, Blake, I'm from Jersey, so I sort of root for you guys. I'm very conflicted. My mom loves you, by the way, she thinks you're the best goalie we've had since Frank Parrish."

Blake smiles, his cheeks faintly pink. "That's very nice of her to say."

"She'll absolutely lose it when I tell her that I met you. Oh, could you…" Lou pulls a notebook out her bag. "Would you sign this for her? Her name is Jane."

"For sure," Blake says and takes the notebook from her, writes, *Thank you for your support, Jane*, then signs it and puts a 33 and a drawing of a little fish next to it.

"Oh no, the fish. It's so cute," Lou says. "Thank you so much."

"My pleasure," Blake says.

Lou thanks him one more time, gives Elliot's arm a squeeze and then returns to Adam, who only sighs, resigned, and leans over to kiss her temple.

"Adam told me he wasn't sure if he could date her when they first met because she was a Knights fan," Elliot says.

"Seems like it worked out in the end," Blake says.

"Yeah, I think he eventually realized that she's a catch." Elliot gives Blake a nudge. "Didn't expect to see you here tonight."

"I didn't expect to see me here tonight either," Blake mutters. "Charlie needed someone to hold his hand. For like three seconds. So I came here with him. The food is good."

"So good," Elliot says.

"The next time you cook for me, you have to make tiny burgers."

"Who said that I'm cooking for you again?"

Blake pulls a face. "Sorry, shouldn't have assumed…"

"No, I mean, I totally will. Tiny burgers sound good. I might try to make some of that other fancy stuff, too. Quiche or whatever."

Blake grins. He looks good tonight, but he always does. He's wearing a sweater that looks incredibly soft and that Elliot would want to bury his face in if he'd had more drinks.

"Did you have a good time with your parents?" Blake asks.

"Yeah, it was nice to have them around. I miss them sometimes." Elliot kinda wants to kick himself for that one. Blake doesn't even have parents anymore. "Sorry, that was—"

"Elliot, come on, it's okay. You know it's okay."

Elliot lets out a soft breath.

"I'm glad you got to see them," Blake says and taps Elliot's back with his knuckles. "Hey, uh—"

"Blake." Blake's teammate has appeared behind them, looking apologetic. "Hey, sorry, do you have a minute?"

"Yeah, sure…" Blake nods at Elliot. "I'll talk to you later?"

"Yeah, absolutely," Elliot says.

He tries really hard not to be mad at Charlie Trainor for stealing Blake away.

He doesn't manage.

It takes Elliot over half an hour to find Blake again.

Adam calls him over right after Charlie tugged Blake away, then Adam introduces a girl to him and her only interest seems to be finding someone to kiss at midnight, because she mentions it about half a dozen times in the five minutes that Elliot spends talking to her. Elliot slips away, quite rudely, when she's distracted for a second, saying hello to a friend who walked past them.

Elliot wanders around the party, starting to wonder if Blake might have gone home, or maybe to another party. He can't see Charlie anywhere either. Blake probably doesn't owe him a goodbye or anything; it's not like they came here together, but the thought of Blake being gone leaves him weirdly disappointed.

He's on his way back to Adam when a glass door ahead of him opens and two girls come stumbling into the hallway, accompanied by a gust of cold air. Elliot peers outside, at a mostly deserted balcony. They're still over an hour away from midnight and it's freezing out there. Two people are making out, leaning against the wall a few feet away, barely visible in the low light, and a group is huddled together over by the edge of the balcony, cigarettes lighting up orange in the night. And then, as far away from them as possible, there's Blake, face illuminated by his phone screen, hair mostly hiding his features. He's bundled into his coat, his breath clouding in the winter air.

"I thought you might have left," Elliot says. It takes some focus to make the words come out the way he wants them to.

Blake looks up, his phone screen going dark a second later. "I'm about to, but…" He shrugs. "Charlie left and he gave me permission to go home. I was trying to find you, but I must have missed you in there."

"And then you decided to hide on the balcony?" Elliot asks. "It's fucking freezing out here."

Blake huffs and shrugs off his coat to drape it over Elliot's shoulders. "It's not so bad," he says. "Anyway. Happy New Year, Elliot. If I'm not totally wrong, I'll see you in three weeks."

Yes, they'll see each other in three weeks, but Elliot wants to see him before that and he doesn't want him to go home either. He'll stand out here for the rest of the night if he has to, but he wants Blake to stand here with him. And because Elliot's had too many drinks and has therefore managed to convince himself that he doesn't care anymore, he reaches out to curl his fingers around Blake's wrist. Blake's skin is warm under his fingertips.

Blake doesn't move, frozen to the spot, eyes on Elliot, clearly asking him what the fuck he's doing. Elliot doesn't have an answer to that question. He doesn't want Blake to leave. There. That's the answer.

He glances over his shoulder. The two people who are making out are still there, all the way across the balcony, out of earshot. The smokers have gone back inside without Elliot even noticing. It probably looks like they're having a conversation, maybe standing a little closer than you normally would, but it's not like anyone would question it. At least Elliot hopes not. Blake hasn't tugged his arm away yet, but he's quiet, waiting, like he doesn't want to make the next move.

Elliot doesn't know where to go from here either. He started something and never considered how to finish it.

"You wanna stay a little longer?" Elliot asks.

Blake looks down at him, licking his lips. "Elliot..."

There's so much in that one word, a quiet warning, and longing, too, like Blake can't fucking stand Elliot's fingers on his skin but can't bring himself to tell him to stop, because he wants this, too. Elliot is dying to press closer, get his hands all over Blake, on that soft sweater and then under it, get his thigh between Blake's legs, wants to feel him shiver, wants to be the reason for it.

Blake lets out an unsteady breath, like he was reading Elliot's mind.

Elliot squeezes his wrist and drags his thumb over his skin, where a tattoo is peeking out from under Blake's sweater. Elliot's never had a chance to really look at them. He has no idea what the hell he's thinking, just knows he wants Blake's hands on him, Blake's lips on his. He leans closer, only a little, so he can keep his voice low when he says, "Come home with me?"

Blake's breath catches. He doesn't say anything for a moment, then shakes his head ever so slightly. "You don't really... Elliot. No."

"Okay," Elliot says.

"It's a terrible idea."

Elliot knows that. It's the worst idea. But he's also drunk and wants to plaster himself against Blake and never let go. "I want you to," Elliot says.

"I'll meet you downstairs in ten minutes," Blake mumbles and takes back his coat, goes inside without looking back and Elliot stays on the balcony for a moment longer and breathes in the cold night air and tries to wrap his head around what he just did.

His heart is fluttering in his chest, excited, scared, urging him to move, to stop standing here, contemplating what this means.

It means that Blake is coming home with him. That's all that matters right now.

He doesn't say goodbye to Adam, because Adam wouldn't let him leave before midnight, so he goes to grab his coat, which takes a lot longer than he expected it would, because all the coats look the same and Elliot barely even remembers what brand his coat is, but he eventually stumbles across it and confirms that it's his when he digs through the pockets and finds a receipt from his favorite dumpling place and a Subway ticket.

Elliot is the only one on the elevator, goes down, nods at the doorman as he leaves. No one's out front. He probably took more than ten minutes to come down here. Maybe Blake thought he changed his mind, thought he wouldn't come and went home. Maybe Blake changed his mind and left, not even waiting for Elliot to show up.

"Elliot."

He whips around and finds Blake behind him. "Fuck, you scared me."

"Sorry," Blake says, smiling a little.

"Let's go," Elliot says and starts towards the street. It takes him forever to flag down a cab and by the time they slide into the backseat of one, his hands are blocks of ice and the tip of his nose is freezing cold.

Blake is quiet on the ride to Elliot's, and Elliot desperately wants to say something, but all the things he wants to say are things he doesn't want their cab driver to hear. He reaches out instead and takes Blake's hand, his fingers warm against Elliot's. Blake gives them a squeeze and wraps his other hand around them, too.

The ride is too long.

He can't handle sitting here with Blake holding his hand when all he really wants to do is climb in Blake's lap and kiss him until they're both out of breath. Elliot slowly tugs his hand away from Blake's and puts it on his thigh.

Blake shoots him a look, Elliot can tell, even though he has his eyes on their cab driver, to make sure that he doesn't get interested in where exactly Elliot's putting his hand. Elliot squeezes, gently, hears Blake's breath hitch, the tiniest bit, and Elliot's fingers give another twitch.

When their cab driver turns into Elliot's street, he pulls his hand away and gets his wallet to pay, shaking his head at Blake before he can think about offering to pay half. Elliot thanks the driver and nudges Blake out of the car, trying to convince himself that he has to be patient a little while longer, that he can't put his hands on Blake right here and right now.

He sways a little on his way to the door and Blake reaches for him to steady him, hand gone a second later when Elliot walks on without falling over.

Elliot laughs and finds Blake smiling at him when he ushers him into the building.

Blake absolutely isn't drunk enough to go through with this.

Elliot stays close in the elevator, so close they're almost touching, so close that all Blake would have to do is move his pinky finger and he'd be touching Elliot's hand. The hand that was on his thigh no five minutes ago. He can still feel it somehow, the warmth of the palm of Elliot's hand.

It takes Elliot some jiggling and soft cursing to get his door unlocked, hands unsteady, and Blake can't tell if it's nerves or the drinks Elliot had at the party. Blake won't say he has second thoughts, because he made a choice here, knowing full well how wrong this could go, how much it could screw everything up, but the more he watches Elliot, fiddling with his key, tripping over the threshold, stumbling out of his boots, the less convinced Blake is that this is the right decision.

"Hey," Elliot says as soon as the door is closed and then he's right there, hands on Blake's sides, tipping his head up and Blake meets him halfway, kisses him, a soft whine escaping Elliot's throat before he kisses him back, pushes, until Blake's back hits the door.

Elliot gets out of his coat, drops it, his lips still on Blake's, moving down the side of his neck when his fingers move on to undo the buttons of Blake's coat. It joins Elliot's on the floor. His hands are everywhere, running down Blake's chest, then back up, one curled around the back of his neck, the other one tugging off his hat, getting caught in Blake's hair, and Blake can barely focus, wraps his arms around Elliot and keeps him close.

There's nothing careful about the way Elliot is kissing him right now, it's like he's been waiting for this, has been starving for it and can't get enough, teeth grazing Blake's bottom lip when he pulls away, only to press a kiss to Blake's throat, hands finding their way under Blake's sweater, burning hot against his skin.

Blake gets his fingers into Elliot's hair, tugs, and Elliot moans, lips still on Blake's throat.

"Come on," Elliot says, pulls him away from the door and down the hall. He trips over absolutely nothing on the way and laughs.

"Elliot," Blake says, but can't finish because Elliot is kissing him again as he guides him into his bedroom.

Elliot doesn't turn on the lights, so the room's all shadows, but Blake can see Elliot's bed, part of it illuminated by the hallway light.

"Elliot, how drunk are you?" Blake asks, because he honestly can't tell right now.

"Not drunk."

"Yeah, you are."

"A little," Elliot says, fingers digging into Blake's sides. "I want to... Blake. I don't just want this because I'm drunk."

"Okay, but…"

"You don't want to," Elliot says.

"We shouldn't."

Blake hates this so much. Two minutes ago, he was willing to let Elliot do whatever he wants with him.

Elliot takes a step back and lets out a breath. "I'm not that drunk."

"I know, I… I'm sorry."

"No, it's fine," Elliot says and that's probably a lie. He looks small, like he wants to hide from Blake, turns his face away when Blake tries to look him in the eyes.

"Elliot."

"I'm not mad because you don't want to sleep with me," Elliot says.

Blake believes him, because Elliot isn't that kind of guy, but he's mad about something, and it's probably Blake's fault.

"This is so fucked up, I'm so sorry," Elliot says. "I shouldn't have asked you to come in the first place."

"I can go," Blake says. It's not that late. He'll go home and think about his life and his choices and he'll sleep in his own bed and maybe he'll let the cats sleep on his bed, because by the time he makes it home, he'll be miserable.

Elliot frowns. "Do you have to?"

"No, but… It sort of sounded like you wanted me to?"

"Please stay."

"Okay," Blake says and Elliot goes in for a hug, face pressed into the crook of Blake's neck, arms wrapped around him tightly. They stand there like that as the minutes tick by, neither of them letting go.

Elliot eventually tugs himself away, finds Blake a shirt to borrow, disappears in his closet and comes back out in boxers and a shirt, then disappears into the bathroom while Blake pulls on the shirt that Elliot handed to him. Blake dumps his jeans and his sweater on a chair in the corner, then slips into the bathroom when Elliot is done.

Elliot left out a toothbrush for him. He's already in bed, sitting up, when Blake pads back into the bedroom. He's over on the left, leaving room for Blake, which means Blake probably isn't sleeping on the couch. Blake climbs in next to him and it's less awkward than he thought it would be.

He's done this before, it's familiar even though it's been years.

"Okay?" Elliot asks. It's an echo of the first time they slept in the same bed, back in Norwalk, where they were supposed to be sharing Blake's room, Blake on a mattress and Elliot in his bed. It was the same question back then, when Elliot had already settled against Blake, breath tickling his neck.

Blake nods and reaches out, relieved when Elliot flops against him, with very little grace, and tucks himself against Blake, the exact same way he used to. Blake kisses the top of Elliot's head because he can't help himself, then scoots down a little to get comfortable.

"Happy New Year," Blake mumbles. It must be midnight by now.

Elliot hums, curls his finger into Blake's shirt. "We'll talk in the morning, okay?"

Blake sees that as what it is, a request for him to not sneak out in the middle of the night. Which, honestly, he hadn't considered yet, but likely would have considered if he'd woken up before Elliot and had found himself with a choice to make. Now that Elliot said that, though, Blake can't. As much as he'd rather write tonight off as a slip-up they should forget about quickly, he knows this is more, and they do need to talk about it, even though he doesn't know what the hell he's supposed to tell Elliot when tomorrow rolls around.

He does say, "Okay," and hopes that he'll miraculously have all the answers in the morning.

15

When Elliot wakes up, he's pleasantly warm, sheets still pulled up to his chin, his knee pressed against more warm skin. He blinks, finds Blake next to him, still asleep, breathing slow and even. Elliot sneaks out of bed to go to the bathroom and is almost surprised when he returns and finds Blake exactly where he left him.

Blake has one arm stuck under his pillow, but the other one is between them, fingers splayed on the mattress. Elliot takes a peek at his tattoos, at the waves that splash across Blake's arm in ink, the fish scales that belong to some kind of sea monster, the leaves of some kind of underwater plant that look like they're swaying in the waves, a play of dark and light, ink and skin. Elliot wants to touch, trace all the lines with the tip of his finger. He wonders how much it hurt, if Blake needed someone to hold his hand. Elliot's far too big of a wimp to get a tattoo, wouldn't know what to get either, but he loves Blake's and would stare at them for hours if he could.

Blake shifts, mumbles something. His hair is all over the place and a few strands in his face seem to tickle him. He scrunches up his nose, blinks, and wipes them away. "Hmm," he says.

"Good morning," Elliot whispers.

Blake squints at him. "Five more minutes."

"Yeah," Elliot says. They both have the day off. Coach told them he didn't want to see their hungover asses anywhere close to their practice rink, so they have all day and Elliot isn't in a rush to disturb the peace. "Come closer?" he tries.

Blake does, scoots over until he bumps into Elliot and wraps his arm around him, nose smushed into Elliot's hair.

The weight in the pit of Elliot's stomach doesn't seem quite so heavy now. Last night was a mess, right from the start. He didn't think this through, didn't think about what it would mean for them if he asked Blake to come home with him. He wanted this and he was selfish

168

enough to ask for it, but Blake had every right to turn him down in the end. Elliot gets it, he wasn't exactly sober, but he still wants Blake's hands on him now, wants to kiss him, see his lips wet and red and bitten again, like they were last night.

"When are we talking?" Blake asks. His hand is splayed on Elliot's stomach, and it could dip a little lower so easily. Blake is barely touching him and it's already driving him insane.

Elliot wiggles, pushes back against Blake. "Later."

Blake shifts, nosing along the back of Elliot's neck, breath tickling his skin. "You sure?"

"So sure," Elliot says and Blake's fingers twitch, hitch up his shirt. Elliot doesn't remember how to breathe. Blake's hand gently moves across the plane of his stomach, then down, skimming along the waistband of his briefs, down his thigh, everywhere but where Elliot really wants that hand.

Blake presses a kiss to the back of his neck, then his hand comes up again, fingers just so skimming over the fabric of his briefs and Elliot's hips jerk against his hand. He wishes he wasn't embarrassed.

The first time they did this together he lasted for about five seconds.

Blake's teeth graze Elliot's skin, but it's gentle, not enough to leave a mark. A brush of lips follows, hands going up now, blunt fingernails brushing over a nipple, and Elliot shivers, then Blake says, "What do you want?"

Elliot wants *everything*.

He remembers what Blake likes, but it's been so long and Elliot is too impatient to make a plan, he just wants to touch and touch and touch.

"I..." Another hint of teeth and Elliot completely loses his train of thought. "*Blake*."

"Yeah?"

"Fuck."

"Hmm..." Blake palms him through his briefs. "So?"

Elliot has an answer on the tip of his tongue and forgets it immediately. He didn't know he'd missed this. The way they were always so easy together, even if things were awkward. He never felt shy around Blake and it's the same now, it's familiar, despite all the years in between then and now.

"Lie back," Elliot says and Blake goes, obediently, and lies down, blue eyes following Elliot as he sits up and pulls off his shirt. He moves to straddle Blake's hips and bends down to kiss him, morning breath be damned. Blake clearly doesn't care and kisses him back, stubble scratchy against Elliot's face. Elliot wants to find out what that might feel like against his thighs. Later.

Elliot looks down at him, thinks of Blake before they were drafted, already tall, but somehow smaller than this. His cheekbones are sharper now and he has a tiny scar at the base of his throat that he didn't have before. And the tattoos, of course, those are new, still fascinate Elliot, would hold his attention if there weren't more pressing issues. He glimpses the outline of Connecticut on Blake's other arm, feathers that probably go with the bird on his upper arm, more waves, and dark, evergreen trees.

Blake is looking back at him, silent, waiting. He was never in a particular hurry, always took his time, except for the first few times, when everything was new, when everything felt urgent.

Elliot leans back down, nose bumping against Blake's. He stays there for a moment, not quite kissing him yet. He runs his fingers through Blake's hair and it's exactly as soft as it looks, trails his knuckles down the side of his face, his thumb across Blake's lips. Blake smiles and kisses the pad of his thumb, and Elliot knows that they've been here before, but he suddenly feels eighteen again, only for a few seconds, like he did when they did this for the very first time.

Elliot kisses him then, slowly, and only stops to get Blake out of the shirt he let him borrow last night, trails his fingers down, letting them get caught in the small patch of hair on Blake's chest and bends down to kiss the soft skin of his stomach, follows the trail of coarse hair down, gets Blake's boxers out of the way and gets his mouth on Blake without any further ado.

Blake groans like he wasn't expecting that. Maybe Elliot should have taken it a little slower, given the fact that he hasn't done this in years, but it seems that Blake cares very little for Elliot's technique. Elliot is happy to find that Blake still makes those soft little noises as Elliot gets him off.

There wasn't much finesse to it, but Blake looks wrecked anyway.

"Fuck," Blake whispers.

Elliot grins and flops down next to Blake, who's flushed from head to toe, breathing heavily, and Elliot can't help but be a little proud of himself. He kisses the top of Blake's shoulder, going easily when Blake reaches for him, kisses him, tugging at Elliot's briefs, getting a hand around him.

He does last longer than five seconds, but Blake pulls at his hair again, which is not something Elliot even knew he liked, and it does something for him, makes him gasp against Blake's mouth, and Elliot doesn't manage to hold on much longer, just gives in to it and ends up tucked against Blake, nose pressed against the side of his neck, trying to catch his breath.

Blake's fingers are back in his hair, much gentler now, carefully untangling knotted curls while Elliot gets his breathing back to normal. "You okay?" Blake eventually asks, hand coming to a rest on the back of Elliot's neck.

"Yeah," Elliot says, but that's all he manages right now. He nudges Blake with his nose. "Cold."

Blake huffs, then sits up to tug at the sheets, his arm trapped under Elliot. "Hey…"

"Hm?"

"Let me up, I need to go to the bathroom."

"Ugh," Elliot says, but lets him go. He'll come back. Always does. Blake is secretly really into cuddling. Or at least he used to be. Blake tugs at the sheets to make sure Elliot is tucked in.

Something in Elliot feels heavy again as he watches Blake shuffle away.

He doesn't know why he's worried. Maybe because this was a mistake. Maybe because they play for different teams whose schedules never line up. Maybe because they can't be what Elliot wants them to be, because that's not the kind of life they chose when they decided to stick with hockey.

Whatever they will be when Blake walks out his door later, it'll be a compromise.

Blake returns to him quickly, entirely unbothered by how naked he is, and slips back into bed. He doesn't complain when Elliot fits himself back against him.

"I'll make breakfast in a bit," Elliot mumbles. Then they'll talk.

Blake hums.

"Before we have breakfast, though…" Elliot reaches up, drags his thumb over Blake's stubble. "Will you do something for me?"

There's a smile on Blake's face when he says, "Of course."

Blake is fiddling with Elliot's coffeemaker, hair wet, dripping on the shirt he slept in. He's pretty sure that Elliot has a hairdryer somewhere, but he didn't want to ask. Honestly, he doesn't care so much. It usually dries a little wavy, which is fine. He's thinking about his hair and coffee, so he doesn't have to think about anything else.

Like Elliot, who slipped into the bathroom when Blake was done, still naked, hand finding the small of Blake's back in passing before he stepped into the shower. Blake left, picked up yesterday's clothes, and then, for some ridiculous reason, decided to put on the shirt that Elliot gave him last night. It's even a size too big on Blake and it's old and worn, a souvenir from Nashville, Tennessee, by the looks of it.

So, yes, he's wearing that shirt for a reason he can't explain to himself, trying to make coffee. He's close to figuring it out. Elliot said he'd make breakfast, so there isn't much else Blake can do, other than wait for him. And his coffee.

He goes through whatever he missed last night, teammates – the ones who were still capable – sending everyone Happy New Year messages, a text from Evan that's just emojis, a text from Charlie from this morning, thanking him for his sacrifice, promising he'll pay Blake back for the cab he presumably took back to Newark last night. Blake does not tell him that he's an idiot who didn't take a cab back to Newark last night like he fucking should have.

Every decision he made after he agreed to coming home with Elliot last night was objectively a bad one. Because what the fuck are they going to do now? Be boyfriends? Yeah, right.

There's no way they can pull this off.

There's no way he can be for Elliot what Noah was to him. Blake would always want more than that. And he can't ask Elliot to give him more than that, because he could go out there and find himself a nice girlfriend and be happy and not fucking hide from everyone.

Elliot comes into the kitchen in a Ravens shirt and sweatpants and comes straight over to Blake, plasters himself against him, dripping on him, too.

"I was scared you'd leave," Elliot mumbles.

"Come on."

"Okay, maybe not really, but… I'm… not scared, but…"

"Yeah," Blake says, "me, too."

"We're talking now?" Elliot asks.

Blake isn't good at talking, never was. Noah made him, even though it turned out that Noah hid, like, a whole fucking bucket of feelings from him. Sometimes he wonders if he should have noticed. They talked a lot, curled up in the same bed, some space between them, because Noah didn't cuddle, or maybe he just didn't cuddle with Blake.

"Blake?"

"I don't know what to say," Blake says.

Elliot lets out a slow breath. "I'm making breakfast."

He does. He makes pancakes and eggs and little sausages and they don't say much to each other, feet pressed together under the table.

Blake does the dishes after, Elliot leaning against the counter, watching him, handing him plates and pans to put into the dishwasher.

"What do you want, Blake?" Elliot asks, all casual, as he hands him an empty mug.

Blake wants Elliot, but it's not that simple. It never was. He wanted Elliot when they were eighteen, but he couldn't have him. Nothing changed. He straightens up and looks at Elliot, whose face has gone serious, no trace of a smile.

"I mean," Elliot goes on, "was this a one-time thing?"

"It should be," Blake says, and when Elliot's expression becomes stony, he adds, "And you know that as well as I do."

Elliot slowly drags his fingers across the counter, pushing crumbs into the sink. "I don't want this to be the only time."

"Okay, so let's say we keep this going somehow and we pull off some sort of friends with benefits thing..." Blake shrugs. "Wouldn't you rather be with someone you don't have to hide?"

Elliot stares at him and Blake can basically watch it sink in. "No," Elliot says, sounding ridiculously offended. "No, I wouldn't rather... I want you. And I don't want to be friends with benefits either."

"What, you want to be boyfriends?" Blake asks, like the thought hasn't occurred to him, like part of him isn't hoping that that's exactly what will happen. But that's the part of him that *wants*, not the part of him that *thinks*.

"You don't?" Elliot asks.

"That's not what I said." Blake wants to reach for him, because he looks lost now, brow furrowed, no trace of a smile.

"So what are you saying?"

This is going to hurt. Blake knew this was going to hurt all along. "What I'm saying is... Remember before the Draft? When we were practically together and then we broke things off, because it was the smart thing to do?"

Elliot ducks his head.

"You didn't want this because of what it could have done to your career if anyone had found out," Blake goes on. "What changed?"

"I wasn't ready for this back in juniors."

"This is still your career. You're right in the middle of it. And you're ready *now*?"

Elliot is quiet for a long moment. "I don't know," he says eventually.

"Yeah. That's exactly it," Blake says. "You don't know. And it's okay that you don't know, but... What if we do this and what if you change your mind? What if you... What if this ends exactly like last time?"

"But you knew—"

"Yes, I knew we weren't gonna last in juniors, but that doesn't mean that it didn't fucking hurt," Blake says.

Elliot's eyes are back on his feet.

"Elliot..."

"No, you're right, I don't... I'm sorry."

Blake sighs and steps closer, gathers Elliot into his arms and holds him close, fingers in the short hair at the base of Elliot's skull, scratching lightly. "I don't want this to be like last time," Blake says lowly. He can't do it again. "So you'll think about what you want. Take your time, okay?"

Elliot nods, fingers tightening in Blake's shirt. "Can you stay for a bit?"

"I…"

Elliot pushes closer, even though he's basically as close as possible already.

"Okay," Blake says. Bad idea, the *worst* idea.

"You wanna watch the Winter Classic?"

"Yeah, okay."

"I can cook if—"

"Elliot, you don't have to talk me into staying, I'm not going anywhere," Blake says. A few more hours, then he'll go. Fuck knows when they'll see each other again after he walks out the door.

"Okay," Elliot says. "This is weird."

"I'm sorry," Blake mutters. He just can't dive into this headfirst. He needs to make sure that he makes it out in one piece.

"No, it's fine."

"Elliot, it's not fine. Stop saying it's fine. Maybe I should go."

"Please don't."

Blake sighs. "Okay. I'll stay for a few more hours and then I'll go home and we'll give each other a break."

Elliot pulls back, probably just so he can frown up at Blake. "Can I still talk to you, though?"

"Yeah, you can talk to me. I meant… no sex. No kissing."

Elliot nods. "If that's what you want."

"I— Yeah. Yeah, it's what I want." Blake doesn't want to get used to anything that won't last. Because if Elliot does realize that this is too much of a risk for him after all, Blake isn't sure if he can deal with Elliot walking away from him again.

And, sure, last time the walking away from each other was mutual, but maybe, if Elliot had been willing, Blake might have considered giving them a chance. Not that there's any guarantee that it would have lasted. The point is that maybe, just maybe, Blake was a little bit in love with Elliot back then. And he can't afford to fall back in love with him now, when Elliot isn't really sure what he wants out of this.

It'll fucking break him.

Elliot, selfishly, without asking for permission, curls himself around Blake as they watch the Winter Classic.

Blake said he wanted space, something he probably wouldn't have even told Elliot a couple of years ago. He would have gotten cagey and would have refused to talk about it. And Elliot will do his best to stay away, but for now Blake's still here and he will make the most of it, because he has no idea what's going to happen next.

They order pizza, eat it in front of the TV, and Elliot sits with his arm brushing against Blake's and Blake lets him.

Elliot hates that he hurt Blake. They were just kids back then and he did what he thought was right for them, thought Blake didn't want to take any unnecessary risks either. He gets why Blake doesn't want to take this too far now. He gets it. And Elliot would never hurt him, not on purpose.

As much as Elliot would like to say that he can deal with this, the hiding, the lying that would come with being with Blake, as much as he wants to say that he's already made up his mind, that he wants to try, Blake is right. Elliot isn't sure. He's scared of what the repercussions might be if someone found out, he's scared of even just telling his teammates that the person he's dating is a man.

Blake is trying to give him an actual choice here, is offering to wait for him to figure out what he wants. But for how long is he going to wait? A month? Two?

"Elliot..."

"Yeah?"

"You're..." Blake drags his hand up and down Elliot's back. "Tense."

"I was just thinking..."

"About?"

"You said you wanted me to think about this."

"Yeah."

"You also said we should give each other a break."

"Yeah."

"So, are we... basically hitting pause?" Elliot asks. "Or are we... hitting stop?"

"Both?"

Elliot huffs. "No, it's not the same thing."

"Then what's the difference?"

"The difference is that in the first case we're sort of on hold, but we're not... I don't know. Are you gonna see other people?"

"What?"

"While we give each other a break, are you gonna–"

"No," Blake says.

"What if I still don't know what I want in a year? Are you willing to wait for that long? Even if I..." Elliot trails off, because he doesn't want to say, *Even if I realize that I can't do this.*

Blake fingers are back in his hair, soothing. "How about we talk about this again at the beginning of summer?"

"Okay," Elliot says. Time passes fast once the season starts to wind down and then suddenly you only have ten games left to play, and then you're getting your playoff schedule and then it's just game after game after game until you're done, or until you win it all.

He can figure this out for himself before the summer. He has to.

Elliot falls asleep sometime during the third period and when he wakes up, Blake is asleep, too. He doesn't wake up when Elliot sits up. The game isn't on TV anymore. Fuck knows who won. Elliot leans down to kiss Blake's forehead, drags his fingers though his hair. "Hey…"

Blake's eyelids flutter, lashes dark against his pale skin. "Come here," he says and reaches for Elliot.

They kiss, lazily, without a care in the world, limbs tangled, Blake's hand on the small of Elliot's back, thumb dipping under his shirt, smoothing over his skin and Elliot is clinging to him like he can somehow get closer to him and keep him here.

Blake doesn't stay for dinner, and maybe Elliot expected as much, but he's still disappointed when Blake says he needs to go. "Gotta feed the kids," he says.

"Give Angus a hug from me," Elliot says.

Blake grabs his sweater, then looks down at the shirt he's wearing. Elliot tells him to keep it and Blake doesn't smile when he pulls on his sweater over it, but he also doesn't *not* smile. It's one of those weird Blake things. He somehow manages to look happy without a real smile on his face.

Elliot kisses him before he pulls on his coat, then kisses him again before he buttons it, then kisses him one more time before Blake leaves, gently squeezing Elliot's hand before he goes. Three kisses, because three has always been his lucky number, and when he was seventeen there was nothing as lucky as kissing Blake Samuels.

When Blake is gone, when the door is closed, and it's just Elliot and his apartment is suddenly quiet, he stands in the hallway, probably for a few minutes, entertaining the absolutely insane idea to run after Blake and tell him to come back, that they'll figure it out somehow. Today.

He knows it's ridiculous.

He still goes hunting for his phone, which he hasn't looked at in… a very long time. He has five missed calls from Adam and a text. *im gonna assume ur hungover but lemme know if ur ded ok?*

Elliot calls him back, because he sort of went off the grid and while he doesn't understand why people should be available to others day and night, it sounds like Adam might have been worried about him.

"Oh, hey, you're not dead," Adam says. "Or are you calling from the afterlife?"

"Sorry," Elliot says. He's grabbing his charger, because he has seven percent battery left and now is not a good time for Adam to think that Elliot hung up on him.

"Did you leave before midnight?"

"Maybe."

"Did you leave alone?"

It takes Elliot a second too long to say, "Yes."

"Are you lying to me right now?" Adam asks. He gasps. "What the fuck?"

"I figured you'd chirp me either way," Elliot says, which is probably a good enough excuse.

Adam tuts at him. "Sooo, did she just leave? Is that why you didn't touch your phone all fucking day?"

"Can we not talk about this?"

"So I'm guessing you're not seeing her again?"

Elliot only sighs in reply.

"I'm just invested in your wellbeing."

"This has nothing to do with my wellbeing," Elliot grumbles.

"*Moo.*"

"What? Stop being overdramatic."

"I'm not. I want you to be happy. Are you happy?"

Elliot is not happy. He still has memories of Blake tugging at him — Blake in his bed, Blake's lips on his, Blake's fingers pulling at his hair, Blake's stubble rubbing against the skin of his thighs. Maybe you could still see it. Maybe he has a mark where Blake kissed his thigh, a hint of teeth following his lips.

"You're not happy," Adam says, interpreting Elliot's silence as just that. "You got laid and you're unhappy."

"Yeah, thanks for the summary."

"Was it bad?"

"No."

"Was it... good?"

"Adam."

"So it was good. Is that the problem? Did she blow your mind and you didn't ask for her number? If she was at the party, we can probably track her down, you know?"

"It's not..." Elliot sighs. He could tell Adam that it was a guy, because Adam knows, but they only ever talked about it *once* and Elliot would rather not bring it up again. "Can we drop it? Please?"

Adam's silence is somehow judgmental. "Tell me if you change your mind," he finally says. "I can find her."

Elliot doesn't doubt that Adam could find her. If she was an actual person that existed.

Blake goes home, feeds Squid and Angus, who are both waiting for him by the door, judging him on his walk of shame down the hallway. He takes off the sweater and he takes off the jeans, but he leaves on the shirt Elliot gave him this morning, and pulls on a pair of sweatpants.

He gets a premade meal out of the freezer and gets it cooking, then he texts Noah and asks him to call him when he has a minute. Afterwards he replies to Charlie and tells him he doesn't need to pay for his cab, that he stayed at a friend's place and took the train back today.

Charlie replies almost instantly: *ill pay for the train then :) sorry i talked u into coming last night, I kno u didnt rly want to go.*

Blake tells him not to worry about it, but doesn't see Charlie's reply, because Noah calls him and greets him with a cheerful, "Tell me you miss me, babe."

"That your girl, Noah?" someone asks.

"No, it's Blake Samuels."

The someone in the background laughs.

"Really?" Blake says.

Noah cackles. "Sorry. You know me, I love to tease and my buddy Phil just can't stop asking stupid questions."

"*Hey,*" says Phil. Presumably.

There's some mumbling, then Noah says, "He left."

"You didn't have to kick him out," Blake says.

"No, I did, it's my room and I'm guessing whatever you want to talk about several hours after midnight on New Year's Eve when all the kissing happens isn't meant for anyone else's ears."

Blake huffs.

"Who'd you kiss?"

"I'm an idiot," Blake says.

"Wow, okay, sure, let's start that way, then," Noah says. "Tell me more, Fishy."

Blake tells him. Everything. Not every single detail, of course, and he mostly focuses on the conversation he had with Elliot this morning, not on what happened last night. Noah hums every now and then, probably in agreement, which seems strange because Blake thought Noah might agree that he's an idiot.

He finishes with, "And now we'll pretend that we're just friends. I'm sure that'll work out great."

"No, but..." Noah hums again. "What you did there... That was a smart choice. Because if you get involved with him and fall in love with him, and I mean more than you already are, and he decides that he's had enough, it'll..."

"Yeah," Blake says. Noah doesn't have to finish.

"Take it from someone who's sleeping with a guy who can't even admit he's gay... you don't need that bullshit in your life."

"Dude, you okay?" Blake says, because Noah doesn't sound okay.

"No, not really, but... I don't know. I don't wanna talk too much about it, because I obviously can't let you figure out who he is, so... Anyway,

178

Fishy, I'm glad that one of us is making reasonable choices instead of constantly running back to a guy who breaks your heart over and over again."

"Noah—"

"No, let's not even talk about it. I know you didn't think I'd turn out to be the bigger idiot here, but I am. I totally am. And it's totally a competition. I won."

"I'm sorry you won," Blake says.

"Yeah, it's... I should tell him not to call me anymore. Or maybe I should stop answering the phone when he calls. I'm the master of my own misery, babe," Noah says. "You and Cowell will figure things out, though."

"Are you just saying that to make me feel better?"

Noah laughs. "Is it working?"

"Not really."

"Aw, damn."

"It's just..." Blake trails off when Squid jumps into his lap, purring as he rolls up into a big orange ball.

"It's just *what*?"

"What if he decides that his career is more important? Or that he doesn't want to do long distance?"

"Long distance? You live as close to him as you possibly can without being on the same team. You hit the fucking jackpot."

"You know what I mean," Blake grumbles.

"Yeah, I know. But you and I made it work."

"We weren't boyfriends, though."

"Wow, way to rub it in."

"Sorry," Blake says. That one's probably overdue. "Really, I'm sorry I hurt you, I honestly didn't—"

"Blake," Noah interrupts, "I'm just teasing. That's ancient history. It's not like you forced me to have feelings for you. They just sort of happened. I got out of there, because sometimes I do make smart choices. We're all good, okay?"

"Okay."

"Good talk," Noah says. "Back to your bullshit. If he decides that hockey is more important, then... maybe you dodged a bullet. I don't know. Blake?"

"Yeah?"

"You deserve someone who loves you more than anything else in the world. Even more than hockey."

Blake isn't sure what to say to that, so he mumbles, "Thank you." It comes out sounding like a question.

"You're welcome, babe. I– Give me one second, someone's knocking."

Blake hears parts of a conversation about dinner, Noah calls someone a dipshit, something about the Emperor of Austria, some mumbling, then, "Hurry the fuck up."

When Noah gets back on the phone, he says, "The guys wanna head out for dinner, can I leave you or do you need more emotional support?"

"I'm okay," Blake says. "Thanks for calling."

"Always, boo. Always."

"Have fun with the guys."

"Thank you. I'll talk to you soon."

Blake hangs up, replies to Charlie and goes to his conversation with Elliot. They haven't actually sent texts back and forth during the last three days. Nothing would really indicate that everything changed last night.

Hi, Blake types.

He deletes it.

Hey, he tries next.

Deletes it.

He looks down at Squid. "I don't care what Noah says, I am an idiot."

Squid looks up at him, blinks, and then goes back to sleep.

"Not helpful," Blake mumbles. "Angus… Hey, Angus, buddy…"

Angus, on the other end of the couch, is looking at him like, *What, me?*

"Come here," Blake says and wiggles his fingers at him. "Come here… that's a good kitty… the best…"

Angus comes over slowly, lets Blake scratch his head, and then makes himself comfortable on a pillow next to Blake, which is great, because now Blake can snap a picture of him.

He sends it to Elliot and says, *Angus says hi :)*

Elliot sends back a bunch of hearts and says, *pet him for me.*

"You're the best cat," Blake says as he gives Angus a pat. Then he does the same with Squid. "And you are the best cat, too."

180

16

Blake gets invited to the All Star Game that season.

"You got too many shutouts, it was inevitable," Charlie says when they announce the roster.

Elliot is going, too, because of course he is. So is Noah, because... yeah. That's just how Blake's life is going these days.

He and Elliot talk. Not a lot. Blake sends pictures of the cats when he misses talking to him, and Elliot sends pictures of his food. They won't play against each other again until the middle of February and Blake isn't even close to New York for two weeks while they're in the West. His cat sitter sends him pictures of the boys, so Blake still has something to send to Elliot, other than photos of palm trees and cacti.

Blake plays against Evan on the road. Evan doesn't score on him and Charlie nearly murders Evan when he nudges Blake after another scoring attempt.

"Call off your dog, dude," Evan shouts.

Blake doesn't, because Charlie probably wouldn't actually punch Blake's brother in the face. They go out for drinks after and Charlie buys the first round and ten minutes later he and Evan are telling each other jokes, Blake sitting between them in silence, thinking he should have probably seen it coming, wondering why he didn't prevent it.

A bunch of girls join them at their table, one of them basically in Evan's lap, and he eventually excuses himself, gives Blake a hug before he goes, and Blake and Charlie wander back to their hotel for curfew.

"Your brother is a bit of a ladies man, huh?" Charlie says.

"I guess. We... don't really talk about that stuff."

"Oh..." Charlie stubbornly stares straight ahead, which probably means that he has something else to say that's currently working its way to the surface. "I still don't know how they all do it."

"Do what?"

"Meet girls," Charlie says. "Do they just walk up to them and talk to them?"

"Uh…"

"How do you do it?" Charlie asks.

"I don't really…" Blake shrugs. He talks to girls because he doesn't want to be rude, but that obviously never goes anywhere. "I was in a relationship a while ago and… I don't really want to get back into one right now." It's not a total lie, because he and Elliot technically were in a relationship, and he and Noah technically were also in some sort of relationship, although it's likely not what Charlie is imagining now.

"Oh, sorry," Charlie says.

"You know, I'm sure the guys wouldn't mind helping you out," Blake says. Brammer loves to play Cupid; he'd be delighted.

Charlie ducks his head. "I don't wanna ask, they're gonna be mean about it."

Blake gets it. He was surprised when Charlie asked him to come to that New Year's party with him. Stuff like that leads to excessive chirping when you ask the wrong guy.

He wouldn't, especially not when it's a guy like Charlie, who looks genuinely hurt when the guys are getting a little too mean in the locker room and blushes when their resident innuendo squad is having a field day. Charlie's great, though. In the room and in front of Blake on the ice.

When Blake is on the bench for the second half of back-to-back games, Charlie is in front of him in the tunnel and holds out his hand.

Blake bumps it with his blocker and Charlie laughs.

"Oh, wait… So Mattie and I hold hands when we go out. We started doing it like a week ago and I've been having really good games and…" Charlie's cheeks turn pink. "You don't have to."

Blake holds out his catching glove and Charlie curls his gloved fingers into it.

Charlie scores a goal and gets two assists and then happily tells the media that it was because Blake held his hand before warm-ups when they all crowd around him after the game. Blake listens to the interview with half an ear, hears one of the reporters asking if Charlie has had an easy time adjusting to a new locker room.

The answer that follows is basically just Charlie going on and on about how kind Blake was to him when he first came into town and how easy he made it for him. "My only complaint is that he didn't keep the guys from giving me ridiculous nicknames," Charlie finishes and Blake chucks a ball of tape at him.

Things are good for the Knights before the All Star break, they're second in their division, which is great, considering their season started with an onslaught of injuries, but they're all back now and Paulie's going to the All Star Game with Blake.

He gets a lot of questions about it before he leaves, how it feels to be going, who he wants to play with. He says Josh Roy, who'll be one of the captains, and it's met by surprise. They probably thought he'd say that it'll be an honor to play with every single player who got invited, which he does add, because that's the expectation here and PR will thank him for it later.

The day before he and Paulie fly to Seattle, where the Sailors are hosting the game, Elliot sends him a text, just *see you tomorrow* and a variety of smiley faces.

Blake forgets to reply because Squid tries to eat his dinner and Blake has to shoo him off the table.

Elliot doesn't deserve a spot at the All Star Game, even though it's his numbers that count here, and his numbers are consistent. He's on pace for more goals than he had last season, but it's strange to go when his team has been struggling, especially during the last four weeks. They're not even in a playoff spot right now.

He texts Blake the day before he flies to Seattle, but Blake doesn't reply. He's probably just busy. Or maybe he'd rather not see Elliot tomorrow, maybe he wishes the All Star Game wasn't forcing them into the same place. Elliot was hoping that he'd get to play with Blake instead of against him for once.

He says hello to Blake when he sees him. Blake says hello to him. He smiles a little. Just the tiniest bit. Could be worse. He could be glaring.

Blake gets drafted before Elliot, to Josh Roy's team, and they pick Elliot, too, two rounds later.

After, Josh Roy is talking to Blake, joking around, saying he only picked Blake because he heard that Blake really wanted to play with him, and Blake's face goes red and Josh laughs and claps his back, turning to Noah Andersson, who's excellent on the ice, and loud-mouthed off it. Elliot doesn't know if he likes him, but when they're all gathered for drinks afterwards, Noah doesn't keep Elliot from going over to Blake, who's talking to Noah, laughing at something he's saying.

Elliot doesn't like that someone else is making Blake laugh like that.

"Oh, look, Elliot Cowell," Noah says, "to what do we owe the honor?"

"Hey," Elliot says.

"Hi," Blake replies.

"I think I'll, uh…" Noah trails off when the Eagles' Morgan Boyle joins them as well and Blake ends up signing a hockey card for Morgan's brother and promises to get him a stick after the game.

Elliot doesn't know much about Morgan, only that the media's always giving him a hard time. He's a quiet guy, but he always plays by the rules, which Elliot appreciates. Their conversation quickly derails into all of them showing each other pictures of their pets, then Morgan and Noah finally leave Elliot alone with Blake. Noah winks at Blake before he goes.

"He's so…" Elliot starts, but trails off when Blake raises his eyebrows at him. "How are you?"

"I'm all right," Blake says. "You?"

"All good," Elliot says. "Nice to be on the same team again. It's been a while."

"Yeah."

Elliot smiles.

"Stop it," Blake mumbles.

"What?"

"You're smiling."

"And I'm not allowed to smile?" Elliot asks.

"No," Blake says and he looks very serious about it.

Elliot ducks his head. "Fine, I'll go smile somewhere else."

Blake rolls his eyes, just when his fellow goaltender, Flynn Jacobi from the Colorado Hawks comes into view and puts an arm around him.

"Samuels, how's it going?"

Elliot excuses himself, because he really can't stand here and listen to Blake and Jacobi talk about goalie shit, and finds someone else to talk to. He ends up standing with Morgan Boyle again, talking about the season so far. And maybe Morgan's a little serious, speaks very softly and doesn't easily crack a smile, but Elliot quickly realizes that it's nothing personal, it's just the way he talks. Like he's cautious, trying not to offend anyone.

Some of the guys come over to them, always talking to Elliot first, nodding at Morgan second and Elliot tries to keep him in those conversations, throws a few questions his way, so he won't just awkwardly hover next to them.

When the guys slowly start to disperse, Morgan says, "I'll head back to my room. It was nice talking to you, Elliot."

Elliot decides to head back as well, looking around to find Blake before he leaves but he's apparently gone already or hiding somewhere. His phone is heavy in his pocket. The last time he sent Blake a text, he didn't even reply, and maybe he's already asleep.

He looks at his phone.

He shouldn't text him. Because they're giving each other a break. And Elliot's stomach still turns when he thinks about telling more people that he's not straight, his heartbeat still becomes unsteady when he imagines someone finding out, so he can't in all honesty say that he's made up his mind about what he wants to do.

But he wants to see Blake.

He still shouldn't text him.

Elliot grabs his phone.

you wanna hang out? he asks, and quickly adds, *it's ok if you say no.*

Blake almost doesn't check his phone when it buzzes. He's changing into his pajamas, doing a terrible job at brushing his teeth as he pulls up his pants.

His phone buzzes again.

He's sort of expecting Noah to chirp him about something when he finally grabs his phone, but then finds two texts from Elliot, asking if he wants to hang out in the first one, saying it's okay if Blake says no in the second.

Blake sighs.

He should say no.

He sends Elliot his room number instead.

Then he pulls on a shirt. He doesn't usually sleep in one when it's just him, but it seems like a good idea. Because they're really only hanging out. Nothing else. Blake will stick with that, anything else will make things more complicated.

Elliot knocks on his door five minutes later, looking much less polished than he did earlier, wearing sweatpants and an All Star Game shirt, his hair messy. Soft.

Blake steps back to let him in without a word, pushes the door shut, and then Elliot is hovering there and it would be so easy to reach out, to pull him in, kiss him until they're both breathless and then splay him out on his bed, get those sweatpants off, press his lips against the soft skin of Elliot's thighs...

"I swear I'm not here to..." Elliot shrugs. "I really just wanted to see you."

"Yeah," Blake says. *Yeah,* because that's exactly what he asked for. "You wanna watch a movie or something?"

Elliot nods and, with some reluctance, makes himself comfortable on Blake's bed, Blake next to him, making sure there's some space between them. He lets Elliot pick the movie. They don't say much, only mumbling to each other now and again to comment on how terrible the movie is.

Blake isn't really expecting Elliot's finger to land on his arm.

"Did those hurt?" Elliot asks, tracing a line of waves on Blake's forearm.

"Yeah," Blake says, because they really did. Took a long time, too. He didn't get them all at the same time.

Elliot hums, fingers curled around Blake's wrist, turning over his arm. "I like them a lot." He nods at the sleeve of Blake's shirt. "Can you..."

Blake pulls it up as far as it'll go. This isn't the first time that someone's looking at his tattoos; he's used to it. Brammer lost his shit the first time he saw the full sleeve, kept turning Blake's arm over until Blake told him to knock it off, grabbing Mattie's stick to poke him until he escaped across the room. Loads of people have asked to see it. But when it's Elliot's fingers on his skin, it's different. His cheeks turn hot with Elliot's eyes on him.

"What about the other side?" Elliot asks.

"You want me to turn over?"

Elliot shrugs. "You don't have to."

Blake shifts, lies on his side so Elliot can see the other arm, his fingers quickly finding Connecticut, the line of trees above it.

"Your parents birthdates?" Elliot asks when the tip of his finger stops on the line of numbers that is hiding in the feathers on Blake's forearm.

Blake nods and turns his arms so Elliot can see the others.

"And your grandma's?"

Blake hums.

"And… Evan's?"

"Yeah."

"That's nice," Elliot says. His fingers linger on Blake's arm for a moment, then he pulls them away, lies down on his side as well, facing Blake, and says, "I'm sorry."

"About what?"

"About… this," Elliot says.

Ah. Yeah. *This*.

"I shouldn't even have to make a decision," Elliot says. "It shouldn't be… How can you even still want to be with me when I can't say, 'Yes, Blake, I want to be with you,' right now?"

"Because it's not that easy. I know it's not that easy."

"Aren't you scared?" Elliot asks. "That someone could find out? And then…"

Blake has to think about it for a moment, because the thought of someone finding out doesn't sit well with him at all, but is he really *scared* of it? "I think the chances of someone finding out are relatively slim," Blake says. "And I think that our teams would probably mind their own business if they knew…" He bites his lip, another thought about to slip out. He's not sure if he wants to put it out there. "Half my team probably knows that I'm gay."

Elliot frowns. "How?"

"I don't have a girlfriend. I've never had one. And they stopped asking after a while and they stopped trying to set me up and all that. So the guys that have been around long enough… They probably know."

"But they haven't said anything."

"No."

"And you haven't said anything."

"No," Blake says. "I was thinking about telling Charlie. And Mattie. I just... never did."

"I don't know how I managed to tell you," Elliot mumbles.

"Was it because of the lesbians?" Blake asks. His grandma was friends with two lesbians who frequently dropped by. One of them still lives across the street. Elliot met them the first time he was at Blake's house, a little taken aback when his grandma told them that the lesbians were coming over for dinner.

Elliot laughs. "Yeah, it was probably because of the lesbians. What happened to them?"

"One of them died a few years ago. Martha," Blake says. "I think she was eighty-seven. And Gladys is still alive and Evan said she came by when he was home during the summer and brought him a casserole."

"That's nice of her," Elliot says. He yawns and curls in on himself a little.

"Yeah."

"That was a good summer." Elliot is starting to sound sleepy, eyelids fluttering. "When I was there... and we were..." He smiles.

Blake should kick him out before he falls asleep, because he knows he won't if Elliot falls asleep in his bed. "Have you been to Iceland yet?" Blake asks.

"No," Elliot says.

"Seriously? Why not?"

"I don't know." Elliot's eyes are definitely closed now. "You should go with me."

"I..." Blake sighs. "Elliot?"

"Hmmm."

"Elliot."

"Hm."

"You're fucking killing me," Blake says. "Go back to your room."

This time he doesn't even get the vaguest of sounds in reply.

When Elliot wakes up, it's three in the morning and he's still in Blake's bed.

He knew he was starting to get tired and could have left, and then *didn't*. And Blake clearly didn't wake him up. Elliot wouldn't have woken him up either if he'd fallen asleep in his bed. He gets up slowly, careful not to shake the mattress, grabs his phone and his room key, pulls on his shoes, and then tiptoes around the bed, tripping over one of Blake's shoes.

Blake doesn't wake up when Elliot curses loudly. Blake is on his back now, snoring quietly. Elliot wants to lie back down next to him so badly, pretend that he didn't wake up and just sleep here, with a few inches between them, but then he'd hope that he'd roll against Blake in the night, that Blake would put his arm around him and that he'd wake up with Blake's breath tickling the back of his neck.

Most of the time, sleeping that close to someone isn't that great anyway, it gets too hot and you end up with someone's knee jamming into your thigh or someone's elbow in your ribs, and it's really not that romantic. But Elliot still stares at Blake for at least a minute, contemplating how cross he'd be with himself in the morning.

He really needs to go.

At least he manages to get out of Blake's room without tripping over anything else and the door shuts behind him with a quiet click.

He's halfway down the hall to the elevators — his room is one floor up — when a door opens behind him and Noah Andersson not-very-stealthily slips out into the hallway. He freezes when he sees Elliot, who's also frozen to the spot, because there's really not a good explanation for sneaking out of someone else's room at three in the morning. And, okay, Elliot is standing in the hallway, but there's also no good explanation for standing in the hallway at three in the morning.

Noah walks up to him, somehow managing to look casual about it. His shoes aren't tied and his shirt is buttoned up the wrong way.

"Headed for the elevator?" Noah asks.

"Yeah," Elliot says and starts walking again, with Noah following at his heels.

"What a coincidence," Noah says, "so am I."

Elliot pushes the button for the elevator and it takes forever to come, and they're only going up one floor, both of them, Elliot nodding when Noah hits the button for the fifth floor, and it still seems like the longest elevator ride in Elliot's life.

"Hey, uh, if I don't mention this to anyone and you don't mention this to anyone," Noah says, "it'll sort of be like it never even happened."

"Yeah," Elliot says. "Great. Let's… never mention this to anyone."

The doors glide open, Noah nods at him and quickly struts away.

Elliot follows, but walks the other way, to his room, fumbles with the key card, nearly drops it, and then jams it into the slot with a little too much force, eager to get out of this hallway.

He lets out a deep sigh when he's finally in his room and then lies awake in bed for half an hour.

Elliot doesn't have a chance to talk to Blake the next day, at least not in private. They're around each other and they do talk, but there's always someone else there. Someone asks for a picture of the two of them, since they were on the same team in juniors and Elliot sees later that their junior team retweeted the picture, adding another one from when they were still on the team. Elliot doesn't remember that picture even being taken – it's just him and Blake on the ice, probably after practice, Blake covering Elliot's head with his catching glove.

"Do you remember this?" Elliot asks when he shows Blake.

"Yeah," Blake says, "I have that one at home somewhere."

"Huh," Elliot says and looks down at it again.

They're interrupted by George Tremblay's kid, who's been making her way around the locker room with a jersey and a sharpie, asking them very politely if they could please sign her jersey. Her dad, probably one of the biggest and scariest D-men in the league, is looking on fondly. He doesn't usually look fond on the ice and Elliot is happy that he'll be on their team tomorrow.

There's some interviews, then the skills competition, and Elliot borrows Tremblay's kid for the breakaway challenge and apparently he's her new favorite person after that, because she won't go back to her dad and sits with Elliot until her dad forcibly removes her. She finds Elliot again afterwards and tugs him with her so her mom can take a picture of them.

Then there's more interviews.

That night, Elliot goes to sleep in his own bed and he doesn't ask Blake if he can come to his room again.

They win the game the next day and Elliot scores twice with Morgan Boyle on his line. They exchange sticks after the game, and then Elliot takes one of his other sticks over to Blake, who's in the middle of taking off his pads, and gives him a tap.

"You wanna exchange sticks?" Elliot asks. It's ridiculous, because they're good enough friends that Elliot can ask Blake for a stick whenever he wants and Blake would probably give it to him, but this is a special occasion and if there's anyone's stick that Elliot wants to take home with him, it's Blake's. "If you still have one left."

"Yeah, I only promised one to Morgan," Blake says and gets up to grab one of his sticks. "Want me to sign it?"

"You have to do the fish," Elliot says.

"I always do the fish, but I'll make it really big for you and give him a face, okay?" Blake says with the straightest face imaginable and then turns around to ask someone for a sharpie.

Elliot signs his stick for Blake in the meantime and Josh Roy comes by to give each of them a pat and to thank them for playing well.

They end up on the same flight back to New York, but Blake's sitting next to his teammate and they're talking about how weird it was to be on different teams when Elliot passes them to sit down behind them. Paul Mooney nods at him, and Blake smiles, just a little.

189

Elliot sits down, buckles in, gets his headphones and goes right to sleep, because that's really the only way of dealing with sitting behind Blake for several hours.

17

The Ravens clinch their playoff spot in their second to last game of the season, on the road, in Hartford, of all places. They haven't won a game against the Cardinals all season and the boys are in good spirits in the locker room after. There's a good chance that they'll be playing against them during the first round, unless the Knights knock them out of the first seed. If the Knights win their game on Saturday and the Cardinals lose their last game of the season, the Ravens will be seeing the Knights early on.

Elliot keeps telling himself that he has no control over the outcome anyway, that it doesn't matter who they end up playing against, because they'll try to win either way. There's no way of telling which opponent will be easier, there's no guarantees during the playoffs. Teams that won the President's Trophy sometimes don't make it to the finals, teams that had to claw their way into a wildcard spot sometimes end up taking their opponents by surprise. Elliot daydreams about being one of those teams, season after season fighting for a playoff spot, barely making it, and then going far one year, giving the team some confidence.

He knows it's really just that. A daydream.

They're lucky they're making the playoffs at all.

Elliot goes out for drinks with the guys after the game, but he doesn't stay for long. He's tired and he blocked a shot during the game, his thigh throbbing dully now, and he wants nothing more than to curl up in bed and stay there for a week, but he doesn't get that kind of luxury.

They're going to Boston tomorrow, to play their last game of the season on Saturday. They already had their last game at home, a 7-2 loss against Toronto. It wasn't exactly a great way to close out the season at home, but at least they'll be back for the first round of playoffs and they'll have more than one chance to redeem themselves.

"Hey, Moo, wait for me."

Elliot turns around and finds Adam speed-walking up to him. "Hey," Elliot says. "Heading back, too?"

"Yeah, not gonna lie, I'm tired as fuck," Adam mumbles.

Elliot nods and gives him a pat on the back.

They're mostly silent as they walk, until Adam clears his throat and says, "Are you ever scared that we're just... never gonna win the Cup? Like, what if it's just us barely making it for the next ten years or something?"

It's not like Elliot hasn't thought about it. There are so many variables to this sort of thing. Of course, you can always sign with another team, or even ask to be traded when you think the team you're on isn't going anywhere, but then maybe the next year is your team's year and you're somewhere else, watching your former team win the Cup from afar.

It's not like Elliot is unhappy in New York. He loves his team, he loves the city, their fans, and if someone asked him if he wanted to leave right now, Elliot would say no, absolutely not, he'll stay as long as they'll have him, but he knows where Adam's coming from. And Adam only has about a year left on his contract.

"Are you thinking about leaving?" Elliot asks.

"No, not really," Adam says. "Just... Don't you think about it sometimes?"

"I do. Sometimes."

"There are so many players that are so, so good, like... Blake MacDonald? Hasn't won a Cup with the Sailors. Or Ian Grey with the Lions? No Cup. How is that fair?"

Elliot only shrugs, because he doesn't have an explanation for it either.

"I'm not going to leave you, though, Moo, I swear," Adam says. "You'll never get rid of me. Unless the Ravens get rid of me."

"They wouldn't," Elliot says. He can't even imagine being on a line with someone other than Andreas and Adam. They're his guys. They work together, they produce, they get along well off the ice, too. They've had a couple of coaching changes over the years, but every single coach they've had saw that they were better together.

That doesn't change that guys come and go, though. Magnus was great on his line, too. He still got traded.

"Maybe this year is our year," Adam says.

Elliot nods, says, "Yeah, maybe," his stomach in knots when he realizes that he doesn't actually mean it.

"Hey, Moo..."

"Yeah?"

Adam smirks. "Can you keep a secret?"

"Sure," Elliot says.

"Don't tell anyone, yeah?" Adam leans closer, like he does sometimes when he pretends that he has something important to say and then just flicks Elliot's nose and cackles. This time, he doesn't. He says, "I'm gonna be a dad, Moo."

"For real?"

"Yeah, Lou's pregnant."

Elliot has never been told how to react when your best friend tells you that he'll be a father, so he hugs Adam and says, "That's great, Adam." He's pretty sure that Adam is excited about this. Adam sounded excited.

It's such a grown-up thing to do. And it's not that Elliot can't see Adam as a dad, but the thought simply never occurred to him. That this is an imminent development in their lives.

Elliot's parents have been asking him if he's seeing anyone and Elliot has so far evaded those questions, changing the subject whenever anything relationship-related came up. His mom did ask him if he's *looking* not too long ago and Elliot said something non-committal. He knows his parents want grandchildren, talk about it whenever a major holiday rolls around and it gives Elliot anxiety, because he's too young to even think about having children, although Adam, who's only about a year older than him, is about to become a dad.

"But, seriously," Adam says, "don't tell anyone yet, the thing has only been hanging out in there for like seven weeks and Lou doesn't really want to spread it around yet."

"The *thing*?"

"I don't know what it is yet," Adam says with a shrug. "It's a thing. Cell Blob. Lou hates it when I call it that, but she calls it an alien, so who the fuck is the worse parent here?"

Elliot laughs. "So you are gonna find out what it is?"

"Probably. Lou likes knowing stuff like that. Maybe she'll know and I won't. I don't know. I kinda really want a girl. Which is weird, because all the guys always want boys, but a girl would be nice, I... Not that I'd be disappointed if it's a boy." Adam groans. "I'm such a terrible dad already."

"Nah, you'll be fine," Elliot says.

Adam reaches over to pat his head. "How does it feel to be an uncle?"

"I'm not actually an uncle."

"You will be in a couple of months."

Elliot gives Adam another hug. The Ravens would be a much worse team without him.

The last game of the season actually means something for the Knights this year. There are no call-ups on the ice. It's their regular roster that gets dressed for the game, it's Blake in the crease.

Mattie, in the stall next to him, looks a little wistful when he puts on his baseball cap. He's played his last game of the season, maybe even the last game of his career. Blake doesn't know what he'll do without him.

"Don't look at me like that," Mattie grumbles.

Blake looks away.

"Gonna fuckin' make me cry," Mattie says and waddles away, giving Brammer a shove when he passes him.

Brammer splutters and falls silent halfway through his rendition of 'Let It Go'. Half the room applauds and Mattie salutes them before he ducks out of the room. Blake can see it on the guys' faces, the exact way he feels, thinking about not having Mattie around anymore next year. He's the oldest guy on the roster right now, the rest of the team relatively young. They're down to a handful of guys who were already here when Blake played his first full season with the team.

There are tons of signs for Mattie pressed against the glass during warmups, and Mattie's out there throwing pucks to people. Blake doesn't know what to do with himself. Mattie told him he wasn't going to keep playing. Blake knew and it still hurts. So much for seeing it coming.

He hasn't announced it officially yet, but whenever Mattie talked to the media, questions came up, about Mattie's contract, about his plans, and every time Mattie said that now was not the time to worry about that, but the media drew their conclusions and most of them hit the nail on the head – Jake Matthews is likely to retire at the end of the season.

The game itself is actually fun once Blake manages to focus and gets his head in the game, his eyes on the ice, on the puck.

He doesn't think about getting into the first seed.

He doesn't think about which team they'll end up facing in the first round, if it'll be the Eagles or the Ravens.

He doesn't think about Elliot.

He doesn't think about winning the Cup for Mattie.

He thinks about the puck.

The arena is loud tonight, the fans excited for the playoffs, not caring whether the Knights will end up in the first or second seed. They'll have home ice either way. They'll be back here soon and then the real fight begins.

Blake is vaguely aware of the fans chanting his name when he makes save after save, the scoreboard showing two goals in the Knights' favor at the end of the second period. No goals for Ottawa.

They pull their goalie with two minutes left in the game and things get heated around Blake's net. Ottawa is so far out of playoff contention that a win would do absolutely nothing for them, but they have some fight left in them. Players get tangled up, Blake ends up with some room in front of the net and the puck on his stick and he hurls it out of the zone with as much force as he can.

He doesn't mean to score a goal. He's tried before, but it never went in and he's pretty sure that the angle's off.

Everyone starts racing after the puck, but no one manages to catch up with it before it slides into the net. A few inches to the left and it would have gone right past it.

Charlie jumps into Blake's arms when the goal horn goes, the rest of the guys not far behind. He gets first star of the game and the crowd is losing it. Blake has never seen that many people still in the stands after a game. He's dead-tired, but after he's done his interview, he sticks around to sign some jerseys, bump some fists, and then disappears down the tunnel where the team is waiting for him, everyone shouting as he waddles into the locker room.

It's Mattie who hands him his puck, and they take a picture together, and afterwards Blake hugs him very, very tightly and tries very, very hard not to cry.

As they're all getting out of their gear, someone announces that the Cardinals lost their game tonight, which means the Knights will see the Ravens next week. Blake wonders if Elliot already knows. He doesn't have time to check his phone, because he has to talk to the media tonight. He probably would have had to talk to them even without the goal. He got a shutout on top of it all, so they're all crowding around him, forcing Mattie and Charlie out of their stalls.

The questions aren't that hard to deal with, mostly because they're all about the goal. Blake wishes he'd had a chance to watch a replay of it, because he barely even remembers how it happened. He tried to get it away from his net, he wasn't exactly planning on putting it in the other one.

They all go out for drinks after the game and invade one of their favorite pubs. They seem to have known that they were coming, probably because Paulie called ahead. Mattie goes out with them tonight as well, usually one of the first ones to beg off, and he buys Blake his first drink.

A lot of people want to buy Blake drinks tonight.

He tries not to overdo it, starts to politely decline more offers, and has to start declining other offers, too, when Brammer's girlfriend and her friends arrive, three of them crowding around him to ask him about the goal he scored. Blake manages to escape and basically hides behind Mattie, who's actually an inch shorter than him.

"You wanna go home, kid?" Mattie asks. "I'll sneak you out."

A bunch of the guys have left and Blake wasn't planning on sticking around much longer either, so he nods.

"Choo Choo already left, huh? Need a ride home?"

"Yeah, thanks, Mattie," Blake says.

Mattie rarely has more than one beer and is happy to drive home anyone who needs a ride. He's looking around the bar now to see if anyone else might need a ride, but most of the guys that are left don't live too far from the arena. Anyway, they can easily afford a cab.

"Mattie," Blake says when they're in the car.

"If you say anything sappy, I'll make you walk," Mattie says, grinning as he starts the car. "I haven't retired yet."

"I know."

"It's time, kid."

Blake nods.

They drive in silence, the radio turned down so low that Blake can barely hear it. The streets are mostly quiet.

Something's ending right now, it's been ending all season. He wants to ask Mattie if he'll stay in the area of if he'll take his family to Canada, but decides that he's not ready to hear the answer to that, if Mattie even has one.

The drive to his place is short, only takes a few minutes. Mattie pulls over outside the door and gives Blake's thigh a pat. "Nice goal tonight, kid. You'll remember that one for a while."

Blake smiles. "Yeah." He doesn't get out of the car yet. There's something strange about tonight, like nothing's the way it's supposed to be. "Mattie…"

"Yeah?"

"I'm gay." Blake takes a deep breath. It helps that he's managed to convince himself that Mattie probably already knew. "You probably guessed that already, but…"

"Listen, kid, your private life isn't any of my business. I wasn't guessing."

"Really?"

"I've been around a little longer than you and you're not the first guy who's never brought a girlfriend and who looked like he wanted to go into hiding whenever anyone asked, so…" Mattie shrugs, then reaches out to put his hand on Blake's shoulder. "I don't want you to think that anything changed here. I'm still me and you're still you, and you should come over for dinner tomorrow."

Blake desperately wants to ask about the other guys, but Mattie would never tell him. In the end, he just says okay to dinner.

"If you have a boyfriend," Mattie says, "he's always welcome at my house, too."

Blake clears his throat. "No boyfriend."

"It's not an offer that expires," Mattie says.

"Thank you," Blake replies, and tries not to think about showing up for dinner at Mattie's house with Elliot in tow.

Elliot and Blake agree that for the duration of the first round of the playoffs, they're not friends. They won't talk to each other. No chirping, not even unrelated cat and food pictures. Nothing.

They'll go dead silent.

The day before the game, they send each other good luck texts. And that's it.

Elliot can barely focus before their first game against the Knights. It's the same thing every year. Once playoffs roll around, it's like he's playing hockey for the first time.

Their first game goes into overtime and the Knights win it, the arena exploding in cheers as the Ravens make their way off the ice. It's only one game and it's not over until they've lost four, but the room is quiet after the game and Elliot isn't in the mood for post-game interviews at all.

One of the reporters asks him how he's feeling about the loss and Elliot stares at him for a few long seconds before he says, "Not great."

When he gets home that night he's still pissed off. He texts Blake, because he doesn't give a shit about the deal they made the day before and Blake sends back a sad face no five minutes later. Elliot almost calls him, but can't think of a thing to say, because he lost against Blake's team and how the hell is Blake supposed to cheer him up? Blake is probably busy celebrating right now. Elliot nearly scored on him in overtime, but he made the save, allowing Paul Mooney to grab the rebound and take off with it. The game was over less than a minute later.

They play in Newark again two days later. Another loss, this one a lot clearer. It's a 4-1 win for the Knights, the Ravens' lone goal scored by Andreas.

And yet, nothing's decided. They'll play in New York next, two games on home ice and they have a chance to tie up the series again, win two at home, take it to Game 5. After the game, Blake has already sent him a sad face and Elliot sends a sad face back, because he has nothing else to say anyway. He wishes he could go home and have Blake waiting for him in bed, curl against him, have Blake hold him close.

Elliot's bed is cold when he curls himself into a ball under the covers. He barely sleeps that night, wakes up every so often and stares into the darkness of his room.

The guys are exhausted when he sees them for their next morning skate. Everyone's tired, the look on Coach Peterson's face is grim. Elliot doesn't expect him to be around next season if the Ravens don't make it far into the playoffs. He's scared to think about what their roster will look like.

Elliot tells himself to get it together. They've lost two games. It's not like they've lost it all.

They fight hard during Game 3.

They still lose.

It's not the first time they've been here, looking a sweep in the eye.

Elliot sits in his stall, with half his gear still on, long after the reporters have dispersed. There's barely a chance of coming back from this. Maybe they'll manage to win the next game. Maybe they'll even manage to win two. But four? It's not impossible, but the entire room knows that it's unlikely. All they can do the day after tomorrow is to play like they haven't already lost.

He gets home late, exhausted.

When he checks his phone, he has a missed call from Blake and a voicemail. Elliot crawls into bed without listening to it, closes his eyes, but doesn't fall asleep. He finally grabs his phone and listens to Blake's message after all.

"Hey, uh, it's Blake," he says, "I know you probably don't want to talk to me right now and we're not even friends until all of this is over, but... I don't know, you looked... I just wanted to make sure you're okay. You don't deserve this. You're such a pain in the ass to play against, you know? I don't... Well, you don't need me to tell you that this sucks... Anyway. I probably shouldn't have called. And I'm sorry. I... I'll talk to you soon. Bye."

Elliot sighs. Something heavy is sitting on his chest, something restless is living under his skin.

He is so, so tired.

It's a clean sweep in the end.

Elliot scores twice in Game 4, Andreas scores, Crab scores, but the Knights are always one goal ahead of them and eventually the clock runs down and leaves them with a score of 5-4, the Ravens eliminated from the playoffs, the Knights celebrating on the other end of the ice, crowding around Blake.

Elliot starts to lead the handshake line. They want to get off the ice. Elliot puts an arm around Crab while they wait for Brian Kelly to lead the Knights their way.

Kelly hugs Elliot, tells him they fought hard, that he could tell that Elliot did everything in his power to drag his team to the next round. Elliot tells him to win it all. They'd all rather lose to the team that ends up winning the Cup than to a team that'll get eliminated during the next round. Kelly smiles at him, pats his head and sends him on his way.

Elliot dreads making it to Blake, not sure if he should shake his hand or hug him. Blake takes the decision away from him, because he's the one who goes in for a hug in the end. They say something meaningless. A few more players, coaches, then Elliot can finally get off the ice.

Elliot is pretty sure that Crab is close to tears, probably blaming himself for the last goal the Knights scored. Elliot goes and hugs him tightly, then he makes his way over to Swanson, to give his shoulder a squeeze. Swanson scowls.

The post-game interviews are torture, as they've been for the entire postseason. Nothing new there. It's all, yes, of course they're not happy with this outcome, and, yes, everyone fought hard and, yes, Elliot is still proud of every single player on his team, but the Knights outplayed them in the end.

He stays in the shower for a long time, goes home, goes to bed, on edge, like his brain hasn't caught up with what happened and still thinks they'll play another game a few days from now.

They have the next day off and Elliot invites the team out for brunch at a place they sometimes go to after practice. Elliot calls them, his name enough to get them a private room on short notice without any problems.

The next day they have exit interviews, locker room clean-out. Adam invites him over for dinner. "You know, in a week or something. When we've got most of the moping out of the way."

Elliot nods and shuffles away to hug the guys that are leaving town soon – Crab, who's going to his parents' place in Halifax, and Andreas, who'll go to Germany for the summer.

He's still at the Ravens' practice facility when he gets a call from Team USA, asking if he's interested in playing at the World Cup. He says yes without even thinking about it. He's not done with hockey this season.

Gear in his trunk, Elliot sits in the driver's seat, staring down at his phone. He thinks about calling Blake.

The Knights have some time off now, because whoever will be their opponent in the next round isn't decided yet. The Cardinals-Eagles series is tied at two, so they'll play at least two more games. Blake is probably home.

Elliot should call Blake before he goes all the way to fucking Newark.

He doesn't. He just starts driving.

Blake is taking a nap with Squid when his doorbell rings. It's the middle of the afternoon. When Blake fell asleep the sun was shining, now it's pouring down rain.

He gets up, makes sure he doesn't look too rumpled, in case it's anyone other than Charlie outside his door, and then shuffles into the hallway.

It's not Charlie outside his door. He should have known, because Charlie knocks.

It's Elliot.

And he's dripping.

"You're all wet," Blake says.

"It's raining," Elliot replies.

"Oh."

"Yeah."

Blake looks at him, at the Ravens shirt plastered to his chest and the dripping curls sticking to his forehead. He looks absolutely miserable.

"I'm sorry," Elliot says, "Some guy who felt bad for me let me in through the front door and I guess I should have called, but I was scared that you'd tell me not to come and—"

"Hey," Blake says and tugs Elliot into his apartment. "It's fine."

Elliot nods, breath catching when Blake pulls him into a hug. Blake's shirt is getting wet now, too, but he doesn't let go for at least a few minutes. Elliot clearly needs this hug, has probably needed it ever since they lost the first game against the Knights.

Blake doesn't say he's sorry, because Elliot likely wouldn't want to hear it anyway.

"Here, let's…" Blake gently pats Elliot's back. "Let's find you something dry to wear and I'll throw your stuff in the dryer. Did you walk here from the station?"

"No, I parked my car in the parking garage down the street and I didn't have an umbrella," Elliot mutters as he takes off his shoes.

Blake finds him a shirt and a pair of sweatpants, and then gets a shirt for himself, too, because he didn't stay dry when he hugged Elliot either.

"You want anything to eat?" Blake asks as he wanders out of his bedroom, because he'd rather not hover next to Elliot while he's changing.

"No."

"Water? Or a beer?"

"What time is it?"

"Not sure if that matters today," Blake says.

"Water is fine." Elliot comes out of Blake's bedroom, tugging at the shirt Blake gave him, a little big on him, and Blake instantly wants to pull him in again. He leads the way into the kitchen instead.

"Ice cream?" Blake asks.

Elliot hesitates for a moment. "I guess…"

Blake nods at the freezer. "Get whatever you want."

Elliot grabs a pint of Phish Food and a big spoon while Blake grabs them two glasses of water.

"What do you wanna do?" Blake asks.

The look Elliot shoots him is probing. "Movie?"

"Okay."

"Can I…"

"What?" Blake asks.

Elliot shakes his head.

"What?" Blake asks again. Today Elliot can have whatever the hell he wants and Elliot probably knows that. There's no way Blake will say no to a single thing.

"I don't wanna go back home."

Blake nods. Elliot can stay. Hell, he can stay for a week.

"Really?" Elliot asks.

"We have practice tomorrow, but you can stay as long as you want."

"I'll make you breakfast," Elliot says.

"You don't have to," Blake mumbles and sits down in his favorite corner on the couch, Elliot next to him, right there, not even pretending that he's trying to leave some space between them.

Elliot picks a movie they've both seen a million times, then glances at Blake, glances at the TV, then back at Blake.

"Here," Blake says and reaches for him, pulls him closer until Elliot's head is on his chest. His hair is still damp.

"I'm so tired of losing all the time," Elliot whispers. "I know we're better than this, I don't know why we never make it."

Blake doesn't know what to say. For the past couple of years, the Ravens were okay. They weren't terrible, but they weren't great either, always only barely making the playoffs, sometimes slipping out of a wildcard spot altogether. They only made it past the first round once. It's better than not making it at all, but Blake gets it. He would probably be hiding in bed for a week if his team got swept in the first round. He curls his fingers around the back of Elliot's neck and drags his thumb over the soft skin there.

Elliot sniffles.

Blake doesn't try to talk to him, leaves him be, because there's nothing he can say anyway. The Ravens lost. It's part of the game. And it hurts. And Elliot will get another chance next year, but next year is ages away. Blake can't believe Elliot came to him after all this, sort of wants to ask him how he can even stand being in the same room as him right now.

He stays very still, and doesn't realize that Elliot has fallen asleep until Angus joins them on the couch and Elliot doesn't reach out to pet him. Blake runs his fingers through his hair for a while, grabs his phone and texts Noah.

Elliot sleeps through the entire movie and Blake isn't really paying attention either, scrolling through Twitter and Instagram, posting another picture of Squid that he took this morning.

"Hey, Angus," Elliot whispers, scaring the crap out of Blake.

He nearly drops his phone on Elliot's head.

"Did I just... nap on you?" Elliot sits up and tugs his fingers through his hair. "Sorry, I haven't been sleeping and I—"

"It's okay," Blake says quickly. "Hungry?"

Elliot nods. "You know," he says, "I think you owe me fifty dumplings."

"You want those today?" Blake asks.

"Nah, I think I can wait," Elliot says and gently pats Blake's chest, then pulls his hand away and sits up.

Blake almost wants to pull him back against him. "I'll throw something together for dinner, okay?"

"Do you mind if I cook?"

"Um... if you want to?"

So he ends up watching Elliot dig through his kitchen, putting together a stir-fry, shooing Blake away every time he asks if he can help, giving him the evil eye – which is not very evil in Elliot's case – every time he tries to steal raw vegetables from Elliot's cutting board.

"Careful," Elliot hisses. "I'm gonna cut off your fingers and then what?"

Blake snorts and ducks out of the way, grabbing them two plates while Elliot mutters about how Blake's pans are all inadequate somehow. He does manage to cook their food in the end, frowning down at his chosen pan like this is part of some high-stakes operation, like they can't order pizza if dinner doesn't turn out to be edible.

And it does turn out fine, even though Elliot is grumbling about how the chicken isn't exactly the way he wanted it to be.

"The chicken is great," Blake says.

"But I wanted to—"

Blake kicks him under the table, and Elliot kicks him back, and then it goes back and forth a couple of times until Elliot winces.

"You okay?"

"Yeah, I just have a gigantic bruise on my leg, it's fine, though, don't worry."

"Sorry," Blake says.

Elliot shrugs and kicks him back one more time.

Elliot arrived at Blake's without much of a plan, fully expecting that Blake would tell him to go home.

He realizes that he's making things harder for both of them, because Elliot is far from making up his mind about anything, has barely had time to gather even a handful of coherent thoughts. He dragged himself through their playoff games, one game after the other, worried about nothing but hockey. He doesn't know what's going to happen next, other than that he'll be on his way to Prague soon.

"I'm going to play at Worlds," Elliot tells Blake when they're cleaning up after dinner.

Blake's smile is soft. "I'm glad."

"And you'll go as far as you can."

"Obviously."

"Until you win the Cup."

Blake rolls his eyes at him. "I'll do what I can."

"I know you will," Elliot says. "I want you to win it."

"Elliot, everyone wants to win it. But there's thirty-two teams in the league and half of them get a playoff spot. Even if you're in the playoffs, you're still competing against fifteen other teams."

"I know, but... what's the point if you don't believe in winning it?"

"I'm trying to be realistic," Blake says with a shrug.

Elliot chews on his bottom lip, trying to keep all his thoughts in. He knows that most of the stuff he's thinking is completely ridiculous and he's putting himself down, because that's what you do after a loss like that.

"Hey," Blake says, because of fucking course he can see it all on his face, and then Blake's hand is cupping his cheek and Elliot can't keep it in after that.

"I stopped thinking we could win against you at some point," Elliot says. "What if I jinxed it because I thought there was no way we could win it anymore after we'd lost three?"

"Elliot," Blake says, stepping closer.

"I know it's stupid, but I can't stop thinking about it. I thought about it all of last night. I didn't do enough and—"

"You did *everything*."

"But it wasn't enough."

"You're not the only guy on your team," Blake says.

He pulls Elliot closer, against his chest, and Elliot doesn't really cry easily, maybe he'll have tears in his eyes after a sad movie, but you won't really find him on the couch, sobbing into his bowl of popcorn or anything.

He cries now, though, because he's been trying to hold it back for days, telling his guys in the locker room that they'd get another chance next season, that he's proud of them for giving everything, that he couldn't possibly have any better teammates. But now, with Blake, he doesn't have to be strong or hopeful or proud of anything.

Blake doesn't say anything, just holds him tightly and kisses the top of his head, hand running up and down Elliot's back. He doesn't let go.

Elliot doesn't pull away either, head bent down, face pressed into Blake's shirt. Even when he's done crying, he holds on, just can't bring himself to let go. Blake doesn't seem to get tired of it either, pulling Elliot with him when he leans back against the counter, keeping his arms firmly wrapped around Elliot. Blake will hold him like this however long Elliot needs him to, won't even ask if they can sit down, so Elliot eventually convinces himself to pull back and says, "What now?"

"I don't know," Blake says and reaches out to wipe a tear off Elliot's cheek. "What do you need?"

"I'm okay. Do whatever you'd do if I wasn't here."

Blake brushes his hair back and scrunches up his nose. "I sort of need to feed the cats and clean their litter box."

"Okay, you do that and I'll... I'll go sit on the couch. Unless you want help. I can help."

"No, go sit down and pick something to watch and we'll... hang out."

Elliot nods and shuffles into the living room. He pulls up Netflix and starts clicking through movies, eventually flopping down on his side, Squid hopping up onto the couch, curling up next to Elliot's chest, purring as soon as Elliot starts scratching his head. He can hear Blake move about the apartment, softly saying something in another room, probably to Angus. Squid leaves when Blake puts out some food in the kitchen.

Blake comes back, sits down next to Elliot's head and pulls a pillow into his lap, patting it gently. Elliot takes that as the invitation that it is and scoots closer to put his head in Blake's lap and closes his eyes. He's not really tired, but his eyes are itchy now, and he doesn't want to watch a movie either. Lying here is great, he'll keep doing that.

"You can watch the Eagles-Cardinals game if you want to," Elliot mumbles.

Blake is very quiet for a moment, which means that he probably wants to. "No, you don't–"

"It's honestly okay." Elliot gets it. He'd want to watch it if he was in Blake's position. Blake will be playing against one of those teams soon and it's in his best interest to watch it.

"Really?"

"Really," Elliot says. He'll probably fall asleep anyway.

Blake's fingers sneak into his hair, then Blake leans forward to get the remote. At first there's silence, then the telltale sounds of a hockey game, skates on the ice, sticks hitting the puck, then the voice of an announcer, telling his audience Josh Roy's goals per game average in the playoffs. It's more than one goal a game. Elliot's is more than one goal a game, too, but he hasn't played as many playoff games as Josh Roy.

Elliot drifts in and out of sleep, squinting at the TV whenever the goal horn goes off, the Cardinals lighting up the Eagles. Elliot grumbles at Blake when he gets up during the second intermission, almost disappointed when he doesn't get to put his head back in Blake's lap afterwards, but Blake's hand is back in his hair a moment later, barely even moving, just *there*.

Blake wakes him up after the game, the TV already off when Elliot sits up.

"Who won?" Elliot asks.

"Cardinals, six-two," Blake mumbles and stands up. "You wanna go to bed?"

"Sure…" Elliot has no idea how he can be this tired after dozing on Blake's couch for three hours, but here they are. "I can sleep on the couch if you want."

Blake hums. "Because you totally want to sleep on the couch, right?"

"I'm not trying to…" Elliot sighs. "I feel bad for showing up here out of the blue and I've already imposed on you enough, so I don't want you to–"

"Elliot," Blake says and gently nudges him towards the door. "Just come to bed with me, okay?"

"Yeah?"

"Yeah."

Elliot just looks at him for a moment, then he says, "Blake?"

"Hm?"

"Thank you."

Blake only nods.

He finds Elliot a toothbrush and a towel and then slips into bed with him later, keeping a few inches of space between them.

Elliot doesn't like it. He can't stand it. "Blake?" he says.

"Yes, you can come over here, but only if you promise that you won't kick me during the night."

"I'll try," Elliot whispers.

"I guess that's good enough," Blake mutters and wraps his arm around Elliot once he's scooted against him, and Elliot wishes, more than anything, that he could come back to this after every loss.

18

Elliot plays his heart out at Worlds.

While he's in Europe, Blake is nominated for the Vezina and the Knights tear through the Cardinals in five games. Blake plays his first game of the Eastern Conference finals against the Boston Grizzlies the day before Elliot plays in the gold medal game in Prague.

The Grizzlies win Game 1.

Elliot wins the gold medal.

Blake somehow finds the time to call him after, sounding tired in the message he leaves. Elliot doesn't hear it until later, when he's already in bed, smiling as he listens to Blake's voice. Then he listens again. And again.

"Hey, I just saw that you won gold." A short pause. "Well done." A long pause. "I didn't manage to watch all the games, but I did my best." A longer pause. "Anyway, congrats and..." The longest pause yet. "I miss you. Let me know when you're back in New York, okay? Have fun celebrating."

Elliot smiles.

Listens again.

It's the part where Blake says that he misses him, quietly, like it's a secret, that he wants to hear over and over again.

Elliot misses him, too.

He falls asleep while listening to the message for what must be the twentieth time. He's drunk and he'll have the worst headache of his life in the morning, he's sore all over, bruises blooming all over his body, but he'll go home with a gold medal, and Blake misses him.

Elliot flies back to Canada with the team and then goes to Oshawa. His parents were in Prague for two games, but couldn't stay for the finals, so when he's home, his mom takes a few days off and they cook together, dig up old recipes, slipping back into Spanish while they cook. His grandma taught his mom Spanish, so his mom insisted on teaching

Elliot as well. He wasn't the most diligent student and he doesn't exactly get to practice very often these days, so he keeps trailing off, his mom mumbling the words he's looking for. He learned some Swedish from Magnus while he was still on the team, but he's forgotten most of it. Andreas has been trying to teach him German and Elliot can at least have a basic conversation now. He knows how to order a beer. They saw each other at Worlds, too, but didn't end up playing against each other.

It's nice to be home now. It's nice to take a break, sleep in every day, eat whatever he wants, just for a few days, before he goes back to running in the morning and watching what he eats and going to the gym. A bunch of the regular Toronto guys are already in town, those whose seasons ended early, some of the guys who played at Worlds with him, and they meet up for scrimmages, and sometimes Elliot plays in the street with the neighborhood kids.

His parents watch the playoffs, cheering for Blake. The first time Elliot sees his mom cheering for the Knights is jarring. Then he remembers that Boston beat Toronto, so of course his mom wouldn't cheer for the Grizzlies in a million years. His dad is from Vancouver, so his loyalties lie elsewhere. Elliot quietly supports Blake, his mom clearly in the know, because she looks over at him every time Blake makes a save.

"Are you boys still in touch?" his mom asks during Game 4. It looks like the Knights are about to tie up the series.

"Huh?"

"You and Blake Samuels. You were such good friends."

"Oh, yeah, we're... yeah."

"I remember going to your games, you know, we could already tell back then that he'd be big one day. And look at him now. He's basically winning those boys the game."

"Yeah," Elliot says.

On TV, Blake just threw himself onto the puck, like a starfish on the ice, his teammates pushing away Grizzlies players. Blake gets up when the whistle goes, slowly, grabs his water bottle, leans against the net, gives the crossbar a pat.

Elliot has been thinking about calling him. The last time they talked was a few days ago, when Elliot told him that he'd be staying in Oshawa for a while. Elliot misses hearing his voice. He watched a few interviews, Blake looking tired, but seemingly in good spirits, not really smiling, but not scowling either.

"That's nice, that you stayed friends," Elliot's mom says. "How's his brother? I didn't really follow him much when he wasn't playing with you anymore."

"Oh, last I heard, he was doing pretty well," Elliot says. All he knows about Evan, he knows from Blake. He should probably text him to catch up, ask him how he's doing.

During the next intermission, Adam sends him five texts in a row, the first one about car seats, the next one about high chairs, then *wtf how do people have babies*, and *i'm not even the one who has to have the baby*, and then, *helppp*.

"Everything okay?" Elliot's mom asks.

"Yeah, Adam's just having a crisis about becoming a dad, I think," Elliot says and tells Adam to take a deep breath.

not helpful, is the reply he gets a minute later.

"Tell him that nobody knows what they're doing," Elliot's dad pipes up. "I didn't know what to do with you either. Neither did your mom. We managed."

"You were crying a lot," his mom adds.

"All the time."

"We didn't sleep."

"I'm sorry?" Elliot says.

"Oh, sweetie, don't worry, that's what babies do. Don't tell Adam that, though."

"Or do tell him, so he's prepared."

Elliot's mom shakes her head. "Don't let us scare you, though," she says. "It's rewarding to watch a child grow up. I mean, look at you now. Captain of your team. Just won a gold medal."

"Yeah, we didn't think they'd even draft you," his dad says, voice mocking.

"Dad…"

"Come on, I'm a little bit funny."

"No," Elliot says and tells Adam to please be a cool dad and lay off the Brandon Cowell humor.

plz i love your dad, Adam replies.

"Are they having a boy or a girl?"

"I don't know. Because Adam doesn't know."

"Oh, a surprise. Lovely." Elliot's mom reaches over to pat Elliot's arm. "When you have children one day, do you think you'll want it to be a surprise?"

"Isa," Elliot's dad says. "Leave him alone."

"It's just a question."

"Let's not act like you didn't try to set him up with the neighbors' daughter two days ago."

"She's a very nice girl."

"Elliot doesn't need our help to find a very nice girl. He'll do fine on his own."

Elliot silently thanks his dad for his support.

"And maybe he and the very nice girl will decide that they don't want children and that'll be fine with us, too."

"Don't be ridiculous, Brandon."

Elliot really wants to remove himself from the room before this turns into a discussion about his future that he won't even be part of. He's really not sure if he wants kids. He's really not sure if he'll ever want to be with anyone as much as he wants to be with Blake, no other man, no other woman.

"Excuse me," Elliot says quietly, his parents barely noticing over their bickering.

He slips out the backdoor and sits on the porch. The game's second intermission is over now and he gets a goal notification on his phone no two minutes after he's sat down. Goal for the Knights, scored by Paul Mooney.

He takes a deep breath.

Sometimes he wants to tell his parents about Blake. Or maybe not even about Blake, just that he's not straight, that he might come home with a guy one day.

Elliot's phone chimes with another goal notification.

The Knights just scored again.

The series against the Grizzlies goes to seven games.

With Games 5 and 6 going into overtime, Blake nearly lies down on the ice when the final buzzer sounds after Game 7.

They won it.

Somehow.

He has no idea how he made it to the end. His teammates come crashing into him, and they take off the net, and Blake ends up with his back against the boards, hands patting his head, everyone shouting.

They're going to the finals, most of them for the first time in their careers. Charlie is still clinging to him when the other guys start to detach themselves for the handshake line. Charlie plants an unmistakable smooch on the side of Blake's mask and then grabs him by his catching glove and tugs him along to shake hands with the Grizzlies.

They'll be facing San Diego in the final round. Nobody thought the Seals would make it this far, a third-seed team that fought its way through two seven-game series and then through a six-game series, hungry, ready for the final round. The media call them dangerous, unstoppable, the secret favorite.

The Knights will have home ice, but home ice means little. The Grizzlies had home ice, too, and now they just lost Game 7 at home.

They shake hands.

The Knights get the Price of Wales trophy and Kells puts his hands all over it and so does everyone else. They take it to the locker room and

Brammer loudly suggests that maybe they should lick it. He settles for rubbing his cheek against it, which isn't much better, but at least they can all go to bed knowing that Bram didn't slobber all over it.

They go out for drinks after the game and Blake ends up squeezed into a booth with Lehts, Mattie, Kells and Charlie, two pitchers in the middle of the table. Charlie's head starts to droop before they've even managed to finish them, and his head drops onto Blake's shoulder.

"Aw," Mattie says and taps the tip of Charlie's nose.

Charlie jerks upright, looking around frantically, nearly knocking over his cup. "Wha…"

"I think it's time for bed, eh?" Kells says and reaches over Blake to ruffle Charlie's hair.

"I'm not tired," Charlie says, rubbing his eyes.

"Sure," Blake says and puts his arm around him.

Charlie grins and leans back against him. "Totally awake."

Blake yawns.

"Kids," Kells says. "Please don't fall asleep on me when we play the Seals."

Mattie cackles.

"We have a couple of days to take a really long nap," Lehts says.

"Thank fuck," Charlie mumbles and closes his eyes again.

"Yeah, I think Choo Choo and I are gonna head back to the hotel."

"Don't call me Choo Choo," Charlie says with the most betrayed face. "You were the only person I trusted on this team."

"Come on," Blake says, "*Charles.*"

Charlie sticks out his tongue at him, but quits joking around on the way back to the hotel, hugging Blake tightly before they go their separate ways.

They keep playing.

They're in the final round, but hockey games are still hockey games. They have to win four of them.

Only four.

"I couldn't sleep last night," Charlie mutters when they get on the plane to fly to California for Game 3. They won one and lost one in Newark, so they don't have an advantage going into this. Ideally, they'll come home with two more wins. They can't afford two losses.

Blake holds Charlie's hand when the plane takes off and they don't go out that evening. Charlie hangs out in Blake's room with him and they order room service and watch a movie and they both fall asleep in Blake's bed before it's even ten o'clock. Blake wakes up sometime after midnight and nudges Charlie awake. Charlie mumbles an apology, red in the face, and goes back to his own room.

Charlie sits next to him during breakfast the next morning, like he always does, cheeks turning pink when their eyes meet. Blake wants to tell him that it's okay, that he doesn't need to be embarrassed, but by the time they get on the ice later that day, Charlie is once again talking to him the way he usually does, so maybe Charlie was scared that Blake would be weird about it.

They hang out in Lehts and Sasha's room that night, because they have two double beds, nine guys squeezed onto them, watching Star Wars. Lehts is the first one to nod off and Sasha very graciously saves him from having a dick drawn on his face. Brammer turns to Charlie next, because he's sleeping with his head on Blake's shoulder again, but all Blake has to do is glare to keep Brammer away.

They play well the next day and leave the Seals' arena with a win, but return to Newark with the series tied.

Coach tells them to get some rest between games, and Charlie comes home with Blake and they order food and Charlie ends up sleeping on Blake's couch.

Blake texts Elliot that night until he falls asleep, skirting entirely around the topic of Blake playing for the Cup. He asks Elliot to tell him about Oshawa, so Elliot does, a quick back and forth that calms Blake down like nothing else in the world. He almost wants to call, but it's late, and he only manages to stay awake for about five more minutes anyway.

In the morning, his phone is still next to him, a few texts from Elliot waiting for him, first a reply to the last text he sent, then *I guess you fell asleep*, and then, a few minutes later, *good night*.

Blake replies to apologize for going silent last night and then crawls out of bed to see if the cats have eaten Charlie. They're next to him, Angus by his feet, Squid next to his chest, both of them asleep, Charlie snoring loudly.

Blake starts making coffee and stares blankly at his depressingly empty fridge. He's already halfway through a cup of coffee when Charlie shuffles into the kitchen, rubbing his eyes.

"I'm so sorry, Fish, I don't know why the fuck I keep falling asleep everywhere," Charlie says.

"No worries. You wanna go out for breakfast? I don't have any food."

"Oh. Sure. I'll…" Charlie nods at the ceiling. "I'll go take a shower. Meet you downstairs in twenty?"

Blake nods and hands him a coffee. "For the long way upstairs."

"You're the best," Charlie whispers and shuffles away.

The Cup is in the building for Game 6.

If the Knights win this game, they– Blake can't even think about it. He's jittery before the game and Charlie's face is white as a sheet.

211

"I've never been this scared of fucking up a game," Blake whispers.

"You're not the only player on the team, kid," Mattie says gruffly.

"Yeah, I could be the one who fucks it all up," Charlie throws in.

"You're also not the only player on the team."

Charlie makes a weird sort of choking sound. "I want to die."

Blake hums. He can relate.

A hand lands on his back and he can barely feel it through the pads, but Blake has never been so glad to have Mattie next to him.

They have a handful of fans in the building that made the trip from Newark, but they're undoubtedly deep in enemy territory. It would be nice to win the Cup at home, but if he had a choice, he'd rather get it over with right now. He doesn't want to play Game 7, he wants to win it today.

When Blake is in the crease, he doesn't think about it anymore. He doesn't hear the crowd. He sees his teammates, sees the Seals, sees the puck. That's it. Just them and the puck, and a save, a save, another save.

The Seals score late in the first and get on the board first.

After that, nothing happens. Well, not nothing. But no goals get scored during the second. Charlie nearly gets murdered right in front of him, Blake tries to murder a Seal in retaliation and doesn't even see who the hell he's grabbing. During the playoffs that sort of shit is legal. They eventually get separated by the refs.

"You okay?" Blake asks.

Charlie nods and skates to the bench, where one of their trainers is already waiting for him with a towel to wipe away the blood on Charlie's face.

Things don't get any less rough after that. Blake ends up with a Seal in his net, the puck's in there somewhere, too, but it's ruled no goal because the net was off before the puck went in.

They go into the second intermission with the score unchanged. Coach Fitzgerald comes into the room, looks around, and says, "Someone needs to score a goal. I don't care which one of you does it."

Blake doesn't care either. Nobody cares who does it.

It's Paulie who comes to their rescue halfway through the third, ties up the game for them and all they need after that is one goal.

Charlie is the one who gets credit for it, but it's not a pretty goal. The puck bounces off at least three people, including the Seals' goalie, before it falls into the net. Blake has his eyes on the board, watching the replay. There's not a single goalie in the world who would have managed that save. It's an unlucky bounce, but they'll take it.

The Seals pull their goalie, and Paulie gets the empty netter, and they still have thirty-two seconds on the clock, but it's starting to sink in now, that they're close, that the Cup is in the building and that they'll hold it in their hands.

Thirty-two seconds.

They run down faster than Blake would have imagined.

He doesn't even remember hearing the final horn. It's like when they won the Eastern Conference Finals, except he's pretty sure that Charlie is actually crying when he hugs him this time. He's pretty sure that Kells is crying, too. Blake hugs every guy he can get to, but mostly he wants to find Mattie.

He's at the very outside of their large and sweaty huddle, but the boys let him through and Mattie puts a baseball hat on Blake that says that they're Stanley Cup Champions. He hugs Mattie until Mattie tells him that he needs to let go, because the Seals are waiting for handshakes.

There are a bunch of Knights fans down by the glass now and when they're done shaking hands, Blake skates over to them to throw himself against the glass. Quickly, because then the Cup is coming out and Kells is skating over to take it from Joe Watson. It goes from Kells to Mattie, from Mattie to Paulie, from Paulie to Juice, and then Juice is skating over to Blake.

He takes it for a spin and then hands it over to Charlie, because he was the one who scored the game winner.

They've let everyone's families on the ice now, too, and Blake finds Evan with Mattie's family and Evan pulls him into a crushing hug. Neither of them says that they wish their grandma was here, that they wish their parents could see this. All Evan says in the end is, "I won't fucking touch it."

Blake laughs, barely has time to hug Mattie's kids before he's pulled away for an interview. That's how his night is going. Photos, interviews, more photos, then the locker room, and the Cup, champagne getting poured everywhere.

Evan told him he wouldn't come out to celebrate with them, because he's insanely jealous and he has to be on a flight to Hartford at nine the next morning because he's helping out at a hockey camp back home.

The team takes the party to a club and Blake wonders how he's supposed to remember winning the Cup when he's handed drink after drink. He gets talked into dancing and he dances and he hugs everyone who's close enough to hug and then someone hands him another drink, and after that he needs to sit down. He eventually escapes to the bathroom, where the music is nothing more than a dull throb and he has a second to breathe. It smells terrible. He's overcome with a strange sense of déjà vu, but doesn't pause to figure out why.

He hides in a stall and gets his phone out of his pocket, his brain hurting from seeing all the missed calls and texts, and finds Elliot's number. It's early morning in Toronto, not that Blake realizes that when he hits call.

Elliot picks up, voice sleepy when he says, "Hey, Stanley Cup champion Blake Samuels."

"That's what you've saved in your phone?"

"Not yet, but I'll take care of that in a couple of hours when I'm actually awake."

"Sorry," Blake says.

"No, you're not."

"I'm not," Blake confirms. "I miss you."

"Blake."

"I do."

"I know. But you're only telling me that because you're drunk."

"Still true."

Elliot sighs. "I miss you, too."

"When are you coming back to New York?"

"I don't know. I... I'm doing the same camp in Toronto that I always do."

"But it's not starting yet."

"No, not yet."

"So when are you coming back to New York?"

"Can we talk about this when you're not drunk? Because you just won the Cup. And this is... I'm not even awake."

"Okay," Blake says, because Elliot has a point and it is okay. "I miss you," he adds, to make sure Elliot understood him the first time.

"Yeah, I heard you."

"You said you miss me, too."

"Yeah, I said that."

Blake hums, because he was going to say something else, but now he can't remember. "I'll call you."

"Okay."

"Tomorrow."

"Whenever you have time."

"Yeah. Tomorrow."

"Blake."

"Maybe the day after tomorrow."

"That's probably more realistic," Elliot says.

"Are you smiling?" Blake asks.

"Maybe."

"Knew it."

"Drink some water."

"Wow," Blake says. "*Wow*."

"That was probably good advice."

"Yeah, not my fault you didn't take it."

Elliot laughs. It's Blake's favorite sound.

"You should go back to sleep," Blake says. "I'm sorry I woke you up."

"You're still not sorry," Elliot mumbles, "but that's okay. Have fun, eh?"

"Yeah," Blake says, and, "Sleep well," and then he hangs up.

"Fish, did you hide in the bathroom to call your... whoever that was?"

Blake opens the door of his bathroom stall and finds Paulie by the sinks, drying his hands. Right. There are other people in the world. He's not the only one. He tries to remember if he said Elliot's name. He doesn't think he did.

"It's okay," Paulie says. "Why's your... whoever... not here?"

"Because," Blake says, and leaves it at that, because Paulie is one of the guys who's been around for a while, got drafted two years before Blake, and he's one of those guys who has probably realized that Blake has never brought a girlfriend to any of their team events and who stopped asking at some point.

Paulie gives him a hug for some reason.

Blake returns to the rest of the team, most of which look like they're about ready to go to bed. He's tired, too, and if he sat down right now, he'd probably fall asleep immediately.

"Okay," Kells shouts over the music, "I'm taking Bram. Blake, you don't look as wasted as some of these idiots, can you grab Choo Choo?"

Blake grabs Charlie, nearly falling over with him when Charlie leans against him.

He's not sure how they make it back to the hotel and he's even less sure how he manages to drag Charlie all the way to his room, Charlie giggling as he tries to get his wallet out of his pocket.

"There, *there*..." Charlie says and holds up the wallet, triumphant.

"Okay, here, let me..."

Blake swipes the card for him and ushers Charlie inside, catching him by the arm before he can trip over a pair of sneakers by the door.

"Whoops," Charlie says and stumbles against Blake. "Sorry. I'm not that drunk, I swear."

"Right," Blake says.

Charlie grins at him, eyes fixed on Blake's face, dipping down to his lips, then back up again. Charlie's eyes are the deepest, darkest brown, warm and soft. Kind. He's definitely staring right now, in a way that you usually wouldn't stare at a teammate, but the rules don't apply when you're wasted because you just won the Cup. Since Blake is marginally less wasted, he knows that something's up here, but his brain is too slow to figure it out.

He's too slow when Charlie leans in and kisses him. Blake kisses him back, only for a split-second, before he gently pushes Charlie away.

"Time for bed," Blake says and nudges Charlie over to his bed.

"I..."

"It's okay."

"Blake."

"It's okay," Blake says again and decides that Charlie is not too drunk to figure out how to put his own ass in his bed and maybe even take off some of his clothes. He quickly bids him a good night and gets the hell out of his room.

Blake's own room is three doors down and he has just opened the door when a handful of his teammates come tumbling out of the elevator, laughing, shushing each other as they loudly sneak down the hallway.

Blake grins at them and Sasha waves at him, nearly tripping over his own feet.

They're all going to be close to death on the flight home in the morning.

They fly home and Charlie sits next to Kells on the plane, so Blake hovers next to Mattie until Mattie offers him the empty seat next to him. There's food on the flight that Blake considers, since he does need to eat something at some point, but his stomach seems to be unsure if it wants him to eat food ever again.

He eventually goes to sleep. It's a long flight and he's exhausted. He doesn't have to worry about anyone drawing dicks on his face, because the rest of the team is fucking exhausted, too. Everyone's hungover and Bram looks a little green in the face, like he's about to throw up all over the plane. Brammer's never been this quiet in his life. Kells seems concerned, shooting glances his way until he passes out.

Blake wakes up at some point halfway through the flight and decides to finally eat something, the plane less quiet now. At least Bram is still asleep, which means he probably hasn't made another attempt to lick the Cup.

Blake goes and sits with the guys that are awake, somehow ending up getting shoved into Kells's lap. Kells doesn't seem to mind as long as Blake lets him steal food off his plate, grumbling about being an old man and then sending Blake back to the buffet to get more food. Charlie is still sitting next to Kells, at first asleep, then avoiding Blake's eyes.

By the time they land in Newark, the boys are all awake and back to partying – as much as they can on a plane. There'll be a lot of that, interviews with the local media, too, and the parade, and then their Cup days in the summer. They're all going to head out again tonight, to celebrate at home. They do all head back to their respective houses and apartments first, though, which means that Charlie has to stop avoiding Blake, because Blake gave him a ride to the airport and they live in the same building, so if Charlie asks someone else for a ride, they'll know that something's up. After they've greeted the fans that are around, probably carefully picked by the organization, Charlie follows him off the plane and to his car, completely silent.

The drive home isn't that long. Neither of them is saying a word. It's not that Blake is expecting an apology or anything, but he's pretty sure that Charlie hasn't forgotten what happened last night, considering that he's been avoiding him all day.

"Charlie," Blake says when he's parked the car.

Charlie takes a deep breath. "I'm so sorry, Blake, I honestly don't know why I did that, I swear I won't do it again. I was just drunk. I don't know... But I'm really sorry. And I won't... Please don't tell anyone."

"I won't," Blake says. "It's okay, honestly."

Charlie nods. "Thank you. And I'm so sorry."

"It's okay."

Eyes on his knees, hands clenched in his lap, Charlie says, "I'm not gay."

"Okay."

"I swear. And, like, I don't mind gay guys. You know I don't. But I'm not. I like girls."

"Okay," Blake says again, because this is not the conversation he thought they'd be having, but it's clearly something Charlie needs to say.

"I just..."

"What?"

"I'm not gay," Charlie says again.

And maybe he isn't, and Blake absolutely believes him when he says that he has nothing against gay guys, because he has proven on many occasions that he doesn't, but there's something going on here, Blake can tell. You don't go and kiss a guy just because you're drunk. "Okay, but, Charlie?" Blake says. "I am." Maybe Charlie needs someone who's definitely on his side right now.

"You're what?"

"I'm gay. And—" Blake stops talking when Charlie looks up. Maybe he shouldn't have said that. He has no clue why he thought that might help.

"You are?" Charlie asks.

Well, he probably can't take it back now. "Yeah."

"But... Really?"

"Charlie."

"I'm sorry," Charlie says. "But isn't it… In juniors it was…" He shakes his head. "Everyone said… all that stuff. You know what they were saying, right?"

"Yeah, I know," Blake says. He hasn't forgotten. He wasn't usually the one all that *stuff* was directed at, and often the other guys were just joking around, but he heard it. He somehow made it out on the other side.

"And I'm not gay," Charlie says, "but…"

Blake waits. He's had a conversation like this with Elliot, once upon a time.

"I had a crush on a guy when I was fifteen," Charlie mumbles. "But I… wasn't supposed to. And I like girls. So…" He looks at Blake. "But now…"

Blake is trying really hard to fill in the blanks and maybe he understands what Charlie is trying so hard to say, but in the end all he can do is guess. "Charlie," Blake says, "it's okay if you like men and women."

"Is it, though?" Charlie asks, red in the face. He glances at Blake. "And you like guys?"

Blake nods.

Charlie blinks at him. "So when I kissed you…"

"I…" Blake takes a deep breath. This is the really awkward bit. "I'm seeing someone. So now I sort of have to explain to him that I kissed another guy." Not that he *really* kissed Charlie, but Blake still isn't looking forward to it. Elliot will be mad. He'll say *it's fine*, but he'll be mad.

"Oh no, I'm so sorry, you can tell him that it's totally my fault, I did it and you didn't, and it's… I'm so sorry." Charlie has tears in his eyes now. "I fucked everything up, I'm so sorry."

"Hey, it's okay." Blake reaches over to put an arm around him. "It's all gonna be fine."

Charlie hiccups. "I'm not fine."

"I'm sorry."

"I'm gonna stop having a crush on you right now, I promise."

Blake has to bite down a smile. It's not really funny.

"You're just so nice," Charlie whispers.

"I'm sorry," Blake says again.

"It's like you're Canadian," Charlie mumbles and pulls away, wiping his eyes. "Please, can we forget that all of this happened?"

"If you want to."

Charlie nods.

"You wanna sit in the car for a few more minutes?" Blake asks.

Charlie wipes his eyes again. "Yeah."

"Okay."

Blake doesn't call him the day after he won the Cup, which Elliot didn't think he'd have time for anyway, considering that the Knights have to fly all the way back from California. He's seen some pictures from the Knights' night with the Cup, has seen pictures of them on the plane, one of Blake with his head on Jake Matthews's shoulder, fast asleep. It seems that the team went out to party again once they'd safely landed in Newark.

In the meantime, Blake has sent him a picture of his entire head in the Cup, hair hanging over the rim. *I swear I won't keep sending cup pics,* he said after.

Elliot is actually mostly okay with the Cup pics, even though part of him is insanely jealous, but he's also proud of Blake, so he tells him to send as many pictures as he wants. Elliot will see them on Twitter eventually anyway.

Blake calls him the day before the Knights have their parade, while Elliot is having dinner with his parents. He excuses himself, his mom looking slightly annoyed until Elliot says, "It's Blake."

There are some calls that are allowed to interrupt dinner. Calls from Elliot's agent. Calls from the team. And calls from Stanley Cup champions.

"Hey," Elliot says. He decides to take his phone all the way up to his bedroom, because he has no idea how long this call is going to take. Even though he wasn't quite awake, he does remember Blake calling him in the middle of the night, asking him to come back to New York and that's not something he wants to talk about with his parents listening in.

He hopes Blake remembers that part.

"Hi," Blake says. His voice is low, sounding rough. He's probably been screaming his lungs out. "How are you?"

"I'm okay," Elliot says. "How are you?"

"I'm so fucking tired," Blake groans.

Elliot laughs. "Go to bed."

"No, I have to talk to you first."

"Okay. I'm all yours."

"This is not gonna be fun," Blake says. "And I'm sorry. And, for the record, I'm not lying when I say that I didn't want any of this to happen."

Elliot doesn't like the sound of that at all. His brain tries to be super helpful and immediately supplies him with the thought of Blake hooking up with some guy after he won the Cup. And now he doesn't really want to be with Elliot anymore, because Elliot is taking too long to make up his mind about what the hell he wants and that's it for them.

It's not like Blake cheated on him, they're not even together and Blake doesn't owe him anything. He did say that he won't be seeing anyone else, but–

"You still there?" Blake asks.

"Yeah," Elliot says. Swallows hard. "What happened?"

"Um, so, the night we won the Cup, there were several very drunk people, and one of those very drunk people kissed me. And–"

"One of your teammates?"

"Elliot."

Elliot knows that Blake is too good of a person to say yes to that, but he doesn't really have to anyway. If it wasn't a teammate, Blake would have said no. "Okay, so *someone* kissed you?"

"Yeah."

"And then?"

"And then I told him to go to bed and I talked to him about it the next day and I told him that I'm not available for any more kissing and he was really embarrassed about it all. It wasn't… It was really just a kiss, Elliot. Nothing else happened."

"Nothing else?"

"No."

Elliot hates all of this. He hates that someone went and kissed his… Shit, Blake's not his boyfriend. He hates that he's jealous. He hates that he's angry, because Blake obviously wasn't walking around begging other dudes to kiss him. It's not his fault.

"Elliot," Blake says, soft. "Are you mad?"

"No, it's f–"

"Don't do that."

"I'm mad," Elliot says. "But not at you. I'm just… mad. I wanna be your boyfriend and not worry about it and I want people to know you're my boyfriend, so no one's gonna go and fucking kiss you."

Blake is quiet for a moment, then he says, "Come to New York."

"You meant that, huh?"

"Yeah."

"Did you mean the other thing, too?" Elliot asks.

"What other thing?"

"You know what thing."

"Tell me what thing," Blake grumbles, but he has to know that Elliot is talking about the *I miss you* thing. It's just that the sober version of Blake can't bring himself to say it and it's a little bit funny. He's said it before, though. When Elliot was at Worlds.

"You said you missed me," Elliot tells him.

"Oh. That." Blake clears his throat. "I meant that, too."

"When do you want me to come?"

"Whenever you— I mean, I sort of have to go to Vegas for the Awards and then there's the Draft and free agency, but... We're not free agents and we're not getting drafted, so..."

"I should spend some time around a phone during the Draft," Elliot says. "I have to call all the new kids."

"Right. Captain."

"I'll come after?"

"Okay."

"Okay," Elliot echoes. "I'll book a flight."

"Good."

"Go to sleep now, okay? Otherwise you'll die during the parade."

"Your mistake is that you're assuming that I'm still alive," Blake says.

Elliot laughs. "Good night, Blake."

"Good night."

The line goes dead. Elliot forgot to tell him something and he calls Blake back before he even remembers what it was.

Blake answers a second later. "Was that an accident or...?"

"No, I..." Elliot shakes his head at himself. "I don't know. It suddenly felt like I wasn't done talking to you."

"You're weird," Blake mumbles, then he says, louder, "Hey, stop it, you little shit."

"Angus?"

"He bit my toe," Blake says, betrayed. "What the hell. Prepare to be eaten alive when you come here."

"When I... So am I gonna come hang out at your place?" Elliot asks. He was sort of assuming that he'd go to his own place and that they'd meet in the middle like they always do. Only now they don't have any other obligations, so they can hang out somewhere together without one of them having to run off.

"I don't know," Blake says. "If you want."

"I thought we're not..." They're not together. Blake didn't want this unless Elliot was sure that he could deal with the possibility of them getting outed somehow, doesn't want him to change his mind a few months later.

Once Elliot lets himself have this, though, he'll stick with Blake no matter what. He wants him and no one else. Never again.

Blake sighs. "I don't care."

"But..."

"We'll figure it out somehow. Just come, okay? And we'll talk when you're here. We said we'd talk in the summer."

"Right, we did say that."

"Okay," Blake says.

"I'll hang up in a minute."

"Sounds great."

Elliot is quiet for a few seconds, then he says, "Are you asleep yet?"

"No, not yet," Blake mutters.

"You have to tell me about the Cup when I get there," Elliot says, even though he doesn't like the jealousy that creeps in when he thinks about Blake and the Cup and the fact that Elliot's team is not the one that won it.

"It's heavy. And silver."

"And it's gonna have your name on it," Elliot says. His heart clenches when he thinks about it.

"*Shit.*"

"What?"

"I kinda… forgot that they're gonna put our names on it."

"It's time to stop drinking," Elliot says drily. "You clearly only have, like, two functioning brain cells left."

"Fuck, it for sure is time to stop."

"You're ridiculous."

"You called me because it felt like we weren't done talking. *You're* ridiculous."

Elliot rolls his eyes. "I think I'm done now."

"Are you sure?"

"Would you answer if I called you again after this?"

"Yeah," Blake says and he clearly means it.

Something's tight in Elliot's chest, but in a good way. "I'll see you soon," he says.

"Can't wait. Bring me a moose from Canada."

"Sure," Elliot says.

Blake laughs, so soft that Elliot barely hears it.

Elliot doesn't call him again after he's hung up the phone, but he stays in his room for another minute or two to school his expression into something more neutral and something less besotted.

19

Adam gets traded the day before the Awards.

Elliot is in his parents' backyard, having an existential crisis about whether or not he's too old to spend half his summer at his parents' house and if he should find himself an apartment in Toronto. Because he could. He has the money. But then shouldn't he be careful with his money? He doesn't *need* an apartment in Toronto.

He tries to distract himself by going on Twitter, even though he knows that'll make him mad about something, especially if he stumbles across another article about the "ever mediocre" Ravens.

It's not that the article he was fuming about the other day didn't have a point, that was probably why it stung so much, but Elliot disagreed with what they had to say about his teammates. That Adam was a deadweight. That Andreas wasn't worth his money. That Swanson, thirty-two years old, is past his prime. That not a single D-man on the roster deserves to be in the NHL. That Elliot was too positive about their abysmal last season in his exit interview.

The team has already been torn to shreds, Kenny traded for another player, Darren traded for a player and picks, three free agents in contract talks, two of which likely don't want to stay. Elliot suspects that Moby will re-sign with the Ravens before free agency starts, but he's in no way certain.

Their coach got fired. The Ravens haven't announced who'll be the new one, have only said that they're taking their time with the decision to ensure that it's the right one.

Their GM is on thin fucking ice. Has been for a year or two.

It's not even that they're tanking every season, it's just that they can't seem to make it far in the playoffs. Even getting into a wildcard spot is a struggle year after year. Ever mediocre.

Moves are being made before the Draft, before free agency, a trade from Tampa Bay to Toronto here, a trade from DC to Seattle there, and then, from one of the New York reporters, *Adam Ishida to the Scorpions for two draft picks, one of them a first rounder.*

Elliot fights the urge to throw his phone across the lawn.

It's a business.

They don't care if a player is the captain's best friend, they don't care if he has a family, they don't care about any of them, in the end, if they aren't worth their money. Elliot doesn't try to think of their next season, him and Andreas, probably still together on the first line, and someone else, someone they might not even know yet, someone new, someone who's not Adam.

Since all they're getting for Adam is draft picks, Elliot doesn't need to call any new players to welcome them to the team. It's a blessing, because he has no idea how anyone could expect him to sound genuinely excited about someone getting traded to the Ravens right now. He can't be, not if they're losing Adam in the process.

He doesn't know if Adam even knows yet, if they had a chance to call him before someone broke the news on Twitter. He texts Adam and asks him to call him when he gets a chance.

It takes half an hour, Elliot still in the backyard, flat on his back in the shade of a tree, somehow unable to convince himself to move and do something productive. Blake has texted him a sad face that Elliot hasn't even replied to yet, knowing that Blake has his own shit going on with the NHL Awards. If he heard Blake's voice right now, if Blake said a single kind word to him, about a guy that isn't even Blake's teammate, Elliot would probably burst into tears.

"Hi," Adam says when Elliot picks up the phone, "I only have, like, ten seconds, because Lou is losing her shit."

"I'm sorry," Elliot says. He let him down.

Adam sighs. "I mean… at least it's not Edmonton, right?"

"Right," Elliot says.

"I'll give you another call later, but I really need to talk to Lou about this. Because the universe is like, here, on top of having to move to Satan's asshole, you can have a freaked-out pregnant wife as well. Yay."

"Let me know if there's anything I can do to help."

"Yeah, promise you won't love your new winger as much as you love me."

"I think I won't even take a new winger, it'll just be me and Andreas."

Adam laughs. "Fuck, this is terrible," he says. "I'll talk to you soon, okay?"

"Okay," Elliot says.

Adam doesn't call him for a while.

Elliot's mom gets home, gives him a hug, because of course she's seen the news, then she asks him what he wants for dinner, if she should make cookies and Elliot says yes to the pity cookies. He replies to Blake, sends him a sad face in return, because he can't think of anything to say, other than, *Can you please come here right now and hug me for a week?* They'll see each other after the Draft anyway.

The next day, Elliot tries to stick to his schedule, meets with his trainer, buys himself a smoothie on the way home and then goes back to lying in his parents' backyard. He should ask them if they mind that he invades their house every summer. At some point.

Not tonight.

Tonight his dad grumbles about the NHL Awards, because he never agrees with who wins and his mom makes popcorn and grabs the leftover cookies and they settle in to watch the ceremony.

Elliot knows all of those guys, has at least shaken hands with them, has met many of them at the All Star Game, but tonight he really only cares about the Vezina. Everyone agrees that Blake should be the one to win it, everyone acts like it's a sure thing, basically already decided, but Elliot is still nervous, stomach in knots, until they say Blake's name on TV.

"Tell him we're happy for him, eh?" Elliot's dad says, apparently for once in agreement with how the Awards are going.

"Yeah," Elliot says and grabs his phone.

It takes him a good fifteen minutes to find the right words, knowing that Blake likely won't reply for a while. Then he adds a, *can't wait to see you*, because it's the truth and because he thinks he's going to explode if he doesn't say it.

Adam calls him later that evening and Elliot goes out the back door and sits in his favorite chair, hoping he won't get eaten alive. He lights one of the candles that are supposed to keep the mosquitoes away.

"Sorry, it's kinda late, but Lou just went to bed and we spent all day trying to figure things out and looking for houses online and shit," Adam says.

"You okay?" Elliot asks.

"I'm still getting used to the idea that I'm gonna have to move to fucking Arizona. I mean, this isn't… We know this can happen to anyone at any point, but it still took me by surprise. I thought I was gonna stay, you know? I thought they wanted me to stay. Guess not."

"We'll miss you."

Adam takes a deep breath on the other end of the line. "We painted the fucking nursery. In New York," he says. "I'm gonna pay someone to paint the nursery in Arizona, I'm not doing that shit again."

"That's probably a good idea," Elliot says.

"How's everything back home? Your folks okay?"

"Yeah, they're fine."

"And you?"

225

"Also fine," Elliot says.

"Can you say more than two words, Moo? Distract me from my misery. Tell me all the hot Oshawa gossip."

"I met Riley Walsh the other day."

"Aw, he was such a good guy. It sucked when he got traded."

"Yeah. I'll probably have dinner with him when I'm back from New York."

"What are you going to New York for?" Adam asks.

"Oh, uh… visiting someone."

"In New York? We live in New York. I'm in New York. Visit *me*."

"I can swing by and say hello," Elliot says. Blake will understand if Elliot ditches him for a couple of hours to hang out with Adam, considering that Adam will be moving to Arizona.

"Please, we'll have some quality Adam-Elliot time, Lou won't mind. We can–"

"Adam," Elliot says, "I don't think I'll have time."

"Wait, so you *are* visiting someone? I thought you were just fucking around. Who?"

Elliot breathes in and out very slowly. "It's complicated."

"You're not sick or anything, right?"

"No, it's…" Elliot squeezes his eyes shut. Adam already knows. He won't suddenly have an issue with this. "A guy."

"A guy?"

"Yes, a guy."

"What kind of guy?"

"A *guy*, Adam."

"I don't ge– Wait. A guy?"

"That's what I'm saying."

"Like," Adam says slowly, "a boyfriend?"

"No, not really."

"But there's a guy."

"Yeah."

"Okay," Adam says, "tell me about the guy."

"I can't."

"Come on, Moo, I won't… I'm not an asshole, we've talked about this. Tell me about the guy. You'd tell me if it was a girl. Is he hot?"

"Adam."

"Is he?"

"Yeah."

"Nice. You have a picture of him? Oh, oh, wait, can I meet him?"

"I'll ask him," Elliot says, voice low, because he's scared it might crack under the weight of everything he's feeling right now.

"For how long have you known him?"

Elliot thinks about Blake lying in the grass with him, seventeen years old, on a summer day he'll never forget. "A while."

"So it's serious?"

Blake's not even his boyfriend. Is it serious? "I'm in love with him," Elliot says.

Elliot's flight to New York is delayed.

Maybe he shouldn't have booked a flight to Newark. He doesn't know what he was thinking. The flight to LaGuardia that left thirty minutes ago was on time. Maybe he should have gone to LaGuardia instead.

But Newark is where Blake lives and when Elliot sent him his flight info, the first thing Blake said was, *cool I'll pick you up*. So he'll probably go to Blake's place first and they'll take things from there. Maybe they'll go to Elliot's, too. It'd be weird to be so close to home for a week and not spend some time at his own place. Blake can come.

"Excuse me."

Elliot looks up and finds himself face-to-face with a very small child. She's wearing a dress that probably belongs to a Disney princess. Her mother is hovering a few steps behind her, looking apologetic. "Hey, there," Elliot says.

"Are you Elliot Cowell?"

"I am," Elliot says, "and what's your name?"

She holds out her hand for him to shake and says, "I'm Evie."

"It's very nice to meet you, Evie."

"My brother didn't believe that it was really you," Evie tells him. "He wanted to get a sandwich instead."

"Well, it really is me."

The mom clears her throat, tugging at the kid's hand. "Sweetie, let's go, okay? Mr. Cowell is on vacation."

"Don't worry about it," Elliot says. People do shoot him looks when they see him at the airport and sometimes people think he has time for an hour-long conversation about hockey. Little girls aren't much of a problem, though. "Do you want me to sign anything for you?"

Evie's eyes go impossibly wide.

Elliot ends up signing a piece of paper in a coloring book with a purple crayon, then takes a picture with her, crouches down beside her and talks to her for a few more minutes before he excuses himself and goes to his gate.

He gets on the plane without any issues and it looks like they won't change the departure time again. He falls asleep as soon as they've taken off and doesn't wake up until the announcement that they'll be landing soon.

His suitcase is already waiting for him at baggage claim and for once he doesn't regret wasting money on priority access, because that means that he'll see Blake faster.

Blake is already waiting for him and seeing him is akin to walking into a wall. Which is ridiculous. He knows what Blake looks like. Since he won the Cup, pictures of him have been everywhere. He literally saw him on TV a few days ago. But now he's right there in very tight jeans and a very tight black shirt, with his hair in a bun, and then there's the eyes and the tattoos and it's… a lot.

He waves when he sees Elliot and Elliot waves back at him and then they're next to each other and Elliot doesn't know what to do, doesn't know if he should hug him or even touch him at all.

Blake saves him, pats his back and says, "Follow me."

Blake is an insanely good driver. Both hands on the wheel, eyes on the road, using his turn signal. Which is great. Except Elliot is pretty much dying in the passenger seat, the sun burning down outside, the air conditioning doing very little to cool things down.

"Do you need both your hands?" Elliot asks.

Blake snorts. "What?"

"Can I borrow one?" Elliot asks, which is, admittedly, a very strange way of asking someone to hold your hand, but Blake doesn't comment on it, just takes one hand off the wheel and holds it out to Elliot, and Elliot takes it with both his hands, lacing their fingers together.

Elliot gives the hand back when Blake needs to do a little more steering and Blake asks about his flight, asks him what he wants for dinner, if he wants to stop at the grocery store to buy any food and Elliot waves him off. They can order food.

"Are you tired?"

"No, I slept on the plane. I just spent a lot of time at the airport today," Elliot says. He was supposed to be here over two hours ago. "I'm glad I'm here now. There's been lots of stuff going on."

"I'm sorry about Adam."

Elliot sighs. "It's a business." He's been telling himself that. It's a business and there's nothing anyone could have done. The Ravens are going to start the new season with a completely different team, only a handful of players left from last season. Something had to change, but Elliot wishes they could have at least kept Adam.

The Ravens probably aren't done making moves either.

Blake reaches over to put his hand on Elliot's thigh, squeezes, then quickly pulls it away again.

Elliot is about to complain and tell him that he could have left it there, because he didn't mind at all and kind of wants it back, but then Blake turns right into a resident parking garage and Elliot realizes that they've made it to Blake's place.

Blake parks in his spot, then gets Elliot's suitcase for him and grumbles at him when he tries to take it. Elliot follows him into the elevator, suitcase between them, Elliot's eyes fixed on Blake's hand, curled around the handle, his own hands stuffed into the pockets of his pants. There's probably a security camera in the elevator and that's the only thing keeping Elliot from shoving that suitcase out of the way.

It takes Blake about a hundred years to unlock the door to his apartment, a hundred years in which Elliot hovers next to him, shifting his weight as he waits for Blake to fit his damn key into the damn lock.

The door opens and Angus and Squid are waiting a few feet into the hallway, eyeing Elliot with suspicion.

"Hey, Angus," Blake says and grabs him, "your best friend is here."

Elliot is handed a displeased cat, which means his plan to push Blake against a wall and kiss him senseless is out the window. Angus purrs when Elliot hugs him against his chest, eyes on Blake, who's closed the door but hasn't moved otherwise.

"Hey," Blake says.

Gently, Elliot sets down Angus. He still wants to get his hands on Blake, but they're clearly not doing that right now. "Hey," Elliot says.

Blake nods at Elliot's suitcase. "Do you want to sleep here? Or I can drive you to your place later."

Elliot can't help but smile, because Blake has told him several times that the world would have to be ending for him to voluntarily drive to Manhattan. "I'll stay."

"Okay." Blake nods again. "Where do you want to sleep?"

"Uh…"

"I have a guest room," Blake says. "If you want it. Or—"

Elliot's had enough of this. Blake knows where he wants to sleep. Blake knows where he wants him, too, he's just talking his way around it for some reason. Elliot steps closer and kisses him, because that's what he's here for. That's why Blake asked him to come. They're not going to spend the entire week in this apartment, but it's the only place where they can do this, so he's not losing any more time.

Blake makes a surprised sound when Elliot's lips meet his. Elliot isn't gentle about it, not when he's spent days thinking about this, distracted, daydreaming, his mom shaking her head at him when she talked to him and he didn't reply, his thoughts already right here.

When Elliot pulls away, Blake is still leaning against the wall, mouth slack, lips wet, breathing uneven.

"I'll sleep in your bed," Elliot says.

Blake nods, a smile tugging at his lips.

"I told Adam that I'm in love with you."

The smile that was barely there to begin with disappears quickly. "You what?"

"I didn't tell him it was you, just that it was someone. Who happens to be you." Elliot doesn't think he's ever seen that look of Blake's face. "Did I fuck up?"

"No," Blake says. "Just... You did that."

"Yeah."

"Why?"

"Because... I am."

Blake swallows. "You're what?"

"In love with you."

Blake reaches for him then, just for his hand, curls his fingers around Elliot's and holds on.

It's an *I love you, too*, if Elliot has ever seen one.

"Hey... Blake?"

Blake scrunches up his nose.

"Did you go back to sleep?" There's a pause, then there are lips on Blake's forehead, fingers in his hair, and a whispered, "Sorry."

"I'm awake," Blake says and blindly reaches for Elliot.

"It's okay if you wanna go back to sleep," Elliot says, right next to his ear. Elliot kisses his temple and Blake leans into it, cracks an eye open and sees Elliot, in all his early morning glory. Curls messy, cheeks vaguely stubbly, sleep in his eyes. He's completely naked and he's kicked off the sheets. He has freckles on his shoulders.

"No, really," Blake mumbles and leans over to kiss the top of Elliot's shoulder, "I'm awake."

Elliot hums, breath hitching when Blake reaches out to touch him. Elliot moves quickly, straddles Blake's hips, only a thin sheet between them, but Elliot doesn't push it out of the way yet.

He doesn't seem to be in a hurry this morning, keen on taking his time. He finds Blake's hands and pushes them down against the mattress, grinding against him, slowly, Blake impatient under him, burning up with every touch, every single one of Elliot's movements drawing a sound from him, until Elliot takes pity and crawls down, takes the sheet with him, lips finding the inside of Blake's thigh.

Elliot sucks a mark there, teeth sharp against Blake's skin. "You're so beautiful," Elliot says and presses a kiss to the bruise he left yesterday. Blake is pale as a ghost, especially compared to Elliot, bruises easily. He still has some lingering marks from the playoffs, mostly faded now, but Elliot found one of them last night and put his lips on that one, too.

Last night wasn't this lazy, last night was about getting off their clothes and getting to touch skin, Elliot taking whatever he wanted and Blake more than willing to give, fast and desperate. This morning, there's time to linger, and they have all the time in the world, all the time they never thought they'd have. Blake is pretty sure that Elliot said, "I always wanted to do this," three times last night.

They stay in bed all morning, the sheets tangled around their feet. Elliot mumbles something about breakfast and Blake nuzzles into his hair. Blake loves him a lot, so much that he doesn't even know how to say it, because *I love you* sounds too cheesy, and at the same time like it's not enough.

It doesn't matter what he told Elliot in January.

It's too late anyway.

He's in love with him, was in love with him even before they kissed on New Year's Eve, and it's going to hurt either way, whatever they decide to do. If Elliot wants him, in whichever way he chooses, well... he can have Blake. Elliot probably knows that. He must know.

When Blake asked him to come here, he basically asked him to forget what he said before. People always get hurt, no matter how hard you try, and when he asked Elliot to make up his mind first, he hurt him, too. There was no winning for either of them.

They take another nap before they get up, Elliot plastered against him, sticky, sweaty, breath hot against Blake's skin.

Blake wakes up when Elliot moves away and slips out of bed. "Where are you going?"

"I just remembered something," Elliot says. He bends down behind the bed to grab his briefs and then pulls on the shirt Blake was wearing yesterday.

Blake frowns at him.

"I don't want the cats to see me naked," Elliot says before he disappears into the hallway. He obviously doesn't close the door fast enough, so Squid flits into the room, hops onto Blake's bed and meows at him accusingly.

Right. Food. "In a minute," Blake mumbles. He holds out his hand and Squid accepts a few gentle pats.

When Elliot returns he nearly trips over Angus, who's sitting by the door, judging them silently. "Here," Elliot says and drops something brown and fuzzy on Blake's chest.

"Um..." Blake holds it up. "It's a moose."

"You told me to bring you a moose."

"You're so stupid," Blake says, grinning despite himself. He pulls Elliot down for a kiss. "Thank you. I'll give it a name and everything."

"Good," Elliot says. "It took me forever to find a good one."

"A *good* moose?"

"Yeah."

"I can't believe you went moose shopping."

Elliot shrugs. He flops back down next to Blake, leg thrown across Blake's. "So…"

"Hm?"

"What's the plan for today?"

"I don't know," Blake says. "This?"

"Bed? Sex? Cats staring at us?"

"Yeah."

"Okay," Elliot says. "And tomorrow?"

"Tomorrow you can pick."

"I told Adam I'd swing by at some point."

Blake pulls a face, because he doesn't want to share Elliot, but Adam is Elliot's best friend and he just got traded and he might not be in town anymore when Elliot comes back again, so Blake gets it. "Okay."

"You could come." Elliot taps his finger on Blake's chest. "He said he wanted to meet my… guy."

"Your *guy*?" Blake asks.

"What would you like me to call you?"

It's a loaded question. Elliot clearly knows what he's asking here and this should probably be its own conversation, about what they want to be for each other and where this is going.

Elliot blinks at him, waiting.

"I…"

"Yes?" Elliot says, lips twitching. "You wanna be my mistress? My comrade? My partner in crime?"

"All of that sounds better than your *guy*."

Elliot grins.

"Can he keep a secret?" Blake asks. He doesn't like the thought, someone else knowing. Mainly because he doesn't know Adam Ishida. Or, he should say, he only knows him as a player, not as a person.

Elliot nods. "Absolutely."

"You trust him?"

"I trusted him when I told him about me."

"Yeah," Blake says. That should be enough for him.

"We don't have to do this. I can go meet him for lunch and then you and I can hang out after." Elliot leans closer and touches the tip of his nose against Blake's temple. "Think about it. You don't have to decide right now."

"If we… did that…" Blake trails off when Elliot kisses his cheek.

"Yeah?"

"Mattie said…"

"Mattie from your team?"

"Yeah. He said I could bring my boyfriend over for dinner."

"Your boyfriend?"

"Well, if I ever had a boyfriend, he said I could bring him." Blake turns his head to look at Elliot, who's very close, his eyes warm and brown, green flecks in them. Blake could count every single freckle on Elliot's nose right now. "You know, hypothetically."

"And I'm the boyfriend in this hypothetical scenario?"

Blake hums.

"Yeah?" Elliot asks.

"Yeah."

Elliot has never been this scared in his entire life.

Not a joke. Jake Matthews isn't the most intimidating guy in the league, generally kind and good-natured, but when Blake pulls into his driveway, Elliot is sweating and not just because it's a particularly hot day.

He wishes that they were doing the lunch with Adam first, but that's not until the day after tomorrow. He's in enemy territory. Jake Matthews has never liked him, because the Knights just don't like the Ravens, and he probably won't like him now. They're having dinner at his house, and maybe Elliot would have also felt better if they were doing this at Blake's, but Blake has assured him that it'll only be Matthews and his wife, no kids. "But the dogs will probably be there," Blake added.

He was trying to cheer Elliot up, but it didn't help.

When Blake rings the Matthews' doorbell, Elliot is still thinking up reasons why he needs to leave immediately. The worst thing is knowing that Blake would literally let him hide in the car if Elliot asked. If Elliot had said something five minutes ago, Blake would have turned the car around and canceled dinner.

It's too late now, though.

Because the door is swinging open and there's Jake Matthews, who looks so different so far away from hockey. Just… like a normal person. He announced his retirement a few days ago, but to Elliot he's still Blake's teammate.

"Mattie, hey," Blake says and hugs him.

"Hey, kid. Hey, Elliot, come on in."

"Here, we brought dessert," Blake says and hands over the cookies he made with Elliot. Well, Elliot made them. Blake handed him ingredients. He did a great job.

"Thank you," Mattie says and ushers them inside.

There's a bunch of stuff lying around that indicates that children live in this house, but, like Blake said, there's no sign of the kids anywhere.

"I didn't tell the girls that you were coming over tonight," Mattie says when he catches Elliot looking around. "They're having a sleepover at a friend's house."

"I'll come by and take them out for ice cream some other time," Blake says.

"Please don't, they already like you better than me."

Elliot laughs.

"I'm not kidding," Mattie grumbles. "Follow me, you two."

He leads them through the house and out onto the terrace. The grill is on and a woman, Mattie's wife, is putting down plates with steaks and burger patties.

"Elliot, that's my wife, Katie," Mattie says.

Elliot shoots Blake a look, like that'll stop him being jittery all over. Another person who knows about them now. Elliot hasn't even told his parents yet. Blake gives him the smallest of smiles in return, a quick one before Elliot turns back to Mattie's wife. "Nice to meet you," he says.

"Hey," Mattie says, voice low, "we can keep a secret, both of us. We're pretty good at it."

Elliot nods and goes over to shake Katie's hand. She asks him what he likes to eat and two minutes later they're talking about the best steak marinades and Elliot tells her about what he's been cooking with his mom and for the next ten minutes they're swapping recipes. There's no way that Elliot will remember them, but talking about cooking calms him down, because he actually knows what he's talking about and really has something to say.

When he turns around to see what Blake is doing, he find shim sitting at the table, eating potato salad, him and Mattie both looking at them.

Elliot clears his throat. He probably should spend some time talking to Mattie, too.

"Oh, go ahead and try the potato salad," Katie says and nudges him towards the table. "Mattie and I fight about it all the time, because he hates it and I don't, and I have Blake on my side already and I could use some more support."

Elliot sits down and helps himself to a spoonful of potato salad.

It's amazing.

"Oh no," Mattie says. "He likes it. You do, don't you?"

"It's really good."

Mattie turns to Blake. "Of course you had to go find someone who likes the damn potato salad."

Katie laughs. "Yeah, so he doesn't care that you're on the Ravens," she says, making a face that tells Elliot that the Ravens are usually not spoken about kindly in this household, "but the potato salad might be a deal breaker."

"Sorry," Elliot says.

"I'll get over it," Mattie says, lips pursed. "You want a beer, Elliot?"

"Sure, thank you."

Mattie gets up to grab him a beer, then he wanders over to the grill to help out Katie.

Blake reaches over, fingertips brushing against Elliot's wrist.

Elliot pulls his arm away, glancing over at Mattie and Katie, who aren't even looking at him, Katie poking the tongs in Mattie's direction.

"It's okay," Blake says, "they already know."

"Yeah, but..."

Blake puts his hands in his lap. "I won't if you don't want me to."

"No, that's not it," Elliot says and holds out his hand so Blake can do whatever he wants with it. He shoots another glance in Mattie and Katie's direction when Blake takes his hand, thumb rubbing back and forth against his palm. "I've never... really..."

He's never touched another guy like this in front of other people. He's not used to being in a place where he doesn't have to hide this, unless that place is his or Blake's apartment.

It's nice, sitting here with Blake like this.

He takes some more potato salad and Blake starts stealing it off his plate. "Hey," Elliot says. "Get your own."

Blake sticks out his bottom lip and Elliot can't help but kiss him. Blake kisses him back and puts his arm around him after, playing with the fabric of his shirt, fingers tapping out a gentle rhythm.

"Do you kids want steak? Burgers?" Mattie asks as he comes wandering back over to them. "Both, because you're hockey players who'll eat everything?"

Elliot fights the impulse to shake off Blake's arm.

"Like you're not one of them," Katie says.

Neither of them is batting an eye at how close Blake and Elliot are sitting.

"Not anymore," Mattie says.

"Hey," says Blake, offended.

"Aw, kiddo."

Blake shrugs. "I'll miss you."

"I'm not going anywhere," Mattie says. "At least not any time soon."

Blake smiles a little now.

"Anyway, I'm not too worried," Mattie goes on. "You have someone to spend Christmas with now."

"Oh," Blake says, like he hadn't even considered that. Elliot hadn't considered it either.

"Or you can both come to our place," Mattie says.

"I'll make the potato salad," Katie adds. "Elliot, steak?"

"Yes, please."

Elliot eats way too much food, and they throw balls for the dogs in the backyard, and Mattie and Katie are all over the cookies they brought, and they both take them to the door when they leave. Elliot gets a hug from both of them and Mattie tells him to take good care of Blake.

"All good?" Blake asks when he pulls out of Mattie's driveway.

"Less scary than I thought it would be."

"Mattie's all right," Blake says.

"Now I'm scared about you meeting Adam."

"Why?"

"Adam isn't nearly as chill as Mattie."

Blake laughs.

"Promise you'll still love me after I've introduced you to him?"

Blake looks over at him.

Elliot doesn't knows why until he realizes that he just said *love*. "You know what I mean," he says quickly.

"Yeah," Blake says. "I know what you mean. And, yeah, I'll still… yeah."

Elliot smiles.

They're literally about to walk into Central Park where they're going to have lunch with Adam Ishida, when Elliot stops in his tracks and grabs Blake's arm. "Oh, shit."

"You okay?" Blake asks. Elliot is really careful about touching him in public. He looks panicked when their hands brush, and now his fingers are digging into Blake's skin.

"I forgot to tell him that it's you."

"What?"

"I… When I said I was bringing my…" Elliot looks around, voice turning into a whisper, "*boyfriend*, I didn't tell him it was you."

"So, what, he's expecting some random guy?"

"I don't know. Probably?"

"Okay," Blake says. "Can't wait to see his face."

"You still wanna go?"

"Yeah, sure," Blake says. It's honestly the opposite of a problem. "Come on. It'll be funny."

Elliot lets go of him and leads the way down a path that looks exactly like all the other paths. Blake is glad that Elliot knows where they're going, because he would get hopelessly lost in this park. To him, it's probably one of the scariest places in New York City, mostly because you can walk in here with the intention of going for a quick stroll and then end up on what's practically the other side of the city. He told Elliot that and he laughed at him. For at least five minutes.

It took Blake by surprise when Elliot told him that they'd be meeting Adam in the park for a picnic, because it's in public, although it'll just look like two teammates and another hockey player friend hanging out together during the offseason.

"Oh, there he is," Elliot says, and nudges Blake to the left.

Adam Ishida is sitting on a blanket, surrounded by bags, pulling plastic containers out of a backpack. He does not see them coming.

"Hey, Adam," Elliot says and Adam looks up, grinning. "This is Blake."

"Hey," Blake says.

"Oh, hey," Adam says, clearly recognizing Blake. His eyes dart from Blake to Elliot, then back to Blake. He's definitely going through something, connecting dots in his head. "Oh, *hey*. Hey, hey. Have a seat."

They do and Elliot starts unpacking the food they brought. Elliot made it in his own kitchen, with his own pans, whistling as he prepared the food. Blake paid for the ingredients, so he at least made a contribution.

"It's really nice to… well, not *meet* you, but…" Adam shrugs. "You know what I mean. Meet you in this very official capacity."

"Yes, very official," Blake says.

"You could have told me, you know?" Adam says to Elliot. "So I could have, like, not made a complete idiot of myself?" He turns to Blake and adds, "I'm sorry that I sort of… stared at you a bit there, but…"

"Not who you were expecting?" Blake asks.

"Definitely taller than I was expecting," Adam replies. "I didn't think Elliot was into guys that are so much taller than him."

"He's not that much taller than me," Elliot grumbles.

"Only, like, twenty feet."

"Shut up."

"Here, Blake," Adam says, "have some dumplings. I picked them up at this place Elliot and I love a lot."

"Oh, I know the place."

"It's a great place." Adam smiles down at a box of dumplings. "I'll miss that place."

There's a pinch to Elliot's mouth now, so Blake hands him another box of dumplings, because that's pretty much all he can do right now. He'll hug him later. And tomorrow he'll buy him those fifty dumplings he owes him, if he doesn't have enough of them already.

Adam is a nice guy, which isn't exactly surprising, but Blake didn't expect they'd get along so well. Adam eventually leaves, because he's busy packing up his entire life, but offers to leave them his blanket.

Blake and Elliot stick around for a little while longer, Elliot lying on his back, dozing while Blake looks out at the park, watching people and their kids and their dogs, throwing balls and frisbees, chasing each other around the park, reading under trees, sharing food, laughing.

Blake jumps when Elliot touches his elbow.

"Oh, no, I'm sorry," Elliot says, laughing. "I didn't mean to scare you."

"*Fuck.*"

Elliot bites his bottom lip and sits up, fingertips brushing lightly down Blake's arm. "Blake?"

Blake huffs at him.

"I'll buy you ice cream to make up for it?"

"No, don't go anywhere," Blake says gruffly. Although ice cream doesn't sound like the worst idea. "Or let's go together."

Elliot nods and starts grabbing the blanket before Blake has even had a chance to get off, that overeager shit. Blake grumbles at him a little more, following Elliot down a path that leads fuck-knows-where.

Elliot knows where he's going, though, like he did before. They get ice cream and then Elliot pulls him up on a rock, half in the shade of a tree but still pleasantly warm when they sit down. Elliot is close, his arm brushing against Blake's whenever he moves.

"You wanna sleep at my place tonight?" Elliot asks.

"Sure," Blake says.

"Can I make dinner?"

Blake laughs. "Okay."

"Not that I don't like the dinner you make."

"Elliot."

"But... I like cooking."

"You can cook at my place."

"I know. It's not the same, though," Elliot says.

"Because you hate my pans?" Blake says, and he's teasing but he knows that he's right. Elliot hates every single pot and pan in his kitchen. "That's the issue, right?"

"They're not *my* pans," Elliot whines.

"Oh my God."

"I just like having my own stuff, it's not that *yours* is bad, but when I'm in *my* kitchen, I know where everything is and I–"

"It's okay, Elliot. Take a deep breath."

Elliot sticks his tongue out at him. "You have ice cream in your beard."

"It's not a beard." Blake wouldn't voluntarily grow a beard in a million years. He looked ridiculous during the playoffs.

"You're scruffy. Is that better? Have I pleased you with my choice of words? Do you want me to pull up a dictionary so we can find another word?"

"It's called a thesaurus and no, thanks, Elliot, we're all good here."

Elliot laughs and leans into him. His skin is warm against Blake's, little specks of sun on his face, in his hair, eyelashes curved against his cheeks. Some of his chocolate ice cream has dripped onto his shirt. Right onto one of the white stripes. He hasn't noticed yet, but he'll complain about how the stains are always on the light stripes and never on the dark ones, like all striped shirts are cursed somehow.

It won't always be like this. The season will start and they'll go back to their separate lives, but they'll match up their schedules and they'll see what they can do, and they'll see each other on the ice four times next season and… "Elliot, next summer…"

"Iceland?" Elliot asks, eyes bright.

"If you want to."

"I always wanted to go with you," Elliot says. "Remember the first time I said I wanted to go? You said you'd go with me."

Blake nods. Back then, he didn't believe they would.

Elliot smiles, trying to outshine the sun. "I want to kiss you so much right now."

"Do it," Blake says, only because he knows that Elliot won't.

"I can't."

"You can do it later," he says. "Standing invitation." Elliot can kiss him when they're back at his apartment, as much as he wants, for as long as he wants.

"In ten years," Elliot says, "we'll come back here. And I'll kiss you."

Blake snorts. "In ten years?"

"Yeah." Elliot tilts his head. "Okay, maybe five."

"Elliot…"

Elliot raises his eyebrows at him, a silent challenge.

"I meant you could just kiss me *at home*," Blake mutters.

"In five years, Blake," Elliot only says.

"Why?"

"Things might change in five years."

"Or maybe they won't."

"Doesn't matter. I'll kiss you right here. In five years."

"Okay," Blake says.

They'll forget about this.

He doesn't even doubt that they'll make it through five years together. He can see himself sitting here with Elliot in five years, but what are the chances that anything will change? Progress is a slow thing. They're crawling.

Elliot was so scared of this. Seven years ago. Seven years, and maybe now he thinks he'll be willing to take that risk in a few years, but if nothing changes, why should they take that risk? They'll have to tell their agents. Maybe one day he'll tell Evan. Maybe Elliot will tell his parents.

Adam Ishida already knows. Mattie knows. Two teammates who won't be their teammates anymore. As time goes on, they'll tell more people, people they trust, but he can't imagine the whole world knowing.

"Blake," Elliot says.

"Yes, Elliot?" Blake replies.

"You don't believe me."

He thinks about them sitting here together, about Elliot kissing him. Three times, because three is the luckiest number. Blake wants to believe him. He tells him that. He wants to.

Maybe that's enough for now.

Made in the USA
Monee, IL
15 July 2020